SPACE TRAIN

Book 1

By LaMont G. Olsen

Copyright © 2017 by LaMont G. Olsen
All rights reserved.
Green Ivy Publishing
1 Lincoln Centre
18W140 Butterfield Road
Suite 1500
Oakbrook Terrace IL 60181-4843
www.greenivybooks.com
Space Train/ LaMont G. Olsen

ISBN: 978-1-946043-98-6
Ebook: 978-1-946043-99-3

To Ms. Debbie Pollok and Ms. Shawn Caine, who both encouraged me to continue when I was ready to give up.

CHARACTERS

PRIMARY CHARACTERS
(LISTED ALPHABETICALLY BY FIRST NAME)

1. Dr. Amy Momora, prisoner physician and Cindy Wong's friend

2. Ms. Cindy Sunn Wong, prisoner nurse

3. Captain Douglas Quest, train navigator

4. Dr. Ervin Kozenskie, husband of Vidula Kozenskie, helped design much of the train's structure

5. Mr. Glenn Harris, mission coordinator and member of the Federal Prisoner Review Board

6. Mr. Justin LeMoore, chief mental health officer

7. Colonel Mickland Forrester, train copilot

8. Ms. Millie Syster, chief nurse, female cryogenic ward

9. Mr. Milton Slusser, Congressman Richards's assistant

10. Molly, Cindy's friend and advisor. After Cindy was raped by her father, Cindy made Molly up in her head.

11. Colonel Rodney Straight, space train pilot

12. Chaplain Sylvester "Frank" Molony, space train chaplain

13. Dr. Vidula Kozenskie, wife of Ervin Kozenskie, prisoner who helped design the computer system on the train

To Ms. Debbie Pollok and Ms. Shawn Caine, who both encouraged
me to continue when I was ready to give up.

CHARACTERS

SECONDARY CHARACTERS
[LISTED ALPHABETICALLY BY FIRST NAME]

1. Mr. Alex DePaul, security supervisor with Space Corp., also joined the crew on the mission

2. Dr. Amy Dickson, second pharmacist

3. Mr. Aston Young, logistics coordinator, recruited from a luxury cruise line

4. Ms. Billy Jefferson, prisoner cook

5. Mr. Blaine Pustual, physical therapist, male cryogenic ward

6. Mr. Brent Smith, chief communication and signal section

7. Ms. Carol McGregor, assistant nurse on female cryogenic ward

8. Mr. Caesar Garza, gardener at the Dallas training facility

9. Ms. Chang Sun Nam, assistant nutritionist

10. Dr. Charlie Davis, chief department of psychiatry, Tulane University; consultant to Justin and Frank

11. Ms. Courtney Cook, connective seal engineer

12. Congressman Richards, congressional spear head for the train mission, advocate for Drs. Vidula and Ervin Kozenskie

13. Dr. Don Towns, cryogenic specialist and medical director

14. Ms. Elvira French, nurse assistant

15. Mr. Ferrell Logan, nurse assistant who was rejected to be on the train crew

16. Mr. Frank Harris, train structural engineer with Space Corp.

17. Dr. Herman Hockstrasser, Cynthia Wong's selected husband-to-be

18. Mr. Jerry Middlegate, second laboratory specialist

19. Dr. Jose Sanchez, chief dentist

20. Mr. Jimmy Lee, Ms. Cindy's father

21. Mr. Kyle Williams, Space Corp. communication specialist and member of the train crew

22. Ms. Laura Yates, chief of nutrition, replaced Nancy Applegate

23. Mr. Leif Udall, train loadmaster

24. Dr. Leonard Maxwell, ophthalmologist

25. Mr. Lester Bingham, propulsion engineer

26. Ms. Linda Bracket, recreation specialist, George Washington University

27. Ms. Lisa Fierek, physical therapist, female cryogenic ward

28. Ms. Maggie Stringer, assistant nurse, male cryogenic ward

29. Mr. Matt Alton, life science components engineer

30. Mr. Martin Holloway, primary laboratory officer

31. Ms. Mary Tong, second cryogenic physician

32. Ms. Muriel French, prisoner with the Kozenskies

33. Ms. Nancy Applegate, first chief of nutrition, resigned from the crew

34. Dr. Owen Francis, chief physician

35. Dr. Rachael Beck, chief of pharmacy

1

LATE AUGUST 2130

Fly-fishing in Wyoming was always brutal in August. Mosquitoes, midges, deer flies and no-see-ums were prolific and hungry. He had sprayed his face and arms with insect repellant, yet the no-see-ums still found the corners of his eyes. It was Saturday, the last day of their annual fly-fishing trip to Wyoming. Justin LeMoore and his friend Ted Spellman fished the same area along the Snake River below Jackson Hole, Wyoming, every summer.

Both Justin and Ted loved to fly-fish, but it was also an opportunity to get away from their jobs at the federal prison in Leavenworth, Kansas. Justin was a social worker, and Ted was a guard. It was their escape from murders, hard-core drug pushers, child molesters and other social misfits.

They were fishing a stretch of river they had fished many times. They always went to Wyoming in August when the river was low and fly-fishing was at its best.

Justin was fishing what he called the Rooster Tail Hole. The main current of the river was forced between two rock walls making a swift whitewater rooster tail before flowing into a large quiet pool.

He watched the calmer water just below the rooster tail as fish rolled and occasionally jumped for mayflies and other terrestrial flyers. He wasn't interested in the jumpers; they were usually smaller fish. He was looking for bigger fish, or lunkers as he and Ted called them. Big fish watched the surface of the water and sipped hatching larva, ants, grasshoppers or other insects that fell into the river. The only evidence they were there was often just a shadow or a roiling disturbance on the surface.

As he watched, he heard his father's voice in his head. He was twelve years old and his dad was teaching him to fly-fish. It was late afternoon; they were fishing the Logan River in northern Utah. A big fish had just turned, taking a grasshopper off the surface of the water.

Pointing out the fish, his father said, *Now watch, son, it will return to its favorite vantage point where it can see the next tidbit to float by.*

Justin saw where the fish was holding and quickly made a cast spooking the fish.

Justin, if you want to catch fish, especially big fish, you have to be patient, his father had sternly said.

Take your time and think. Watch while the fish makes several runs and look for a pattern. Pay attention to the wind. Is it steady or blustery? What is in your back cast area? How much line will you need? And after you cast, where will your line fall into the water? How fast is the current moving, and where is it? When your line lands on the water, will it float naturally? There is a lot more to fly-fishing than just lashing the water with a fly. You need to place your cast exactly where you want it.

Now, more than twenty years later, his father's words were still in his mind. Justin carefully watched to see if he could tell where the lunker was lying. *I'll only be able to make one cast before spooking it,* he told himself.

He was using polarized glasses to eliminate as much glare as possible on the water. Finally he spotted a shadow as it flashed into the swift water and then retreated to its observation spot.

Okay, now I know where you're lying and where I need to make my presentation. It's taking something large. I'll try a grasshopper fly.

He selected a good-looking grasshopper fly from his box and carefully tied it to his tippet, or end of his leader. Rehearsing the cast in his mind, he judged the distance to be about forty feet. The wind was blustery and the current of the river where he wanted his fly to land was swift.

He checked the wind again. It always blew in spurts, sometimes hard then abruptly stopping. He glanced at the area where his back cast would go, made sure he had plenty of line off the reel, then conducted one last practice cast in his head.

He was ready. He took a couple of deep breaths, brought the rod up and in two false casts had the length of line out he needed. He quickly compensated for a gust of wind and watched as the fly settled onto the water. He watched the one or two seconds it took for the fly to float into the visual range of the fish. It seemed like five minutes. There was a dark flash and with one quick upward jerk of the rod, he set the hook.

As soon as the fish felt the hook sink into its upper jaw, it raced for the swift water. Justin knew if he allowed it to use the current to its advantage, it would break his tippet and be gone.

He jumped up, raced to the water's edge and ran downstream. He was hoping to coax the fish into the slower water of the pool below the rooster tail.

The fish resisted and made another drive back upriver into the swift water. If it swam across the current, it would have the full force of the water to its advantage. That would be dangerous.

As Justin feared, the fish turned and raced against the current, straining his tippet to the point of breaking. A stream of thoughts flooded his mind. *Will my blood knot hold? Should I have used a nine-weight tippet? Can I turn it back into the slower water downstream?*

He was hoping to tire the fish out, but it did not tire. Instead, it cut across the current and jumped, a blur, then another jump trying to dislodge the fly.

In the midst of the most exciting catch he'd made in many years, his communication device vibrated. He, for sure, wasn't going to answer it. However, it broke his concentration for a split second, and the fish made a turn, again heading upstream.

He could feel the line straining and had to react quickly. He allowed more line to race between his fingers, keeping the right tension. The lunker made one last dash in an effort to shake the hook. At the end of its run, Justin was able to lead it out of the swift water and into the deeper, calmer pool. It made several more short bursts but not as vigorous as before.

Justin began calling Ted, who was fishing a hundred yards or so below him. "Ted, can you hear me? Get up here and see what I've caught."

Ted and Justin had been fishing buddies for several years. Ted was not the controlled, calculating fisherman Justin was. He was more of a numbers guy. He didn't care how big his fish were, just keep them coming.

"Ted, get up here," Justin again wailed, "and hurry! I've finally hooked the lunker."

After several more shouts, he heard Ted reply, "I'm coming. Cool your jets." Sounding like a moose crashing through the brush, Ted emerged with scratch marks on his face and arms.

"What's happened? Did you fall into the river?"

"No. I finally hooked the lunker."

"Want me to net it?"

"No, I don't want to take chances of injuring it. All I want you to do is take some pictures."

"Take chances of injuring it! Isn't that bad boy going on your wall?"

"Nope. I just want a few pictures. Then I'm going to release it. Grab my camera. It's in the pocket of my fly vest. Get some pictures of me and the lunker when I get it in."

The fish was tired, and Justin was able to lead it close to shore. He held it in the water until Ted was ready with his new 3-D camera. He then carefully picked up the magnificent eight-pound German brown trout. It had a huge hook jaw; bright-blue, red, and salmon spots along its sides and a snow-white belly.

"Get several shots and a close up with the fly still in its jaw," Justin instructed.

"I can't believe you're not going to have that monster mounted and hung on your wall," Ted complained.

"This monster and I have had a challenging contest. It would be a shame to kill such a beautiful creature just to hang it on a wall and collect dust. I'm going to release it, come back next year and see if I can repeat the contest. I've hooked it two other times, and it outsmarted me by going crosswise to the current and jumping. This time I knew what to expect. It will still be here next year and we have a date to see who will win one more time."

After twenty or more pictures from every angle, Justin carefully put the fish back into the water, removed the hook and released it. It made a quick dash for the deeper water then turned as if to look at the winner of the contest. For one brief moment, their eyes met, it was only for a split second, but something profound happened.

He found a shady spot, reviewed his pictures, and was content. Ted had walked back to the river where he made several casts hooking a small brook trout on a Mackey Special fly before heading back downstream.

Late afternoon was a special time on the river. The water sparkled in the sunlight, shadows began creeping across the water, and the evening hatch would soon begin. Justin sat quietly enjoying the sounds of the river, birds chirping in the trees, and the hum of insects. There were bluish pines and clumps of quaking aspen already starting to show touches of gold in their leaves. It seemed like the river and trees were the only living things around him. At least at that moment.

Awhile later Ted returned having decided to try his luck upstream. They each ate a candy bar and stuffed the wrappers into their pants pockets. They agreed to fish until dark then meet at camp no later than 9:30 PM.

"Since this is our last night, let's have fish for supper," Ted said.

"Sounds good to me."

"Keep six or eight brook trout," Ted yelled as he crashed back into the brush heading upstream.

Justin remained at the lunker hole and caught several smaller rainbows and a couple of brook trout. But his enthusiasm had cooled. Somewhere out there the lunker was brooding and nursing a sore jaw.

He's *the one I want another contest with,* Justin told himself.

As evening progressed, an entire new world emerged with sounds like the soft hooting of an owl, a doe and fawn glided out of nowhere to drink at the river's edge, and pine trees turned from green to a darker bluish black. There was also a change in the smell of the river. During the day it was often hot with more powerful smells that blotted out the quiet subtle odors. In the evening a soft breeze often came up, bringing faint aromas like moss, damp earth, pine, wild rosebushes and other flowers.

Justin switched flies to a Renegade, and as the evening wore on, he focused on catching his dinner. He liked fish about six to ten inches long to eat. Pan fish is what he called them, and this was the time of day to catch them.

He soon had all the fish he could eat and crouched by the river to clean them. It was like heaven. The cool evening air, quiet sounds, and aromatic smells all washed over him. It helped rid him of his normal work stresses of trying to change hateful prisoners who didn't want to change. In addition, there were staff meetings, constant peer reviews, writing in charts and seemingly endless inspections.

As he quietly sat, he again remembered his father. It was he who had instilled his love of nature. On their outings, they would often sit together in the evenings quietly watching and listening to the little sights and sounds as darkness approached.

He grew up on a small farm in northern Utah, which was the perfect place for a boy. He was happy to trail along with his dad as he worked. His father would often point out a pheasant nest or a mother pheasant with her brood following behind. In winter his dad trapped muskrats, beaver, mink, bobcats, coyotes, and other animals for pocket money. Justin also began trapping when he was only eight or nine years old. His dad and an old black Labrador retriever were his best friends.

It seemed like his father was always fixing something around the farm. The old tractor seemed like it always needed some kind of repair, as did the hay mower, the milking machine and other equipment. Justin helped his father build a barn, which included wiring the lights, milking equipment and milk coolers. Although his dad never had any formal training, it didn't seem like there was anything he couldn't build or fix.

Many said Justin was just like his father. He had a knack for understanding machinery and electricity. He planned to be an engineer when he started college, but after his second year, he decided it was more interesting to work with people than machinery. Everyone was shocked when he changed his major to social work.

Sitting alone on the riverbank brought back a profound feeling of emptiness. His father had died suddenly of a heart attack, and at times like this, the loss was still painful as a sore tooth.

He looked at his watch, almost nine fifteen. Time to start back to camp. As he got up to go, he realized he'd fished the same hole all afternoon. He guessed he wanted to be near the lunker. He felt like they'd somehow developed a mental bond and looked forward to next year. Hopefully, he'd be able to repeat today's contest.

When he got to camp, Ted was already there and had the stove going.

"How many did you keep?" Ted asked as he put a half a cube of butter into the frying pan. It sizzled and smelled wonderful.

"Seven," Justin responded.

"I also kept seven. I hope they'll all fit in the pan. You can rinse your fish in the dishpan on the tailgate of the truck. I put some clean water in it."

"Thanks," Justin replied, dumping his fish into the water and giving them a rinse.

Ted put the fish in a bag with flour, shook them vigorously, then laid them in the pan. They sizzled in the hot butter.

"They smell good. I don't think there's anything that smells better than fresh fish frying in butter," Justin remarked.

"I agree. Oh by the way, I called Eve while I was waiting for you." Her name was Evelyn, but everyone called her Eve.

"You've got the perfect wife and mother for your kids," Justin said, as he wiped his hands on a paper towel. "I've never heard her complain about us taking our annual two-week fishing trip up here."

"Nope, but of course, there's a payback. She goes to Arizona every winter and spends ten days or so with her mom and sisters. I'm expected to take vacation time and care for the kids. Oh, and Eve said to tell you hi."

Ted turned the fish over, and Justin said, "That's nice of her. She's sure thoughtful."

"You really should settle down and get married. How old are you now, thirty-five or forty?"

"I'm only twenty-eight for your information. And since you married Eve, there isn't anyone left who'd put up with me."

"Come on. There are plenty of good women out there. What happened between you and Kathleen? I thought you were engaged," Ted chided.

"We were, but we weren't right for each other. She was a city girl and lot more social than me. I couldn't ever keep her happy." Looking into space, an image intruded into his mind. "The breakup was painful. I'm not going to try again until I meet the right person." Still looking away, he asked, "When did you know you wanted to marry Eve?"

"The first time I saw her."

"The first time you saw her?" Justin asked, looking suspicious.

"Yep. I saw her at a college basketball game and knew immediately she was the girl I wanted to marry. After the game I found her, and said, 'Hi, beautiful. Would you like to marry me?'"

"Just like that, you asked her to marry you?"

"Just like that. She looked at me, laughed, and said, 'Maybe we should at least know each other's names before we get married. My name is Evelyn. What's yours?'"

"'Ted,'" I replied.

"'That's better,' she said. 'Now we can get down to business.'

"I took her out to dinner that night, we began dating and six months later we married. Why do you ask? Have you seen someone who had that impact on you?"

Ignoring his question, Justin continued, "So you believe in love at first sight?"

"I do. Not for everyone, but somehow I knew the first time I saw Eve that she was the one. Come on Justin, I know you. You're blushing. You have seen someone you felt that way about. Haven't you?"

"No. No, I haven't," Justin lied, trying to push an image out of his mind. "The fish smell like they're done and this is a fishing trip, not *The Dating Game*. Let's eat."

They sat for a long time sharing stories about this and past fishing trips. The wood smoke smelled like a camp should smell. The cool of the evening made the fire feel good as it cast flickering, gnarled shadows around the area.

Finally Justin said, "We'd better get to bed. We'll have to get up early and pack if we're going to drive all the way to Kansas City tomorrow."

"I guess you're right. I sure hate returning to work," Ted remarked.

"Me too," Justin concurred.

The following morning, they were up before daylight. Justin looked at the sky where the last nighttime stars were fading. Looking into the heavens, he had a dark feeling. He shook it off and they soon had the tent down and stowed in its sack. They packed the rest of their gear in Justin's Dodge truck.

Looking at the empty camp, Justin remarked, "I don't know why, but I have a bad feeling. What if we never get back here again?"

"What are you talking about? We come here every summer," Ted replied.

"Yeah, you're right." Yet Justin wondered: *Why do I feel so empty?*

They drove to Jackson Hole, had breakfast and then began driving east. They were just turning onto Highway 25 when Justin's communicator began vibrating. It was then when he remembered it vibrating while he was catching the lunker.

He looked at the screen, and said, "Oh no, it's the warden. What could he want?"

"I don't know, but you better answer it," Ted said with a worried look.

Justin pushed the button and the 3-D image of the warden appeared. "Hello, Warden. What can I do for you?"

"I tried to call you yesterday. Since you didn't answer, I assumed you probably didn't have communicator contact."

"We were in a remote area," Justin said, winking at Ted.

"When do you expect to be back?"

"Not until late this evening."

The 3-D image momentarily disappeared, and they could hear the warden talking to someone else. When it reappeared, he said, "Justin, it's imperative we talk as soon as you get back. Call me when you get near Kansas City. I don't care what time it is, just call and we'll be here."

"Sir, what is it about? And who is we?"

"I don't want to talk about it over the communicator. Just call me," the warden replied, then disconnected.

"Sounds pretty serious. Especially if he's calling you in on a Sunday," Ted noted.

As they drove, Justin and Ted speculated about what the warden could want. It was a hot day, and the heat from the road made it look like there was a lake or water ahead on the road. It was after seven o'clock by the time they were approaching Kansas City, so Justin called the warden.

"Thanks for calling. I've set the meeting up for eight thirty in hopes you'd be here. You're here earlier than I expected, but that's great. Come to my office as quickly as you can. We'll be waiting," the warden directed.

"Sir, I'll need to stop by my house. I don't have any work clothes with me and all my fishing clothes are dirty. Besides, I haven't shaved in two weeks."

"Don't worry about your clothes or shaving. Come in your fishing boots if you must. Just be here," the warden replied as the image disappeared.

"What can possibly be that important? You're not some kind of child molester or pervert, are you?" Ted laughed.

"I'm sure that's it," Justin replied, giving Ted a withering look.

When they arrived at the prison, Ted dropped Justin off in the staff parking lot. He walked to the gate, slid his ID card through the electronic scanner and stood to have his retina verified. There was a beep, a light turned from red to green and the door opened.

The guard said, "What are you doing here? I thought you and Ted were fishing?"

"We just got back," Justin sulkily responded. "The warden ordered me to come to his office for some kind of meeting."

"Oh, oh, what did you do to warrant a meeting with him at this hour, and on a Sunday to boot?"

"Wish I knew."

"Good luck," the guard replied.

When he arrived at the warden's office, there was a trustee inmate sitting at his secretary's desk.

The trustee looked at his grimy clothes, and sniffing, said, "I'll let the warden know you're here."

The warden's office was palatial. The outer office and waiting area was a mauve color with beautiful landscape pictures. The furniture was also mauve and looked expensive. There must have been an air freshener somewhere. There was a faint smell of pine. It was a poor substitute for what he'd smelled last night.

Justin fidgeted for several minutes before the door opened and Warden Jenkins walked out. "Come in," he said, gesturing toward his office. "Sorry to bring you here on a Sunday and at this time of night. However, I think you'll understand when you hear what we have to say."

The warden was dressed in a dark pin-striped suit, white shirt, a red power tie, and shoes polished like mirrors. Justin felt even more out of place in his jeans with smudges of fish guts on the legs, dirty sneakers and a T-shirt with I LOVE FLY-FISHING on the front.

The office was spacious with a highly polished conference table at one end where the warden held staff meetings with the various department chiefs. Since Justin was not a department chief, he only visited the office from time to time.

As he entered the room, two men, also in dark suits and ties, stood on the other side of the mahogany conference table. *They must be FBI agents,* he thought as every little thing he'd ever done wrong flashed before his eyes.

He pulled a chair out across the table from the two men and sat down. He felt out of place and worried about how he smelled. He sat with his hands in his lap, not wanting to touch the warden's polished table.

The warden took his seat at the head of the table.

"This is Justin LeMoore," Warden Jenkins said, nodding at Justin. "As I told you, he's an outdoorsman. He grew up on a farm, and I'm told he can live on tree bark, roots and berries. I don't know how many of those skills will translate into what you have in mind. But if you want someone who can live on tree frogs and beetles, this is your man. This is Glenn Harris," the warden said, gesturing to the first man.

He was a distinguished-looking black man with steel-gray hair and a suit that looked like it had been hand-tailored for him. He appeared to be about fifty and had kind eyes.

"Glenn and I go back a hundred years," the warden said. "We went through the prison administrative course together. Glenn has been the warden of the Arkansas State Prison and the California State Prison. He's currently the chairman of the Federal Prison Advisory Board in DC."

Mr. Harris stood and reached across the table. Justin also stood and they shook hands. He had big hands and a firm straightforward grip.

I like him, and he isn't from the FBI, Justin thought.

The warden then gestured to the other man. "This is Milton Slusser. Mr. Slusser is Congressman Richard's right-hand man. As you may be aware, Congressman Richards is from Kansas and is the chairperson of the Congressional Prison Reform Committee."

Well goody. He isn't an FBI agent either, Justin thought, and relaxed a smidgen.

Milton Slusser also looked to be about fifty. He had large, pudgy jowls and a neck about two sizes too big for his shirt collar. Justin's first impression was that he was a mole who had just crawled out its tunnel into the light. His eyes were small, close together and set far back in his head.

His shirt, suit, and tie were rumpled, giving the impression he'd slept in them. Mr. Slusser didn't bother to stand, just extended his hand across the table. Justin had to stand and lean over in order to reach it. His hand was small with fingers like sausages, and when Justin touched it, he wanted to yank back. The hand was wet and clammy. After quickly shaking hands, Justin quickly sat back down and tried to unobtrusively wipe his hands on his pants. Although he wasn't sure he wanted to contaminate the smears of fish guts.

Warden Jenkins said, "Glenn and Milton are here to talk to you about a project you may want to participate in."

Justin was dumbfounded. *My entire day was ruined driving back here just to discuss a project?* He was instantly angry and wanted to stand up and shout, *what kind of Mickey Mouse crap is this? Yesterday I caught the lunker, and now you want to discuss a project?*

The office was hot, and as the warden looked at Justin, he said, "Justin, you look tired and frustrated. I apologize for bringing you to a meeting after just getting back from your fishing trip. Did you catch some nice fish?"

"Yes, sir, we did. Then looking at the warden, he asked, "Sir, why am I here?"

"Do you remember about ten years ago when NASA sent forty carefully selected federal convicts to a habitable planet in outer space to start a colony? They sent twenty males and twenty females. Each couple was married prior to departure so they could reproduce and build a new society when they arrived. It took over two years for them to reach the planet traveling faster than the speed of light. It is now time to send a resupply ship back to the colony. Mr. Harris knows more about that project, so I'll let him explain the rest."

Mr. Harris looked at Justin, and with the deepest most resonating voice he had ever heard, said, "I also want to apologize for bringing you here on a Sunday and at this time of night. But, what we have to discuss is urgent. As Warden Jenkins said, we are preparing to send another mission to resupply the first colony and take more individuals to start a second colony. Now, with your indulgence, I'd like to switch gears for a minute. Do you know how many people there are on the Earth today?"

Looking a little irritated, Justin replied, "I'm not sure. I'd guess somewhere around sixteen or eighteen billion."

"Try twenty-four billion. Even with aggressive population reduction methods, we have barely slowed the growth. Are you familiar with the writings of Niccolo Machiavelli? He lived from 1467 to 1527."

"I think I read some of his works in college. As I recall, he was kind of a doomsday author."

"I guess you could say that. He's credited as being the father of modern political theory. He foresaw the world population explosion of our time and had this to say: 'When every province of the world so teems with inhabitants that they can neither subsist where they are nor remove themselves elsewhere . . .the world will purge itself.' The bottom line is we have outgrown our home and need to start looking for somewhere else to colonize. If we don't, as Machiavelli said, the world will find a way to purge itself. We have had terrible pandemics over the course of world history which killed billions of people, and it is likely we will see more.

"Our missions aren't meant to solve the world population problem by transporting large numbers of people to another planet. At this point, they are research endeavors. We learned a tremendous amount from the first mission and have proved that colonization of another planet is possible. But there are still issues to be worked out. For example, the first flight required a lot of living space and a tremendous amount of supplies to support forty prisoners plus twenty crew members on the two-year flight. This mission will answer other questions like, can a vessel more than a mile long maintain faster than light flight? Will the connective seals between the cars hold up in space? And what impact will long-term cryogenic hibernation have on people?

"This mission will be significantly enlarged to accommodate sixty couples. The challenge is how to transport a hundred and twenty people plus a crew of about forty and feed them for two years. We think we have overcome that hurdle though. Are you familiar with the World Cryogenic Society?"

"I can't say that I am," Justin replied.

"I wasn't either until this project was approved by Congress. Since then I have learned a great deal about it, and I'm more than impressed. Cryogenics has been around for over a hundred years. In the twenty-first century, some people had their bodies frozen when they died. They were in hopes at a future date, science would have advanced to a point where they could be revived. The problem is that when you freeze human tissue, the cells burst, so it didn't work.

"About thirty years ago, NASA funded a cryogenic research project and out of that came a breakthrough. After more than a decade, the team found if they just reduced a body's temperature, but did not freeze it, and using a series of drugs, they could put a person into a controlled coma. While asleep, they could feed and hydrate someone for long periods of time. They feel with the proper care, a person could be kept in hibernation for years. That significantly reduces the amount of living space, food and other requirements needed for an extended voyage.

"For our project, the World Cryogenic Society will train a small team of physicians, nurses and other medical personnel. They will monitor each patient's vital signs and provide nourishment, medication and anything else a person will need during the voyage. They will have a physical therapy crew on board to exercise the patients every day to keep their muscles and joints limber and active." Mr. Harris looked at Justin, and said, "Justin, you look tired. Are you with us?"

"Yes, sir. I think so," Justin replied.

"Are you sure? We don't want to overdo you."

"I'm fine. Go ahead."

"Okay, then let me go back to the first mission. We've kept in touch with the first colony, and they are doing remarkably well. They were provided with supplies to get started with, like hand tractors, plows and other farming equipment. Building supplies, hardware, and a supply of dehydrated food was also sent until they could raise their own crops. They are farming and even domesticating some of the indigenous animals. Many couples have had children and they are pretty much self-sufficient."

"And I believe when the crew returned to Earth, they were compensated quite handsomely," Mr. Slusser interjected, giving Justin a big toothy smile.

"Yes, I believe they were." Mr. Harris said, giving Mr. Slusser a dark look for breaking in. "As Warden Jenkins said, it is now time to send a resupply ship back to the colony. But, that's only a small part of the mission. The real purpose is to be a research facility. The participants will be kept in cryogenic hibernation for about two years.

Such an endeavor has never been tried before. We'll also be trying a new hull design for the current vessel and a different and larger motor configuration. We'll also be able to grow food along the way in a self-contained greenhouse."

Looking at Justin, he laughed, and said, "I'm sorry Justin, but I have this picture in my head of you eating frogs and tree bark. My curiosity is killing me. Can you really live on tree bark, frogs and lizards?"

"I used to like doing it when I was younger. But you can only eat so many tree frogs and lizards before you start craving a good bowl of pork and beans. I'm more of a modern camper now."

"You're my kind of man." Mr. Harris laughed. "Okay. Now I can concentrate. Let me explain why we're here."

Finally, Justin thought. *This might be interesting if I was awake, but I'm tired and this is boring.*

"NASA has developed a revolutionary new space ship they call a space train. The train is essentially a series of sixty cars linked together like a train here on Earth. The engineers will give a class as part of the training with a full description of the train and how it works. The train will contain everything the prisoners and crew will require for the mission. Five cars will resupply the first colony. The remaining fifty-five will contain the supplies needed to start a second colony.

"They will have trucks and tractors with the latest engines that run on carbon fuel. In addition, they'll have sawmills and small electricity-generating plants that are solar-powered but can also run on carbon fuel. There will be doors, windows and all the hardware such as hammers, nails, bolts and nuts they will need to build houses. There are large forests on the planet so they will be able to cut their own lumber. I think it is the most exciting thing I've participated in during my entire career."

Mr. Slusser had sat quietly through the explanation, but again broke in. "I assume you'd like to know how all this relates to you?"

"Yes, sir, I would. I can't see how I'd fit into such a project."

"We'll have both prisoner and paid civilians as part of the crew. For example, there are several excellent physicians incarcerated across the country. Many of them have volunteered to go on the mission and then remain on the planet to provide ongoing care to the new community. We'll have at least one highly trained civilian physician to oversee medical services during the entire mission. He'll be augmented by one or two convict physicians on the flight to the New World. As I said, the convict physicians will not only provide medical services during the flight but will also remain with the colony. Likewise, four highly trained civilian nurses will participate on the mission. They'll be augmented by prisoner nurses and nurse assistants. Like the doctors, the prisoner nurses will remain with the colony. Actually about 25 percent of the crew will be prisoners. The return flight to Earth will have a very small crew with only the command module plus about four support cars," Mr. Slusser said.

I thought Mr. Slusser was going to tell me how all this relates to me, Justin thought.

Mr. Slusser pompously continued, "Only prisoners with a sentence of ten years or more, to include life sentences, will be selected. That'll include some with a murder sentence, but not if they have a diagnosis of antisocial personality or psychotic types of disorders. Many of the prisoners are people who committed crimes of passion or made mistakes as youngsters. You know what I mean. They killed someone on impulse, but were not premeditated."

By this time Justin needed a break. He was tired from driving all day, and now after almost an hour in the warden's office, he was fidgeting in his seat.

The warden again looked at Justin, and said, "Justin, you look tired. Let's take a quick break. Are you hungry?"

"I didn't realize it, but yes, sir, I am. We had breakfast in Jackson Hole Wyoming this morning but didn't stop to eat after you called."

The warden stepped to the door and summoned the trustee. "Call the kitchen and have a food tray sent up. Also, have them put some coffee and dessert on the tray for the rest of us."

Justin excused himself, and again thought, *I still have no idea what I'm doing here. I can't see how I could be of any benefit to this project.*

It was after nine o'clock. He took his time in the restroom. He washed his hands and face which helped revive him a little. When he returned, a tray with a small steak, green beans, mashed potatoes, a roll and a big glass of water was at his place at the table. Another tray contained slices of pie and the other three were sipping cups of coffee.

"I hope we all feel better now," the warden said.

Mr. Slusser immediately launched back into his discussion. He had loosened his tie which allowed his neck to recede into his shirt, like a turtle pulling its head into its shell.

"Congressman Richards has been the leading advocate for funding." He was eating a piece of lemon pie, and with his mouth full, said, "You guys eat pretty well around here."

Justin thought, *Mr. Slusser looks like he eats pretty well wherever he goes.*

By this time Justin was feeling confident he was not in trouble, so he said, "All of this is interesting, but I still don't see where I would fit into the project."

"Fit in?" Milton Slusser blurted out, spraying the warden's

polished table with spatters of lemon pie. "We want you to go on the mission as a crew member. I thought we made that clear."

"Go on the mission?" Justin exploded, adding spatters of mashed potatoes and green beans to the lemon pie. "What in the world would I do on the mission?"

"You've been recommended to go as the mental health coordinator," Warden Jenkins quietly commented, as he looked at the spots on his table.

"Me! Recommended? Who recommended me? You want a social worker to be the mental health coordinator? I'd think you'd want a psychiatrist to fill a job like that. Besides, psychiatrists are physicians. Or take a psychologist. They could test everyone all along the way. When it comes to the mental health professions, social workers are at the bottom of the barrel. Are you sure you've got the right person?"

Warden Jenkins broke Justin off, saying, "I heard several questions in there." Turning to Mr. Harris, he continued, "Glenn, go ahead and answer them."

"Thanks, Warden," Mr. Harris said. "We want to answer each of your questions, Mr. LeMoore. First of all, I cannot tell you exactly who recommended you, but let me say it was from more than one source. We are looking for single people who can be away for an extended period and not have a family waiting for them. It is my understanding you're single. Do you have a girlfriend, fiancée or anything like that?"

"No, sir. I don't have a fiancée or a girlfriend."

"That's good. Now to answer your question about why a social worker. Actually, I have found most social workers to be the most down to earth and realistic of the mental health professionals. However, you would be working with a psychiatrist and a research psychologist here on Earth. The psychiatrist and research psychologist are from Tulane

University, in New Orleans. They'll oversee the human side of the research component of the mission and be available for consultation.

"Each member of the crew will be given periodic physical exams by the onboard physicians. You'll be responsible for administering mental status questionnaires and conducting weekly interviews with each crew member. The results of your evaluations will be transmitted back to the consulting psychiatrist and psychologist. They will analyze your data and use it for research purposes. They'll also assist with whatever mental health services that might be required. If a crew member demonstrates a need for mental health services, you will be the primary therapist. There will also be a chaplain on board who will deal with spiritual matters and assist you."

"I appreciate your comments," Justin replied, "but I don't see myself as being that proficient or skilled."

"Based on what your colleagues have said, you are exactly what we need. We want a common-sense individual who can relate to people and has the skills to assist someone who may require services. Social workers are often less threatening than psychiatrists or psychologists. We're looking for someone who can immediately join the paid crew. Then, concentrating, Mr. Harris continued, "I almost forgot. You would also be expected to participate on the final prisoner selection team to determine which prisoners will be selected to go on the mission."

"Although, some of the prisoners have already been selected," Mr. Slusser interjected.

Mr. Harris frowned, and replied, "Yes. Vidula and Ervin Kozenskie."

Ignoring Mr. Harris, Mr. Slusser went on like a grandparent telling about their perfect grandchildren. "Drs. Vidula and Ervin Kozenskie are a husband-and-wife team. They are the most intelligent people I've ever met. Vidula is a computer expert. Before their incarceration, she was a full professor at Harvard and has designed computer systems all over the world. Ervin is a space and mechanical engineer. He has added immensely to making structural changes to the train. We have found that people who are participating and take ownership in the project are extremely devoted. Vidula will also participate in the prisoner selection process as the prisoner representative. I predict they will be leaders in the New World community. I'm sure you'll be impressed with them."

"Hmm," Justin said, looking at Mr. Harris. "You said you wanted someone to start immediately. You must have had someone else in mind and they fell through."

"That's true. We did have another person in mind, but she didn't work out. Your name came up several times, so here we are. I again apologize for approaching you at this late date, but we didn't have a choice. To stay on track we need to complete the crew selections within the next two weeks. Our goal is to bring the crew together and start team training within the next thirty days."

Sitting back in his chair, Mr. Slusser continued, "You haven't asked about the emolument?"

"Emolument?" Justin asked.

"Yes." Mr. Slusser was obviously trying to impress Justin with his vocabulary. "Your salary. Your compensation for the mission."

"I assumed it would be my normal salary," Justin replied.

Mr. Slusser puffed up like a toad, smiled, and said, "If you sign on, there will be a bit of an increase. I've been authorized to offer you two hundred and seventy-five million dollars, plus twenty-five million dollars hazardous duty pay for a five-year contract." As if Justin couldn't add, he leaned forward, and smiling said, "That comes to three hundred million dollars. Also, if you need funds to settle your affairs before departure, I'm authorized to give you three hundred thousand dollars advance pay. Of course that would be deducted from your first year's salary."

Justin stared into space. Those kinds of numbers were beyond his comprehension. After a few moments, he gained his mental composure, looked at Mr. Slusser, and said, "Let's see if I understand. You'll pay me three hundred million dollars for the five-year mission?"

"Yes, that's what I'm saying," Mr. Slusser replied as he beamed all over. "We know this must be overwhelming and we're prepared to give you a day or two to decide."

"I need to decide about a five-year mission and that kind of money in a day or two?"

"It's Sunday, and we'll need to know by Thursday afternoon. That'll give you over three days to decide. I have to return to Washington in about four hours for an important meeting with Congressman Richards. That's the reason we had to have this meeting tonight. I'll return for a final meeting with you on Thursday. Mr. Harris has agreed to remain here during that time to answer any questions you might have. Just think of it as a five-year contract. Plus you'll be on the greatest adventure of your life."

Justin was stunned. He was so tired he could hardly focus, but his mind was going a thousand miles an hour. Warden Jenkins, Mr. Slusser and Mr. Harris all looked at him. Apparently, they were waiting for some kind of response.

"Can we expect a decision by 2:00 PM on Thursday?" Mr. Slusser inquired.

"I'll do my best," was all Justin could say.

"We know this is a big decision to make, but time is of the essence," Mr. Harris noted.

"Sir, I'll do my best. I'll be here Thursday at 2:00 PM."

"I'm staying at the Marriott Hotel just down the street. If you have any questions, call me. We could get together for dinner one night if you'd like. Here is my card with my communication number on it," he said, sliding the card across the table. "We'd also appreciate it if you wouldn't say anything about the offer until we have a chance to talk again."

"I won't say anything. And thank you sir. Right now what I need is some sleep and time to digest all of this." Looking at the warden, he asked, "Could I get a ride home? Ted took my truck to his place."

"Sure. I'll have someone drive you. Oh, and by the way, take the next few days off so you can concentrate on the offer."

"Thank you, sir. I'd appreciate the time."

It was almost 11:00 PM. Between being dead tired, thinking about a five-year space mission, and a salary that was beyond his comprehension, Justin's head was spinning. By the time he cleared the gate and walked to the parking lot, the car was waiting for him.

When he got home, he called Ted.

"Well, what was it about?"

"A job offer."

"At the prison or somewhere else?"

"Somewhere else," Justin replied. "I'm tired right now. I'll call in the morning."

"Okay, you sound tired. I'm dying to hear the details though. Don't keep me waiting."

"Thanks, Ted, you're a great friend," was all Justin could say.

Justin took a hot shower and tried to sleep, but sleep wouldn't come. He tossed, turned, and all he could think of was five years in space and the enormous salary. He got up, paced, tried reading, but by morning he was even more exhausted.

Ted called, and said, "Boy, have you got the staff and inmate rumor mills churning."

"Really?"

"Yes, really. You can't believe it. I guess it all started on Saturday when the two guys in dark suits showed up. Everyone knows they tried to find you. They're convinced you're a child molester, a murderer or something."

"How could rumors get going that fast?"

"You know how fast rumors travel in prison. I think the trustee who was at the warden's office the other night must have started it. The prisoners think the two guys were FBI agents. Then you were summoned by the warden to his office immediately after returning from our fishing trip. At breakfast I heard one inmate say he's bet fourteen cartons of cigarettes that you murdered someone. So what can you tell me to put the rumors to rest?"

"I can't tell you much more than I told you last night. All I can say is I've been offered another job. I've been asked not to say anything about the job until I decide if I'm going to take it."

"Come on Justin, how can a job offer be that secretive?"

"I don't think it's a secret. They just don't want things out until I decide. We have another meeting set up for Thursday afternoon. Maybe I'll be able to say more then."

"That's not going to do much to quell the rumors."

"Let them have their fun. It gives everyone something to speculate about," Justin concluded.

Justin disconnected and had to laugh about the bets. He had a staggering headache, and his eyes felt like they were filled with sand. He took two aspirins and, while standing by the kitchen sink, thought, *The salary alone makes it hard to turn down, but five years is a long time to be away. The lunker will have been replaced by a new lunker before I get back.*

Justin had purchased a small home on the outskirts of the city, which he'd have to sell. He was not worried though; he had a realtor friend and was sure he'd help.

For the rest of Monday and all day Tuesday he moped around, unable to decide. He had a hard time sleeping and by Wednesday evening was exhausted. Not knowing what to do, he went to the porch, sat in a lounge chair and stared at the horizon. He fell asleep, and when he awoke two hours later, his neck hurt and his legs were asleep. He got up, paced around the yard, and decided to take a couple of sleeping pills. He went back to bed and either from sheer exhaustion or from the medication, he slept the rest of the night.

He hoped by morning he'd be able to make a decision, yet when he awoke, he was still undecided. He sat at the kitchen table and made list after list of the pros and cons. There were arguments both ways. By lunch, he still couldn't decide. He showered, shaved, got dressed and slowly drove to the prison.

Justin promptly arrived at the warden's office at 2:00 PM.

The warden's secretary said, "Go right in. They're waiting for you."

This time he was wearing slacks, penny loafers, a brown tweed blazer and a tie with a trout jumping out of the water on it. The warden and the two federal guys were back. Each stood when he entered.

Mr. Harris was dressed in another tailor-made pin-stripe suit, crisp white shirt, cufflinks, a red check power tie and a pair of highly polished shoes. Mr. Slusser looked like he hadn't taken his suit off.

He might have slept in it and added a spot or two on his tie, but other than that, he looked the same.

Justin wondered what Congressman Richards must be like to keep a pet like Milton Slusser around.

"Have you made a decision?" Mr. Harris asked.

"No, sir. Not yet."

Mr. Slusser raised his bushy eyebrows. "Since you didn't call Mr. Harris or have dinner with him, we'd hoped you had made a decision."

"I apologize," Justin replied. "I've given your offer a great deal of thought. To tell you the truth, I'm still pretty overwhelmed."

"Unfortunately," Mr. Slusser growled, "we're under a time constraint and we both need to leave today. Congressman Richards is extremely anxious to keep the project on schedule. If you're not interested, just tell us so we can discuss the opportunity with others who may be more forward thinking."

"Why don't we hear what Justin's questions are? Perhaps we can answer them," Mr. Harries calmly said.

"I do have some questions, and I have to resolve some other issues before I make a final decision."

"Other issues?" Mr. Harris asked. "May I ask what they are?"

"Like being away for five years. Giving up many of the things that makes life worthwhile like hunting, fishing, friends and family."

"Do you think those issues can be resolved?" Mr. Harris asked.

"Yes, sir. I think I can resolve them, but I still have some other questions. You mentioned crew training. Where will that be held? Where will the prisoner training be conducted? You mentioned the New World has animals on it. If I sign up, can I take a few guns with me and do some hunting when we get to the New World? Are there fish in the lakes and streams? And if so, could I do some fishing while we're there?"

They all smiled, and Mr. Harris said, "You're pretty focused on hunting and fishing. Let me start with the easy questions. You'll be housed at the Norfolk Naval Base in Virginia. That's where the crew training and prisoner selection will take place. They also have some extra space in the old base prison, which we can use for the prisoner interviews. The second phase of training will be for both the crew and prisoners. It will be conducted in Houston, Texas.

"Your questions about hunting and fishing are more difficult. Are you talking about taking phaser-type weapons or conventional guns that shoot bullets?"

"Conventional hunting guns, sir. There's no sport in shooting an electronic weapon that sights itself and can kill an animal several hundred yards away. That's not hunting. That's just killing. I'd want to take standard hunting guns to hunt with, as we do here on Earth."

"The train will have a weapons vault, and like the first mission, phasers will be provided. Once you arrive, they will be given to the colony for food gathering and protection. I don't know how the board would see you taking private weapons. I'll have to ask that question. If you sign on, I'll do my best to get permission for you to take a gun or two along. Of course, they would have to be quarantined in the weapons locker. They wouldn't be accessible until you arrive at the New World. Would that be acceptable?"

"Yes, of course. If I can take a few guns, I'll gladly put them in the weapons locker until the train arrives."

"As far as fishing goes, I am told there are huge fish in the streams. The colony reports catching fish a hundred pounds or more," Mr. Harris said.

"Wow! That sounds great! Just one more question. If I can't

make a decision today, does that mean I'm no longer in the running for the position?"

"Not necessarily, but it does complicate things. We don't want to pressure you and know this is a big decision. But, we can't postpone a decision for more than two or three days at most."

Mr. Slusser was clearly agitated that Justin hadn't come in groveling for the job. "There's one other thing you're missing and should consider. Many government contracts are for places almost as remote as our mission. We're not asking you to do anything that isn't standard practice. And if its distance that's holding you back, even that shouldn't be a problem. You'll be in constant communication with us here on Earth. In addition, Mr. LeMoore, we're offering you a salary that's significantly more than you can make in a lifetime working as a prison social worker. There are several others whom I'm sure would jump at the opportunity to make that kind of money."

Justin ignored Mr. Slusser and, looking directly at Mr. Harris, said, "I'll take the job."

"Well, that was fast," Mr. Harris replied.

"That was too fast. We don't want you to accept the job today and have second thoughts when you start missing your buddies or hunting and fishing," Mr. Slusser said, giving Justin a flinty look.

Justin again ignored Mr. Slusser and continued to only look at Mr. Harris. "Sir, if I tell you I'll take the position today, that will be the same answer tomorrow, next week or even next year."

"That's great, but may I ask what made you reach a decision so quickly?" Mr. Harris asked.

"I'm not sure. It's easy to prostitute yourself for money, but I think the real reason is that it would be exciting to participate in such an adventure. I'd like to see if we can really do it. And as Mr. Slusser said, five years isn't forever."

"Okay," Mr. Harris replied. "It will take about an hour to go over the contract and sign the various forms. If you'd like an attorney to look the documents over, you can electronically transmit them to us in the next day or two."

"I'm comfortable with signing them."

"Well," the warden broke in. " I'm delighted for you, Justin. If I were a young man in your shoes, I'd have done the same thing. I wish you the best of luck. But now I have to do some recruiting of my own."

He got up, shook Justin's hand, and continued, "If you gentlemen will excuse me, I have some other things I need to attend to."

Milton Slusser also excused himself. "I'll see you back at the motel," he said, looking at Mr. Slusser.

Mr. Harris asked, "To start off with, would you like to avail yourself of the advance money we discussed?"

"Yes, please. If I have a problem selling my house, the advance would be helpful."

When they finished signing the contract, Mr. Harris gave Justin a folder and instructed, "This is your application for a base pass at Norfolk. Please complete and forward it to me."

"You'll be given quarters in a wing of the Norfolk Naval Base guest house along with the rest of the paid members who will be on the crew. You'll continue to be paid your current salary until we depart. We have also been authorized to pay you a housing allowance and per diem while you are in training and prior to your departure. The guest house has kitchens on each floor. You can cook there and we would prefer that you do so. We'd like each of you to take turns cooking and everyone eating together as much as possible."

"That could be a problem. I'm not a very good cook."

"As long as you don't cook frogs and tree bark, I'm sure you'll do fine."

After they had concluded their business, Mr. Harris leaned back in his chair, looked at Justin, and asked, "Justin, do you like classical music?"

"Yes, I do. When I'm alone, that's about all I listen to. What makes you ask?"

"I'm not sure. You just seem to be that sort of person. I'm a great fan of classical music. Who are your favorite composers?"

"That's hard to say. I'd have to put Mozart, Beethoven, Bach, Wagner, Tchaikovsky, and Handel at the top of my favorite list."

"You have good taste. I'm also very pleased that you accepted the position."

As they got up to leave, they shook hands and Mr. Harris said, "I feel like we have a great deal in common. I look forward to working with you."

As Mr. Slusser and Mr. Harris were waiting at the Kansas City International Airport for their flight back to Washington, Mr. Slusser said, "Do you think we made the right decision about Justin LeMoore? I have a bad feeling about him. I'm afraid he could be a pain in the ass."

Mr. Harris smiled. "I have just the opposite feeling. I think he's a kindred spirit."

"I did it," Justin told Ted on the phone. "I signed the contract for the new job."

"So when are you going to tell me what the job is, and where it will be?"

Justin explained the mission as best as he could but didn't go into the salary.

When he told Ted about being away for five years, he exploded. "Five years! You're going to be gone for five years!"

"Yes. Five years. When I get back, we'll spend an entire summer fishing in Wyoming, Montana and Alaska."

"I don't know what to say. I hope you know what you're doing. You're not getting any younger, you know. Isn't it about time you found a good woman and settled down? By the time you get back, you'll be over thirty-three and that's a bit late to be starting a family."

"Maybe I'll find someone along the way."

"Yeah sure. Like you're going to fall for one of the convicts. How long before you leave?"

Justin was glad Ted couldn't see his face. "I have to be in Norfolk to begin crew compatibility exercises in thirty days."

Sounding irritated, Ted said, "I guess there isn't much else to say. Let me know if Eve and I can do anything to help you get ready."

It was obvious Ted was not happy about the decision.

2

Justin contacted his realtor friend. "I've taken a new job. I need to sell my home as quickly as possible. I don't need to make any money on the sale and the furniture and appliances can go with the house if someone wants them."

"I know a young couple who are looking for a house. How about I bring them over in the morning?"

"Sure, that would be great," Justin replied.

The next morning, his friend brought the young couple over. It didn't take the couple long to decide. By midafternoon, the house was sold. Ted and Eve invited Justin to stay in their basement until he departed.

With part of the advance money, he rented a storage locker and paid the rent for five years. Ted helped him move his camping stuff and a few other things into the locker.

When they finished, Justin said, as he handed Ted the key, "If it's alright, I'll leave this with you. You're welcome to use whatever you want while I'm gone. And if something should happen and I don't come back, everything in the locker is yours."

The prison had a big farewell party for Justin. He was sad to say good-bye to his colleagues and the inmates he'd worked with. He had dinner with Ted and his family the evening before he departed. It was a somber affair.

On the eighteenth of September at 5:00 AM, just over a month since he caught the Wyoming lunker, Justin signed out of the prison and began driving to Norfolk. He was amazed by how much had happened in those thirty short days.

I'm going to outer space for five years. I have to console and reminded myself that the substantial pay package is an opportunity that will allow me to do things I've never dreamed possible. I can buy hunting permits for myself and Ted all over the world.

Justin found he was more aware of sights, sounds, and smells than he ever remembered as he drove out of Kansas and started across Missouri. There was a morning mist in the trees. Farmers were harvesting their crops, and the colors of fall were starting to appear. When he took a break at a rest stop, there was a warm earthy smell to the air that he hadn't noticed for a long time. Although he'd been told the trip would be safer than flying from one country to another, he still had a twinge of concern. He wondered whether this would be the last time he would see any of this.

He could have driven straight through to Norfolk in one long day, but by the time he got to Virginia, he was tired. He decided to break the trip up and stopped at a motel in Richmond. After dinner, he walked through the historic district and marveled at the old buildings.

I wonder what life must have been like when the first residents arrived and the struggles they went through to build a new life.

As he wandered along the quiet historic brick street lined with old sycamore trees, he wondered, *Will the residents of the New World experience many of the same difficulties and challenges as the early residents of Richmond?*

The next morning, he got up, had a leisurely breakfast and drove the two hours to Norfolk. He arrived at the naval station about mid-morning. He parked at the gate and walked to a building with a sign that read PASS AND GUARD STATION.

A sharp-looking marine checked his driver's license and found his name on a clipboard list. "Sir, you're expected," he said, handing Justin several papers to sign. When the marine was satisfied the signatures on the papers and the one on his driver's license were the same, he handed him a pass. "Please wait here. I've been told to call Mr. Harris upon your arrival."

Mr. Harris soon arrived, and reaching out to shake hands, said, "Welcome to Norfolk. How was the trip?"

"Fine. Long but uneventful."

"I thought you'd arrive yesterday. Did you decide to spend the night somewhere?"

"I stayed in Richmond. I'd never seen the historical section so I stopped and spent the night."

"Good for you. I'm glad you took advantage of the opportunity. It may be awhile before you can do much sightseeing again. Jump into your truck and follow me over to the offices. They're not much to look at, but they're just temporary and serve our purpose."

Mr. Harris was driving a shiny black Lincoln. It was obvious he liked things to look sharp and be shiny. Justin followed him through a maze of buildings to what looked like an old red brick warehouse with large rusty sliding doors. There were no signs or other markings that would suggest the place was anything other than what it looked like. They parked in the front and Justin followed Mr. Harris into the building.

The inside of the building was not in any better repair than the outside. It was old, dark and smelled like a damp warehouse. It had dirty orange carpet on the floor and at one end there were several small cubicles with florescent lights hanging over them.

At first glance, Justin was ready to go back to Leavenworth. As far as he could see the prison was lighter and brighter than this old nasty-looking place. When they got to the cubicles, he was even more shocked. They were made from old dirty room dividers with just enough space for a couple of desks, chairs, and a filing cabinet. The first two cubicles had handwritten signs pinned to the dividers.

One said, "Command/Navigation," the other, "Signal/ Communication."

Mr. Harris, in his booming basement voice, said, "Justin, let me introduce you around and show you where you'll work."

3

"All of this is temporary," he said again. "We have two types of staff working on the mission: those like you who will be part of the away crew, and those who will remain here on Earth to provide support. We're going to spend time in team building for the next couple of weeks with just the away crew. Those in support positions here on Earth will come and participate from time to time. They won't be housed here or participate in the crew training. When the mission is under way, you'll all be communicating from space with your counterparts here on Earth.

"We want you to at least know them so you'll be able to put a face with a name. Dr. Charlie Davis, the psychiatrist, and Dr. Susan Lister, the research psychologist, will be working with you. They'll be here for a few days to coordinate with you and the chaplain. They're both from Tulane University in New Orleans.

"There will be six teams or groups on the mission as part of the crew. This first cubicle, as you can see by their sign, is the Command/Navigation team."

As they walked into the cubicle, there were three men sitting around a small circular table covered with star charts and laser measuring devices.

"Gentleman, this is Justin LeMoore, the social worker. He's the last of the team to arrive. I'm taking him around so he can see the lay of the land."

All three stood. "This is Colonel Rodney Straight. He's the pilot."

Colonel Straight stepped forward and extended his hand. He

was a slim boyish-looking man who appeared to be about fifty-five with sandy frizzy hair. He had a steady gaze and looked the picture of confidence.

"Call me Rod," he said, as he and Justin shook hands.

A second man stepped forward. "I'm Mick Forrester." And he also shook Justin's hand. He was about six feet tall with short grayish hair and ice-blue eyes.

"Colonel. Mickland Forrester is our copilot. He's participated with Colonel Straight on several joint missions so they are used to working together," Mr. Harris noted.

The third man stood back until Colonel Straight and Colonel Forrester moved to the side. He then stepped forward. As he shook hands with Justin, Mr. Harris said, "This is Captain Douglas Quest. He's the navigator."

"I'm glad to meet you," Captain Quest said. "Call me Douglas or Doug."

"I'm also glad to meet you," Justin replied. "I look forward to working with all of you."

"Gentlemen, we don't want to disturb you, so please continue what you were doing," Mr. Harris remarked.

As they stepped away from the cubicle, Mr. Harris said, "We are fortunate to have Colonel Straight as the mission leader again. He was also the pilot on the first mission. He not only knows how to get to the New World and back, but has also been intricately involved in the design and construction of the train.

"Colonel Straight is a retired air force space officer. He has years of navigation, engineering, troubleshooting and systems repair experience. He's a graduate of the United States Air Force Academy in Colorado Springs.

"Colonel Forrester is also a retired air force colonel and a graduate of the Air Force Academy with a degree in space technology. After a thirty-year career in the air force, he retired. Since then he has taught space science at George Washington University here in Washington DC.

"Captain Quest, the navigator, is a graduate of the United States Naval Academy with a degree in oceanography. Are you familiar with military ranks?"

"I know army and air force ranks. I'm not as familiar with navy ranks," Justin replied.

"A captain in the navy is equivalent to a full-bird colonel in the army or air force. It has been said that if Captain Quest is given a map and a stopwatch, he could pilot a car through the streets of New York with all the windows blacked out. He gravitated to space travel toward the end of his naval career. At first he was assigned to work with NASA developing reliable star charts. He has navigated two multiyear missions where his techniques were tested and proven to be accurate.

"Let's keep moving. I want to introduce you to Chaplain Frank Molony, since you'll be working together."

As they walked through the cubicles, Justin noticed the other sections. There were signs that read MEDICAL, NURSING, ENGINEERING/MAINTENANCE, LOGISTICS/SUPPLY, MENTAL HEALTH/ CHAPLAIN, AND, PRISONER LIAISON.

"What's the prisoner liaison section?"

"We're going to have a crew meeting this afternoon and introduce everyone to each other, but we will not meet the prisoner liaison. If you recall our first discussion in Kansas, that person is Dr. Vidula Kozenskie. She'll arrive with her husband, Ervin, when we start the prisoner record reviews. Ervin will not be on the selection team, but they want to be together. We decided to allow him to accompany his wife and continue his work here."

"It seems like the Kozenskies are involved in everything," Justin commented.

"Let's step over to my office where we have a little more privacy," Mr. Harris said, and pointed to a small glassed-in area.

Mr. Harris went around his desk, sat down, and pushed a button on his music device. Justin sat on a metal chair in front. To Justin's surprise, Mr. Harris leaned back in his chair, put his feet up on his desk and closed his eyes as the room filled with classical music.

He sat that way for almost two minutes, before saying, "It's like a balm to my soul. Do you recognize it?"

Justin listened for another minute before replying, "I believe its Mozart's Piano Concerto no. 21."

"Very good! I'm impressed! It is indeed Mozart's Piano Concerto."

They listened for several more minutes before Mr. Harris reached over, turned the music down and opened his eyes. He looked at Justin, and said, "I think you should be aware of my opinion of the Kozenskies since you're going to be the primary mental health person on the crew. I know there are several others who also have questions about them.

"Do you remember about eight years ago there was a sensational court case about a couple who were involved in a massive computer scheme? They tried to take over the economies of several countries?"

"Yes. As I recall they were involved in trying to take over the entire world economy, or something to that effect."

"The Kozenskies are the ones. Ervin is Russian. His father is a multibillionaire who owns a private company that specializes in space technology. Vidula is from India, and her family runs a banking consortium there and in England. She went to college at Cambridge and was recognized as a computer genius.

"They were both full professors at Harvard at the time of their arrests. Ervin taught in the Department of Space Technology, and Vidula taught in the School of Business. She was known as the most influential business strategist in the world. She was a consultant, in one way or another to almost every country on Earth. Little did anyone know she and Ervin were also running the biggest financial scheme the world has ever known.

"Their schemes were not the ordinary hacker who breaks into a company's finance files and transfers a few billion dollars into their own account. They bilked countries out of their entire cash reserves. Vidula used her charm to worm her way into small countries who were struggling with debt. Then as a financial advisor, and using her computer skills, she'd wreck their economies. The Kozenskies then quietly moved in and offered to help with money they'd stolen from the very countries they were assisting. She targeted small countries like Saudi Arabia, Iraqi, Brazil, Turkey, Malaysia, Georgia and several others.

"They had trillions of dollars, and since most of the countries didn't want the world to know what had happened, they allowed the Kozenskies to supposedly help them. Once they gained monetary control of five or six countries, they expanded into four or five more. And it almost worked. By the time they were caught, they controlled the finances of about twenty countries, and as the old saying goes, 'He who controls the purse strings controls the power.' It was their objective to take over the United Nations and essentially control the world economy.

"In their defense, they felt by redistributing and controlling the world economy, they could eliminate world hunger, disease and also resolve world conflict. As we know, most, if not all of the recent wars revolved around water and other dwindling resources. As recently as 2050, World War III was fought over water rights. I know some will argue it had to do with issues between world religions, but the real reason was many countries, especially small countries, felt powerless and disenfranchised."

"So what happened to them?" Justin asked.

"The Kozenskies were like magicians. They propped up entire economies, influenced stock markets, justified wars, influenced elections, and relying on massive misinformation schemes, they controlled public perceptions. But like all power-hungry people when they couldn't achieve their objectives as quickly as they wanted, they set up their own CIA-type organization. They had their own hit men and a small army. They started toppling countries and replacing the leadership with puppet leaders while they ran everything from behind the scenes.

"Their fatal mistake was trying to take control of Canada. They actually sent a squad of hit men to kill the prime minister. The Kozenskies had gone through an elaborate process of not leaving a trail between themselves and their hit teams.

"The attempt on Canada was too big, too aggressive and people started looking at other world events. The press began researching, and little by little tracks began to emerge, which led to the grand scheme and finally to Vidula and Ervin. Amazing, isn't it? For almost ten years they actually ran a good part of the world economy. And, in many respects did a good job. In the countries where they were involved, the standard of living, education, medical care and even per capita income rose for the average family. They were not thieves in the traditional sense, more like modern-day Robin Hoods.

"After their conviction, they were sentenced to two life terms at the Federal Correctional Institution at Beaumont, Texas. They were model prisoners and wrote books, gave lectures from prison and became celebrities.

"They'd just been incarcerated as the first New World mission was completed. When this mission was announced, they managed to get a meeting with Congressman Richards while he was on a tour of the Beaumont prison. They convinced him they should not only be on the mission but that Ervin should also help design the train, and Vidula would assist with the computer system.

"Vidula helped design the computer and communication systems for the entire train. Ervin, using technology developed by his father, became an advisor on using graphite, aluminum and gel-foam lamination. They designed a revolutionary new hull design which would reduce radiation and strengthen the vessel. Over time they have become involved in every aspect of the mission. Their every move is supposed to be monitored by the FBI, but I fear they are smarter than any of us. I constantly worry what is going on behind our backs."

"That's frightening," Justin worriedly commented.

"I don't want to frighten you. As I said, their every move is supposed to be monitored. If I find even a hint of something sour going on, I'll pull the plug on the entire mission. Trust me Justin, I won't intentionally put anyone's life in danger."

"Thank you sir. I appreciate your vigilance and I do trust you."

"Let's go back out. I want to introduce you to your other mental health colleagues."

They walked to the mental health cubicle where a large man was coming out. He had on jeans and a black shirt with a priest collar. He was about five foot eight inches tall, hefty with a pudgy almost-angelic face. He also had a smile that would light up a dark room.

Mr. Harris said, "Father Chaplain Sylvester Molony, just where are you going this time of day?"

"Well sir, I was on my way to the restroom. I wanted to be ready for lunch. I hate being late for anything, but especially for lunch."

"From the looks of it, you're not late very often," Mr. Harris said as he slapped him on the back.

"No, sir, I'm not. I grew up in a good Irish Catholic home of nine brothers and sisters. If you were late for a meal, you went without. Therefore, I've made it a goal to always be on time. As you can see," he said, slapping his ample middle, "I've pretty much attained that goal."

"I'd like you to meet Justin LeMoore," Mr. Harris said, gesturing toward Justin.

Chaplain Molony extended the biggest hand Justin had ever seen, and said, "I've been looking forward to meeting you. I hear we're going to be working together."

"That's also what I hear," Justin said, as they shook hands. "You must've been a football player."

"As a matter of fact I did play some ball, but that was a few years and quite a few pounds ago. I went to seminary at William and Mary. We had a pretty fair football team for a small school. I was a linebacker. If I could get in front of someone, they didn't often get past me," he said with another big smile.

Justin had to also smile, and noted, "I'll bet you could stop just about anything."

"Anything but a loaded dump truck," he replied. He then continued, "I hear you're a Mormon."

Oh boy, Justin thought, *he doesn't waste any time.* All he could do was smile, and say, "Yes, sir. I am."

"Always thought I'd like to be a Mormon. I envied you guys. I can't have one wife and you can have several."

"Not for the past two-hundred-and-fifty years. And if we still could, I wouldn't want to attempt it. Seems to me it would take a saint to keep more than one wife happy. I suspect it would be far worse than you living a celibate life."

With a roar of laughter, Chaplain Molony said, "I hadn't thought of it that way. No, sir. I hadn't considered that, and I think you're right. You know I believe we're going to get along just fine."

"I hope so," Justin noted. "As you said, we're going to be working together for quite a while. By the way, what do I call you: father, chaplain, chaplain father—or what?"

"Well sir, I never liked the idea of calling priests father. If I can't have a wife. How can I be a father? I know I'm supposed to be a father to my flock, but that doesn't always work. I had a congregation in the inner city of New York for several years, and the youngest parishioner was at least eighty-five. I was only in my early twenties. Shucks, how could I be a father to them? I guess chaplain is acceptable if that's the handle you want to use, but I'd rather you just call me Frank."

"Frank? Where did Frank come from?" Justin asked. "Is that your middle name or something?"

"Nope. When I was a kid, I hated the name Sylvester. I must have been about four or five. To me Sylvester sounded like a darn cat. I told my family I wouldn't answer to that name anymore. They wanted to know what they should call me, and I said Frank. It was probably the first name that popped into my head and that's what it's been since."

"Why didn't you have it officially changed?" Justin asked.

"I thought about it, but Sylvester is an old family name. Plus, it confused people about what my real name was and I kind of liked that."

"I'll leave you two to get better acquainted," Mr. Harris laughed. "I've reserved a table at the officer's club for lunch. It's almost that time and I'm going to make an announcement. Oh, by the way, where are Dr. Davis and Dr. Lister?"

"I'm not sure," Frank replied. "They left about an hour ago. I assume they'll be right back."

"Dr. Davis is the psychiatrist, and Dr. Lister is the research psychologist. We're going to be working with them. As far as I can tell, they're like all shrink people. They're kind of nuts, but after we leave, we'll only have to talk to them once in a while," Frank said.

Justin and Frank were just coming out of the restroom when Mr. Harris's voice came on the PA system announcing it was lunchtime. "I've reserved a table at the club for anyone who can attend. The crew meeting will begin at 2:00 PM. It's mandatory for all crew members who are here. Some of the support teams are not available, so we will wait to introduce them at a later time. Since there are several of us going, and parking is tight, let's meet at the front door and carpool."

"We can ride together," Frank suggested. "I have a two-seater. It'll give us time to chat."

"Sounds good to me. I have my truck here if you'd rather ride in that."

"Mine is fine. It's small and easy to park," Frank noted.

The crew met at the front door, but since Frank and Justin were riding together, they left and walked to the parking lot. Frank led the way and stopped at a tiny red sports car. He beeped his key and the doors rose like wings on a bird.

"This sure isn't what I'd have pictured as a priest's car," Justin remarked. "How do you get into it?"

"Just step in and slip down," Frank said. Then with his traditional smile, he demonstrated how to do it. "See," he said, plunking down into the seat. "Nothing to it."

Justin followed the demonstration, slipping down into the seat. Once in, he had to ask, "How do you get out again?"

"That's a bit harder. I'll show you when we get to the club," Frank said as the doors automatically closed and locked.

Frank laid rubber for half a block, squealed around the corner, power-shifted down, sort of stopped at the stop sign and squealed out again.

"Maybe we should have brought my truck. I'm not sure you're safe. I thought priests took some kind of poverty promise or vow. Does the pope know you're driving something like this?" Justin laughed.

"There are some who think I shouldn't be driving a car like this, but it's my only sin in life. I figure since God hasn't struck me down, it must be okay with him. I used to dream of a car like this as a kid but never thought it would be possible coming from a poor Irish Catholic family. Of course, I couldn't have ever afforded this kind of car if I hadn't gone to work for the Federal Bureau of Prisons. But then what's a priest supposed to do with his money since he doesn't have a family?"

"I don't know. Give it to the poor, I guess. I never thought about it," Justin replied.

As they pulled into the parking lot, Frank continued, "I suspect there are all kinds of priests like there are all kinds of Mormons. I've given money to the poor, and I generally live pretty frugally, but everybody has to have a little fun in life."

When they parked, Frank said, "Okay now, watch me. Put one hand on the bar at the top of the window and push the button with your other hand. If you hold on tight, the door will pull you up, then you just step out. Watch." Frank took hold of the bar above the window and pushed the button. The hydraulic door pulled him up and he stepped out.

Justin did as Frank had demonstrated but didn't have a good hold on the handle. He lost his grip and the handle pulled out of his hand. That left him half up and half down, which forced him to crawl out of the car to the amusement of Frank.

"I knew we should have brought my truck," Justin said, as he stood up and dusted his hands off.

"What sport is there riding in a truck? Besides, you'd probably make me ride in the back."

Justin liked this unconventional priest. He liked him a lot. He hated the thoughts of leaving Ted and wondered what he'd do for a friend. It was obvious Frank could be a lot of fun and a good friend. He reminded Justin of a big teddy bear.

They walked into the club just as Mr. Harris was coming in. Frank walked over and punched him on the shoulder. With a big smile, he said, "I think Justin's going to be okay. Yes, sir, I think he'll be just fine."

Justin was aghast. He would no more think of punching Mr. Harris on the arm than hitting his grandma. Frank, on the other hand, didn't seem to care what status one had. Everyone was fair game.

Although there could have been fifteen or more people at the lunch, there were only seven. Several others arrived that morning and had gone over to lodging to unpack, so they were not aware of the lunch.

Just as they sat down, Milton Slusser appeared from out of nowhere. He again looked like he'd just emerged from his winter's hibernation. He oozed into a chair next to Mr. Harris and Colonel Straight. They spent most of the time discussing something to do with changes to the computer specifications of the train and additional costs.

Frank wanted to hear about the fishing trip and all about camping. Apparently, Mr. Harris had told him about the Wyoming fishing trip.

"I've only slept in a tent a few times. My family used to visit my uncle and aunt in the country, and there weren't enough beds in the house for all of us kids. I, my brothers, sisters and cousins had to sleep in tents. I hated it.

"When you grow up in the city, your security is a metal door and dead bolts. I felt like I was totally exposed to the world sleeping in that drafty, flimsy tent. I was afraid some bad guy was going to come and take me away. Besides, there were strange noises all night. Cows mooed, dogs barked, and a skunk came right up to our tent. I didn't sleep very much when I had to camp out. Aren't you afraid of bears and stuff when you're camping in the woods?" Frank asked.

"Not really. I'm more concerned about two-legged critters than bears. I'm probably safer in the woods than you are in the city behind a steel door."

"You're probably right, but I still like four walls around me."

They talked about the mission and what they'd both heard. They also wondered just how much work there would be for them once the mission was under way.

"I heard we'll be busy for the next several months," Frank said.

They all left just before 2:00 PM and returned to the office. Frank was right; once Justin knew what to expect, he was able to get in and out of the sports car without a problem.

4

Once back to the offices, everyone congregated in a large area in the corner of the warehouse where a sign read, "CONFERENCE AREA." There were two large gray laminated tables set end to end with florescent lights hanging over them. Around the table were gray government-issued metal folding chairs.

They were not comfortable. Justin had long legs and liked to lean back, but the chairs were so flimsy he didn't dare do it. The floor had more dirty orange outdoor carpet on it. Justin was not sure if it was just his imagination, but he thought he could smell mold or mildew. It was hard to tell as the entire area was so dark, dirty and dingy.

Mr. Harris sat at the head of the table, with Mr. Slusser slouching in the chair to his right. Everyone stopped talking and looked toward Mr. Harris when he tapped his fountain pen on the table.

Mr. Slusser immediately spoke up, and said, "Before we begin, I'd like to say a few words," as he folded his hands across his belly. "Congressman Richards wanted to be here but he was detained on the floor, so he asked that I represent him."

Congressman Richards must be pretty hard up having to use you as a substitute, Justin thought. He felt momentarily guilty about his reaction toward Mr. Slusser, but there was something about him that made his skin crawl.

"Congressman Richards sends his regards and excitement about the project," Mr. Slusser gushed. "The mission has been the congressman's pet for several years. He's lobbied his colleagues for resources, which I believe contains some pretty substantial salary packages for each of you."

Then for the next fifteen minutes, he continued to extol the virtues of the congressman. He explained how he'd almost single-handedly fought for funding and was anxious for the mission to remain on track. What he didn't say was everyone there were minions to make the congressman look good, which translated into votes.

Thankfully, when Mr. Slusser stopped to take a breath, Mr. Harris broke in. "We all appreciate the congressman's good wishes and I'm sure each of us will do our best to make the mission a success."

It was obvious Mr. Slusser was taken aback by not being able to conclude. He sputtered, "Ah yes, both the congressman and I have the utmost confidence in you all." He concluded with, "Like the congressman, I'm very busy," and excused himself.

I'm tired of that shit-head Harris cutting me off like that, Mr. Slusser told himself.

Boy, was that a bunch of flummox, Justin thought to himself.

Mr. Harris welcomed each of the crew members. "I'm happy to finally have everyone in one place. I have personally been involved in selecting each of you. I did not make my selections easily. I looked for people who are doers, thinkers, problem solvers and able to get along with others. I wanted people who will work until the job is done, no matter how long it takes. In addition, I want people who know how to unwind and relax when given the opportunity.

"Some of you came from within the federal prison system, some from the military, some from civilian life and several even come from different countries. I'm convinced we have found the best team of dedicated people anywhere.

"Mr. Slusser has already told you of the political side and I do not belittle that. And before we go further, let me address a point Mr.

Slusser made. You're going to receive substantial salary packages, but you are also going to earn them. You're going to take risks and you will deserve every dollar of pay you get.

"Most important, I want you to know that I am here for you. If you have a problem or want to talk, come see me. I don't want anyone to have issues that could fester and degrade the mission. I don't care what time it is or what day it is. If you have a concern, call me."

He went to a whiteboard and wrote his communication device code down. "My wife passed away two years ago and my children are either in school or on their own. The mission has become my life. Although I have discussed the mission with each of you during the hiring process, I want to briefly go back over it so everyone hears the same thing."

Mr. Harris went back to the mission of sending about one-hundred-and-twenty federal convicts to the New World. "We anticipate it will take around four months to select the final group of prisoners to go on the mission, finish preparations and complete the train. Some of the train is already in orbit, but there are other modules, to include the cryogenic units, which are not finished. The contractor has guaranteed us the remaining modules will be completed and placed into orbit by the first of March."

Frank leaned over to Justin, and said with a big grin, "Wanna bet? When have you ever seen a government contract finished on time?"

Justin whispered, "I don't bet on sure losers."

"Now, I would like to go around the table and have you tell us your name and what position you will have. In the interest of time, you do not need to go into much detail. I have prepared a pamphlet that has a paragraph covering the background, education and experience of each paid crew member. You can review that at your leisure. I'm impressed by the qualifications and depth of experiences each of you are bringing to the mission. Hopefully, over the next several weeks, you will be able to spend time getting to know one another. Since you are going to be spending several years together, I hope you'll all be friends."

The introductions took more than an hour. It was interesting to hear from each person.

After the introductions, Mr. Harris said, "I almost forgot a couple of other items. Several of the engineers and others on the support team will be coming to spend a few days with us as their schedules permit. While I'm thinking about it, and for your information, in addition to the crew physicians, there will be at least one prisoner physician who will assist on the mission. He or she will remain at the New World site to provide medical support to the colony. There will also be a prisoner nurse, four to six assistant nurses, several physical therapy assistants, two prisoner cooks and others who will accompany you.

"I know some of you have not been able to check into lodging yet. We'll cut today a little short so you can unpack and get settled. We've been given the entire second floor of the base guest house for our crew. I think you'll find it adequate for the time we'll be here. The communal kitchen has been stocked with food, and starting tonight, we expect you to cook for yourselves. I know you may not want to eat in every night, but I'd like you to spend as much time together as possible. There is no duty roster, so how you decide who cooks is up to you all. You'll find a shopping list on the cupboard door. The housekeeping crew will make a run to the commissary twice a week. So whatever you need, just add it to the shopping list. If you want to make your mother's favorite recipe, let the housekeepers know. They will do their best to find the ingredients.

"Tomorrow we'll start our team building, so wear something comfortable. We'll be doing group exercises for the next three days, which may include some floor time. Don't wear anything you don't want to get dirty. Have a great evening. I'll see you in the morning at 0800 sharp. By the way, we use military time which will be important when the mission starts. Once in space, there won't be a sun in the sky or other ways to tell whether it's AM or PM. For example, it's 4:00 PM NOW, which is 1600 hours military time. Don't worry, in a week or so it will become second nature."

With that, Mr. Harris left the room and everyone followed.

Frank said, "Let me show you our cubicle."

There were three large black binders on each desk. Justin was curious and picked one up.

"You don't want to look at that now. They're the mental health research protocols: permission forms, questionnaires, testing crap and enough other stuff to choke a horse. I think the boys and girls at Tulane have way too much time on their hands. Dr. Davis and Dr. Lister will be up here for two more weeks. They want to spend time going over all of this with us."

"I can't wait," Justin said, with a sarcastic smile as he laid the binder back down on the desk.

"For now, let's go over and get you unpacked. You have the room next to mine. They're both right across the hall from the kitchen, so we'll be well taken care of."

Justin followed Frank to the navy lodging as best he could. The building looked new, one of the only new structures on the base as far as Justin could tell.

"I'm sure glad you're not driving the space train," Justin said, as he got out of his truck."

"Shoot, if I were driving, we could probably cut at least a year off the trip."

"Yeah, if you didn't wrap the train around a meteor first."

"You could be right about that. Yes, sir, you just might be right. But at least there wouldn't be any cops up there giving speeding tickets." Frank smiled.

"How many tickets do you get?"

"My son, that's an issue between me, the city, and God," Frank replied.

After checking in, Frank helped Justin carry his luggage up to the room. Justin left the door to his room open while Frank was checking the kitchen.

"They've got enough steaks in the freezer to feed a small army," he shouted. "There's salad fixings, sodas and beer in the fridge. They've thought of everything. There is even steak sauce in the cupboard. There's a nice patio behind the building with a gazebo, a gas grill and a dozen or so picnic tables. Maybe we should take the cooking duty tonight. We could get our night over with and not have to work hard."

"Sounds good to me," Justin yelled back. "If you'll run down and start the grill, so it will warm up, I'll wash my hands and get the steaks ready. We can make a salad together."

Frank left, and when he returned, he spread the word that dinner would be ready at 1830 outside on the patio. Everyone was excited that Frank and Justin had taken the cooking duties the first night.

While Frank was gone, Justin got the steaks out and laid them on cookie sheets. Justin preferred rib-eye steaks, and what was there were New York steaks, but they would do. He was putting seasoning salt on them when Frank returned. Together they made a big salad and put it in the refrigerator.

A little after 1700, they carried the food and eating utensils down to the patio. It was on the west side of the building, and by 1800 it was catching the last of the afternoon sun. The air was warm, but there was also a subtle hint of cool. The area was surrounded by woods and the air smelled like fall. The trees were mostly birch and maple. They were just starting to turn orange.

The building was red brick, and at first the area was warm with the sun reflecting off it. The patio floor was made of gray flagstone with a dozen or more picnic tables and lawn chairs scattered around. There was a large fire pit off to one side with a stack of wood beside it. There was also a large gazebo with a gas grill. It was well equipped with a sink and even a large stainless steel table for food preparation.

Frank set several tables with paper plates, napkins and plastic eating utensils. Justin was preparing to put the steaks on when Colonel Straight, Colonel Forrester and Captain Quest arrived. They were talking between themselves and only briefly acknowledged Justin and Frank. They sat down in the lawn chairs and quietly continued their conversation.

It was not long before two others arrived. Justin recognized the woman to be the chief nurse for the female cryogenic ward, Millie Syster. The other was a man who looked like a weightlifter.

Frank said, "He's Tony Tonnick, the chief nurse for the male cryogenic ward."

Nurse Syster looked like she may have strayed into the wrong place. She was wearing a black leather miniskirt, a revealing low-cut pink silk blouse, fish-net hose and flashy pink high-heel shoes. She had blond shoulder-length hair with a pink bow in it. It was hard to tell what the true color of her eyes were, as her lashes were so thick and long it was like looking for a rabbit in a briar patch. She wore bright-pink lipstick and smelled like a perfume factory.

Tony Tonnick looked like a pro-wrestler. He had thin long blond hair, huge biceps, a chest like a steel barrel and a neck that had to have been twenty-five inches around. He had small close together eyes and a flat nose that looked like it had been broken more than once.

Frank walked into the gazebo, poked Justin, and looking at Millie, whispered, "Bet those aren't real."

"Frank," Justin whispered back. "I thought priests weren't supposed to notice such things."

"How can you not notice headlights like those?"

Justin ignored Frank's last comment, and said, "It looks like Tony is into bodybuilding."

"Yeah, it does. It also looks like ole Tony better watch out or Millie might want to do some bodybuilding on him. They look like a pair."

Several others soon arrived, so Justin called out, "I just started cooking a few steaks. If you'll come into the gazebo, you can pick the one you want."

Dinner went well for the first night, and everyone seemed to be comfortable with one another. As they ate, the conversation revolved around the crew meeting and what would happen in the days to come. After everyone had their steak, Justin cooked one for himself and Frank. Justin sat down next to an attractive lady to eat his steak. She appeared to be about twenty-five with short curly hair, a thin face, big eyes and full lips.

"I know Mr. Harris introduced us all at the crew meeting, but I'm terrible with names. I'm Justin LeMoore, the social worker," he said, extending his hand.

"I'm Carol McGregor, one of the nurses," she replied, shaking his hand.

Trying to make conversation, Justin asked where she had gone to school.

"I received my RN degree from Mississippi State University, School of Nursing."

"How did you end up on the mission?" Justin asked.

"I worked for a home health care agency for eight years. Many of our patients were bedridden. When I saw an advertisement in a nursing magazine about the mission and taking care of cryogenic patients, I applied."

As they were talking, another person sat down and introduced himself as Blaine Pustual. I'm in the physical therapy section. I'll be working on the male cryogenic ward."

Blaine was tall, slim with dark hair, which he wore in a ponytail. He had brown eyes and a Santa Claus smile. He said he was a Choctaw Native American.

"We certainly have an interesting mix of people and professions on the mission. What will you do as a physical therapist?" Justin asked.

"When someone is in cryogenic hibernation, it's important they are moved and their muscles worked every day. That prevents them from atrophying and becoming stiff. Each patient must be what we call patterned. That entails moving, massaging, rotating and exercising their limbs each day."

They talked for several minutes until someone yelled, "The sun's gone down and it's getting chilly. Can we build a fire in the fire pit?"

"I can't see why not," Justin responded.

He got up and between himself and several others, they soon had a roaring fire going. Everyone picked up a lawn chair and crowded around. The warmth of the fire felt good, and the smell of smoke reminded Justin of his and Ted's last fishing trip. In his mind's eye, he could see the lunker he caught and wondered if he would ever get the chance to catch it again.

At first everyone was trying to get to know one another and the conversation was lively. During a lull in the chitchat, Justin commented, "I've heard a lot about the Kozenskies. Does anyone know any details about them?" He didn't say anything about having talked to Mr. Harris.

"I heard they bought their way into the project," Millie replied.

"That's nonsense," Colonel Forrester retorted. "They were brought into the mission by Congressman Richards. He recognized they're the most intelligent people alive. Dr. Vidula Kozenskie has done some remarkable things with computers and Dr. Ervin Kozenskie is a genius at space engineering. They have both contributed to safety features that are decades ahead of their time. They made a mistake which landed them in prison, but that doesn't mean they shouldn't have a second chance."

"That's partially true," Justin replied. "Prison statistics suggest that recidivism is still well over fifty percent."

"So you don't think people can change?" Colonel Straight demanded.

"I didn't say that, sir. What I said was over half the prisoners incarcerated will reoffend after getting out. From the little I know about the Kozenskies, they appear hungry for power and control. Even in regard to the train, they appear to be seeking involvement and control in everything. That suggests they have not significantly changed from their previous behavior."

A thin nervous-looking lady spoke up, and said, "I've heard they have all kinds of secret stuff hidden away in the computers."

"I'm sorry, I didn't catch your name," Justin said.

"My name is Nancy Applegate. I'm the chief of nutrition," she responded.

Nancy looked to be about fifty-five, a wrinkled face and bleached blond long hair. She had bluish eyes and a mouth that never changed from a steady frown.

The argument was getting out of hand with some saying they were mission essential and others saying the Kozenskies were dangerous.

"I'm friends with a social worker at the Beaumont prison where the Kozenskies were incarcerated. I could give him a call and see what his opinion is. If anyone would like me to," Justin said.

"I'd like to know," Frank, Millie and several others eagerly stated.

"Alright," Justin said. He made the call reaching his buddy at home. He told him about the mission and that several people on the crew wanted to know more about Drs. Vidula and Ervin Kozenskie.

There was a long pause before his friend said, "Can you get out of going?"

"No, I've signed a contract," Justin replied.

"I wish you could. I think the Kozenskies are two of the most dangerous people on the face of this earth. Vidula is a charmer and can talk up a storm about how they want to help create a perfect society. Don't trust them. They're both power hungry and will do anything it takes to get and keep their power. They have surrounded themselves with about a dozen other prisoners as kind of bodyguards.

"One of their so-called friends somehow got into the female ward and broke a guard's arm. Although the female ward is a restricted area for males, he somehow gained access and was supposedly defending Vidula. I think their intention is to have their prison militia go on the mission, and if that happens, I feel sorry for whoever crosses them. Ferrell Logan is the big guy who broke into the female ward. He's a psychopath. He enjoys inflicting pain and fights to kill. After the female inmate incident, they put him in solitary confinement and started an investigation. But it didn't go anywhere. The Kozenskies saw to that. In my opinion, the Kozenskies are not only intelligent but also dangerous. They somehow manipulated their way into the New World project by conning some congressman. Now they're recognized as world authorities on cryogenics, space ship fabrication, celestial navigation and a host of other things.

"They both have photographic memories and not just for broad stuff. They can read a technical journal and recite page for page what they've read. What's more amazing is they understand what they read and can discuss the material with the best in the field. It's scary. They are so much smarter than anyone else, that I don't think there is any way to control them. They were forbidden from using any computer equipment while in prison, but when they were accepted for your mission their computer privileges were restored. Now they're back using the federal prison network to do research and heaven knows what else. Everything they access supposedly goes through the FBI server and is monitored, but I don't think there's anyone in the FBI smart enough to know what they're doing. They even had space engineers coming to the prison to discuss issues with them. I don't know what they will do, but I'll lay odds they're up to something. If you're going on that mission, I pity you. I think you're a sheep entering a lion's den."

"You're not painting a very pretty picture," Justin said.

"I'm just calling it as I see it," his friend responded.

"Then there's Milton Slusser. Have you met him yet?"

"Unfortunately yes, and I don't trust him either."

"You're right, don't trust him. He came down here and began

meeting with the Kozenskies about four years ago. The next thing we knew, they were telling us what to do. They and Slusser would meet for hours at a time discussing finances, computer systems and who knows what else. I think they somehow bought off Congressman Richards and Mr. Slusser. I've been told they still have multibillions of dollars stashed away in secret accounts around the world."

"Have you met Congressman Richards?" Justin asked.

"Nope. He came several years back. I didn't see him though. Since then everything comes from that beady-eyed Slusser guy. I don't know what else to tell you. Just be careful."

"Thanks for the information, although you sure haven't done much to relieve my anxiety," Justin said. "Have a great evening and I'll keep you informed."

"You just keep your eyes, ears and any other senses you have wide open. We're all glad to have them out of our facility."

"That was interesting," Justin said, as he disconnected his communication device and reported his conversation.

Several said they'd heard similar things and wanted an explanation from Mr. Harris; otherwise, they'd pull out of the project.

Dr. Tegan Holly and Won Cho from the engineering section spoke up, and said, "We support the Kozenskies. They've made the train far safer than it would have been without their assistance."

Dr. Tegan Holly looked like a college professor. He appeared to be about forty with graying hair, a reddish complexion and green eyes. Won Cho was a tall Oriental man with stiff black hair, a roundish face and dark eyes.

Brent and Zagar from the communication and signal sections also spoke up, and said, "They've been helpful in designing the train's communication system" Brent said.

"I think Vidula is manipulative and has designed software that no one except she can access," Zagar commented.

Brent Smith was a short man who looked to be about forty. He had light-brown hair, hazel eyes and bushy eyebrows.

Zagar Hamzah was from Iraq. He was about five foot six inches tall, dark complexion, black hair and a heavy black mustache.

Captain Quest piped up, saying, "I support the Kozenskies. Ervin's seen things in the star charts that I've never noticed."

There were definitely two camps, those who swore by the Kozenskies and those with questions.

After Justin, Frank, and several others finished cleaning up, they each returned to their rooms. For some reason, Justin found Millie Syster intriguing, despite her appearance. He was curious, so he got the pamphlet out that Mr. Harris had given everyone. Millie received her nursing degree from the University of Maryland School of Nursing. She'd worked for the past ten years at the UCLA Medical Center where she'd been responsible for long-term chronically ill patients.

After all that had gone on, Justin found it hard to sleep his first night. Everything was overwhelming, but mostly he kept hearing his friend say, 'Can you get out of the mission? Keep your eyes, ears and all your other senses wide open. Don't trust the Kozenskies.'

5

Breakfast was on your own and everyone congregated in the kitchen. Apparently, Justin wasn't the only one who had a hard time sleeping, as the topic of conversation around the table was again the Kozenskies. After another lengthy discussion, Nancy Applegate and several others felt they had to clear the air with Mr. Harris before any team building could take place.

When they all arrived at the office area, Mr. Harris was in the conference room wearing a maroon turtleneck T-shirt, crisp ironed tan slacks and new white tennis shoes.

Several said, "We thought you told us to wear clothes we could get dirty. Why are you dressed like you're going to a concert?"

"That's correct. I said for you to wear clothes you can get dirty. I didn't say anything about me." Then turning to the two people sitting next to him, he said, "I'd like to start by introducing Linda Bracket and Norman Israelson. Linda and Norman are George Washington University recreation graduate students. For the next three days, they're going to help us get to know one another. After Linda and Norman finish their material, we'll be going to Marine Corps Base Camp Lejeune. Several young energetic marines will take us through the confidence course and other outdoor activities. So, with that, I'd like to turn the time over to Linda and Norman."

Raising her hand, Nancy Applegate, said, "Sir."

"Yes, Nancy, what can I do for you?"

"Sir, we need to discuss the Kozenskies before we begin. We spent a lot of time talking about them last night. Some of us are concerned about the role they're playing in the mission."

The two graduate students took their seats as Mr. Harris slowly stood. To the students, he said, "Please wait for me in my office. It appears we have some things to discuss before we can begin."

"Okay Nancy, what are your concerns?"

"Last night some of us discussed the Kozenskies at length and we're uncomfortable about them. They nearly brought war to the world, bankrupted entire countries, had their own underground hit squad and now they're almost running the mission. We talked to an individual who works at the Beaumont prison, where they've been detained for the past four years. He said they can't be trusted."

"What individual?" Mr. Harris pointedly asked.

"Sir, I called one of my social work buddies who has worked with the Kozenskies for the past four years," Justin responded.

Mr. Harris remained standing and looked at each person. "I don't know what I can say to reassure those of you who have questions. I've talked to the FBI and they have not seen anything that suggests a problem. I've probed into everything I can think of to see if I can find something others may have missed. I haven't found anything either."

"Sir," Colonel Straight said. "May I say something?"

Hesitantly Mr. Harris replied, "If you have something constructive to say."

"Yes, sir, I believe I do. The Kozenskies are the smartest people on this planet. Were they manipulative and dangerous in society? Of course they were and they're where they should be, in prison. However, the mission has given them an outlet for their genius. They now have a purpose for their intelligence and they've embraced that challenge. And according to some of our own crew, they are fully engaged in making the ship safer. We all agree that prior to their incarceration, they were off track and let power go to their heads in their attempt to control the world economy. But the concept of creating a more effective block of smaller countries, increasing the GNP of those countries, and raising their standard of living was in and of itself a noble goal.

"As far as the mission goes, all I can say is yes, they are intelligent, but they have used their intelligence to make the train a better vehicle. So what is the down side of them participating in the mission? They aren't going to do anything to jeopardize their own safety."

Mr. Harris listened, and then said, "For the most part, I concur with you, Colonel Straight. Vidula and Ervin have contributed a great deal to the mission. This mission is also important to me, but it is not as important as any one of your lives. I hope each of you can trust me in that regard. If I find evidence something could be wrong from the Kozenskies, or from anywhere else, I'll be the first to shut the entire project down. I will never knowingly let any of you enter into harm's way."

After a pause, and looking around the room, Mr. Harris continued. "Will there be dangers on the mission? Of course there will. Space travel is always dangerous. But as Tegan and Won have said, the Kozenskies have made safety improvements that would have gone undetected without their genius."

Then again pausing and looking around the room, he continued, "It is obvious there are still many of you with concerns, so let's clear the air. I'd like to hear what you all have to say."

For the next forty-five minutes, many of the crew argued the Kozenskies had been given too much authority. They had access to every vital component of the ship, which made many crew members nervous.

Justin told Mr. Harris what his friend had said: "Never trust them. Keep your eyes, ears and any other senses you have on alert."

It was uncanny but the door opened, and who should be standing there but Mr. Milton Slusser. He walked in, placed his hands on the table while his beady little eyes darted from person to person.

"I thought I'd stop in and see how things are going. From what I can see, it doesn't look like much team building is going on."

"There's been some questions about the Kozenskies which had to be resolved before any meaningful team building could take place," Mr. Harris replied.

"So have they been resolved?"

"Most of the issues have been discussed."

"Good," Mr. Slusser stated. "For the past five years Congressman Richards has worked hard to obtain and maintain funding for this project. He's had an uphill battle. But when the Kozenskies became involved, he's had a much easier time."

"Sir, last night I spoke to one of my social work friends who works at the Beaumont prison. He wasn't as complimentary about them as you are. In fact, he suggested they are dangerous and shouldn't be trusted," Justin stated.

Mr. Slusser's face turned almost purple. "Mr. LeMoore, just what exactly did your friend say you shouldn't trust? Let's see. Perhaps that they've improved the structural integrity of the train. Or perhaps they've built redundant systems to ensure your safety if one, two or even three should fail? Or perhaps it's because they've become world experts on cryogenics and made medical contributions, which I think even Dr. Towns would acknowledge as valuable. And with all of that you talk about some buddy who says he doesn't trust them? Can this friend produce one shred of solid evidence of a diabolical plot they are accused of hatching? Well, Mr. LeMoore! Have you any such evidence?"

"No, sir, I don't think there's any hard evidence. But he did say—"

Mr. Slusser broke in, "No evidence! Do you all hear that bullshit? Some no-name social work buddy has a gut feeling. No evidence, just a feeling. And he wants that to stand against the mounting contributions they've made to ensure the mission is safer, faster and more comfortable for everyone. He sits there as a mental health expert disputing that they may have seen the light and changed. Isn't that part of why mental health exists? To help people change? Or don't you believe people can change, Mr. LeMoore?"

"I think people can change. But people have to want to change, or see a need for change before anything meaningful will take place."

Quivering with anger, Mr. Slusser walked to Justin, leaned over him and shouted, "Hell-all-mighty, don't you think over four years in a federal prison would make someone want to change? As a mental health professional, it's your responsibility to help inmates see it's in their best interest to change. That's called working through resistance. Perhaps you're not familiar with that term. You appear to be more interested in catching fish than assisting those you're paid to help."

Mr. Harris jumped to his feet and took Mr. Slusser by the arm. "Milton, that's enough! We'll work through the issue. You're only complicating things."

At first it appeared Mr. Slusser was going to hit Mr. Harris, but he paid no attention and led Milton to his seat.

Mr. Harris then went on, "I know some of you still have questions. If any of you cannot trust that I will continue to be vigilant to any issue that could jeopardize your safety or the mission, I'd like to immediately know about them. If you feel you can't or don't want to continue with the mission, I'll release you from your contract with no hard feelings."

"And if you can't refrain from causing trouble or calling your buddies who have no damn credibility, it would be best for everyone if you did leave the mission," Mr. Slusser shouted in a quivering voice as he looked at Justin.

"Milton, I'm responsible for the crew, and I won't allow any person to jeopardize the success of the mission. You've said your piece and now we need to get to work. So if you'll excuse us, we shall do just that."

He escorted Mr. Slusser to the door, and they walked out into the cubicles where he began yelling and waving his arms. "I've had a bad feeling about that damn Justin LeMoore from the first night we met him. I think he should be dismissed. He's a troublemaker. We can't have people like him calling their buddies and stirring the crew up. All the primary players think the Kozenskies have been nothing but helpful. Now one social worker, based on a call to his buddies, has everyone on edge. I'm going to discuss this with the congressman and I'm sure he'll support me. You need to get rid of him!"

"Milton, don't tell me how to manage the crew," Mr. Harris angrily stated. "I'm responsible for the paid staff. I like Justin. He's a leader, but he's not a yes-man. I'm not going to remove him, so if you want to talk to the congressman, go ahead."

"I intend to, and you can expect a call."

"That will be fine," Mr. Harris replied, as he turned back toward the conference room.

Mr. Harris returned, sat down, and said, "Well, that was a heck of a way to start our team-building session. I want each of you to remain on the crew. I have the utmost confidence in you and I hope you have faith in me. I was also dead serious when I said any of you can resign your position with no hard feelings. If you wish to leave, I need to know now."

Then looking at each person, he asked, "Is there anyone who feels they'd like to resign?"

No one responded until Nancy again spoke up. "Do we have to decide immediately?"

"I'm afraid so. We don't have the luxury of much time."

Looking around the group, he asked again, "Is there anyone who is having second thoughts about remaining with the mission?"

Like before, no one responded. "And one last thing," Mr. Harris said. "If you're going to call your friends and get second or third-hand information or opinions, please let me know."

Justin's ears burned. It was obvious who that remark was aimed at.

"With that, I want to briefly meet with each of you in my office. Nancy, I'd like to start with you."

Nancy and Mr. Harris walked to his office and closed the door and blinds.

"That was interesting," Frank said.

Colonel Straight was obviously angry. He stood and looking directly at Justin, said, "All of this is scandalous and as far as I can see, you're nothing but a scaremonger. Until I see something factual, I support the Kozenskies and all the good work they've done. Furthermore, I agree with Mr. Harris. It may be better if someone resigns if all they want to do is dig up dirt about others."

With that, he left the table and walked outside. Several others voiced the same opinion. Suddenly the tide had changed and the majority of the crew seemed to be supportive of the Kozenskies.

Frank looked at Justin, and whispered, "Are you okay?"

"I'm all right. Mr. Slusser and Colonel Straight are right. We don't have any evidence other than hearsay about the Kozenskies doing anything wrong."

It was over an hour before Mr. Harris returned. Nancy was not with him.

Mr. Harris sat down, and said, "Nancy has decided to leave the mission. She doesn't want her negative attitude to impact the rest of the team. I've called a backup nutritionist. She will be here tomorrow as she works in Washington DC and is immediately available. We will postpone the start of the team building until tomorrow. Since it is almost lunchtime, I have taken the liberty of ordering pizza and sodas. It should be here any minute. After we eat, I'd like to meet with each of you and verify your commitment to the mission. If you are thinking of leaving, please make up your mind now so we can get on with what we need to do."

The pizza soon arrived, and everyone sat around the conference room table eating in almost complete silence. Each person seemed to be contemplating his or her individual feelings. After everyone had eaten, there were still two large pizzas left.

Martin said, "I'm cooking tonight. We're having pizza."

Everyone could see that Mr. Harris had received a call in his office. Holding his communicator he again closed his door and blinds.

When Mr. Harris completed the call he returned to the group. "Okay, guys and gals, I want to see each of you alone in my office for about ten minutes each. Afterward, we will meet here as a team, so don't wander off. When we leave this afternoon, either we are unified as a team, or you have decided to leave the mission. Justin, let's start with you since you talked to your buddy and also seem to have strong feelings."

Justin did have strong feelings, which he voiced to Mr. Harris. It was also true he didn't have any facts or evidence. He again told Mr. Harris about his buddy's feelings that the Kozenskies have something up their sleeves. "He thinks they have put together their own prison militia and are plotting to get several of those individuals on the mission."

Bach's Concerto no. 6 was playing in the background, as Mr. Harris said, "I've heard rumors to that effect, but until I have proof, I can't do anything about it. Justin, I like you. We seem to be kindred spirits. You are a key player, and I can see you are a natural leader. But,

I cannot have you going behind my back. I even received a call from Congressman Richards himself about the issue. If you have a question or want to call a buddy, please talk to me first."

"Yes, sir, I will. And I apologize for my indiscretion. It won't happen again. Would you like me to resign?"

"Thank you. And no I do not want you to resign. I know I can trust you," Mr. Harris said. "Now, do you know what music is playing?"

"I believe it's one of Bach's Concertos, but I can't put my finger on which one."

"Your right. You certainly seem to know your classical composers," Mr. Harris noted admiringly.

Everyone had a brief individual meeting with Mr. Harris, and no one else opted to leave. After meeting with each person, Mr. Harris asked, "Does anyone have anything more you would like to say?"

No one raised their hand.

"I take the silence to mean you're all on board and willing to see the mission through. Is that correct?

"Justin?"

"Count me in sir."

"Frank?"

"I'm in."

"Colonel?" he said, looking at Colonel Straight.

"I've always been supportive."

"Mick, what about you?"

"Like Colonel Straight, I've never had a problem with the Kozenskies."

Mr. Harris continued around the room and every person said they were committed.

"All right, as far as I am concerned this issue is over. It is almost 1600, so we'll end for the day and start tomorrow with the team-building activities. I suggest you all go hit the pool or fitness center and relax."

Martin picked up the pizza boxes and again announced, "Dinner will be served in the kitchen. Take what you want. If you desire to warm it, feel free to utilize the microwave."

Everyone seemed like they wanted to be by themselves that evening. Justin needed to talk about something other than the Kozenskies, so he called Ted. They talked about fly tying, and Ted announced they'd both drawn an elk license for the Colorado, Flat Top Mountain hunt in November. Ted said he had a friend who was contacting the Colorado Fish and Wildlife Conservation Office to see if he could buy Justin's license and have it transferred to his name.

That makes me feel pretty lousy, Justin said to himself.

They continued talking, but the conversation was frustratingly difficult. There was an edge in Ted's voice. Things had changed between the two of them.

After the call, Justin felt even more depressed, so he took Mr. Harris's advice. He went to the base pool where he swam until he almost couldn't crawl out. He returned to the guest house, ate the last slice of cold pizza, drank a glass of milk and ate an apple. He went to bed with a bad feeling in the pit of his stomach.

I wonder if I should follow Ms. Applegate and resign. He knew he wouldn't though; something was driving him to see the mission through.

6

The next morning when everyone had taken their seats, Mr. Harris said, "I assume our interchange yesterday settled everything. Are there any lingering issues we need to discuss before we begin?"

No one said anything.

"Good. Then I assume everyone is fully committed to the successful completion of the mission. Am I correct ladies and gentlemen?"

Almost in unison they all responded, "Yes, sir."

The two graduate students were again sitting next to Mr. Harris. Turning to them, he said, "It appears we are ready to begin. Oh, I almost forgot. We have a new crew member with us this morning." He was pointing to a woman sitting next to Millie. "Ms. Laura Yates will replace Ms. Applegate."

Laura Yates looked like a pixie. She was only about five foot two, couldn't have weighed more than a hundred pounds and appeared to be about sixteen.

"When we interviewed to fill the nutrition position, it was a toss-up between my choosing Ms. Applegate or Ms. Yates. I chose Ms. Applegate due to her years of experience, but I could have gone either way. Ms. Yates received her master's degree in nutrition from Georgetown University just three years ago and has worked for the Bethesda Naval Hospital as a nutritionist since then. The navy has been working on their own cryogenic studies and she has been in the forefront of the nutrition section. Her boss was not happy when I called, but she will be even more valuable to him when she returns.

Laura has been fully briefed on our discussion yesterday and is committed to the mission. Is that right, Laura?"

Laura nodded her consent.

Gesturing toward the two graduate students, Mr. Harris said, "I introduced Linda and Norman yesterday, but let me do it again for the benefit of Laura. Linda Bracket and Norman Israelson are recreation graduate students from George Washington University. We were going to spend three days with them, but since we lost yesterday, we will just have today and tomorrow. They are going to help us get to know one another and to work effectively with each other. With that I would like to turn the time over to them."

Justin looked at Frank and whispered, "I hate these stupid get-to-know-you games."

"Me too," Frank responded.

Much to Justin and Frank's delight, the first day was enjoyable. The graduate students kept the group laughing the entire time. They went through several get-to-know-you exercises, and both Justin and Frank had to admit they actually enjoyed them.

Dinner that night was much more animated than the previous night.

Won Cho said, "I've made my mother's favorite recipe of fried rice."

Brent said, "I've made my mother's recipe of spaghetti and meatballs. You can pick one or try some of each."

After dinner, everyone sat around and talked. The Kozenskies never came up.

The following day, Linda and Norman had problem-solving tasks that were either completed by the entire group or by smaller sections. They again made it fun and not stressful for anyone.

At the end of the second day, the students asked permission from the group to use pictures they'd taken of the two-day exercise. "It will help fill one of the requirements for a community recreation class we are taking," Linda stated.

Before they broke for the evening, Mr. Harris said, "Wear camping clothes tomorrow. We'll be going to Camp Lejeune where the marines will take you through four days of the confidence course and other training. A bus will pick you up at the guest house at 0530."

That elicited a groan from everyone.

The next morning was clear but cool. Everyone staggered to the parking lot in front of the guest house at 0530 where a bus was waiting. Mr. Harris was there in a turtleneck sweater, crisp-ironed slacks, and clean white tennis shoes. Everyone wanted to know how he was going to remain clean in those clothes. He just smiled.

Justin saw Nurse Millie sitting by herself, so he asked if she would mind if he sat with her for the ride. She was all decked out in yellow shorts, a light-green blouse, pink tennis shoes and not a hair out of place. She sure didn't look like she was going to do anything that would get her dirty. Justin had never spent any time with her, so it was a good opportunity for both of them to get to know each other.

"How did you learn about the mission?" Justin asked.

"I heard about it through a nurse friend and contacted Mr. Harris. He thought I'd be a good fit for the mission and offered me a position. How did you get on the mission?"

Justin quickly told her about being recruited by Mr. Harris and Mr. Slusser.

"You seem to have strong feelings about the Kozenskies," she noted.

"Having worked in a prison, I'm careful to look at not only what people say, but also where they come from, what got them into trouble and how they operate in prison. People don't usually change unless they see a need for change. Based on what I've heard, the Kozenskies haven't changed. They still appear to be seeking power. They're still manipulative and use other people for their own benefit. For me that makes them hard to trust."

"I agree," Millie said as she began rummaging around in her purse. After a minute she looked up and said, "Damn, I forgot my lip gloss."

Frank was sitting several seats behind Justin and Millie, and Justin could tell he was listening. When they arrived, Justin stepped into the aisle, letting Millie go ahead. After both Frank and Justin exited, Frank quietly asked, "What do you think of our little floozy?"

"She's a little rough around the edges and uses some colorful language, but I like her. I like her a lot. I think you see what you get. She says what she thinks and I like that too."

Looking around, everyone noticed several ominous-looking towers, an obstacle course and a sign that read GAS TRAINING. Captain Quest said it brought back old memories from his navy boot camp training. Both Colonel Straight and Colonel Forrester agreed.

Millie was standing next to Justin and Frank as they were looking at the various obstacles. "I don't climb shit like that, and I for damn sure ain't gonna jump off of one." She was pointing at a tower with a zip line that went from the top far out into a field.

Justin looked at Frank, who just smiled.

"I can pump iron all day long, but I don't like heights either," Tony said.

"Just concentrate on one piece at a time. The marines won't put anyone at risk. Think of it as going to Seven Flags or some other amusement park," Colonel Straight suggested.

"I don't go to amusement parks either. And they damn well can't make me climb up there and jump off. If they want my little pink butt up there, they're going to have to carry me!" Millie responded.

Although Tony was a hulk, he also looked frightened and quietly said, "I don't do amusement parks either."

Four youthful marines appeared. One of them, a slim black sergeant with highly polished boots and a crisp-ironed uniform, asked, "Mr. Harris, would you please identify yourself." Mr. Harris stepped forward and the two of them walked off a little way and discussed the plans for the day.

Carol McGregor from nursing quietly said, "I assume they're plotting about how to kill us in slow, agonizing degrees."

Her comment brought a nervous laugh from the group. Then the sergeant came back and addressed, or rather shouted at everyone. "Welcome to the Camp Lejeune training center ladies and gentlemen. My name is Sergeant George Thaddeus Washington. And this," he said pointing to the various obstacles, "is where we make marines out of civilians like you. You're not going to get the whole training course. We're only going to give you a taste of what you see. I've been told your experience will be for team building. Let me assure you, it will take a team to get through the training over the next four days.

"I noticed several of you looking at the towers. Don't let them or any of the other obstacles scare you. Thousands of marines go through this course each year and only about twenty-five percent die." Then looking at several frightened faces in the group, he followed up with, "Just joking. Actually we have a one-hundred percent safety record, so don't be worried."

The sergeant then shouted, pointing at the various events, "Each obstacle or training device is designed to teach two objectives: First, you're stronger and tougher than you think, which builds individual confidence. Second, some of the training will be obstacles that can't be accomplished alone. It will take you and your buddies to complete them. You're going to encourage one another, help one another and in four days you'll know who you can count on and who you can't."

Sergeant Washington smiled and continued, "We're going to start off with a little two-mile run to get our muscles warmed up and working."

"Two miles!" Several people groaned in unison. "I don't walk two miles in a week."

"All right, I want everyone to fall in," the Sergeant shouted. No one, except the three former solders, seemed to know exactly what that term meant, so he yelled, "People! That means line up! Move! Move!"

Everyone quickly lined up and the group staggered around the two-mile track with Sergeant Washington singing military cadence, or Jody songs. When they returned, Millie was bending over with her hands on her knees huffing and puffing.

Justin asked, "Are you all right?"

She wheezed, "Hell no, I'm not all right. Do I look alright? If I'd have known we had to do this kind of crap, I'd never have signed up."

Several others who were either lying on the ground or trying to breathe, agreed.

The rest of the day was spent sliding down ropes, making rope bridges or crawling through tires. For lunch, they ate cold Meals Ready To Eat, or MREs as the sergeant called them. By the end of the day, every member of the group was dirty, stiff, sore and tired.

Millie's yellow shorts were black, and she had long angry welts up and down her legs. Her neatly cut blouse had three buttons torn off and her hair had sticks and mud caked in it. Even Tony, the nurse hulk, who had a T-shirt that read BONES ARE FOR BREAKING, was tired and acted like several of his bones had been broken.

Mr. Harris was still neat, clean and seemed to be enjoying everyone else's misery.

Justin rode back with Frank, but there was very little conversation.

When the bus pulled into the guest house parking lot, Mr. Harris announced, "Tomorrow we will meet here at 0500."

"Why 0500 tomorrow? After today we won't even be able to get out of bed. This wasn't in our contract," Jerry Johnson, the laboratory specialist said.

With a big smile, Mr. Harris replied, "Oh yes, it is. Your contract states prior to departure you will engage in team building and other duties. So don't whine."

After Mr. Harris departed, Colonel Forrester said, "I don't think it's right that Mr. Harris isn't joining in the fun. I suggest the last day we make sure he gets a little dirty."

"I second that," Justin said.

"I'm going to have a bath and I'm not getting out until tomorrow morning," Rachael Beck from Pharmacy whined.

Frank replied, "And I think dinner should be up to the individual. For me, I'm going to skip dinner, take a long hot shower and go to bed."

"I thought missing a meal was something you refused to do coming from a big Irish Catholic family," Justin teased.

"It is a first. I'll admit that. But I'm so tired I don't think I could lift a spoon."

They were a sorry sight the next morning as they limped into the parking lot at 0500. Mr. Harris was there looking sharp as usual in a pair of gray slacks, tennis shoes, another turtleneck sweater and a tweed jacket. Everyone else wore blue jeans and long-sleeve shirts. Millie was sporting a pair of new long jeans and a long-sleeve blue sweatshirt. She still had her pink signature tennis shoes on though.

When several people commented on her new outfit, she retorted, "Hell, fashion only goes so far when someone is trying to kill you."

There was very little talk on the bus. They all seemed to be contemplating what misery was in store for them upon arrival.

Sergeant Washington was waiting for them wearing sweat clothes. After another staggering two-mile run, it was a team log carry and then three hours of emergency medical training.

"Okay, boys and girls," Sergeant Washington announced, "You're in for a real treat. The dreaded tower jump is next. Actually you're going to love it. It's so much fun you'll all want to do it again. Heck, we should be charging for the ride."

Shove it up your butt, Millie said under her breath.

After some safety instruction, Sergeant Washington said, "One person at a time will climb the tower. There will be two helpful marines at the top who will strap you into a harness. Your harness will be attached to the slide cable, and when the instructor tells you to jump, you jump. Just hold on to your harness and enjoy the ride. Now doesn't that sound like fun?"

"Why don't you demonstrate how to do it," Tony asked in a worried voice.

"I've done it hundreds of times. It's a piece of cake. Don't worry, once you've done it, you'll want to do it again."

"Wanna bet?" Tony said.

Justin volunteered to go first thinking it would be exciting. When he was told to jump, he jumped. The cable acted like a spring throwing him into the air; then he raced to the bottom of the slide into a sawdust pit where two marines sort of caught him.

"You can go to hell if you think I'm going to climb that thing," Millie said again. However, she was eventually forced into it. She cursed and cussed all the way up, and when she got to the top, her blood turned to ice.

It took the two husky marines several minutes of enduring Millie's cursing before they were able to manhandle her into the harness. Although they seemed to enjoy it. Once strapped in, she stood on the platform paralyzed. After trying to coax her to jump, one of the marines gave her a push and away she went. It sounded like a banshee war cry as she careened down the cable and into the sawdust pit.

Getting up and spitting sawdust, she wailed, "Hell almighty. I peed my pants."

Like Millie, Tony had to almost be carried up the tower and pushed off. No one was sure if he wet his pants or not.

After another lunch of cold MREs, the afternoon was spent in gas mask training.

Sergeant Washington said, "The gas chamber is to provide confidence in a gas mask or oxygen mask."

"When in the hell, are we ever going to need a gas mask on the mission?" Millie asked.

"You probably won't," Mr. Harris interjected. "But if there was a fire on the train, there could be dangerous gases. If you can wear a mask in a gas chamber, then you'll have confidence that you can wear one anywhere."

By the end of the second day, most had blisters on their hands and feet—and again hurt all over.

Before they boarded the bus, Sergeant Washington said he needed to talk to everyone. "We have a real treat for you tomorrow. We'll be assembling at the airfield. Then we're going take you on a little plane ride. Have any of you experienced weightlessness?"

Only the command crew raised their hands. "Well, tomorrow you'll all have that opportunity. I suggest you don't eat breakfast. Barfing in weightlessness is a messy experience. Everything just floats around in the cabin. Cheerios, milk, half-digested bacon, pancakes and cheese burritos are all right there to see and taste again if you want. The first time I went up, almost the entire group of us puked our guts out. And when we landed, we had to clean the plane. I never saw such a mess and several of us started puking again."

"We get the picture," Millie said. "We don't need a damn blow-by-blow description."

"I just don't want to surprise anyone tomorrow. Also, wear long pants, tennis shoes and a warm jacket. The plane gets pretty cold at more than fifty thousand feet."

When the group got back to the guest house, everyone again went to their rooms for more hot baths, showers and plenty of aspirin or Tylenol.

The group was in hopes they'd get out of the two-mile run on the third day, but there was Sergeant Washington waiting for the bus in his marine sweat clothes. Singing at the top of his voice, he led them on their two-mile stagger around the airfield. After the run, they loaded into the airplane and were off.

On the way up, Sgt. Washington and someone from the flight crew gave a briefing on weightlessness. They were told that at fifty thousand, the plane would go into a steep dive and for several minutes they would be weightless.

"Anyone have a big breakfast?" Sergeant Washington yelled over the roar of the plane's engines.

No one raised their hand. "That's too bad. I was hoping to identify who'd be volunteering to clean the plane when we land. It looks like everyone will have to pitch in. We'll make about four dives today, so you'll all get a good exposure to what weightlessness feels like."

The group did well. No one lost their breakfast and the experience turned out to be exciting for everyone. They were like children bouncing off one another, laughing and having a wonderful time.

They landed shortly before noon, and after cleaning the plane, they ate another lunch of cold MREs. In the afternoon they had a class on the effects of weightlessness and space medicine.

"Tomorrow bring a swimming suit. The final day will be conducted at the base swimming pool. You'll put on space suits and do underwater drills," Sergeant Washington yelled. "Working in self-contained space suits, underwater, is as close to working in space as anything you can experience on Earth."

The final day again started with the much-dreaded two-mile

run. Everyone had blisters on top of blisters, and it was painful just to walk, let alone run. After the run, they were told to put their swimming suits on. They were then fitted with heavy bulky space suits and told to pair up. Each person was given an air tank, which had two hours of air in it. After a brief familiarization drill, each pair was given what looked like a small window with an aluminum frame and a number on it.The window unit was white on one side, black on the other and was held together with screws. Each pair was given a tool belt and told to toss their window into the pool.

Sergeant Washington then instructed them. "Ease into the pool, drop to the bottom and find your window. Together with your buddy you'll unscrew the assembly, change it from the white side to the black side, screw it back together, then lift it out and have it examined by one of the instructors."

Getting used to being in an unfamiliar environment, breathing out of tanks and a regulator was at first challenging. Trying to use screwdrivers and small end wrenches with clumsy gloves on was maddening. Many dropped their tools and tried to take each other's screws. If a pair brought out an assembly without all the screws, they were given another tank of air and sent back into the pool. Some spent the better part of the morning before they accomplished the task.

After a final cold MRE lunch, the group spent the afternoon going through the individual obstacle course in the rain. One event had a rope hanging over a small muddy creek. Each person had to grab the rope, swing across the creek, then swing the rope back to the next person. The rope was wet and slick, which meant almost everyone took a dunking. Mr. Harris stood nearby smiling and holding his umbrella in his pressed slacks, golf shoes, another warm turtleneck sweater and a sport jacket.

After Justin took a dunking, he moved over to Colonel Forrester. "I think Mr. Harris should join in the fun." Several others agreed.

Justin, Colonel Forrester, Frank and Dr. Won Cho casually walked over, picked Mr. Harris up, carried him to the creek and tossed him in. He came up spluttering, coughing and by the time he crawled up the muddy creek bank, he looked like everyone else. Glaring at everyone with mud hanging on his eyelashes, he said, "Beware. I don't get mad, but I do get even."

Of course those who had not participated protested that they should not be held accountable.

"This is team training. And since everyone laughed and cheered, you are all culpable. As they say, payback is hell, so be prepared," Mr. Harris said.

The four days revealed who could be counted on under stress, who wasn't reliable, who was frightened of what, who was willing to risk and who hung back when things got tough.

Millie was the surprise of the group. At first everyone thought she'd be a prissy miss and above getting her hands dirty. She fooled everyone though. She slid down ropes, crawled across walls, low crawled through mud and was the perfect cheerleader. Millie liked to look good and talk rough, but when the chips were down, she was willing to get as dirty as anyone else. She became the group mother, always flitting around making sure everyone was okay, encouraging, smiling and helping where she could.

Chaplain Frank Molony was the teddy bear of the group. He struggled running and with many of the physical demands, but was always happy, helpful and interested in everyone. As unlikely as it seemed, Frank and Millie were the two most parental figures of the group. Everyone was sure they'd butt heads on everything, but instead they ended up liking and working with each other.

Everyone thanked the marines for four well-executed days. Although sore, cold, and miserable, everyone said they had learned a lot about themselves and one another.

When the bus arrived at the guest house, Mr. Harris said, "I had planned to give everyone off tomorrow, as it will be Sunday. But since I was thrown into the creek, which injured my pride, it will be an office-party day. Do you know what an office party is?"

No hands were raised.

"Okay, then I'll tell you. We will meet at 0430 and clean the office until it shines. The bathrooms will be polished and the rafters dusted. All the cubicles will be moved, the nasty orange carpet removed and the floors painted before the end of the day."

Several of the crew said, "That for sure isn't in the contract. We're not in the army you know."

"Not only is it not in our contract, but it's also horseshit," Millie exclaimed.

"I beg your pardon," Mr. Harris said, looking at Millie. "This is an important lesson for you all to learn. Does anyone know what that is?"

"Don't mess with the boss?" Laura Yates nervously replied.

"Very good, Laura. Don't mess with the boss. In addition, there's no better way of learning about your fellow teammates than working together. Especially on a Sunday."

There was another collective groan from the group.

Then with a twinkle in his eye, Mr. Harris said with a smile, "Just kidding. Take the day off. You all need to go to church and ask for forgiveness. We'll meet at the office Monday morning at 0730. Tegan, Holly, and Won Cho from Engineering, along with some of the contract crew who designed and built the train, will give you a two-day overview of the vessel. I think you'll all be confident in the train after their review. Thanks for your hard work. You were all great. Have a relaxing day off. I'll see you Monday morning."

Many of the crew did go to church, including Justin and Frank even went with him. Frank had said he might like to attend a Mormon service sometime and Justin was delighted to take him.

In the evening, Justin and Frank made hunter stew and fresh-baked Dutch oven corn bread. After being out in the cold all day, the warm food was not only good but also comforting. There was a great deal of chatter and everyone felt they'd learned a lot about one another. They were friends, and for the most part, everyone felt comfortable with one another.

7

Monday was sunny but cool, so everyone wore jackets. Dr. Tegan Holly, Dr. Won Cho, and five others, they didn't recognize, were all at the warehouse dressed in business suits. When everyone was seated in the conference room, Mr. Harris stood and asked if they all had a good day off.

"It was wonderful," several said.

"I'd like to tell you that we'll have weekends off, but with the short time we have to complete the ground portion of the project, I can't guarantee how many you'll get. Currently the train is to leave the docking station, eight-hundred miles above Earth, the last week in March. That means we are on a tight schedule.

"Okay," he said, looking at the group. "I'd like to turn the time over to Tegan and Won. As you can see, we also have some visitors. I'll let Tegan introduce them."

Tegan stood, and said, "I'm glad for the opportunity to give you an overview of the Space Train. We're all proud of it, and I'm sure you will be too. Notice I didn't say spaceship. A space ship denotes just what it says, a vessel with an outside hull and everything enclosed within it. Normally, a space ship has a command area, and all command and communication flows through that area. We've designed a new concept. A Space Train.

"With that said, let me introduce you to my colleagues. These are only part of the engineering team who helped design the vessel. Some are now overseeing the construction and assembly of the train. To my right is Mr. Van Johnson, who is the primary engineer. Van and his colleagues work for Space Corp. They are known worldwide for designing and building state-of-the-art space ships and about anything else that's space related. Next, we have Mr. Frank Harris, no relation to our Mr. Harris. Frank is the structural engineer. Along with Dr. Ervin Kozenskie, they developed the carbon, aluminum, and gel-foam-laminate hull. Their vision and technical know-how has revolutionized spacecraft hulls."

Then gesturing toward the only woman on the team, he said, "This is Ms. Courtney Cook. Courtney is a connective seal expert. She designed the connective links and seals which allows each car to move independently.

"To Courtney's right is Mr. Lester Bingham, the propulsion engineer. He's designed propulsion motors for everything from space battle cruisers to space tugs. The motors Lester designed for the mission are the most innovative, advanced space motors available. They're fueled by a mixture of synthetic plasma and carbon, which is misted into the combustion chamber. The design has proven to be reliable and easy to use.

"The last person is Mr. Matthew Alton. Matt is a life science system specialist. He was responsible for designing the air, water, sanitation, heat and cooling systems for the train.

"There are two other individuals who've been instrumental in making everything come together. They are Drs. Vidula and Ervin Kozenskie. They've been helpful in the problem-solving process and I've come to deeply respect their work."

Flipping a small 3-D projector on, a large picture of the space train appeared as if floating in air. Some cars had windows, but most looked like big silver tubes. "This is a rendition of what the space train will look like when it's assembled at the US space dock. The command car is currently complete and in Houston waiting to be ferried to the train. The other sections are in various stages of completion. They should be finished within the next few months. It's a race against time to get everything constructed, assembled, tested, ferried into space and all the supplies loaded before the end of March.

"Currently there are four cars which are totally complete and in space. The rest are being ferried up to the assembly site as they are constructed. None of us are willing to compromise on safety though. Even if it takes longer, we'll take as much time as required to ensure each piece of the train is built to specification. They will then be tested both on the ground and in space.

"The train will have sixty cars when completed. Each car is a hundred yards long, forty-eight feet wide, forty-five feet high and weighs over three hundred tons empty. The cars with the windows are primarily living space," he said, pointing to several cars with rows of black squares.

"This is the command car," he noted, pointing to the front of the ship with a V-shaped nose section and what appeared to be a wraparound thin black line.

Pointing to the black line, Tegan continued. "This is a window that allows a one-hundred-and-eighty-degree view. It's six inches thick and can withstand and deflect meteors up to the size of a small car. The window is not just to see out of. It serves as a microwave detection device. That allows the command group to see objects as small as a pea up to five million miles away and warn the command of potential collision dangers.

"That sounds like a lot of distance, but with a train as big as this"—he pointed—"going faster than the speed of light, it can't turn on a dime. The command crew will need all the time possible to make course corrections. In addition to meteors, there are solar storms that can send gamma and X-rays spewing into space at near the velocity of light. A large geomagnetic storm could induce electrical currents that might cause transformers and other electrical equipment to overheat, catch fire or explode. Such damage could be catastrophic. At best, it would fry all the electronic equipment. At worst, it could kill everyone on board and turn the train into a zombie craft, adrift and dead in space.

"If I've frightened everyone, let me reassure you we have planned for such events. We have helioseismology equipment on board that will map solar flares and storms from millions of miles away, allowing us to detour around them."

For the next two days, the engineers continued to give a detailed explanation of the entire train. They explained the function of each car along with the numerous safety features. Although interesting, most explanations were so far above the heads of the audience that many had a hard time remaining awake.

On the morning of the third day, Tegan opened by saying, "I know we've bored some of you to tears with engineering details, which you may not be interested in. I hope our discussion, and all the detail, has given you a sense of confidence in the train. It truly is a marvel. And as you can see, all of us who have worked on the train are proud of what we've collectively accomplished. So with that, we'd like to answer any questions you may have. I'm confident between all of us, we can answer any question you may have."

"You've told us about the train in detail, but what about supplies?" Frank asked. "I'd like to hear about food."

After a chuckle from the group, Tegan continued. "The train will hold enough supplies and equipment to build a small city. That also includes food. Not only will it have a store-house of preserved foods, but one entire floor is also nothing but a gigantic freezer. It is stocked like a cruise ship with some pretty exotic stuff, like ice cream, crab, steaks and lots of other goodies. The middle floor of the same car is a greenhouse, which will grow fresh vegetables and fruit. I'll guarantee, you won't starve on the mission. Did that answer your question, Chaplain?"

"Yes. Thank you. That puts my mind to rest," Frank responded.

Leonard Maxwell raised his hand, and asked, "I know what you said about the command car being able to deflect meteors or shooting space rocks, but what if the command car is damaged or destroyed? Will we all die and the train be nothing but a piece of space junk?"

"Heaven forbid. If that were to happen, the train could successfully be guided to its destination with nothing more than a handheld computer from any car in the train. It wouldn't be as comfortable as the command car, but it could be done."

Tegan then said, "Matt, would you please address the life-support issue?"

"Sure," Matt responded. "Each life-support function has at least three backup systems. If a space rock should hit one car and damage the life-support equipment, the affected car would instantly seal itself from the cars to its front and rear. At least three other life-support systems in other cars would instantly assume responsibility for unaffected areas in the damaged car. Once repairs have been accomplished, the original equipment can take over again."

"What would happen to a person who was in a car that was hit by a meteor?" Leonard went on.

Courtney stood, and said, "I think I can answer that. The reality is this: If you're in a car when compression is lost or there's a hull breach, there will be nothing you can do. In less than point three seconds, the doors will close and seal the affected area off. Everything that's not secured will be sucked out, which includes crew members. Space is almost a total vacuum and several hundred degrees below zero. Human flesh would instantly freeze solid. But let me emphasize that such an event is extremely remote."

Tegan stepped over to a table, and said, "Let me show you something. I thought this might come up, so I've brought two pieces of spacecraft hulls. This is a piece of hull from the first ship." He was holding up a metal square about two feet in diameter.

Holding it sidewise, he pointed, "You can see it's made of five layers of hardened aluminum. "Each plate is about an inch apart. Then turning it to the front, he pointed at a small dark spot. This is a tiny hole. It was made by an atomic test gun at the space agency test area in New Mexico. The projectile was the size of a grain of rice and shot at twenty thousand miles an hour. Now look at this side," he said turning the piece around. As the object went through one layer to the next, the hole got bigger and bigger until in the fifth plate it's three inches across."

"Now," he said, bending over and straining to pick up another piece of hull. "This is a piece of our current train hull. As you can see, it's eighteen inches thick."

Pointing at each layer, he continued. "It has a three-eighth-inch-thick layer of laminated hardened aluminum, graphite and steel on the outside. Then there is a layer of gelatin foam, another layer of one-fourth-inch hardened laminated aluminum graphite, then a one-fourth-inch steel plate, five more layers of gel-foam with a one-fourth-inch inner plastic wall. We've tested hundreds of combinations to find a hull structure that would withstand a meteor impact. This one has proven to be the best. This test section was shot the same as the first one I showed you."

Turning the section around so everyone could see the outside skin and pointing at another dark spot, he said, "Here's the entry hole." He smiled and turned it around to the inner side. There wasn't a mark. "The projectile only went through the first few layers," he proudly said. "The object pierced the first layer just like the other section I showed, but the gel foam dissipated the energy, so it didn't puncture the inner skin. We're confident the train hull can withstand ninety-five percent of all meteor impacts."

Tegan followed up, saying, "If the train should be hit, the affected area would instantly seal itself off as Courtney said. There are hull sections on board that can be brought to the breach site, and by cutting the damaged section out, a new one can be chemically welded into place. Within an hour or two, the damaged section can be re-pressurized and then other repairs on the inside of the car can be accomplished."

"We don't anticipate any collisions though," Won stated. "The space agency has developed a force field that works like a shield and will deflect almost anything out there. It's like a magnet. As you all know, a magnet's negative field will repel another magnet's negative field. Space debris either has a negative or positive charge. The aluminum and steel skin of the train pulsates between positive and negative several hundred times a second, which will deflect all but the largest space debris."

"So what about the big stuff?" Millie asked.

"I'm glad you asked," Frank replied. "Large chunks of meteor will be detected far enough away so the train can take evasive action, or use two plasma cannons located in the nose of the command car. The plasma cannons are something new and can shoot several million miles in the vacuum of space. They're so powerful, they can disintegrate a meteor as large as a football field. We really don't anticipate using the cannons very often though. The first space mission didn't have them and they didn't encounter anything that couldn't be maneuvered around. Isn't that right, Colonel Straight?"

"Yes, that's correct. But I'm glad we have the cannons just in case."

"I've read that it isn't just meteors that are dangerous. It's also radiation. I know you touched on it, but could you explain it again?" Jose asked.

Van stood, and said, "You may have read about the first moon landing back in the twentieth century. It was a mad dash to the moon and back. In part it was to allow the mission to be completed between solar flares. In the infancy of space travel, no one had built a craft that could protect astronauts against solar flares, large doses of gamma rays or radiation. Their only defense was mass. But with mass comes weight. And they didn't have motors that could boost that much weight into orbit. Here on Earth, solar flares are of less concern because the atmosphere and the magnetic field between the north and south poles deflect almost all harmful radiation.

"As we've already discussed, the train, like Earth, has a magnetic field that pulsates from negative to positive. The field will not only protect against meteors, but it will also repulse radiation. So combined with the eighteen inches of mass in the walls, it will eliminate ninety-seven percent of all harmful radiation and gamma rays."

"All of this is reassuring, but with so many experimental, or relatively new components, it seems to reason that not everything will work as planned. Are you confident once we've passed the point of being able to return to Earth for repairs, that whatever breaks can be fixed?" Blaine from the physical therapy section asked.

Won stood, and said, "Yes, I am. For example, we have hull components that will allow us to repair a dozen or more breaches if need be. In addition, we'll have enough computer and communication equipment to almost replace the entire system if required. We have four extra motors, heating and cooling units and other parts to repair anything that might be damaged or fail. Like Tegan, I wouldn't volunteer to go on a mission that had even the slightest uncalculated danger to it. In addition, our motor designs are not all that new.

"Using carbon and plasma as fuel is relatively new but has been tested over and over in space. Those bugs have been worked out. As we've told you, we currently have four cars completed and in space. The motors, heating units and other components have worked flawlessly for more than six months. Each of the engineering team has spent more than a month at a time working on the train and they're totally confident in them.

"Now, with all that said, the mission is an experimental mission. Every component of the train will be monitored both by the engineers and command module on the ship. Each component will also constantly be analyzed here on earth."

Then thinking, Won asked, "How many black boxes would you suspect is on a commercial airliner?"

"Ten or fifteen," Justin said.

"There are a few more than that," Won corrected. "Actually a commercial airliner has about fifty or so, depending on what type of plane it is. The train has over three thousand."

"Three thousand?" several people asked.

"Yes, three thousand. Actually there are over three thousand. Every component of the train has a monitoring system. The engines each have almost a dozen themselves. They measure everything from engine output, oil pressure, temperature, structural integrity and even vibration. The hull is monitored for its integrity; the magnetic shield is checked for its proper function. I could go on and on, but believe me, every possible component is monitored and a constant flow of data is fed to a central transmitter. The transmitter sends the data to the bridge and also back here to Earth. There are NASA engineers and other personnel on duty twenty-four hours a day, seven days a week overseeing every shred of data that comes from the train. Even you all will be monitored."

"What? Nobody told me about that," Millie questioned.

"No?" Won asked. "Well, here is the fact. Each of you will be fitted with a monitoring device, as will each cryogenic patient. It will record blood pressure, heart rate, stress level and a host of other data."

"You mean to tell me somebody will know every time I take a crap?" Millie demanded.

"I hadn't exactly focused on that," Won laughed. "But I guess somebody could."

"Shit, that's all I needed to hear," Millie said, making everyone laugh.

"That's a good point about privacy. There is nothing secret about the train. The data that is sent to Earth can be accessed by everyone from our engineers, to scientists around the world or even laypersons who are interested. I've even been told that many grade schools are going to adopt a cryogenic patient and follow him or her through the mission."

The crew had so many concerns and queries about the train that Mr. Harris gave the engineers one more day to make sure no one had additional questions. Schematics were laid out along with pictures, diagrams, or whatever else needed to put everyone's minds at ease.

At the conclusion of the additional day, Mr. Harris reminded everyone, "Colonel Straight has made the voyage before and the first vessel was far inferior to the one you'll be on. The train is the most comfortable, safe and reliable space vehicle ever built. I'm absolutely confident in a little over five years, we'll all be reunited again."

After thanking the engineers who presented, Mr. Harris said, "This will conclude the team building. The medical team will relocate to Tulane and work on the cryogenic procedures. The engineering, communication and the logistics/supply teams will relocate to Houston. Only the prisoner selection team will remain here at the naval station.

"Just for everyone's information, the prisoner selection team will consist of Colonel Mickland Forrester, Mr. Justin LeMoore, Chaplain Frank Molony, Dr. Charlie Davis, Dr. Susan Lister, Dr. Mary Tong, Ms. Millie Syster, Ms. Laura Yates, Mr. Blaine Pustual, and Dr. Vidula

Kozenskie.

8

The prison was located in an obscure part of the base and looked like the setting for an old, World War II movie. There were double twelve-foot chain-link and barbed-wire fences, guard towers every fifty yards and the buildings inside looked to be mid two-thousand vintage.

When everyone arrived, Mr. Harris and a guard escorted the group to the security office where they were each photographed, retina scanned and given badges which allowed them into the prisoner area. Once that was accomplished, they were taken to the work area which had been set up for them. It was a cold cement-gray-walled meeting room about twenty-by-forty feet long. The room was normally used for prisoner activities like meetings, parole boards and other administrative functions.

Ten tables had been set up, each with a team member's name on it. Each work station had a computer, a writing tablet, pen and an in and out box. Mr. Harris had a table at the head of the room facing the rest of the group. There was a person whom no one had met sitting next to him.

"This is Mr. Dillon. He's the records administrator. He'll be doing the computations and developing the order-of-merit list."

The front table facing Mr. Harris had a name plate, which read DR. VIDULA KOZENSKIE.

Mr. Harris said, "I expect Dr. Kozenskie will be here shortly. Until she arrives, I'll explain how the prisoner selections will be made. When we made the announcement to the various federal prisons about the New World mission, we received several-thousand applications. A group of prison physicians made up the first selection team. They screened out violent, mentally ill and those inmates who would be unable to function as team players.

"After several weeks of record reviews, the applications were narrowed down to three hundred men and three hundred women applicants. From that first list, your job will be to select seventy-five men and seventy-five women to be the initial candidates. The selection process will be done by record review and personal interviews. The seventy-five men and seventy-five women selectees will be placed on an order-of-merit list. The top sixty men and top sixty women will be the primary candidates. The fifteen remaining men and fifteen women will serve as alternates."

As Mr. Harris was talking, the door opened. Milton Slusser and two guards entered the room with a woman and a man in handcuffs, leg irons and wearing prisoner-orange jumpsuits. They were obviously the Kozenskies.

Dr. Vidula Kozenskie looked to be about forty years old with short grayish hair combed like a male. She was more than six feet tall and looked masculine. She had olive skin, wide dark eyes and almost black eyebrows. Standing with her legs as far apart as her leg irons would allow, she looked like a prize fighter. She looked confidently at each person in the room and smiled as her handcuffs and leg irons were removed. She rubbed her wrists a few times before taking her seat at the table with her name on it.

"Dr. Ervin Kozenskie will not be part of the team," Mr. Harris reiterated. "But I felt it would be good to have him introduced."

He was about four inches shorter than his wife with a pudgy build and a short blond crew cut. He had narrow light-blue eyes and a square head that looked two or three sizes larger than what should fit with his body.

Since he would not be remaining to participate on the selection team, his handcuffs and leg irons were not removed. He only glanced at the others in the room. He stood stiffly and did not smile.

Mr. Slusser stood next to the Kozenskies looking like he was still wearing the same suit as the first time Justin saw him.

"Ladies and gentlemen, it's my pleasure to introduce Drs. Vidula and Ervin Kozenskie. Congressman Richards met the Kozenskies at the Federal Correctional Institution at Beaumont, Texas, several years ago. He was so impressed with their intelligence that he invited them to participate in the New World mission. Congressman Richards wants you to know how much he trusts them. They're both dedicated, driven scientists and respected by many of your own crew colleagues. Colonel Straight, Colonel Forrester, Captain Quest and many of the engineers have worked with the Kozenskies. They know firsthand of their dedication and commitment to the mission.

"As you all know, both of these fine people have been intricately involved in the New World mission, and they've participated in every aspect of the train's construction. They've become world-renowned in their expertise of every facet of the train. The opportunity to be involved in the design and assembly, not to mention establishing a new society, has been a captivating challenge for them both.

"Unfortunately, we all make mistakes. They were involved in some things prior to our mission that turned out to be problematic and necessitated a change in their living arrangements. I've had the privilege of getting to know and spend a great deal of time with the Kozenskies over the past four years. I've found them to be good and decent people."

At that, both Kozenskies smiled and nodded.

"Congressman Richards also wants you to know how much he admires each of you. He has personally reviewed each of your records and feels you are the pioneers of the future. You're the men and women of tomorrow. Your expertise and experiences will be invaluable to future long-term space travel."

Mr. Slusser continued his discursive dialogue for the next thirty minutes, extolling the virtues of Congressman Richards and the Kozenskies.

Justin whispered to Frank and Millie, "I feel like I'm buying a used car from one of those hyper multimedia salesmen."

Millie said, "I feel like I've just been given an enema without lubrication."

Frank smiled, and whispered, "Millie, you need to tone down your language."

Millie smiled her little-girl smile, and replied, "If you don't like it, close your saintly ears."

Finally Mr. Harris stood, and said, "Thank you for that eloquent introduction of the Kozenskies. Although Dr. Ervin Kozenskie will not be participating in the prisoner selection process, he will be housed here, so he can be near his wife. Before we go any further, would either of you like to say anything?"

Dr. Vidula Kozenskie stood and spoke like she had a mouthful of gold. "I can't tell you how happy we are to be here. As Mr. Slusser said, my husband and I are totally committed to the mission and ensuring its success. If you'll indulge me, I'd like to share our philosophy. Ervin was born and raised in Russia. I was born and raised in India. We come from overpopulated nations and have been committed to improving the quality of life of third world countries all our professional lives. Our goal is to build a society on happiness, contentment and appreciation of one another no matter what our differences are.

"Here on Earth, we have all kinds of material goods. What we don't have is contentment and true happiness. When we arrive at the New World, we'll love one another and be content with what we have. What more could we want?"

Dr. Ervin Kozenskie, standing next to his wife, and in a voice an octave higher than hers, said, "Like Vidula, I'm thrilled to be here. I only wish we had found this project ten years ago. We have longed for someplace where we can invest our considerable intelligence and make a difference."

"Thank you, Drs. Kozenskie," Mr. Harris said. "We also look forward to working with you."

There was an imperceptible look between Dr. Vidula Kozenskie and Mr. Harris that suggested everything between them may not be on the best of terms.

After the brief introduction, Mr. Slusser and the two guards escorted Dr. Ervin Kozenskie from the room.

Mr. Harris followed up with, "For Dr. Kozenskie's sake, let me introduce the members of the team."

Dr. Koznskie turned and looked at each person as they were introduced. For some reason, Justin felt she paid particular attention to him, and as their eyes met, an icy feeling gripped him.

Mr. Harris said, "We will now continue with the selection process overview. As I was saying prior to the Kozenskies' arrival, we will select seventy-five males and seventy-five females.

"One of the requirements for each candidate is to be single and agree to wed a person selected for them. It is like it was in Japan and other places several centuries ago. Actually, if you go back in history, many cultures had arranged marriages. Research reveals many of those relationships were more successful than the system we have today. Often, we rely on emotions and sometimes hormones to determine compatibility.

"The first group sent to the New World has seen a one-hundred percent success rate in compatibility and marital satisfaction. Of course they must rely on their mates in a different way than we do here on Earth. Maybe we should apply at least some of the selection techniques here where we see less than forty-five percent of marriages truly succeed.

"Once the prisoner selections have been made, we'll work with a mating service to match the various men and women to be husbands and wives. We'll use the same mating service used for the first group. They have a wealth of tools to collect personal data on each prisoner, which will be used in the pairing process.

"As I've mentioned, there are a number of talented individuals in the prison system who have specialized knowledge and or skills. For example, there is Dr. Herman Hockstrasser, who is a renowned agricultural botanist. He received his PhD from the University of Heidelberg, in Heidelberg, Germany. He came to America to work in crop research with a colleague at Texas Tech University. His colleagues used Dr. Hockstrasser's research to develop a strain of weevil-resistant alfalfa, which he patented and sold for millions of dollars.

"Dr. Hockstrasser confronted his colleague about stealing his research, but to no avail. After a heated argument, he laced his colleague's lunch with foxglove leaves which killed him. Foxglove leaves contain a form of digitalis which stopped his colleague's heart. Dr. Hockstrasser was arrested and ultimately sentenced to life in prison. Since his confinement, he has continued his plant research and jumped at the chance to go to the New World. He is excited to hopefully find and work with new plant varieties.

"As Tegan explained, there will be an entire floor in one of the cars devoted to seed storage and a garden under lights. In prison, Dr. Hockstrasser proved he can raise abundant crops under lights. He will be a valuable asset to the mission.

"Dr. Hockstrasser and several other prisoners with special talents have been nominated and will be presented to the group to be validated for specific positions with the crew. In most cases, these individuals will be selected to marry, although some may go as a single person.

"For those prisoners selected to be in the male and female cryogenic groups, the selection process will be much like a military promotion board. The three hundred male and three hundred female prison records will be available on your computers. That means you will each have six hundred records to review plus about fifteen nominations for validation. If at all possible, they need to be completed within thirty days.

"Look for individuals with skills to contribute to the New World community. You will vote each record from ten minus to ten plus. That means you will have a thirty-point spread with which to evaluate a candidate. Does that make sense to everyone?" Mr. Harris inquired, looking at each person in the room.

"Since no one is raising their hand, I assume it is clear. Before we start on the actual records, we will look at five male and five female records for practice. You will find all ten on your computers. Take your time. Carefully read them and then vote using the ten-minus to ten-plus system."

For the next two hours, the team read and voted on the practice records. The results were tallied over lunch. During lunch, which was brought to them, the team had an opportunity to personally meet Dr. Kozenskie. She was charming and had nothing but flattering words for everyone. Making sure she had everyone's attention, she said, "Just for your information, my name is Vidula. In our Hindi language, it means *intelligent*. I'd like to be friends with each of you and I hope you will call me Vidula.

"We're so impressed with how intelligent and dedicated each of you are. It's refreshing to work with people like you. We've always had the dream of making a positive difference in the lives of people. We are also excited for the chance to share in the creation of a society from the ground up. The opportunity is beyond our imagination. We can't wait to get to know each of you individually and blend our intelligence with yours."

After lunch, Mr. Slusser again appeared, and said, "It's wonderful to see the selection team coming together. Congressman Richards is working hard to ensure that funding remains on track and is resolving any obstacles to the mission. As usual, he sends his appreciation and support for all that you are doing."

"I feel like I've just been smeared with honey," Justin whispered to Frank.

"Remember, everything that's sticky isn't honey," Frank responded. "I get the feeling Vidula is more black widow than honey bee and fully equipped with venomous fangs."

With a frown, Mr. Harris again cut Mr. Slusser off and continued with his briefing. "When the records review is completed, and an order-of-merit list has been established, the top seventy-five males and seventy-five females will receive a face-to-face interview with each of you. Let me caution you not to discuss the merits of any one individual with each other. We don't want anyone to be influenced by another member on the team." Mr. Harris looked directly at Vidula who simply smiled. Mr. Slusser gave Mr. Harris a look that would wither a tree and soon disappeared.

"What do you know about Justin LeMoore?" Vidula asked that evening when she'd returned to her and Ervin's cell.

"Probably about the same as you. I know Milton doesn't like him. He was a social worker at the federal penitentiary in Kansas City. He's never been married, likes outdoor sports and is reported to be a straight arrow. He belongs to one of those fringe churches like Jehovah's Witness, Mormon or something."

"I think he's going to be a troublemaker," Vidula answered.

"What makes you say that?"

"Maybe just intuition. When I looked at him, something told me he was going to a problem. Milton said he even called one of his social work buddies from Beaumont to get his opinion about us. We need to keep a close eye on him. He may even need to be eliminated."

"Vidula, please, we can't start eliminating people and forcing our will. That's what got us in trouble before. Promise me you won't do anything," Ervin almost pleaded.

"Ervin, chill out. I'm not going to do anything to jeopardize our plans. Maybe he will decide to resign," Vidula said as she looked the other way.

"Vidula—" Ervin started to say.

She cut him off and kissed him on the forehead. Ervin knew better than to follow up.

The records review progressed well. The first few records took a little longer, but once they got into a rhythm, the team was able to read and vote on a record about every twenty minutes.

Vidula made an effort to single out and chat with a different person during each break. When Justin's turn came, she was gracious and wanted to know all about him.

She noted, "I hear you're an artist when it comes to fly-fishing. I was also told you're thinking about taking some of your tackle along to the New World. Tackle is what you call fishing gear, isn't it?"

"Yes, *tackle* is the correct term. I don't think of myself as a fishing artist though. I'm just someone who likes the out of doors."

"You don't give yourself enough credit," Dr. Vidula said. "May I call you Justin?"

"Sure. Justin is fine with me."

"I'd be pleased if you'd call me Vidula. We're going to be a close, intimate team and since we all know each other's academic accomplishments, there's no need for formalities."

Yes, we all know our abilities and our place in the pecking order, Justin thought.

"You must be part entomologist and intelligent in order to read the water and know where big fish are lying."

It was obvious Vidula had done some quick reading about fly-fishing. Justin's mental picture was again that he had been smeared with honey. Although Frank's analogy may have been more accurate. She was more like a spider who was weaving a web for him to get tangled in.

As Vidula walked away, she said to herself, *I don't like him. One way or another he's got to go.*

Frank was given the same treatment. Vidula had read up on the priesthood and even knew what parishes he had worked with. After their encounter, Frank told Justin, "I don't see Vidula as a spider anymore. She's more like a cobra waving back and forth with venom dripping from her fangs."

Vidula talked to Millie, but she was her usual blunt, sometimes-crude self. It was obvious the two women did not like each other, so her session didn't last long.

After her interview with Vidula, Millie approached Justin and Frank. "Vidula makes my ass ache. I feel like I've just been squeezed by a big slimy python."

It was in the third week of the record review. Like most everyone else, Justin had evaluated more than 80 percent of the records. Everyone was confident they'd complete the review within the month.

Mr. Harris continually complimented the team for their hard work. In fact, Mr. Harris was so happy he gave the team the next weekend off.

Justin was delighted and spent all day Saturday looking at guns at several local gun shops. He was shopping for a large-caliber rifle to take on the mission. So far he hadn't found exactly what he wanted, but had a good time looking.

After the relaxing weekend, it took everyone a record or two to get back into the swing of things. It was the second record of the day for Justin. He read the name on the record, Cynthia Sunn Wong. His heart almost stopped. He knew that name. He then scrolled down to the picture. Normally he didn't pay much attention to pictures. Prison photos weren't very flattering. However, when he looked at Ms. Wong's picture, it was like an electric charge went through him. Although everyone was dressed in the standard orange oversized jumpsuit, and looked like a pumpkin mechanic, he couldn't take his eyes off her image. His heart was also beating like a brass drum.

It's her, he thought.

Over a year ago, he attended a federal prison conference in California. It was titled Working with Professionals in Confinement. He was asked to be on a panel, and Ms. Wong was an interviewee. As she was led into the room, he was instantly attracted to her. He felt he knew her, but couldn't remember ever actually meeting her. Looking at her, his heart beat faster and his mouth went dry. Luckily the psychiatrist and psychologist on the panel dominated the conversation.

He did ask one salient question: "Ms. Wong, it almost sounds like you are comfortable in prison. Is that correct?"

For the first time, she looked at Justin. When she did, she began to stammer. "Well, ah, yes. Sort of I guess. I never felt comfortable at home, especially when my father was drinking. He'd often beat me and my mother. He raped me when I was sixteen and forced me to marry my husband, Yan when I turned eighteen. Father bet me on a hand of cards, which he lost. Yan, my husband, also beat me, locked me in the house and forced me to spend nights with his friends. Like my father, Yan often threatened to kill me, especially when he was drunk. The only good thing Yan ever did for me was to enroll me in nursing school. Of course he only did that so when I graduated, he'd have a steady income. In prison I have friends. I can use my nursing skills and the bars keep me safe. If I go back outside, no one would want me. So yes, prison is the safest place I've ever been in my life."

"It sounds like killing your husband was self-defense to me," the psychiatrist said. "Have you tried for an appeal?"

"Sort of. A women's advocate group asked me for permission to have an attorney pursue an appeal. I wish I hadn't allowed them to do it. I hope it doesn't go through."

This can't be happening, Justin told himself. He'd dismissed the thought of the impact she'd had on him at the conference and never expected to see her again. Yet after looking at her picture several times, he was paralyzed, suspended somewhere between awe and nausea. He had to swallow a couple of times to gain his composure before looking at the rest of the file. He was having the same reaction as when he saw her at the conference over a year ago.

Could Ted be right about love at first sight? But an attraction to a convict is wrong. Professionally and morally wrong. I could never allow myself to fall in love with a convict.

He looked farther into her file, which said what he already knew. She'd been convicted of first-degree murder for the alleged premeditated murder of her husband of five years. According to the record, she shot Yan five times. The shooting had happened just two years ago. She claimed her husband had been abusive and she had shot him in self-defense. The jury found her guilty of killing her husband, "execution style," and sentenced her to fifteen years to life in the California State Prison in Los Angeles.

The record did confirm her case was being reviewed by the appellate court. It appeared, she had a decent chance of having the conviction overturned.

Justin told himself, *That's an issue I'll need to resolve in the individual interview.*

She didn't have any criminal history prior to the shooting. Her mother was Caucasian, her father was from Taiwan. She reported her father was an alcoholic and abusive to both her mother and herself. Her father, now deceased, owned a landscaping business and a plant nursery. She was an only child. Her mother, now also deceased, appeared to have been nurturing and loving.

Ms. Wong had a master's degree as a nurse clinician and had worked as a trauma nurse at a large hospital in California. She had been a model prisoner and was known as a motivated, compassionate person on the prison medical unit. Her hobbies included gardening, cooking and sewing. Her record read, "Eager to join the mission and help provide medical care for members of the New World community."

Justin was overwhelmed with emotion. He couldn't understand why she had such an impact on him and looked at the picture again. She was a pretty woman, but he wouldn't say she was a raving beauty. Yet his heart was pounding and he had a hard time breathing. His emotions were so raw, so powerful there were no words to explain it. He got up, went to the refrigerator, and removed a bottle of sparkling water which he gulped down. After a short break, he returned and reviewed the file again.

He was upset for letting himself get so emotional and decided to put the record aside. He'd go back to it later. He worked the rest of the morning without a reaction to any other record.

When lunch came, Frank asked, "You look troubled. Are you okay?"

Justin was shocked. *Was it so obvious?* He asked himself. "I'll tell you later. I don't want to talk about it here."

Frank looked at Justin, and said, "Okay. Come over to my room tonight."

"How about after dinner? I think Dr. Lister is cooking tonight, so it'll be either takeout or canned spaghetti."

"Fine," Frank replied.

After lunch, Justin went back to the Wong record and found his heart racing again. He put it back into his hold box for the second time. By late afternoon he was almost afraid of going back to the record. Although he did. Actually, she seemed like the perfect candidate, yet he was befuddled about how to rate her.

If I rate her too high, that may be a tip off to my stupid reaction to her. Maybe I should rate her low and try to disqualify her. But that isn't honest. But, is it honest to feel the way I do?

Justin's fingers wavered above the keyboard. *I could easily justify a one on the grounds that her case is up for appeal, and if it was successful, she may want to back out. I could also justify a ten plus, although I've never given anyone such a high rating. But she has a valuable skill as a nurse clinician. She'd be an asset to those on the New World. I can't stand it any longer. It either has to be a one or a ten. There isn't anything in between.* He was so flustered he felt dizzy as his finger floated back and forth until his fingers, almost of their own will, pushed the buttons. Ten plus.

Justin had become close to the big teddy bear priest and found it easy to confide in him. But what would a priest know about the kinds of feelings he was having? He'd never felt this way about a woman and it was aggravating.

As predicted, Dr. Lister went to the local Chinese restaurant and brought back three different pans of fried rice, spring rolls and salad. Dinner was fast. Thankfully everyone lingered after eating to talk. Justin was in no hurry to face Frank and didn't have anything more to tell him anyway. It was almost 2200 before the conversations died down and everyone straggled off to their separate rooms.

Frank got up and said in a loud enough voice for all to hear, "Justin, come over to my room. I need to talk to you."

Then addressing Justin, he said in a normal voice, "I thought that would take any suspicion off you."

Justin was in a testy mood anyway, and Frank's announcement only added to it. "What suspicion? Are you nuts? We visit all the time. Why would anyone be suspicious tonight?"

"Because you're acting like a twit," Frank said. "You stare off into space and act like you've got ants in your pants."

"It couldn't be that bad," Justin denied. "Nobody besides you seemed to notice anything."

Frank just smiled. "Come in, my Mormon son. Tell Father Frank everything."

"Is this supposed to be like a confessional or something?"

"I don't know. I'll have to see how large the sin is." Then sitting down in an easy chair with one leg over the arm, he continued, "Come on Justin, what's going on?"

Justin sat staring into space for several seconds before hesitantly beginning. "I opened the second record of the day, and when I looked at the picture, my heart started pounding. I couldn't take my eyes off the image. I briefly met a woman by the name of Ms. Cynthia Wong at a Federal Prison Conference that I attended about a year ago. The conference was on working with inmates with professional degrees. I was on a panel that interviewed Ms. Wong. She claimed to have killed her husband in self-defense. Her case is currently at the appeals court for review and I think she could get off on the grounds of self-defense. I can't understand why she'd even consider going on the mission if there's a chance of her conviction being overturned."

"Perhaps she just wants to get away and doesn't care if her conviction is overturned or not. So you know her?"

"Well, sort of. As I said, I was on a panel of prison mental health professionals who interviewed her. That's all. I've only seen her that one time. This is silly Frank. I feel like a fourteen-year-old school kid with a crush on a movie-star picture. I don't get involved with prisoners, and I've never had a reaction like that to any other woman."

"What did you say the inmate's name was?"

"Cynthia Wong."

"I remember the name from the records review. All I remember is that she's a nurse. I'll take a look at her file tomorrow. Maybe we'll have to arm wrestle over her."

"I'm tired Frank, and I don't know what else to say," Justin said, getting up. "I'm going to bed."

Justin didn't see Frank go down to Millie's room. She'd also thought Justin had seemed different during the day, but hadn't said anything. Frank decided he needed to get her opinion. Justin, Frank, and Millie had become good friends.

Sleep didn't come easily, and when Justin did doze off, he had mixed up dreams about his colleagues laughing at him and Ms. Wong coming and going. He got up early, went for a run, had a hot shower and ate breakfast alone. Driving to the prison, he felt like everyone was looking at him.

I've never thought people were looking at me. Now whenever someone looks in my direction, I feel totally transparent, he thought.

"I waited to ride over together," Frank said, as he walked into the computer room.

"I went for a run this morning and left early. Sorry. I should have told you I was leaving."

"How'd you sleep last night?"

"Would you shut up?" Justin angrily whispered.

"Shut up? Asking how a buddy slept last night doesn't seem like such a private question."

"Naw. You're right. I apologize. Actually, I didn't sleep very well. I had lots of screwy dreams. That's why I got up and went for a run. Perhaps we can talk again tonight after dinner. I got a little behind yesterday so I'm going to work hard today and get back on track."

"Sure," Frank replied.

By now most of the other team members had arrived and Vidula was escorted in by two marine guards. As usual, Mr. Harris welcomed everyone, and said, "For the most part, you're all on track to finish in six or seven days. There are a few who need to pick up the pace a little, but overall I'm pleased with the progress."

Justin was sure Mr. Harris was speaking directly to him, although he'd never been behind before. To avoid any further problems, he didn't open the Wong file all day. He also remained an additional two hours that evening so he'd be a little ahead.

He didn't want to see anyone, so he drove off base and bought a sandwich for supper. When he arrived back to the guest house, he went directly to his room hoping to ignore Frank. Frank must have read his mind. Justin had barely closed the door when Frank knocked and walked in.

"Where ya been?" Frank asked.

Justin felt irritated but tried his best not to show it. "I stayed for a while to make sure I was caught up, then drove over to the Piggly Wiggly. I bought a sandwich and ate in the truck. I don't think I'm up to talking tonight."

Totally undaunted, Frank drove on, "I reviewed the Wong file and we don't need to arm wrestle. Don't get me wrong, she's all right looking from what you can see of her in a prison jumpsuit. She didn't make my heart beat any faster though. From the record, she was probably convicted for premeditated murder because she took a self-defense course just a month before she killed her husband. She even took her husband's pistol to the range to practice with. That may not have set well with the jury. The shot in the face probably also gave the prosecuting attorney the opportunity to claim she did it execution style.

"Apparently her defense attorney couldn't or didn't get the point across to the jury that she'd been physically and sexually abused by her creepy husband. Bottom line is, her defense attorney dropped the ball as far as I can see. I suspect any rational person on the appeals board will recognize what the truth is. I suspect they'll either throw the conviction out altogether or demand a new trial. Did you look at the file again today?"

"Nope, and I'm not going to. Frank, I'm tired. I appreciate you reviewing the record, but I'm ready for bed. I didn't sleep well last night so I'm going to take a shower, read a little and hit the sack."

"Sounds like a plan. You want to ride together tomorrow?"

"Yeah sure. I'll see you for breakfast," Justin said.

After work the next day, Justin and Frank left together. As they walked to the car, Frank inquired, "How was your day?"

"Pretty good," Justin replied. "Another good-night's sleep and I'll be back to myself again."

"Did you review the Wong file again?"

"What record did you say?" Justin asked.

"Don't play silly buggers with me," Frank teased. "You know very well which file."

"If you're talking about the one that caused me some distress, the answer is no." Although that was not the truth. Justin had pulled the Wong record up not only once but many times during the day. Each time he had the same reaction.

The remainder of the ride to the guest house was accomplished in crushing silence. When they arrived, Justin quickly extricated himself from Frank's car, and said, "I'm going for a run before we eat. Since it's your turn to prepare supper, I expect a gourmet meal. Not some takeout crap."

"We're having chili. Millie and I started it in four Crock-Pots early this morning. It should be great by now. I know it's going to be a smashing hit. If you're late, there may not be any left."

"I have no doubt it'll be delicious. And knowing you and Millie, you'll probably pay people to have a third and fourth bowl so there won't be any left by the time I return," Justin joked.

There was plenty of chili when Justin got back.

The rest of the record review was completed a week later, and the order-of-merit list was established for both men and women.

Mr. Harris thanked everyone, and said, "There's just one more chore to complete. We need to review and vote on the inmates with a critical expertise who have been nominated to serve on the crew. The votes will be up or down, so you'll either approve or disapprove them. You're the ones who will have to live with these individuals for the next two-plus years, so I want you to have the primary voice in the decisions. Since it's at the end of the day, I suggest we put the review off until tomorrow. We should be able to knock them out in one day."

The next morning, the group assembled around the conference table. Mr. Harris passed out the order-of-merit lists, which had a line drawn below the seventy-fifth name on both the male and female lists.

No one except Vidula paid much attention to the lists, although Justin checked to see if Ms. Wong was above the cutoff line. She was at the top of the list, which gave him mixed feelings. On one hand, he was relieved. On the other, if she'd been voted off, the issue of his attraction to her would have been resolved.

Vidula read and reread the order-of-merit list. She counted, *One, two, three.*

Oh no, she said to herself. *I must have missed some names. Mr. Slusser said he'd have at least eight on the list, four on the crew list and four in the cryogenic group. We need all eight to implement our plan.*

She quickly reread the list again, looking carefully at each name and prisoner number. She could still only find three names: Elvira Strong on the crew list; Muriel French and Safire Strong in the cryogenic group. Sue Spector, Ferrell Logan and three others were all at the very bottom of the lists.

We can't do what needs to be done with only three people plus Ervin and me. I'm going to kill Slusser! He hasn't lived up to one agreement, Vidula complained to herself.

Mr. Harris asked, "Has everyone reviewed the list?"

At first no one said anything. Then Vidula spoke up. "I think the list must have been altered by mistake. There are two names that I'm sure have been extruded from the list."

"Oh," Mr. Harris said, looking bewildered. "How would you know that?"

"Because I know them both and they're well qualified." She picked the two most important to her, and said, "Sir, I respectfully request we review the records of Mr. Ferrell Logan and Ms. Sue Spector again. They're both nurse assistants."

After carefully reviewing his list, Mr. Harris looked at Vidula. "They both fell well below the cutoff line. In fact, they're at the very bottom of the list."

"Yes, I realize that. But Ervin and I know these individuals and I'd like to request that they be moved up. They're both dedicated to the mission and I can personally vouch for their good character."

Mr. Harris raised his eyebrows, looked at his list again, then at Vidula before responding. "Dr. Kozenskie, as I've already noted, these two individuals fell well below the cutoff line. I see no reason to review them again."

"Sir, I know it's unusual, but Ervin and I are friends with them. They are wonderful, down-to-earth workers. They would add immensely to the mission if given a chance. I'd deeply appreciate it if they were added to the up-or-down list."

"The people being considered must have a specialized skill like Dr. Hockstrasser." Boring in on Vidula, Mr. Harris asked, "What specialized skills do these two people have?"

"They're nurses."

"Are they nurses or nurse assistants?" Millie asked.

"They are nurses."

"To hell they are! Nurse assistants aren't nurses. According to their records, they're nurse assistants," Millie replied with fire in her eyes.

"Thank you, but they're exactly what the contract specifications call for."

"As I recall, there were several nurse assistants on the list. What's so special about the two you want?" Millie demanded.

"I've already answered that. Both Ervin and I know Logan and Spector. We can vouch for their skills," Vidula answered, looking like a tornado about to touch down.

"So, you're a medical doctor or nurse? And you have the background to evaluate their medical skills?" Millie demanded.

"No, Ms. Fancy Panties, the doctors at the medical clinic told me they were extremely qualified."

Most of the team said they couldn't even remember Mr. Logan or Ms. Spector, so Mr. Harris told everyone to quickly review their records again.

While everyone was at their computers, Vidula went over to Mr. Harris's desk and leaned down and whispered. "I also want to discuss the elimination of Mr. Kyle Williams. He's a computer contract employee with Space Corp. He's dangerous. He meddles in everything."

"Vidula, we're not here to discuss contract employees. This meeting is to discuss inmates who may be part of the crew. If you have a problem with a contract employee, that needs to be addressed to the contractor," Mr. Harris quietly replied.

Justin walked over to Mr. Harris's table and handed him a paper copy of the two files. He quickly reviewed the documents before turning to Vidula. "I see no reason to even discuss these two records.

They don't have specialized skills and their names are far below the cutoff line."

"Sir, these are two of the finest people I know. Ervin and I like to help those who haven't had a fair chance in life. These two individuals are in that category. With individual attention they've blossomed and have grown beyond our wildest expectations. I'm pleading with you to give them a chance. I can guarantee they will make us all proud."

"Vidula, they have been given a fair chance. It was the opinion of the group that others are more qualified," Mr. Harris replied.

Vidula pleadingly looked at Mr. Harris. "I'm begging you not to make a final decision on these two individuals until we've had a chance to discuss them further."

Finally, to appease Vidula, Mr. Harris relented, "Out of courtesy to you, I'll allow you to quickly discuss them. However, the decision will be up to the group. Whatever they decide will be the final decision."

"Has everyone reviewed the records?" Mr. Harris asked.

Everyone nodded yes, so he continued, "Let's start with Mr. Logan."

There was a long silence. Then Dr. Mary Tong said, "I voted no for Mr. Logan. Although he's a nurse assistant, he has a violent background. His prison record isn't very flattering either. He's been repeatedly cited for aggression and fighting with both other inmates and guards while in prison."

"I also voted no," Justin said. "Mr. Logan's past history of interpersonal conflicts with both other inmates and the prison staff suggests he can't be trusted."

Vidula smiled as if everyone was missing something. "If you will all look at Mr. Logan's record, he's been a model prisoner for the past ten months. All he needed was someone to give him a chance and some guidance."

"There's another nurse on the list and she's a real nurse," Justin noted.

"Who might that be? Ms. Cynthia Wong?" Vidula asked.

"Yes, she's the one," Justin replied.

"I don't think we should even consider her. Ms. Wong's conviction is most likely going to be overturned on appeal. We should eliminate her altogether and take Mr. Logan. We know he'll be willing to go. He's also physically strong, which will be important when working with the cryogenic patients."

Before Justin had thought it through, he looked at Vidula, and in that instant more was communicated between them than any words could have conveyed. "How can you even compare a master's degree nurse clinician with a nurse assistant like Mr. Logan? And as far as Ms. Wong not going on the mission, we don't know if her appeal will even go through."

Vidula didn't miss a thing as she watched Justin's body language. *I think Mr. LeMoore is attracted to Ms. Wong? An attraction between a federal correctional employee and a convict? That could be useful at the right time,* she told herself. "If your murder conviction and life sentence was overturned, would you go?"

"Appeals take forever to get through the system. Plus, Ms. Wong may want to go even if her conviction is overturned. Perhaps someone should ask her. Scrolling down Mr. Logan's file, he continued, "Mr. Logan has had three convictions for rape. He murdered his last victim while forcing her husband to watch as he repeatedly raped and then killed his wife. While in prison he's had multiple altercations with groups of other prisoners. In fact, just last month he was involved in some kind of altercation. Reading further into the file, Justin continued, "Now that's interesting. It appears you were also involved." Justin noted.

With another forced smile, Vidula continued, "The so-called altercation you're referring to was a time when Mr. Logan was defending me. You don't know what the prison environment is like. I was being accosted by other prisoners. Mr. Logan came to my aid."

"Oh, come on, Vidula," Justin said, looking angrily at her. "This man's a violent criminal. I've worked in a prison for several years now and I understand the environment very well. According to the record, the altercation took place on the women's cell block. I didn't know males were allowed on a female block. What in the world was Mr. Logan doing in a male restricted area?"

Vidula smiled at Justin as if explaining the obvious to a child. "You may not know it, but women can be just as aggressive as men. Mr. Logan was in the area and heard my pleas for help."

"How did he get into a restricted area like the women's cell block to hear your pleas?" Justin inquired.

"Actually . . . he was coming to . . . see me," she stammered. "Ervin and I have been helping him deal with his early childhood trauma."

"So you're also a psychiatrist?"

"You don't have to be a psychiatrist to help someone."

"Hmm. And you were conducting therapy with a male in the women's cell block?"

"I had approval to see him," Vidula said, knowing she'd trapped herself in a lie.

"The Federal Correctional Institution at Beaumont must be different than other prisons. I'm unaware male prisoners are ever allowed on female blocks—for any reason. And if you were providing therapy, why didn't you meet in the library or some other public place?"

Now it was her turn to ignore Justin's question. "Everything isn't as black and white as you prison people would like it to be. Things happen. I was being assaulted and Ferrell did what he had to do to defend me. We've worked with him and know what kind of a person he is. When we get to the New World, we'll need people like him to make things work."

Returning to the original issue, Justin continued, "Vidula, Mr. Logan isn't a nurse. He's a nurse assistant."

"He's as good as any nurse. He's been working in the prison medical clinic for quite some time now. He knows what he's doing. I trust him as much as any of your book-learned nurses," Vidula countered.

"Oh bullshit. He only received his nurse assistant certificate a few months ago, so he can't have that much experience. In addition, can he order medication, or can he diagnose like nurse clinicians can? Is he aware of the indicators that could mean life or death to a patient? All Mr. Logan can do is follow orders and change bedpans," Millie tersely responded.

"That's all he needs to do, my dear. There are doctors and other nurses to diagnose and prescribe medications."

"It sounds like you want Mr. Logan on the mission to be your enforcer," Justin challenged as he again locked eyes with Vidula.

"Mr. LeMoore, are you accusing me of something?" Vidula asked, looking like a tiger waiting to pounce.

"Just making an observation," Justin responded as he maintained eye contact with her.

"Your observation is totally inaccurate. I believe in giving someone a second chance. With another chance Mr. Logan could be a valuable asset to us. I thought you mental health professionals believed in the same thing."

"Vidula, this isn't a therapeutic mission and I'm just quoting what the record says. Mr. Logan accosted a guard, breaking her arm, then forced his way into an unauthorized area. To me that makes him less than a model prisoner. To be honest, I can't understand how his record has gotten this far. It should have been eliminated during the first review."

Mr. Harris stopped the interchange. "Does anyone else have any additional comments about Mr. Logan?" No one responded as he looked from person to person around the table. "If no one else wants to voice support for Mr. Logan, he will not be added to the crew list."

When I'm done with you, Justin big boy, I'll crush you, humiliate you and break your spirit, Vidula told herself.

With tears in her eyes, Vidula turned to the group. "Friends, I beg you to reconsider. You've eliminated a person who would have been of immense support and value to the mission. Ervin and I have lived with this man. He has potential. If you deny him the opportunity to participate, it will destroy him. He'll probably have to be locked in solitary confinement when he could have been a productive citizen in the New World."

"Dr. Kozenskie, that's enough," Mr. Harris said. "The discussion about Mr. Logan is over. The other person you wanted to discuss is Ms. Sue Spector. She also fell below the cutoff line. I'd like a short discussion to determine if she should be added to the crew list."

For several minutes no one spoke. Everyone seemed to be intrigued with their shoes, their fingernails or something in space that no one else could see.

Finally Justin spoke up. "I voted no because her training and record just wasn't that impressive. Her record also states she was a member of a prison gang. In addition, it notes you and she were friends, Vidula."

Everyone's attention was on Vidula. She'd dried her tears and looked from person to person in the group. "My dear friends, I don't think any of you know what it's like to be in prison as a professional. Prison is hard on everyone, but for most prisoners they're with people of their own background and caliber. Ervin and I were intellectually superior to everyone else around us. We had never been in a situation where our personal safety was constantly threatened. The verbal taunts, constant threats and never knowing if we could even go to the bathroom in safety was overwhelming. Ervin and I were at first separated and didn't see each other for days on end. We couldn't even look to each other for safety or consolation. Fortunately, Ms. Spector and Mr. Logan befriended us, which stopped the threats and harassment. And if you'd like to check your computer, you'll see Ms. Spector didn't assault anyone."

"That's true, as I've already noted. But, by reading between the lines in her record, it suggests Ms. Specter was a leader in a prison gang. It appears she arranged to have your dirty work done," Justin said.

"Mr. LeMoore, I take exception to your accusing Ms. Specter of doing my 'dirty work,' as you call it. Ms. Spector is a leader, and thankfully when we became friends, the threats ceased. That allowed us to concentrate on assisting with the mission."

"So you're saying Mr. Ferrell and Ms. Spector were in essence your bodyguards and protectors. Is that right?"

Vidula smiled. "You have to understand something. In the prison you're either strong enough to protect yourself or you have friends who are willing to assist you. Neither Ervin nor I are physically strong people. We resolve issues with our intelligence, but in prison intelligence is scorned. Mr. Logan and Ms. Specter were friends who recognized our superior intellectual abilities and were willing to help us."

Millie piped up, "Vidula, you make me sick with your superior-intelligence bullshit. The way I see it, Mr. Logan and Ms. Specter were coordinating attacks on inmates and in some cases they caused serious injuries on your behalf."

"They simply did what any friend would do. They watched out for us," Vidula quietly said. "For people like us with superior intelligence, prison was like dying with your eyes open."

"Wow! Like dying with your eyes open. That's pretty profound," Justin commented. "But isn't it true that you and your husband were moved into the same cell? And isn't it also true that your cell was not even on the general cell block?"

"Yes, after Congressman Richards and Mr. Slusser intervened. But even then Ervin and I were constantly in fear for our lives. Without friends like Ms. Spector and Mr. Logan, Ervin and I would most certainly be dead by now. That would have meant the mission wouldn't have had the opportunity to use our considerable assistance."

Justin looked at Vidula, and said in an accusatory voice, "Dr. Kozenskie, many of us have worked in prisons for several years and have seen the effects of protection groups or gangs. They always turned out to be dangerous and were manipulated by people who thought they were superior to the rest of the population. By using privileges, or other devices, they were able to direct their gang to meet their own needs. It appears you had such a group who were protecting you. It also looks like you made some kind of deal with Spector and Logan. It appears you told them you'd get them on the mission. So again I have to conclude that you want them to be your enforcers."

"My friends," Vidula said with a forced smile. "You're again making judgments about issues you know nothing about. Besides, we were told by Mr. Sluss . . . well, nothing."

"Please go on, Dr. Kozenskie. What exactly did Mr. Slusser tell you?" Mr. Harris asked.

"Ervin and I have invested so much in this mission, and you're all sitting around making judgments on issues from computer records."

Then ignoring Mr. Harris, she continued, "Ms. Spector and Mr. Logan are good people. They're trying to pull themselves up by their boot straps. They deserve a chance. Please help me give them that chance."

"We need to move on. Can I have a vote on Ms. Spector?" Mr. Harris said.

The vote was negative except for Colonel Forrester. He voted thumbs up. Mr. Harris noted Colonel. Forrester's positive vote, but said, "For the record, the decision is negative and has been made by the group. Neither Mr. Logan nor Ms. Specter will be added to the crew list."

With a flair for the dramatic, Vidula put her hand to her forehead, and said, "I have a headache. I need to lie down. Please excuse me." With that, she stood and walked toward the door where she was met by two guards. They handcuffed, then shackled her and escorted her back to her cell.

There was total silence when Vidula departed until Mr. Harris said, "I don't want this to change anyone's opinion toward the issues we have discussed. You have come to a conclusion and voted based on what you saw in the records. You are the ones who will live with the various unpaid crew members. You should have the final say in who goes and who stays. We will now continue the discussion on the other individuals."

"I don't know about anyone else, but I'd like some clarification about what Vidula meant when she said, 'Mr. Slusser told us.' She didn't finish her sentence, but it sounded like Mr. Slusser told Vidula and Ervin they could 'choose' some of the crew members to go on the mission. If Mr. Slusser or Congressman Richards have given the Kozenskies authority to select certain individuals, I think we're on dangerous ground," Justin said.

Colonel Forrester spoke up again. "I don't see what the big deal is with the Kozenskies being able to select some of the members of the team. It's obvious they'll be leaders when they get to the New World. Personally I think they should be able to choose people they can work with. I think some of you are being too critical. If we were in the Kozenskies' place, we'd want to have people we trust and can work with on our team."

"Can work with or a gang who'll force their will about how things will be run in the New World?" Justin asked.

"It's going to take strong leadership to build a society at the New World. We need to remember the members of the colony will still be convicts. I think the Kozenskies have a valid point about other prisoners being critical of their intelligence and could still want to do them harm. Having someone they can count on to maintain their security makes sense to me," Colonel Forrester continued.

"We want a democratic elected government in the colony, not a dictatorship or a kingdom," Mr. Harris said. "If there's any hint that one group is going to use force to conscript others into subjection, we don't want those people in the New World population. In addition, the first colony didn't have anyone like the Kozenskies. And through a democratic process, they have elected two presidents and have been able to successfully resolve problems."

The discussion became heated with Colonel Forrester extolling the Kozenskies' accomplishments and contributions to the mission. He continued to argue they should be able to choose some of their colleagues to assist them.

Laura Yates changed her mind and supported Colonel Forrester's position. The rest continued to support the group decision.

Mr. Harris spoke up, and said, "The discussion about the Kozenskies' request for specific individuals is finished. Our task now is to vote on the other convicts who have been nominated to be part of the crew. Since it almost noon, let's go to lunch. Be back here by 1300."

As they were breaking for lunch, Justin met Mr. Harris in the hall, and asked, "Since the Kozenskies are prisoners, why didn't we vote on them? Also, are they going to be in the cryogenic group or part of the crew?"

"Their acceptance to be part of the mission took place years ago. Congressman Richards and Mr. Slusser took care of that even before I came on board. The issue of them being part of the cryogenic group has never come up. I don't see any reason it couldn't be discussed though. Are you ready to take that tiger on?"

"What's your opinion?" Justin asked.

Mr. Harris looked the other way for a moment, and then said, "I think the issue should be decided by the group."

When the group reconvened, there was little discussion about the other candidates. They all had professional credentials and positive histories from their respective institutions.

Once the selection business was finished, Mr. Harris said, "Let me quickly discuss Mr. Kyle Williams. While you were reviewing Mr. Logan's file, Dr. Kozenskie came to me and wanted to talk. She wants to have Mr. Williams removed from working on the train. Since she brought it up, I need to clarify his position. Mr. Williams is not a convict. He's a contractor who works for Space Corp. He's a communication specialist and one of the brightest computer hardware and software individuals I'm aware of.

"Kyle, Tegan, and Vidula designed much of the communication system on the train, and at first, they all seemed to get along very well. As time went along, Kyle began accusing Vidula of requesting hardware units that were not in the original design. Vidula said she was building redundant systems for safety, but then Kyle started finding software packages that were encrypted.

"Now, Kyle and Vidula disagree on everything and she's trying to have him eliminated from the project. She alleges Kyle is cutting corners and putting safety at risk. Most of the crew back Kyle but Vidula has elevated her concerns to Mr. Slusser, making it political.

"The truth of the matter is that we're wasting our time even discussing Kyle Williams. He's a contractor and we can't eliminate a contractor, even if we had cause to. The only thing we could do is go to the contract representative and present our reason for wanting him dismissed. But from all indications, Mr. Williams is competent and of enormous value to the mission.

"As far as I'm concerned, the issue is dead and need not be discussed further. I simply wanted to bring it up and have it out in the open. Now, is there anything else that needs to be discussed?"

No one responded.

"Since no one seems to have anything further to say, I suggest we adjourn. We've had a long day with a lot of emotion. I think we all need to go relax, hit the gym or go to a movie to unwind. I don't want you to discuss what has gone on here with anyone else. What went on in this room must remain in this room. Now, go get some rest and relax."

9

It had been over a month since the medication tray Nurse Cindy Wong had been carrying clattered to the floor. Little plastic cups, pills and a carafe of water were all scattered across the polished black-and-white tile floor of the prison medical clinic.

It was Monday morning at the California State Prison, the same day Justin reviewed Cindy's prison record for the first time. Dr. Amy Momora, the prison physician and Cindy's best friend, rushed across the room to her. Cindy was on her hands and knees picking up the cups and pills.

Bending down and picking up the carafe, Dr. Momora asked, "Cindy what happened? Did you trip over something?"

"No," Cindy replied, continuing to clean up the mess.

"Then what happened? Are you all right?"

Cindy put most of the items back on the tray. Dr. Momora took the tray, stood and laid it on her desk. "Here, let me help you up," she said. "Honey, you look like you've seen a ghost. She then led Cindy to a vacant bed and helped her lie down. Quickly removing her stethoscope from around her neck, she checked Cindy's pulse. She then placed the bell on her chest in various spots, checking her heart, respiration and other vital signs. She was concerned Cindy may have had a slight stroke, heart attack or other problem.

Finding nothing that could be readily detected, she again asked, "What happened?"

"You'll think I'm crazy. Do you remember about a year ago when you were supposed to go to a prison conference to be interviewed?

The conference was titled Professionals in Prison, or something like that. You were not feeling well, so I went in your place."

"Yes, I remember."

"Do you recall me telling you that I thought I knew one of the interviewers, but couldn't place him?"

"Yes, and as I recall he made quite an impression on you," Dr. Momora said with a wink and a smile.

"It was nothing," Cindy replied, with a frown. Although she knew Amy's observation was correct. The attraction she felt toward Mr. LeMoore had been overpowering. And when she returned from the conference, it took several weeks to get him out of her mind. In fact, from time to time, she still allowed herself to fantasize about him, knowing she'd never see him again. And since he was a federal correctional employee, nothing could come from such a relationship anyway.

"As I recall, you were pretty stirred up for a couple of weeks after you got back," Dr. Momora noted.

"Go blow it out your ear. You're making that up," Cindy retorted.

"Have it your way, but you know I'm right. Anyway, are you sure it was even the same person?"

"Amy, it was like I was looking through a window. I saw his face as clearly as I can see you. But why would I see his face? It was as if I was being told something, but I don't know what it could be."

"Just lie there for a few minutes and let's see if it happens again. We've been working hard. I suspect you're just tired. Applying to go on the mission is also emotionally upsetting. It was probably just something your unconscious mind brought forward."

Cindy tried to put the event out of her mind, but Molly, her imaginary friend she'd made up after being raped by her father, said in her head, *I have a bad feeling. You need to be careful and stay with me behind our wall.*

Since going to prison, Cindy and Molly had not talked very much, but for some reason she was back.

She saw the face several other times that day and over the next couple of weeks. She kept the visions, or whatever they were, to herself.

The next morning, she took the plunge and approached Dr. Momora. "Amy, I don't want to go on the mission. Please, let's cancel our applications and stay where we're at. We've got a good deal here. We're able to run the clinic the way we like and it isn't that bad. This is the only safe place I've ever lived and I don't want to lose it. If we go on the mission, we don't know who we'll be forced to marry or what they'll be like. Please, let's cancel our applications."

"Cindy, you've got to get out of your rut. It will be an adventure, a chance to make a difference in a new society."

"Please, for my sake. I want to cancel our applications. Besides, what about my medical tests?" Cindy asked.

"Don't worry about your medical report. I've taken care of that. This is all about the face you saw, isn't it?"

"Yes, in part, I guess." Then thinking, she continued, "But it's more than that. Doesn't it frighten you to marry someone you've never met?"

"Not really. They have a dating agency that is making the selections. I'm told those on the first mission are doing very well. All I can do is trust the man they select will be a good person."

"I wish I had that kind of faith."

"Wouldn't you like to be normal, fall in love and have a family?" Amy asked.

Molly again intruded into Cindy's mind, *Sure you would, but you're damaged goods. You can never have a meaningful relationship with a man. No man is ever going to want you. You're too tall, you don't have an hourglass figure, your breasts are too small and you're hands are too big. You're not beautiful and can never return a man's love.*

"I'd like to be a normal person and have a family, but I'll never be able to have that kind of relationship with a man," Cindy replied.

10

"I don't care where he is. I want to talk to him now!" Vidula shouted into the secure communication device that had been secretly provided to her and Ervin by Mr. Slusser.

"I'm sorry, Mr. Slusser is in a meeting with Congressman Richards. He can't be disturbed," the frustrated receptionist responded.

"I don't care if he's meeting with the president himself. You tell him Dr. Vidula Kozenskie is on the secure device. You can also tell him if he doesn't get his ass out of the meeting and on the communicator, the agreement is off."

"One moment please," the receptionist said as the device began playing soft music.

"Mr. Slusser better get his fat you-know-what on the phone," Vidula told Ervin. "We had an agreement and he damn well better live up to it. I'll carve off about a pound of his butt if he doesn't get over here."

"Vidula, honey, we need to find out what may have happened before we jump to conclusions," Ervin said, trying to calm his wife down.

"Don't honey me," Vidula shouted as she continued to stare at the device. "We had a deal. And if that worm Slusser, or even the high and mighty Congressman tries to wiggle out of it, they'll wish they'd never met us."

"Vidula, what in the world is the matter?" Milton said, as his image appeared on the communication screen.

"We need you over here now," Vidula shouted. "Things have fallen totally apart."

"Vidula, calm down," Milton said.

"Calm down?" Vidula again shouted. "We had an agreement and it's completely unraveled. I don't want to discuss the issue over this device, so you need to come over here now. Do you hear me?"

"Vidula, I hear you loud and clear," Milton stated with fear creeping into his voice. "But I can't drop everything this instant. Its 1610 now. It'll take another hour to finish our meeting. Then I'll come over. Oh, I forgot. I have a dinner engagement with an important lobbyist at 1900. I'll hurry. I should be able to be at your location at about 2100."

"We're also important lobbyists and just because we're confined doesn't mean we still can't make things happen. Do you hear me, Milton?" Vidula demanded.

"Vidula, I won't discuss this issue further over the airways. I'll be at your location as close to 2100 as I can. Until then, I suggest you calm down. I'm sure we can resolve whatever the problem is. Good afternoon Vidula. I'll see you and Ervin this evening."

"That no-good, slime-sucking politician," Vidula bellowed as she paced back and forth in their cell. "His kind used to bow and scrape at the mere mention of our names. Now he has to finish a meeting with that little weasel Congressman Richards, then have dinner with his important lobbyist. If he's not here by 2100, he's dead. I'll kill him with my bare hands. If they think they have problems getting the train to work now, just let this group of do-gooders continue to eliminate our team. They'll find the life-support system will fail about six months into their wonderful mission."

Then thinking to herself, she said, *Slusser has no idea how hard he and the good congressman are going to fall.*

"Hush, Vidula," Ervin said. "You don't know whose listening. It sounds like you made enough of a scene by leaving the group. We don't need anyone to start eavesdropping and trying to eliminate us altogether."

"There isn't anyone smart enough in this dump to eliminate us, Ervin dear," Vidula said, with the veins on her neck standing out like a purple road map.

"Honey, let's just relax and gain our composure. I received some new data from my two Russian astronomer friends who are working with long-range laser telescopes. I think they may have found the data were looking for," Ervin excitedly stated as he rubbed Vidula's neck and back.

As they were talking, a young marine guard appeared at their cell door, and said, "Ah, sir, ma'am. Ah, my office received a call from Congressman Richards's office about a meeting you are to have with someone by the name of Mr. Slusser about 2100."

"Yes. Thank you. We're aware of the meeting," Ervin said.

"Ah, you'll be escorted to a private room when Mr. Slusser arrives," the guard politely noted.

The brig had made a special cell for the Kozenskies in what had been a group treatment room. It was just a cement room, but it had a queen-size bed, a large bookcase, two standard gray government desks, a communication device and two computers. They could have used the desk communication device to call Mr. Slusser, but Vidula didn't trust it wasn't being monitored. That was the reason she'd used the secure device Mr. Slusser had given them. According to Mr. Slusser, no one knew they had the device except him and Congressman Richards.

Knowing the meeting with Mr. Slusser was set, Vidula and Ervin began working on their individual projects. Dinner would not be brought to them for another hour, so Ervin went to work analyzing the data from the two Russian astronomers.

Vidula logged in to her computer and sent an encrypted message to a trusted colleague. The message was brief: "Eliminate numbers 6646787 and 5198243. Payment will be as usual."

With that finished, she turned to her husband, and asked, "You don't think Kyle will decide to go on the mission, do you?"

Looking up from his work, Ervin responded, "I doubt it. I suspect he'll have had enough of us by the time the mission begins."

"If he does decide to go, Slusser better have a way to get rid of him. I also want that meddling Justin LeMoore off the project. I hate him, along with his pudgy little priest buddy and that nurse. A Mormon, a Catholic and a prostitute as friends and allies. That's just plain sick and wrong. If Slusser can't eliminate Kyle and LeMoore, they may have an accident," Vidula said.

Ignoring his wife, Ervin focused on his printer, which was printing page after page of data. As he scanned the data back into his computer, a star map began to emerge on the screen. Each star on the map had a designated number with a string of analytical data associated with it. Ervin entered and reentered the data, and each time the same result came out.

After studying the map, he said in a whisper, "Vidula, I've found it! I've really found it!"

By 2100 Vidula was pacing up and down in their room. By 2115, she was almost walking across the ceiling. "Where is that jerk? When I get through with him, he'll be willing to take a job flipping burgers."

"Vidula, I know you're upset, but now that I have the data, we need to be careful. We're on the brink of a historical opportunity that will never come our way again. We can't do anything to jeopardize it."

"Jeopardize the mission? We're heading for a train wreck if we don't have the crew we need. That's what could jeopardize the mission. Just you remember that."

Ervin knew better than to make any comment when Vidula had her dander up. He contented himself by rereading the data and basking in his discovery.

At 2130, the guard knocked at their door, and announced, "Mr. Slusser is waiting for you in the interview room."

Vidula and Ervin were put in leg irons and the guard followed them to the room. They found Milton sitting at a table.

"I thought you said 2100," Vidula sarcastically remarked as she sat and tried to adjust her leg irons. She then turned to the guard, "Is it all right if we go out into the exercise yard? It's stuffy in here. I also think I smell mold."

"I'll have to check with the shift commander. I'll be right back," the guard replied, locking them all in the interview room. "I don't think anyone here is intelligent enough to bug this place," Vidula said, as she carefully examined the walls and ceiling. "But I don't want to take any chances,"

"Vidula, what in the world is the matter?" Mr. Slusser asked, looking contrite.

Vidula continued to look around the room, but before she could respond the guard returned. "The shift commander has given permission for you to go out into the exercise yard. Please follow me."

The exercise yard was about twenty-five yards square. Two sides were made from the same red brick as the prison and extended out to the open end. The end had a twelve-foot chain-link fence topped with razor wire across it. There were basketball backboards cemented into the concrete along two sides, and an old picnic table, gray with age, sat next to the building. As they stepped into the yard, floodlights snapped on, making the area brighter than noonday and causing all three to squint.

Vidula shuffled to the far end of the yard next to the chain-link fence with Ervin and Milton following. When they arrived at the fence, she turned with the veins again standing out on her neck. "Slusser, do we have a deal or not?"

Milton responded, almost in a whisper, "We have several deals. Let's not play games. What's going on?"

"Didn't we agree Ervin and I could identify eight individuals to accompany us on the mission?"

"I think we discussed something like that," Milton returned.

"Something like that!" Vidula exploded. "Milton, there's no thinking about it. That was one of the conditions we agreed on before we ever signed onto the project. You were going to take care of the computer so all eight names would appear on the master roster. Ferrell Logan and Sue Spector were both voted off the crew."

"What about the other nurse and physical therapy assistants you wanted? Were they also eliminated?" Milton asked.

"Only one was accepted. That means all we have are two in hibernation and one physical therapy assistant on the crew." With her hands on her hips and looking like a rabid dog, she said, "We worked for over six months to groom and train the eight people we identified. Ferrell Logan and Sue Spector, along with the other three, were supposed to be on the crew."

"Vidula, Glenn Harris is such a straight arrow. I'm sure he wears starched and ironed underwear. He seems to be suspicious about something, and according to an informant, he takes the lists home each night to ensure they haven't been changed. Besides, if he thinks there's something fishy going on, he'll shut the entire project down. I can't just go in and tell him to reverse something that's been done. He wants everything to be transparent and all decisions made by the selection group."

Thinking quickly, he went on, "If five have been eliminated, that still leaves you with three. Isn't there any way you can work with someone else?"

"Milton, think it through! How can we train anyone else now? And if all of this isn't bad enough, I'm hearing rumors that Kyle Williams is considering going on the mission. If he continues snooping around, he could botch our entire plan."

"You really don't think he's smart enough to break into your encrypted programs, do you?" Milton hopefully asked.

"No, but as I said, he could inadvertently change things enough to create a problem." Vidula stepped close to Milton, and reaching up, she pinched his cheek, and said, "Milton, you have a couple of problems that need to be fixed. Remember, we're already serving life sentences. If you can't follow through with your agreements and something was to leak out about you and Congressman Richards making deals, I suspect it would cause quite a stir. And if a revealing investigation should take place, that wouldn't help good old Congressman Richards win his next election either. Would it? You need to do some serious planning about how you're going to resolve these little issues."

Leaning toward Milton again, she whispered, "Get us some additional help and get rid of Kyle." She gave him a maniacal smile, then stood and stomped away with her leg iron chains jingling between her ankles.

"Vidula!" Milton called as she crossed the exercise yard.

She paid no attention as she entered the building.

Milton's trepidation rose to a volcanic state as he watched her go. Turning to Ervin, he pleaded, "Ervin, I hope you understand how touchy this whole business is? I can't go throwing my weight around or we'll all be in trouble. I know Vidula is upset, but even if I'm not able to get the five individuals back, you still have three. That's a pretty good percentage."

"I understand," Ervin said. "Vidula can be difficult when she's upset. I'll do what I can, but you know Vidula. Once she takes a position it's hard to change her mind. We need at least eight individuals to make everything come together. I don't think three can do what needs to be done."

"I'll see what I can do," Milton worriedly said, mopping his brow with a handkerchief as they walked back across the exercise yard. "What about recruiting some others when you get to Texas? You must know someone you could contact."

"That's a possibility, although they wouldn't be trained." Scratching the stubble on his chin, Ervin said, "But perhaps that could be done on the job. We haven't considered that option. I'll run the idea by Vidula."

"Please do. There must be someone you could contact to help you recruit some of the other prisoners to help you. You know how difficult these things can be for the congressman and myself. One wrong word and we could all be in trouble," Mr. Slusser pleaded.

They walked toward the building and a guard opened the door. As they entered, Mr. Slusser again pleaded with Ervin to calm Vidula down. The guard immediately fell in step with them. Ervin and Milton shook hands and Milton proceeded toward the exit.

Turning around, he called back, "Please Ervin, do what you can."

"I'll do what I can," he replied, as the guard escorted him toward his and Vidula's cell.

"We escorted your wife back to your cell," the guard said as they walked along. "She must have gotten a little cold out there."

"Yes, it did get chilly," Ervin responded.

As they were getting ready for bed, Ervin discussed the possibility of recruiting several members from the hibernation list to assist. Vidula actually thought it was a good idea and quickly sent a message to a trusted friend.

The communicator rang in Mr. Harris's office at 0700. When he answered, Milton Slusser's image was on the screen.

"Glenn," Milton said in a cheery voice. "I need to talk to you as soon as possible." Without asking if it was okay, he continued, "I'm in the car and just pulling into your parking area. I'll be up in about three minutes. It won't take long."

Mr. Harris turned his music down, and thought, *Now what? Obviously the Kozenskie blowup yesterday has already been reported to the big boys.*

In less than two minutes Milton arrived with what looked like powdered sugar down the front of his suit. "Glenn, how in the heck are you?" he asked out of breath but with a big smile. "You must have a thousand things going on. I hear you're through with the records and crew review."

Leaning back in his chair, Mr. Harris said, "Yes, we finished yesterday with the list of prisoners who were nominated to be on the crew. I'll be giving the selection group their instructions on interviewing the top seventy-five individuals on the male and female order-of-merit lists today. If we remain on track, we'll be finished by Christmas. I assume since you're here, you must have heard about the conflict between Vidula and the selection group?"

"Yes. I received a call from Vidula last night," Milton replied.

"I noticed you were here about 2130. I understand you had a

meeting with the Kozenskies in the exercise area for fifty minutes," Mr. Harris noted, looking over the top of his glasses at Mr. Slusser.

"You don't miss much, do you?" Milton noted with a forced chuckle.

"I can't afford to. So, what can I do for you, Milton?"

"Ahem. When Congressman Richards and I first discovered the Kozenskies and realized how important they could be to the mission, they asked for several key players to be on the crew with them."

"Milton, you know it's up to the group to make the decisions on who will be on the crew. I suspect what you're really talking about are the two individuals the group didn't feel were qualified."

Mr. Slusser fidgeted in his seat, brushed at the powdered sugar on his tie, and smiling said, "When the group arrives at the New World and they start the colony, there'll be a need for strong people with medical training."

"Finding inmates with medical skills isn't difficult to do. In fact, we have two sound prisoner medical personnel, Dr. Momora, a family practice physician and Ms. Wong, a nurse practitioner."

Keeping his eyes locked on Mr. Slusser, he continued, "Unless you're talking about another skill, like being an enforcer or goon for those who want to be king and queen."

Mr. Slusser knew he couldn't sway Mr. Harris and his panic was rising like a thermometer on a hot day. With a nervous laugh, he said, "What are you talking about king and queen?"

"The way you're talking, Vidula and Ervin are setting themselves up to be king and queen."

"That's nonsense," Milton replied.

Mr. Harris leaned forward, locking eyes with Mr. Slusser. "One of the two individuals who wasn't selected didn't meet the minimal medical training. In addition, he has a background of violent behavior and has had several aggressive altercations in prison. Vidula wanted to disqualify a person who was much higher on the list and have a guy at the bottom of the list replace her. The other individual Vidula wanted was also professionally questionable. She appeared to have been involved with a prison gang. Interestingly enough, several altercations at the prison involved the Kozenskies in some way. It appeared to the group that both Ms. Spector and Nurse Assistant Logan were working for the Kozenskies to enforce their position at the prison."

"The Kozenskies say Spector and Logan were simply trying to defend them."

"Milton," Mr. Harris said, continuing to lean across his desk with an angry intense stare. "You and I both know the altercations were not defensive. That Logan guy even broke one of the female guard's arms as he forced himself onto the women's cell block. If you want to open an investigation, I'm more than willing to do so. However, based on what I've seen, any rational individual or group will come to the same conclusion."

Looking away, Milton changed directions. "Vidula thinks Dr. Momora and Ms. Wong may sexually involved. Do you know anything about that?"

"Oh, for heaven's sake Milton, that's ridiculous," Mr. Harris angrily stated as he stood. "I have to go over my notes one more time before I brief the group. I hope you'll excuse me. I really need to go. And one other thing, Milton, you keep talking like the Kozenskies are going to be part of the crew. What makes you so sure they won't be part of the cryogenic group?"

Milton almost fell off his chair. "Part of the cryogenic group! Where did that come from! It's always been clearly understood the Kozenskies would be part of the crew. They either designed or helped design almost every component of the train. They have to be available as a resource to the rest of the crew."

"I'm fully confident between the crew and the engineers here on Earth, the train will have all the technical expertise they'll need. The first voyage to the New World was accomplished without the Kozenskies and this one can do the same."

"You can't be serious," Milton said.

"I'm dead serious Milton. It hasn't come up yet, but I can guarantee it will. In fact, I'll bet you a steak dinner on it. Now, if you'll excuse me, I have a briefing to give in fifteen minutes." With that, Mr. Harris walked toward the office door.

Mr. Slusser's astonishment somehow vetoed prudence, and as Mr. Harris walked through the door, he swung around in his seat, blurting out, "Glenn, would you allow the two assistants who were voted out to enter the pool for the cryogenic group?"

"Absolutely not. If they'd have made the list, I wouldn't have a problem. But they didn't. The selection group made the decision and I won't reverse it."

Milton sat for several minutes with his head in his hands until a guard saw him through the open door and inquired, "Sir, are you okay?"

"Yes, yes, I'm all right," he responded.

But he wasn't all right. He felt like his insides were on fire. *How am I going to break this to Vidula and Ervin?* He asked himself.

Mr. Harris explained, "The team will interview the top seventy-five males and seventy-five females on the order-of-merit lists. Each team member will see eight prisoners a day for twenty minutes each. There are nine of you, so we should be able to complete the interviews by the first week of December. If we can get the job done on schedule, I think I can arrange a couple of weeks off for everyone over the holidays."

Justin had pretty much recovered from the impact of viewing Ms. Cynthia Wong's record, but as Mr. Harris talked, he started to have a queasy feeling in the pit of his stomach. The interview rooms were small cement rooms, no windows and a nine-foot ceiling with high fluorescent lights. The floors were carpeted with outdoor carpet in another shade of orange. There was a small metal desk, an old gray swivel chair for the interviewer and a metal folding chair for the prisoner. Each interview would be recorded, so there was a camera on a tripod capturing both the interviewer and the interviewee.

To keep track of the time for each interview, a bell was rung at the beginning, two bells at the fifteen-minute mark and three bells at the end of the interview. The first interviews began at 1000 and seemed to go pretty well.

At the end of the first day, the group met and reviewed one or two recordings from each member. Some interviewers looked as stiff as scarecrows to begin with, but by the end of the day everyone was much more relaxed. For the following twenty days, everything went well. Prisoners seemed anxious to participate in the mission and there were few discrepancies from what was in their records. Most decisions of where each person fell on the order-of-merit list remained the same.

At the end of each day, the interviewers received the names of the prisoners to be interviewed the next day. It was the first of December and the last group of prisoners had just arrived. Justin had tried hard to put Ms. Wong out of his mind, but it hadn't worked. Her impending interview was there, tucked away in a secluded corner of his brain. Since he hadn't interviewed her, he knew she'd be in the last group, but didn't know exactly which day.

It was the second day and the end was finally in sight. A guard knocked on the door of Justin's office after his last interview. Justin answered the door and a guard handed him a paper.

"This is the interview list for tomorrow," he said, handing Justin a clipboard.

Justin reviewed the names and there it was. Ms. Cynthia Wong, 1325. He could feel his face flush and was afraid Frank would see his discomfort. He attempted to avoid Frank, but as he was getting into his truck he came out of the compound.

"Hey, Justin," Frank hollered. "Wait up. I need to chat with you."

Dang, Justin thought, *this is exactly what I didn't want to happen.*

Frank loped over to the truck, and said, "Guess you saw the list for tomorrow. Are you going to be okay?"

"I'll be fine," Justin lied. "I'm over it. It won't be any big deal. I've got a date to look at some new fly-fishing equipment so I can't talk. I'll check in on you later."

"I think you're avoiding the issue and not telling me the truth. I'm going over to the gym for a while, but I'll be in my room by 1900."

"Great," Justin said. Needless to say, he didn't make it to Frank's room that night.

The next morning was clear and cold. Rather than having breakfast at the guest house, Justin drove off base and bought a bottle of orange juice and a bagel at a local corner store. The interviews started at 0800 each day. Justin waited until right at 0755 to slip into his office.

He was out of sorts and couldn't get into his rhythm all morning. He waited in his office until everyone left for lunch, then slipped out and drove to the Military Shoppette. He bought a bottle of water and a candy bar. He drove back to the prison, quickly went through the pass check and quietly slipped back into his office.

The 1300 interviewee arrived, but he was so anxious he had a hard time concentrating. All too quickly 1325 came. The bell rang, the guard knocked, opened the door and Ms. Wong walked in. She looked much like her picture, not ravishing but poised and pretty. She looked taller than in her picture. Justin guessed her to be almost six feet. She had brown eyes, with a slight Oriental look about them. To Justin it made her appear somewhat exotic. Her brunette hair was pulled back in a ponytail and longer than her file showed. She had a medium build with a light complexion, large hands and long slender fingers. Anything else about her figure was hidden by the orange prison jumpsuit.

She entered the office, and when she made eye contact, her expression was one of utter shock. She stared, transfixed by Justin's face, as her knees buckled causing her to almost fall. When Justin stood, he also felt like his knees were going to give out, but seeing Ms. Wong almost fall he rushed around the desk to help her.

Like all prisoners, she was wearing leg irons and handcuffs so it was easy to trip. But when Justin reached out to steady her, it was as if he was charged with electricity. A spark jumped from his hand to her arm. Despite the shock, Justin extended his hand and she reached for it. She then stood as if momentarily frozen in place.

His professional resolve was gone. "Aaaahh . . . my name is Justin LeMoore," he stammered. "Please have a seat." He let go of her hand and gestured to the chair in front of his desk.

Ms. Wong looked at the chair, then back to Justin before shuffling forward. Her eyes went from his face to the floor several more times as she felt for the chair and eased onto it.

When Justin returned to his seat behind the desk, his mind was blank. Finally he said, "I think I remember meeting you at a prison conference about a year ago. I was on a panel that interviewed several professional prisoners."

"Yes, I remember," she quietly replied as she looked at the floor.

"As I remember, you are a nurse. Is that right?" he asked, even though he had her file on his computer in front of him.

"Yes, I'm a nurse clinician."

Molly said, *I have a bad feeling about him. Be careful what you say. There's something dangerous about him.*

Justin drew a deep breath and forced himself to regain enough composure to stumble through the typical questions. "Why are you interested in going on the mission? How long have you been incarcerated? Are you concerned about the cryogenic process?"

She responded to his questions, but he couldn't remember any of her answers. Then he recalled the issue of her appeal. "I understand your conviction is under appeal and could be overturned?"

"Yes, but I want to participate in the mission whether my conviction is overturned or not. I didn't start the appeal. It was started by a domestic violence group. But," she blurted out, "I won't go if my friend Dr. Amy Momora isn't also accepted. We've been friends since I was incarcerated. It would be impossible for me to go without her."

"Let me see," Justin said as he reviewed the list for the next day. "Dr. Momora's name is on the list to be interviewed tomorrow, but I can't guarantee anything. The decision about who goes is a group decision, not mine to make alone."

"Is it possible to put in a good word for her?" Ms. Wong asked.

"After I've had the opportunity to interview her, I'll honestly evaluate her and vote according to what I see. That's about as much as I can guarantee."

"I'm sure you'll be impressed. She's an incredible physician and would be a valuable asset," Ms. Wong pleaded.

"You seem to be very attached to Dr. Momora. Are the two of you intimately involved in any way?"

"Good heavens no!" Ms. Wong replied, briefly making eye contact with Justin. "I love her, but it's like loving a sister. She's the only person I've ever been able to confide in and trust. If we're together, we'll be able to continue that support."

Then not knowing what else to say, she continued, "I understand we will be expected to marry. I look forward to that," she lied.

Be careful, Molly said. *You know you're damaged goods. You can't ever really love a man or be a real wife.*

"I'm sorry to ask such a question, but I had to clarify the issue. I hope you understand," Justin said.

"I understand," Ms. Wong replied.

"Have you asked other interviewers to ensure Dr. Momora is on the mission?"

"No, I haven't," she replied.

"Why not?" Justin asked.

"I don't know. I just didn't feel right about it."

It was as if Justin's mind had been wiped clean as he stared at Ms. Wong. She was looking at the floor.

"I could swear we know each other from somewhere else other than the prison conference panel interview," Justin said.

"I feel the same way," she replied, fleetingly looking at Justin, "although I'm sure we haven't."

The fifteen-minute bell rang twice to Justin's relief. He couldn't remember having such a long interview or feeling more uncomfortable.

"Do you like camping?" Justin asked. He had no idea where that question came from. It just popped into his head.

"Yes, as a matter of fact I do," she replied. "But I've only been camping a few times. My father didn't like camping so we never went as a family. I was briefly in Girl Scouts and camping was my favorite thing to do. I could spend hours just walking through the woods and looking at everything.

"Night was my favorite time. I loved to lie on my back, look at the billions of stars and listen to all the night sounds. I used to wonder what it would be like to fly up into the stars. I wanted to see what they really looked like up close. When I was a girl, I'd also ride my bike out of town into the country. There were some farms about four miles from our home. One of them had a lot of trees and a creek that ran through it. I'd catch crawfish, frogs and all kinds of insects. My mother hated it because I'd take them home and sneak them into my room.

"After I got older and married, camping and my time in the woods stopped. I hope the New World has lots of places to explore. I also hope, if I have children, they'll be able to run free and catch frogs and bugs like I did."

"And will you make a fuss when they bring them back and sneak them into their bedrooms?" Justin asked with a smile.

"Of course, that's what mothers are supposed to do."

The bell rang three times and they both stood. Justin reached over the corner of the desk to shake hands and again there was an electrical charge that jumped between them.

Trying to make a joke, Justin said, "You have an electric personality."

"I think it must be the dry air in here. Probably static electricity," she responded.

They briefly made eye contact and she departed.

This is stupid, absolutely stupid, he told himself. *I made a complete fool of myself. My heart's beating like a school kid over his first crush. And I'm sure anyone who sees the recording will instantly know what's up. What was I thinking asking her a question like her interest in camping? How could I have made such a fool of myself?*

The rest of the afternoon's interviews went better, but Justin couldn't get his mind off Ms. Wong.

Cindy felt like she was coming apart as the guard escorted her to hers and Amy's cell. Dr. Momora looked up from the book she was reading as the door opened. She took one look and asked, "Cindy, what's the matter? Are you sick? You look flushed."

Cindy flopped down on her bed, put her arm over her eyes, and replied, "Do you remember me telling you about the person I met at the prison conference and the face I saw in the medical clinic?"

"Yes, I remember."

"I saw and met him today."

"Really?"

"He was one of the interviewers. It was Mr. Justin LeMoore."

"And?" Dr. Momora's asked, letting the question hang.

"And it was horrible. When I walked into the interview room and recognized him, my knees buckled, my heart started pounding and I couldn't breathe."

Cindy hesitated for a moment as Molly instructed, *We have to leave. This whole thing is wrong. Tell Amy you want to drop out of the mission.*

Gathering her thoughts, she continued, "I almost collapsed so Mr. LeMoore jumped up to help me. It was like electricity jumped from his hand to my arm. It must have been static electricity from the carpet. Oh Amy, I'm so frightened. Please, let's drop out of the mission and go back to prison."

"Drop out? We've had this discussion before. We are not dropping out! There must be a reason you saw his face and there must be a reason you reacted to him the way you did. Did he look dangerous?"

"Not physically dangerous, but I was petrified. I've never had that reaction to a man before."

That's why we have to drop out and leave. He's as dangerous as Yan was. You can't handle your emotions. He could destroy us. Cindy, we have to go back to prison where there are walls to protect us, Molly shouted in her head.

"How did Mr. LeMoore react to you?" Dr. Momora asked.

"I don't know for sure, but I think he was as nervous as I was."

"Sounds to me like it was love at first sight—for both of you," Dr. Momora joked.

"Amy, that's not funny!" Cindy angrily protested. "I have no desire for a relationship with a man. Any man. And besides, he's a prison employee."

Molly quickly insisted, *That's right. You can never have a relationship with any man. I'm your only real friend and we have to drop out of the mission.*

"Maybe God has a plan for you. Maybe you are supposed to work together to do something," Dr. Momora replied.

God has nothing to do with this. You have to trust me, Molly angrily stated. *Have I ever led you astray?*

Cindy felt like a moth being drawn to a flame.

Justin left immediately after his last interview and drove to the guest house. He quickly changed clothes and went for another five-mile run. When he got back dinner was ready, compliments of Millie.

Almost everyone was at dinner and most remained after to talk which helped occupy his mind.

The subject got around to the Kozenskies, and as usual some supported them and some still didn't trust them. Colonel Forrester was the most verbal and continually reminded the group of how much they'd contributed to the mission.

"They've improved almost every system on the train. I don't see how their motives can be anything but genuine. Sure, they're a little eccentric, but aren't all intelligent people a little strange? Look at Albert Einstein, the great music composers, painters and even some of the brilliant minds who have worked on the train. I just don't think they've been given a fair chance."

Frank arrived late for supper, which was not like him. Justin was sure he'd been up to something. Not knowing made Justin even more uncomfortable.

Frank spoke up, and said, "Mick, I hear you, but there's something about the Kozenskies that goes beyond intelligence. I think its cunning. Vidula smiles and says all the right words, but there's a dark undercurrent that makes me feel like I'm being stalked by a vampire."

Justin quickly agreed. "I feel the same way. When you interview people in prison for the first time, you often get the sense that this is really a dangerous person. The hair on the back of your neck prickles and you feel uneasy. It's not the words they say; it's a negative vibe you feel. A good sociopath will tell you anything they think you want to hear. They're good at manipulating people, but beyond the words, there's something wrong. It's like you can feel a dangerous person."

Colonel Forrester asked, "And you think you feel danger in the Kozenskies?"

"Yes, sir, I do."

"I think you give your gut and the hair on your neck too much credit," Colonel Forrester flatly stated. "Show me one shred of evidence that verifies they're anything other than what they say they are. Give me one scrap of wrongdoing and I may change my mind. Until then, I think you're on a witch hunt."

"Mick," Justin responded. "Didn't you spend time as a test pilot?"

"Yeah, almost five years."

"And as you flew those multibillion-dollar planes, you relied strictly on the instruments. You never had to use your senses or intuition. Is that right?"

"I see where you're going," Colonel Forrester responded. "Yes, there were times I had to override the instruments and make a split decision. But when that happened I always tried to figure out what needed to be changed so I could rely on the instruments. Intuition isn't reliable."

"I partially agree, and I'll try to keep an open mind. But people are different from machines. Many will try to outsmart you and say anything they think you want to hear. They'll manipulate you and then stab you in the back. Power-hungry people will do anything to achieve their goals. It's a game with them and many are masters at their art. So based on my experience I've learned not to only listen, but to also pay attention to my senses."

Justin got up to get a drink, and Dr. Tong and Millie followed him out.

"We agree with you. You should talk to Mr. Harris. He seems to trust you. You can articulate what many of us are feeling," Millie said.

"Not on your life. First of all, Mick is right. We don't have any evidence. Second, if we as a group are uncomfortable with the Kozenskies, then we as a group should go talk to Mr. Harris."

The group continued to discuss their opinions. After almost an hour, they finally decided the only thing they could do was to be on guard and keep their eyes open.

Justin tried to unobtrusively go to his room, but Frank fell in step with him. "Okay, we're going to talk. Do you want to go to your room or mine?

"Your room," Justin said. "That way I can leave when I'm tired of your useless prattle."

"Fine with me," Frank replied as he opened his door. "Enter, my befuddled friend."

Justin walked in and sat on the couch. Frank took his usual place in the easy chair with one leg over the arm.

"You successfully avoided me last night and ducked out after your last interview today. The time has come. Out with it. Father Maloney is here to help you."

"What makes you think there's anything wrong? You have a suspicious mind."

"Suspicious my fanny," Frank replied. "Do you want to tell me about the interview, or should I tell you what I saw on your recording?"

"You looked at my recording!" Justin angrily exploded. "The recordings are supposed to be private. You can't go around looking at other people's recordings."

"So sue me," Frank said. "Justin, no one said we can't look at each

other's recordings. The entire group reviews each other's interviews all the time."

"Yes, but that's for training. They're not for your amusement," Justin stated with a frown.

"Mr. Harris said selection decisions must remain with the group. I haven't gone outside the group by looking at your recording. So again, do you want to tell me about the interview, or do you want me to start with what I saw? Which by the way, was one of the worst interviews I've ever seen."

Justin didn't know where to begin. And Frank was right. It was a terrible interview. Finally, he said, "I wish I could tell you. All I can say is that it was horrible and exhilarating at the same time. Since you violated my privacy by watching my recording, what more can I say?"

"What I want to know is what you were feeling up here," Frank said, pointing to his head, "and down here." He continued by pointing to his heart.

"Jumbled up, out of control, silly, incompetent and totally unprofessional," Justin sighed. "Can I go to bed now Father? I have sinned, but I've confessed my sin."

"Oh no my son," Frank said with his usual annoying smile. "You've just said words. Now comes the decision about repentance. Come on Justin, tell me what really happened."

Justin sat back, closed his eyes, and after several seconds began, "She walked into the room and my knees went weak. She stumbled and I went around the desk to help her. When I reached out, it was like a spark jumped between us. I think she also felt it because she jumped when I touched her arm. She then just stood there. I had to almost lead her to the chair. Then I couldn't think of the questions I wanted to ask. I bumbled along until I finally thought to ask about her appeal.

"After her reply, I couldn't think of anything to follow up with. She asked me to make sure a friend of hers is accepted for the mission. Her friend is Dr. Amy Momora. Do you remember reviewing her file?"

"Vaguely," Frank responded. "I can't say I recall any details other than she was a tall black lady and a physician."

"Ms. Wong said they are good friends, and cell mates. She even said if Dr. Momora isn't accepted, she won't go either. Do you think they could be lovers?"

"Naw, I doubt it. I think Dr. Amy Momora is on the list for you to see tomorrow. Perhaps you'll have a better idea after your interview. Perhaps we should go in a little early and take another look at their files. That might tell us if there's something suspicious," Frank said.

"Good idea. What time do you want to go?"

"How about 0600? That should give us enough time to look both files over."

Frank, then began howling with laughter, looked at Justin.

"What's so funny?" Justin demanded.

"Your interview," he giggled. "I can't get it out of my head. I thought your question about camping was particularly salient. I expected you to follow up with something like, 'I like to camp, hunt and fish. Would you like to go with me sometime?' You were about as obvious as an elephant trying to hide behind a picket fence."

"Yeah, that was a pretty dumb question. I have no idea where it even came from. If she wasn't a prisoner, I might do just that. I'd ask for her phone number, take her out and maybe go hiking together. But this isn't a social situation. She's a prisoner! We live in two totally different worlds!"

Frank said, "Here's something to think about. If her appeal should be approved, she wouldn't be a prisoner anymore. Then there would be nothing to stop her from changing her mind. She could request to go as a paid nurse," Frank said.

"Holy mackerel, I didn't think of that," Justin replied.

"Let's say her appeal did go through, and she decided not to go on the mission. Would you consider resigning so you could be with her?"

"No, I've signed a contract," Justin flatly stated. "This is crazy anyway. Why are we even talking about such nonsense? I'm going to bed."

Frank stood as Justin got up to go. "Justin, you said when we were talking about the Kozenskies that you'd keep an open mind. I suggest you do the same about Ms. Wong. Something is going on, and we don't know what God may have in store for us. If you simply dismiss your feelings, you might be making a big mistake."

"Frank, don't you understand? She's a convict. She's going to marry someone who has been selected for her. They're going to live on the New World and I'm going to return to this world. Hopefully I'll be rich and can hunt and fish to my heart's content. There isn't any Ms. Wong in that equation."

Frank just smiled. "My son, keep an open mind."

Justin turned. But as he was leaving the room he turned back. He had to ask, "Was the recording really that bad?"

"I guess someone could conclude you were just a little off today." With another belly laugh, he continued, "Of course they'd have to be deaf and blind. And I can't remember anyone on the team who is either deaf or blind."

"Thanks," Justin said. "I hope your collar chokes you, then you get tangled in your robes and fall down in front of your entire congregation."

Frank just laughed. "My son, both of those things have already happened."

That night, Cindy was so upset she couldn't sleep. She lay in bed looking at the bumps on the cement ceiling. *Why did I react like that?* She asked herself. *Why does my heart race and I feel like I can't breathe when I think about Mr. LeMoore? And what will I do if the appeal does go through? I was so content in prison. If I don't go, I might have to leave Amy, and what will I do if I'm forced to marry someone like Yan? And how will I relate to Mr. LeMoore when we land? I'm so mixed up. I wish we had never applied for this.*

As she pondered the questions, she dozed off and saw herself and Mr. LeMoore sitting at classroom desks. There was a tall dark-haired woman standing over them. She was shouting, *You've both been bad and have to be separated.*

Sweating, Cindy woke with a start. Her heart was racing, and she was having a hard time breathing. *Why was I dreaming about me and Mr. LeMoore? What could the dream mean, and why would we need to be separated?*

Molly was beside herself. *This is an omen. You and Mr. LeMoore will do something that gets us into trouble. If you continue, you're risking everything. We both could be destroyed. Please, you have to resign and return to prison. That's the only place where we're safe.*

Cindy got up and paced the floor in the dark for more than an hour before lying back down. Still unable to sleep, she again stared at the ceiling. She briefly dozed off and felt herself falling, spiraling down toward an evil misty abyss. She knew if she fell into the mist, she'd be lost forever. Desperately looking up for light, or hope, she saw the same tall dark-haired woman standing above hysterically laughing. The woman was holding some kind of clock or device, which she was trying to set.

Cindy woke crying and gasping for air. Reality rushed in wrapping a frosty grip around her, freezing her very soul. Molly was going crazy. *Can't you see the danger we're in? There's something evil about the mission. If you go, we'll both be destroyed.*

When morning finally came and Amy began to stir, Cindy went over and sat on the edge of her bed. Looking at her friend, she pleaded, "Amy, please, we have to resign from the mission."

She then recounted her dreams and again begged, "We had a good life at the prison. I don't want to risk what could happen on the mission. I've never felt such a dark, cold sensation. If I go on the mission I'll be destroyed. I know I will. Please Amy. Prison is the only place where I can be safe."

Amy sat up, wiped the sleep from her eyes and looked at her friend. "You're just reacting to the emotional events over the past few days. Your dreams were the result of your unconscious, internal fears and nothing more. Your outlook on life is too restricted and your vision for the future too narrow. You need to look beyond your past life. You walk under a cloud of fear and depression. You have to move out into the sunshine. All men aren't bad."

Then taking hold of Cindy's wrist and looking into her eyes, she continued, "You can stay if you want, but I'm going on the mission. I'm not going to spend the rest of my life in prison when I could be helping start something special."

Cindy was caught. She couldn't face leaving Amy, yet in her heart she knew the black hole was real. She'd seen and experienced it before in the dark days of her life. It came on after being raped by her father, and again when she was forced to marry Yan. She knew she could be consumed by it, but didn't have a choice. She'd go on the mission and pretend she was happy, all the while knowing she was risking her very existence.

When Justin finally got to bed, he also had a hard time sleeping, even though he'd taken two PM tablets. Like Ms. Wong, when he finally did sleep, he had crazy, mixed-up dreams. In one dream he was running across an open field. He had a large backpack and was trying to run. His entire body felt ponderous. His feet felt like they weighed fifty pounds each. He was moving in slow motion. Then he was in some kind of dark place or cave. Ms. Wong was there but she was asleep. Around the room, chains hung from the walls. Some had women in them screaming and trying to clutch at him. Vidula was coming toward him shrieking, *I'm going to kill you.* Before she could carry out her threat, some kind of animal charged from out of nowhere and ate her.

He awoke in a panic, relieved to find he was just dreaming. He was wet with sweat and his heart was pounding. He got up and looked out the window into the dark for a long time.

Why am I having nightmares? Even as a kid I never had bad dreams. Other kids were afraid of the dark, monsters under their beds, or like Frank, frightened when he had to sleep in a tent. I never had those kinds of fears.

He was not sure what time it was. It was still dark but he had to do something.

I'm going to go for a run, he decided. As he left the building, the cold early morning air washed over him. It helped to clear his mind.

The dreams are just the result of so many significant emotional events that have taken place over the past several days, he told himself.

When he returned from his run, it was starting to get light. He took a hot shower and waited for Frank to get up. He'd turned the entertainment center on and was watching the early news when Frank knocked and walked in.

"You up and ready to go review those two records?"

"Sure," Justin responded.

"You look like you didn't sleep very well last night," Frank noted.

"I didn't," Justin replied.

"You had a lot on your mind. Hopefully today will go better."

"I hope so," Justin responded.

They went to Frank's office and pulled up Dr. Amy Momora's and Cynthia Wong's files. They'd seen their files during the records review, and Justin knew Ms. Wong's file by heart. Frank, on the other hand, couldn't remember many details about either one of them.

Dr. Momora's picture showed an extremely tall, slender, intensely black lady. According to her file, she was raised in Somalia. When the country fell into anarchy, her father used his connections with the American ambassador to have Amy and her brother sent to America.

Amy had been attending medical school and when she moved to America, she applied and was accepted into John Hopkins University Medical School to finish her degree. After completing her medical degree, she went on to the David Geffen School of Medicine at UCLA for her residency.

Amy's parents were ultimately killed in the political unrest. Both she and her brother requested asylum in America. Their request was granted and eventually both received their US citizenship. Amy's brother became an attorney and over time the two drifted apart.

After completing her residency, Dr. Momora took a job as the medical consultant for several nursing homes and assisted-living centers. She had difficulty seeing so many patients who were essentially warehoused, just waiting and wanting to die. Experiencing such horrible misery, she eventually became interested in the right-to-die movement. In addition to pain, many lived in endless boredom, helpless and unable to manage their own lives.

The right-to-die issue had been debated for over two hundred years, but the wheels of government grind slowly. Dr. Momora decided to indirectly assist some of her worst patients to take their own lives.

Her file said she'd assisted ten patients to commit suicide when somehow word got out. She was arrested, the trial was well publicized and in the end, she was sentenced to life in prison.

Since she was a skilled physician, she was assigned to the prison medical clinic.

After reviewing Dr. Momora's file, they quickly looked at Ms. Wong's file, but didn't find anything of significance. When Cindy arrived at the prison, and since she was a nurse, she was also assigned to the medical clinic. Not long after her assignment, Dr. Momora and Ms. Wong became cell mates.

I don't see any indication they're lovers or intimately involved," Justin said.

"Me neither. I guess we'll just have to see what comes out of the interviews. You're going to see Dr. Momora today and I'm going to see Ms. Wong," Frank commented.

The day went better, and Justin's interview with Dr. Amy Momora went fairly smooth. Her picture did not do her justice. When she was escorted into his office, Justin was shocked. She had to bend down to enter the room. She had to be at least seven feet tall. She was a beautiful woman with dark flashing eyes, intensely white teeth and a natural warm smile. Justin rose from his chair and reached out to her.

At least no lightning bolts, he thought as they shook hands.

He motioned her to the chair and she sat. She maintained constant eye contact, answering every question straightforward.

"Yesterday I interviewed Ms. Wong, which I assume you're aware of?"

"Yes, she told me all about it," Dr. Momora said, with almost-a-straight face.

Justin could feel the color rising in his face, so he quickly drove on. "Dr. Momora, I need to ask the same question I asked Ms. Wong yesterday."

Her eyes twinkled, and Justin had the distinct impression she was a mischievous person.

"I assume you want to know if Cindy and I are lovers. Cindy told me you asked her about it yesterday."

I wonder what else she told you, Justin thought. "So you discussed the interview?"

"Of course. You're talking about prison. We talk about everything."

Justin thought his face must be beet red by now. "Yes, I'm familiar with how information travels in prisons."

Then taking over the interview, she asked, "Do you know why I'm in prison?"

"Your file said you were convicted of assisting elderly patients in nursing homes to terminate their lives."

"Yes, and it cost me life in prison. The court wanted to make an example out of me." Then looking at Justin, she asked, "Do you know that modern medicine has done too good a job of keeping people alive without any hope of having some kind of quality in their lives? Many have said we should demand that hopeless patients not be allowed to live. Or at least they should have the option to end their lives if they wish. That would help a little to decrease the surplus population.

"Can you imagine how many people around the world are living in human warehouses or even with families in relentless pain day after day, month after month and year after year? Many have given up hope of ever having any semblance of meaning, self-worth, respect or dignity in their lives. Most would jump at the chance to end their lives if given the opportunity. I think a human being should be given the dignity to choose, if or when he or she wishes to leave this life. Does that sound wrong to you?"

"We can debate that question all day. Those questions are messy. Religion, individual beliefs, emotions and of course money all enter into such discussions."

"I'm glad you brought money up. Do you know we as a society spend more than half of our national health care resources on people with less than six months to live?"

"No, I didn't know that," Justin replied. "I'm not sure what all of this has to do with my original question about you and Ms. Wong being intimately involved?"

"Nothing really. I was just curious about what you would say. I was wondering how open minded you are. I can see you're pretty conservative. Now, back to your question about Cynthia and me being lovers. The answer is no, we're not. Go ahead and check on us any way you like. You'll find although we love each other like sisters, that's all there is. Now, can I ask you another question?"

"I suppose so," Justin hesitantly responded, wondering where her question would go this time.

"Do you think Cindy and I will both be able to go on the mission?"

"I don't know. Ms. Wong asked the same question. Since you've made it this far, and you're both medical professionals, I'd think you both have a good chance. But, I don't get to make that decision independently."

"Anything you can do to help us both get a bed would be appreciated," Dr. Momora noted.

"I need to ask one last question, Dr. Momora. Ms. Wong's conviction is up for appeal. Is that right?"

"Yes."

"From what I can see, she has a good shot at having her conviction overturned. If that happens, do you think she'll still want to participate in the mission?"

She was momentarily hesitant. It was as if she was returning from some faraway memory. She was thinking of Cindy's dreams last night. Then looking at Justin, she said, "Yes, she will. Cindy didn't initiate the appeal. It was a spouse abuse group who started it. After Cindy applied to go on the mission, she actually asked the attorney to bury it until after we leave."

"Oh," Justin responded, feeling both anxious and relief at the same time.

The third bell rang, and Dr. Momora stood. As she was leaving, she looked back at Justin. With a sly smile, she said, "Cindy didn't get much sleep last night either."

I'm not sure I like her. She's obviously uninhibited and certainly speaks her mind. I can see why Ms. Wong likes her so much, Justin told himself.

The rest of the interviews and reviews were completed by the second week of December, so Mr. Harris gave everyone the next two weeks off. They were all to be back for the last phase of the deliberations by the third of January.

"Vidula, I've tried everything to get Logan and Spector back on the crew, but Glenn won't budge about going over the head of the selection team," Milton Slusser apologetically stated.

"Fine, count me out," Vidula said as she got up and paced back and forth.

Feeling off balance, Mr. Slusser looked at Ervin, who'd been sitting quietly. "Ervin, do you understand what I'm saying?"

"Yes, I understand. But Milton, one way or the other we've got to have more people to make the plan work."

"I know. Did you make contact with anyone to see if some of the people on hibernation list might be interested in assisting you?"

"Even if we found fifty people, they wouldn't be trained," Vidula angrily complained.

"No, but you could train them when the time comes," Milton suggested.

"The bottom line is you failed to live up to the agreement you made to alter the order-of-merit list. We need at least five people on the crew, or our plan won't work."

Vidula sat back down, looked at Milton, and said, "Okay, there may be a way of making it work. Right now one of our selectees will be part of the crew. Two others, Muriel French and Safire Strong are in the hibernation group. Those two need to be moved to the crew. Including Ervin and myself that would give us a total of five who are awake. Even with that, I'll have to automate a lot more to make everything come together."

"I'll have to reconfigure the computer system to automate the awakening process. That means I'll have to have total access to the schematics and add at least two more relay boxes: one on the male cryogenic ward and one on the female ward. They'll be disguised as life-support backups and incorporated into the emergency systems. I'll have to do the programming over the holiday break when the crew won't be there to bother me. In addition, you've got to get Kyle off the crew. He'll want to know what the extra backups are for. If he starts snooping too hard, he could jeopardize everything.

"I think I can take care of the schematics and get you to Houston over the holiday," Milton said.

"Look Milton, the time for 'I think' is over. Do you understand? Somehow we need to move the two individuals from the Snow White group to the crew. We'll also need the schematics and the two new relay boxes."

"You didn't answer about recruiting some others from the cryogenic group to help."

Vidula just looked at Milton, but said nothing.

"Vidula," Ervin submissively said, "with a little creative programming, I think you could still make the plan work."

"We have time over the next two weeks to order the hardware and software. The biggest issue will be getting us to Houston," Vidula noted.

"I'm comfortable I can make that happen," Mr. Slusser quickly replied.

"Good," Ervin said. "We'll need to work out the kinks and call Tegan and Won to let them know we're making more modifications. It will just look like an upgrade. They'll never look for the embedded sleeper program. I think I can camouflage everything so even snoopy Kyle won't pick up on it."

Justin spent a week with Ted hunting pheasants in Kansas and then flew to Colorado where he spent Christmas with his sister and her family. Afterward, he flew back to Kansas where he spent three more days with Ted.

All during the trip, he continued to have the same crazy dreams. In one he was in a prison jumpsuit in what appeared to be a dining area. Vidula was a prison guard. She kept shouting, *the judge gave you to me.*

Now you'll understand what it's like to be a prisoner. I'm going to humiliate and break you.

Justin didn't understand why he was having nightmares almost nightly. It was getting old. He needed just one good-night's sleep.

Just before Christmas, Vidula received a message from a colleague on her communication device with two attached lists. One had twelve male names; the other had sixteen female names. When Vidula showed the list to Ervin, he said, "See Vidula. You just have to have a little patience. We're going to have more assistance than we initially planned on."

"But they won't be trained," Vidula complained.

"Don't worry my love. What we're going to ask them to do doesn't take all that much training. Besides, the ones we trained can train the others in Houston."

"I hope so," Vidula replied.

11

Everyone returned to Virginia after their holiday and New Year's break. The Kozenskies spent the last half of December in Houston working on the two computer relays. Vidula and Ervin were flown back to Virginia on the third of January.

On the fourth of January, Mr. Harris was in the conference room at 0700 chomping at the bit to get started. He wanted to review the order-of-merit list with the group for both the males and females one last time. His plan was to make sure there wasn't any further discussion after people had time to think about the interviews.

"Once we complete everything and inform the various prisons about who has been accepted, we'll all move to Houston. We have a facility that will accommodate the one-hundred-and-twenty primary selectees and the thirty alternates. I hope we can complete the deliberations and wrap everything up in the next two weeks," Mr. Harris said.

"The marriage contractor will send each person on the selected and alternate list a lengthy questionnaire. Using that information, they will make preliminary recommendations and ask for our input. When we transfer to Houston, they'll meet with each person for a face-to-face interview before making any final recommendations.

"Once everything is finalized, we'll meet with the one-hundred-and-twenty primary selectees and share the list of who they'll be mated with. The alternates will be housed in Houston but will not initially be assigned a mate."

"I heard through the grapevine the train may not be ready by March. Is that true?" Justin inquired.

"All I can say is that I've heard the same rumors. My charge is to have all personnel issues completed by the first week in March and that's what I intend to do. If construction of the train is delayed, someone else will have to answer to that."

"Is there room to accommodate both the crew and inmates in Houston if it does take several extra weeks?" Justin continued.

"Yes, there will be plenty of room. The medical and mental health crews will be housed in the complex, as they will be working closely with the inmates. Now, for our current task, I have loaded the seventy-five male and seventy-five female files into the computers. I want to briefly review each individual to see if there is any further discussion needed. Any questions?" Mr. Harris asked.

No one had a question, so Mr. Harris said, "Okay, let's begin."

Over the next few days, there were several opinions expressed about a few of the candidates but none that changed the order-of-merit list.

One morning, Mr. Harris announced, "Number seventeen and fifty on the female list have decided to withdraw from the mission. They were both scheduled to be on the crew. One is a nurse assistant; the other is a physical therapy assistant."

Everyone was shocked. Since the candidates had all gone this far in the selection process, no one expected anyone to withdraw. "That's the reason for having the extra candidates. The first mission had about a ten percent dropout rate. I'm not surprised at all, and I'll be even more surprised if there isn't several more. On the first mission, we had one person opt out as the group was getting ready for transport up to the ship," Mr. Harris noted.

Vidula spoke up, saying, "Since we have to reorder the list anyway, I'd like to address the two crew vacancies. I've been looking down the list. Muriel French is a qualified nurse assistant, and Safire

Strong is a physical therapy assistant. Currently both are in the hibernation group. Could they be transferred to the crew list?"

"Do the two individuals you're referring to happen to come from the institution you were at?" Justin inquired.

"Yes, they do, Mr. LeMoore. That's how I know of their backgrounds. But I don't see what that has to do with anything."

The group conceded the nurse assistant and the physical therapy assistant vacancies needed to be filled, so the Strong and French files were brought up and discussed. Neither was anything outstanding. Ms. French had been a nurse assistant and a home health provider. Ms. Strong had been a physical therapy assistant at a large hospital. Both had been employed for several years prior to their incarcerations. Justin did a quick review of their records but found nothing significant. He kept hoping Frank or someone else would nominate Ms. Wong to fill the nursing vacancy, but no one did.

Finally, he said, "I think we should review everyone on the list who has a nursing background. Not just Ms. French."

Everyone agreed. A review of the records showed Ms. Cynthia Wong was the only other person who had a nursing background. "I suggest we move Ms. Wong from the cryogenic group to the crew," Justin said.

Mr. Harris watched Justin with interest, but didn't comment.

"Ms. Wong is a nurse clinician. As we have said before, the position doesn't require that kind of specialty," Vidula noted. "If you turn to page ninety-six of the *Mission Position Manual*, you'll see that position calls for a nurse assistant. In fact, there are no nurse clinician positions in the manual."

At first Dr. Tong supported having a nurse clinician, but then said, "The two positions are listed as assistant positions. A nurse clinician can do everything a nurse assistant can and a lot more. They can dispense some medications and conduct more thorough medical examinations. They also have a much wider range of experience."

Vidula argued, "A nurse clinician is usually less experienced in working with patients than a nurse assistant who has dealt with bedridden patients day after day. Ms. French has provided services to home health care patients for several years. Therefore, she'll be willing and able to provide that same service to the cryogenic patients. The crew will have three physicians and several nurses. They don't need a nurse clinician."

Dr. Tong reversed her position and sided with Vidula. "We will have physicians to diagnose, so a nurse assistant is all that's needed. What this position requires is physical strength to move the patients, pattern and exercise them. Ms. Wong's skills will be most useful when we get to the New World."

That's a bunch of horseshit. I thought we'd resolved that crap weeks ago," Millie lashed out. "As the chief nurse for the female cryogenic ward, I'll take a nurse clinician any day of the week over a nurse assistant. You all seem to think once people are in a cryogenic state they peacefully slumber and never incur any other problems. The fact is, even asleep people get sick. They get diseases, infections, cancer or even contract pneumonia. There are a hundred other things that a nurse clinician will spot but will go over the head of a nurse assistant."

Justin was perplexed, and looking at Dr. Tong and Vidula, and asked, "Are you saying individuals with higher degrees are less able or unwilling to provide routine nursing services and their diagnostic skills are useless?"

Dr. Tong thoughtfully replied, "I've seen some cases where individuals with advanced degrees were less willing to provide routine services. And, as far as diagnostics go, that's the reason we have physicians. Every patient will be given routine physical exams and we will spot anything that is problematic."

"So you're telling me that between you, Dr. Momora, Dr. Francis, and Dr. Towns, you can cover all one-hundred-and-twenty cryogenic patients and over sixty crew members who will all require services. Are you really saying an extra pair of trained eyes wouldn't be of value?"

"Mr. LeMoore, it sounds to me like you have some personal reason you don't want anyone but Ms. Wong," Vidula pointedly noted as her cat eyes darted around the room looking for support.

"Actually, I'm glad you asked. I'd like to ask you the same question. Why are you so invested in Ms. Strong and French being on the crew? Are you planning something that you'll need specific people for?"

Frank also chimed in, "Vidula, to an observer you have to admit things do look a bit fishy."

Vidula momentarily looked like cold water at been thrown in her face. She quickly recovered, and choosing her words carefully, said, "Ervin and I personally know both Ms. Strong and Ms. French. They are friends, like Dr. Momora and Ms. Wong are friends. These two would have support from each. In addition, they've successfully provided the same kind of care to homebound patients as will be required on the cryogenic wards."

"I've found the more educated one is, the more worth they'll be to the mission," Justin noted.

"Yes, and I second that," Millie responded. "I'm still at a loss about wanting to choose a less-skilled provider over someone with both credentials and experience. Something is rotten here."

Vidula looked back and forth between Justin and Millie. Then smiling sweetly, she said, "It may appear something is going on to you, but it's not true. All Ervin and I care about is doing whatever is best for the mission."

Mr. Harris interrupted, "People! Let's stop the bickering. That won't get us anywhere. I want to take a vote to determine if the group is comfortable with filling the vacant prisoner physical therapy and nurse assistant positions with individuals from the cryogenic list. All those in favor, please raise your hands."

Everyone except Justin, Millie and Frank voted in the affirmative. The motion carried.

Millie jumped up in her black leather mini-dress, high-heeled shoes, low-cut blouse and screamed, "This is bullshit."

Then leaning over the table and looking directly at Vidula, she shouted, "Lady, you've got testicles bigger than a buffalo, but I don't trust you as far as I can spit." She then stomped out, saying, "I need some fresh air. I'm going to the ladies' room."

Everyone laughed except Vidula.

On one hand, Justin was also seething inside. He felt his colleagues had let him down. On the other hand, it may have been better for Ms. Wong to remain in the cryogenic group. What really bothered him was that the group had been swayed yet again by the Kozenskies.

Capitalizing on her win, Vidula continued, "I'd also like to again propose that Kyle Williams from the communication section be eliminated. I know he's a contractor and not a prisoner. I've heard from reliable sources that he is meddling with the programs. And what's worse is that he's trying to change them. A recommendation from this group to the contractor would go a long way in having him removed."

Laura from Nutrition, whom Justin thought was asleep, piped up, and asked, "Vidula, who's your contact?"

Vidula looked at her, and with a patronizing smile, said, "I don't want to get into who said what. Just know my source is reliable."

"But if we don't know who your source is, how can we determine if he or she is credible?"

"Trust me, the individual is one-hundred percent reliable," Vidula responded. "I don't spread rumors."

Millie returned and curled up in her chair with her legs under her. It was obvious she was in a first-class pout.

Justin still had his dander up, so he joined in. "Vidula, you mean to tell us based on your word we're supposed to eliminate an individual whom we've already discussed and can't do anything about?"

"Perhaps we should all go home and leave everything to Vidula and Ervin. They seem to be the only ones to make decisions around here," Millie said with a smirk.

"Millie, we know how much you like to flaunt your underwear, but in this case, you're making a total bare ass of yourself," Vidula angrily spit out.

"Yes, and you can kiss my bare ass!" Millie responded.

Mr. Harris again broke the encounter off. "Ladies stop! This is getting us nowhere. We've already discussed Mr. Williams's status. Neither I nor anyone here has the authority to dismiss him, even if there was cause—which by the way, there isn't. In addition, I have received an official notice by the contractor that he has asked to go on the mission as a crew member."

Vidula gave Justin and Millie a fiery look, and in a voice as hot as boiling lava, said, "Mr. Harris, we will all regret this decision. Mr. Williams will be nothing but trouble."

"I appreciate your observation and opinion, but I'm responsible for the paid crew and I think Mr. Williams will be a positive addition," Mr. Harris replied.

Vidula didn't say anything more, but it was obvious she was

furious. Her mouth twitched and kept tapping the table with her fingernails as she looked off into space.

After the group closed deliberations for the day, Millie and Frank took Justin aside.

"We both want to know what you think should be done about Vidula," Millie said.

"I'm going to see Mr. Harris and share my opinion. That's all I can do. He's responsible for the final decision. But I don't think there is much he can do either. I think you should come with me and let him know what your opinions are."

The three of them waited until everyone else had gone; then they went to Mr. Harris's office. They knocked on the door and Mr. Harris said, "Come in."

When Justin, Frank and Millie entered, he reached over to his entertainment center and turned the music down. "I had a feeling the three of you may want to talk."

"Sir," Justin said. "We can't put our finger on anything specific, but something's not right with the Kozenskies. Do you realize all four of the proposed nursing or physical therapy assistants on the crew now come from the prison where the Kozenskies were incarcerated? And although neither Ms. Strong nor Ms. French appear to be a part of their goon squad, they only seem to want certain people."

"And what's the deal with Dr. Tong?" Millie asked. "She seems to be one of them. No matter what the Kozenskies want, Dr. Tong is right there to support them—even if she has to change her mind to do so."

Mr. Harris leaned back in his chair looking tired. He took his glasses off and rubbed the bridge of his nose. Then reaching over and turning his music back up, he asked, "Do any of you recognize this music?"

Frank and Millie just shrugged their shoulders.

"I'm not sure, but I believe it is Wagner's 'Ride of the Valkyries,'" Justin said.

"Very good Justin," Mr. Harris commented.

Wrinkling her nose, Millie looked at Justin, and said, "Nerd."

Mr. Harris just smiled. "We've discussed this before. I had hoped something would surface that I could take action on, but we don't have any more proof now than when we last discussed the issue. If the Kozenskies are planning something, they have hidden their tracks extremely well. But then I ask myself, once under way, what can they possibly do? There's only one habitable planet that we're aware of within reach of our current technology. It's not like they can hijack the train and go somewhere else. I can't see anything they can do."

"They could kill the crew and take over the train. Then they could start their own colony in space," Justin offered. "With the supplies on board, they could live quite a while. And in the meantime they could try to find another habitable planet."

"That's possible," Mr. Harris agreed. "But the risks are extremely high. If they killed the crew, they couldn't maintain the train by themselves and they know it."

"I'm not so sure they do know it," Justin replied. "They seem to think they can single-handedly operate and maintain the train without any other assistance."

"Neither you nor I trust the Kozenskies. We all agree on that. But we still don't have any proof. Until something surfaces that I can take action on, there is nothing I can do. We have to continue on the same course unless you want to withdraw from the mission," Mr. Harris said.

"I've seriously considered it," Justin replied, knowing he

wouldn't. He craved proof or confirmation that something was going on. But beyond that was the issue of conscience. How could he leave knowing his friends would be in danger? No, he wouldn't leave. But he also knew the outcome was more than uncertain.

"If Justin leaves, I'll leave too. I'm so sick of Vidula, I could puke," Millie said.

"You need to make your own decision. I don't want to be your decision maker, or your spokesperson," Justin said.

"Like it or not you've become the group voice for many of us. If you go, there will be several others of us who will follow," Millie noted.

"Justin is not going anywhere," Mr. Harris said with finality. Looking at Millie and then back to Justin, he stated, "I want you to continue pushing Vidula. Hopefully if they are planning something, they'll make a mistake and then I can do something about it."

Justin, Millie and Frank chitchatted with Mr. Harris for a few minutes longer and then left.

"Are you really considering leaving?" Millie asked after they had departed Mr. Harris's office.

"Depends on the minute," Justin replied. "If you'd asked me today after our altercation with Vidula, I'd have said yes. I've cooled down now. I really want to see the mission through."

"Vidula, you've got to be careful. We can't afford any slipups that could lead to an investigation as to why the original nurse and physical therapy assistant decided to withdraw," Ervin said.

"Oh, quit worrying. It's amazing what a little money and some political pressure can do. There's no way to trace anything back to us," Vidula responded.

Vidula then called Mr. Slusser and demanded an immediate meeting with him. He was angry but finally agreed to a short meeting and drove to the marine base. When he arrived, he was obviously upset, and said, "Vidula, I can't just pop down here every time you want to tell me something. You're going to be leaving for Houston in the next few days and I for sure can't go there every time you want to meet."

"Milton, we have to communicate. When I call you, it's important. Let me tell you what happened today. We were able to get a nurse and a physical therapy assistant moved from the cryogenic group to the crew. They'll fill the two positions that suddenly came vacant. But we couldn't make any headway with eliminating Kyle Williams, and that has to be accomplished. We were also informed he intends to join the mission. If that happens, he'll make every effort to dissect our software. Although we are confident he can't break through our encryptions, he could inadvertently cause problems. He must be eliminated one way or another."

"Listen," Milton said in an angry whisper. "First of all, I need to know if you had any part of the original nurse assistant or the physical therapy assistant deciding to drop out."

"Why no," Vidula said, lying but appearing as innocent as a lamb. "We were as surprised as you were."

"Okay, I believe you. However, there's nothing I can do about Kyle, and if you're talking about something more, I don't want to know about it. The last thing Congressman Richards needs is to be implicated in a scandal about eliminating a member of the mission."

"So what are you saying?" Vidula asked as she leaned close to Mr. Slusser. "Are you saying if you don't know, it's okay?"

"What I'm saying is this: I think you should leave him alone!" Mr. Slusser responded as he leaned back in his chair. "And another thing. I can't run over here whenever you want to meet, but I do agree we need to communicate."

Digging into one of his jacket pockets, he brought out a small plastic box. "This," he said, holding the device out for Vidula and Ervin to look at, "is the latest encryption communication device on the market. It's an upgrade to the one you currently have. I want to take your old one back, and from now on you need to use this one when we talk. Unlike your old one, all you have to do is plug your regular communicator into it. Just push this little green button." Holding it out, he showed them where it was.

"It will only ring on my encryption device. If I can't immediately take a call, I'll text you when I can be reached. You'll see the message on your communicator screen. Everything you say will be encrypted and we can speak freely."

"How do we know everything is encrypted?" Vidula asked.

"My, we are suspicious, aren't we?" Mr. Slusser responded.

"You forget, Milton dear, we've been around for a long time and have learned not to trust anything we can't verify."

"The only way to verify the encryption device works is to use it. The alternative is not use it and not communicate."

"Doesn't look like we have a choice," Vidula suspiciously said.

"Right. But remember, anything that could impact you could also impact me and the congressman. That should give you some sense of security."

"Very little," Vidula noted.

"We'll try it," Ervin broke in. "We understand you're as concerned about security as we are."

During the next week most prisoners were tentatively matched with someone from the opposite sex. In one of their discussions with Mr. Harris, Millie asked, "Why are we forcing people to marry? If you put a bunch of men and women together and leave them alone, they'll know what to do. Hell, you'd have a passel of kids in no time. Let them work their relationships out for themselves."

"The public would never go along with it," Mr. Harris responded. "Although it is 2121, the Bible Belt in the South is even more rigid today than a hundred years ago. People would never go along with a free-sex commune, especially if it is being paid for with tax dollars. The public wants couples going to the New World, and they want them to be married, nice, neat and clean. Besides, thus far relationships with the first group have been very successful."

"The other way sure sounds like a lot more fun to me," Millie concluded.

"Well, you can forget it. That will never happen," Mr. Harris said. "The proposed marital list will not be finalized until the contractor has an opportunity to interview each individual. But it's a start. It's easy to pair up most of the prisoners based on information from the inmate surveys. Some have the same interests, backgrounds and goals for the future. Of course there are always a few who will challenge us. But like with the first group, I'm satisfied most couples will be compatible."

Justin was curious and looked at the list. Cindy was paired with Dr. Herman Hockstrasser, which seemed to be a workable choice as both seemed to be married to their work.

Dr. Momora was coupled with what seemed to be a nice person. Her proposed mate's name was Victor Benchley, a black schoolteacher. Victor had been married but was incarcerated for involuntary manslaughter after drinking too much at a New Year's Eve party. He had an accident on his way home which killed a mother and her infant daughter. Victor pleaded guilty and was sentenced to fifteen years in prison. Almost immediately after his incarceration his wife filed for divorce. He had spent his time in prison helping other inmates get their high school diplomas.

"Do you know the Kozenskies aren't listed on either the cryogenic or the crew lists?" Justin said one evening when he, Millie, and Frank were talking after dinner.

"Naw," Frank responded. "I'm sure they're on the crew list."

"Not unless I've repeatedly missed their names," Justin countered. "I've looked at both lists, and they're not on either of them."

"They have to be on the crew list," Frank said. "I've got a list in my room. I'll go get it."

"I hadn't thought about it, but you're right. They ought to be in the cryogenic group. At least we'd be free of their crap during the two-year trip. You should bring it up to the group tomorrow," Millie commented, as they waited for Frank to return with his list.

"I'm tired of being the leader of this threesome. You bring the idea up and get your head chopped off for once."

"You're right," Frank said as he returned to the kitchen with both the crew and cryogenic lists in his hand.

"I told Justin he should propose that Ervin and Vidula be added to the cryogenic list. That would put that smart-ass Vidula in her place," Millie mused.

"I agree with that," Frank concluded.

"Sure, you big chickens. Why do I always have to do the dirty work?"

"Don't think of it as dirty work," Frank responded. "It's an honor that we trust you enough to do it. Of course we'll be right there behind you."

"That's what I'm worried about," Justin laughed. "You two will be behind all right. Far, far behind."

"Frank is right. You're not only a leader but also a brother to us followers," Millie retorted with a smile.

The discussion continued for over an hour. By the time they split up and went to their rooms, the decision had been made. The Kozenskies should be in the cryogenic group.

The next morning, the three conspirators traded views one last time.

Mr. Harris began the meeting, and said to the group, "I want to tell you how proud I am of everyone. If we can conclude the business today, everyone should be ready to leave for Houston by Saturday. Tomorrow all we'll have to do is clean out our office areas. Before we begin though, I need to ask if anyone has any last-minute issues that have not been resolved."

Justin said, "I have an issue. I've noticed the Kozenskies are not on either the cryogenic list or the crew list."

Vidula whirled around in her chair looking like a rabid dog ready for an attack.

"I suggest," Justin quietly said, "that Vidula and Ervin be put in the cryogenic group."

"Have you totally lost your mind?" Vidula shouted.

Locking eyes with her, Justin continued, "Ma'am, the crew has experts in every area of the train. What value would you add?"

Vidula lost her usual forced composure. Her face flushed and the rabid dog was on the attack. In a shrill voice, she screamed, "Have you been asleep during the past months! Ervin and I are the brains of the train! Without us there wouldn't be a train."

"I concur. You've been extremely valuable in the development of the train," Justin conceded as mildly as he could muster. "But by the time the mission starts, you'll have accomplished everything that needs to be done. It will be up to the various engineer and maintenance sections, both on the train and here on Earth, to work out the bugs and keep the train running."

"Since we designed much of the equipment, don't you think Ervin and I would be the most logical people to work out the bugs?" Vidula spit across the table.

Mr. Harris sat impassive, tapping his pen on the table while looking into space. "Sometimes too many cooks spoil the broth," Frank noted. "I'm also comfortable that the necessary experts will be on the mission. Besides, there's an army of engineers and others here on Earth who will be available to assist if needed."

"I might have guessed you three troublemakers would be the ones to bring up such an idiotic idea." Then looking at Millie, Vidula said, "Don't you have anything more to add to the group, Ms. Fancy Panties?"

"Nothing other than to say I support the idea. I feel you'd be more trouble on the mission than you're worth. Oh, and by the way, they're pink today."

Everyone else gasped, too stunned to speak.

Then Charlie Davis piped up, "We have seen some problematic behavior in the group from the Kozenskies. Well, from Vidula, that is. We haven't seen Dr. Ervin Kozenskie much. As far as Vidula goes, I think it would be positive if she were in the cryogenic group."

"Has everyone gone totally loco?" Vidula asked as she stood. "This is insane. It's always been clearly understood that Ervin and I would be a part of the crew. If something goes wrong and we're asleep, who will bail you out? No one, and I mean no one is as qualified as Ervin and I in resolving problems that could arise on the train."

"I think you're being a bit conceited," Mr. Harris quietly said. "You've been valuable in assisting with the other engineers. But here's another way of looking at the issue. It takes over five tons of food and supplies for each crew member to complete the voyage. It only takes one-and-a-half tons of food and supplies for each cryogenic person. If you and Ervin are in the cryogenic group, we could re-designate seven tons of supplies, which could be used at the New World community."

Still standing, Vidula focused on Mr. Harris. If looks could kill, he'd have withered like a prune. "This is unbelievable. A Mormon who can't find a wife, a prostitute, a fallen priest and then we have Mr. Harris who appears to be afraid of this ragtag threesome. Sir, I can't believe you'd even consider putting Ervin and me to sleep when the difference between success and failure may hang on us."

Laura Yates and big tough Blaine Pustual both looked like they'd been riveted to their chairs and their mouths glued shut. Dr. Lister voiced her opinion, and Dr. Davis said, "I support the others. I see no reason why the Kozenskies couldn't be in the cryogenic group. Sometimes others will see things the designers missed because they only see the project from their perspective."

Trying another tactic, Vidula said, "Friends, I can't believe what I'm hearing. Ervin and I love you. What would happen if there was a crisis while we were in hibernation? It would be devastating. Please, this is not the right thing to do. Think of the consequences. We've been the driving force of the train since its aborning."

"Vidula," Mr. Harris authoritatively said, as he also stood. "I think we should excuse ourselves. I'd like to discuss this privately in my office."

By this time Vidula was sobbing like a schoolgirl who'd lost her first boyfriend. "I knew you'd support them even though they're making a huge mistake. But sir, such an aberrance would be unthinkable for Ervin and myself. Ervin and I have poured our lifeblood into this project. To think we would be in hibernation during the journey is unacceptable. If there's a problem, we want to be there to solve it. You can't possibly ask us to abdicate our hopes and dreams of being a part of the mission."

"Vidula, we need to take a time out and let your emotionalism cool. We'll come back and discuss it again a little later. Please excuse us," Mr. Harris said as he took Vidula by the arm and led her to his office.

"Justin, you sure have a knack for starting trouble," Colonel Forrester angrily remarked. "And for your information, I agree with Vidula. You're going against what you were fighting about regarding education and experience. Vidula and Ervin are the most intelligent people on this project. They know the train inside and out. Why then would you not want them to be part of the crew in case there's a problem?"

"Because they're troublemakers," Justin said. "Look at the way they've tried to bully the group. Besides, I still think they have something going on behind our backs."

"And you haven't caused problems? I think you've also tried to bully the group and sway our thinking. You started the very first night we were together by calling your buddy at Beaumont looking for dirt on the Kozenskies. For some reason, you've had it in for Vidula and Ervin from the very beginning. And I don't want to hear about your gut, or the hairs on the back of your neck standing up either," Colonel Forrester said as he got up to leave. As he stomped toward the door, he turned around and pointing his finger at Justin. "I think you and Vidula are too much alike. You both have to have your way."

About fifteen minutes later, Mr. Harris returned without Vidula. Looking at everyone, he said, "I think we're all too emotionally charged to deal with this issue rationally. Let's take a break. It will do us all good to get away and let our emotions cool." Looking at his watch, he said, "It is now 1030. Let's take a long lunch and be back in our seats at 1300."

"Ervin, you're as nutty as they are!" Vidula shouted.

"Listen, Vidula," Ervin pleaded. "It may not actually be such a bad thing for us to go into the cryogenic group."

"You're crazy."

"Listen my love," Ervin pleaded. "We both know that many on the crew distrust us and are looking for anything to discredit us. If we are not there, that distrust will dissipate. Right?"

"If we're not awake, who will put the plan into action?"

"That's the beauty of it. We can encrypt the programs in the guidance pods. They will activate the awakening program."

"Yes, but what about Kyle?" Vidula asked. "You can bet he'll be trying to hack into our programs? And if we're asleep, who's to say someone may not just pull the plug on us and we'll never wake up? I don't trust LeMoore and several others not to try to kill us while we're sleeping."

"That again is the beauty of it. We're twice as smart as Kyle is. We can encrypt the program so neither Kyle nor anyone else will ever detect what is in them. In fact, it's kind of a game to outsmart him. Look at everything we've done. Not one person from the crew has been able to break into our programs. And as far as killing us while we're in hibernation, neither Justin nor anyone else would dare do such a thing. Everyone would blame him. Besides, the command crew are solidly supportive of us. They wouldn't let anything happen."

Smiling her most evil, self-satisfied smile, Vidula said, "Maybe LeMoore and Kyle should have a hapless event before we leave and be done with them both."

"No! We can't afford a slipup, which could be the kiss of death for us. We can do it without compromising our plans. Besides, we're infinitely more intelligent than anyone else on the mission."

"It's just crazy enough that it might work." *And when we put our plan into action, I'll take care of Kyle and Justin, one way or another. They'll both get their comeuppance,* she said in her head.

"Trust me, my love. It will work. We can have a nice long sleep; the computer will activate and—bingo—we're on our way. I suggest we go back into the meeting and tell the group we've reconsidered. We'll tell them we're both in agreement. It'll completely disarm them."

"I can see your point. I don't like it, but if you feel that strongly, I'll go along. I'll go to the meeting this afternoon and tell them we're willing to concede. We'll be part of cryogenic group. I dislike not being on top of things during the mission, but if we can negotiate being the last to be put to sleep, we could make any needed last-minute adjustments."

"Vidula, how about if I also go to the meeting and let me tell them about our willingness. That would stop them in their tracks. I also think you should come up with a good apology which will win everyone over."

"It won't win Justin and his two sidekicks over. Someday Justin will get his reward. There will come a time when I'll make his life a living hell."

The group trickled in after lunch and braced for more fireworks. Then to their surprise, both Kozenskies arrived. Vidula took her seat with Ervin standing next to her.

When the group quieted down, Ervin looked at Mr. Harris, and asked, "Sir, I wonder if I could address the group?"

"I suppose so. May I ask what you want to address?" Mr. Harris was leery after the interchange with Vidula before lunch.

"I'd like to discuss our being part of the cryogenic group," Ervin flatly said.

Mr. Harris still wasn't sure of the Kozenskies' motives. Looking at both Ervin and Vidula, he stated, "The group has already explored that issue. Your wife made it clear what her position is."

"That's true, and I understand there was a heated interchange on the subject. We discussed it over lunch and we think we've arrived at a solution."

"Oh," Mr. Harris suspiciously responded.

"First of all, I'd like to apologize for the frustration and Vidula's abash before lunch. We've poured our whole lives and souls into the mission, and when something impacts our ability to continue our contribution, it's naturally upsetting. As I said, Vidula and I have discussed being part of the cryogenic group and we think we have come up with a compromise."

All eyes were on Ervin. No one even seemed to be breathing as Vidula looked at each person in the group.

"Vidula and I always want to be team players. As a result, we've decided to allow ourselves to be placed in the cryogenic group. The only thing we ask is that we be allowed to be the last to go into hibernation. That way, if there are last-minute issues to be resolved, we will be there to assist."

Everyone looked at Vidula and Ervin in disbelief. Ervin returned the look waiting for a response while Vidula smiled and nodded her agreement.

Then Vidula added, "I want to apologize for my behavior before lunch. Know we love you all and trust your judgment. It's just that the mission has become the most important thing in our lives. We've tried to play a small part in designing and building the most advanced, safe, dependable and comfortable space vessel ever constructed. But, like any machine, things will go wrong. The vast electronic system may have problems, especially in the beginning and we feel we have the expertise to resolve those issues. We're aware that some feel we've pushed too hard and may have overbuilt certain pieces of equipment. If that's true, it was done in your best interest.

"We've built multiple backups for every function on the train. We recognize there are some who want to minimize costs, sometimes at the expense of safety. And yes, there have been cost overruns. But everything we've done has been to increase our margin of safety. Thankfully Congressman Richards and Mr. Slusser have agreed and managed to increase the budget to accommodate the upgrades we've recommended. We also have to remember that most of the cars we've built will land on the New World and will be utilized for decades to come. So, it's been important to build a lasting product."

Then pausing, she continued, "My heart overflows with love for you all. It is a deep concerned love for each one of you. You're our family. You can trust that your safety and well-being has been our only objective over the past years. Again, I hope you'll forgive my outburst before lunch." And with that, she sat down.

Everyone was stunned. Mr. Harris looked at Vidula and Ervin, and in a surprised voice said, "Thank you, both, for your clarification and willingness to participate in the cryogenic group. We all recognize your devotion and concern for the mission."

Dr. Ervin Kozenskie looked contritely at the group, and said, "I want to thank everyone for letting me attend your meeting and allowing me to speak. I hope Vidula and I have put your minds at ease. Please know we want to be team players and will abide by the team decision."

I'm going to barf right here on the table. They've got some kind of nefarious plan that no one else knows about, Justin thought.

"I didn't and still don't like you going into the cryogenic group," Colonel Forrester said, looking from person to person in the group. "I don't think any of you know how valuable these two, fine people have been to this mission. If we had a need for an analysis or rebuilding a component, they were there. And I personally take exception to Justin ever bringing up the issue. As you heard, they have nothing but our interest at heart."

Dr. Tong chimed in, saying, "I also support the Kozenskies remaining as part of the crew. They've been extremely helpful in enhancing the cryogenic wards. Personally, I'd like to have them available to us in case of a problem or emergency."

Justin said, "I concur with Colonel Forrester and Dr. Tong. The Kozenskies have been extremely helpful and will continue to be valuable as the mission progresses. But once the train is fully operational, there'll be engineers and experts both on board and here on Earth who can resolve any problem that may arise. If something happens that requires their expertise, they can be brought out of cryogenic hibernation."

"By the time they're fully awake, it may well be too late," Colonel Forrester complained. "When something goes wrong, we'll need an instant analysis and plan. It'll take several days for them to be fully competent. We could all be dead by then."

"According to the briefing we received from Dr. Holly and Dr. Cho, the train is the safest vehicle that's ever gone into space," Justin countered. "If that's true, there's no reason the Kozenskies can't join the cryogenic group."

"They were right. The train is the safest, most advanced and reliable bird that's ever gone into space. That doesn't mean there won't be bugs that will develop along the way though. As far as I'm concerned, the decision's been made. Ervin and I will be joining the cryogenic group," Vidula said with more than a hint of sarcasm in her voice.

"Vidula, I salute you. I think you've made the right decision," Millie noted.

Smiling, Vidula responded, "Thank you for your support, but

we don't need your confirmation. Go show your panties to someone who cares."

"I told you before what you can kiss," Millie shouted, her voice echoing off the cement walls.

"Ladies, ladies," Mr. Harris broke in again as he tapped his fountain pen on the table. "The Kozenskies have made a decision and we will let it stand."

"Sir," Colonel. Forrester said as he put both his hands on the table, pushing himself up. "You seem to be rushing this decision and I for one don't like it."

"And I appreciate your opinion, Colonel Forrester," Mr. Harris noted. "Few decisions are cast in concrete, but for now I'm comfortable neither the safety of the crew nor the mission accomplishment will be negatively impacted by the Kozenskies' decision. I think our job here is complete. I want to thank you all for your hard work and dedication. Some of you will be able to take a few days off, but unfortunately, most will need to go directly to Houston. You medical and mental health folks will need to be in Houston not later than the twelfth of January.

"Before we depart, we need to shred any documents with names or other identifying details on them. We will start in this room and then you can go to your individual offices. Bring any documents or papers you may have collected back here."

Justin was carrying bags of shredded paper to the dumpster when he met Colonel Forrester in the hall. "You and your little clique are fuzzy thinkers," he said. "Sometimes I wonder if you have even a flicker of electrical current passing through your brain. You spout off about having the most qualified people available on the crew and then put the two people who've contributed the most to sleep? Are you crazy or just stupid?"

"Sir, I know we see things differently. You see the Kozenskies as benevolent angels sent to be our salvation, and I appreciate that. My job requires me to work with people who'll say anything they think you want to hear. Unfortunately, they usually have a hidden agenda. Normally that agenda involves things that are of no benefit to anyone but themselves."

"Show me one whit of evidence and I'll consider changing my mind," Colonel Forrester flatly stated.

"Sir, I fear when the evidence is revealed, it will be too late."

"Just what do you base your distrust of the Kozenskies on? I hope it isn't just intuition, your gut or the hairs on the back of your neck."

"Some intuition," Justin replied, trying to remain calmer than he felt inside. "Mostly though, it's based on personality types. I see two extremely intelligent people with big egos who crave power. Complete power. I've learned to anticipate the worst from people who crave power at any cost. Look at their history, then look at their current behaviors and tell me what you see."

"What I see"—pointing his finger at Justin— "are two people who've assisted us in making the most advanced space vehicle ever built. I've seen no indication of them taking power. Rather, I've seen you and your buddies snipe at them from the first day you arrived. I'm confident they'd never do anything to harm any of us." With that, he stomped down the hall and slammed his office door.

About 1600, Mr. Harris walked down to Justin's office, and said, "You seem to be a hero to some and a skunk to others."

Thinking Mr. Harris had somehow heard about the hallway interchange, he said, "Colonel Forrester isn't very happy with me right now."

"It will blow over. Everyone has come to rely on the Kozenskies' way too much. But now that they've volunteered to be in the cryogenic group, I aim to hold them to it."

"I thought you were talking about Colonel Forrester and my interchange in the hall an hour or so ago," Justin said.

"I don't know anything about that," Mr. Harris replied, so Justin filled him in.

"Well, don't worry about it. Colonel Forrester is leaving for Houston tomorrow, and we'll start moving the prisoners to the compound in about ten days. I'd like you and Frank to arrive by Tuesday or Wednesday of next week. As I told the group, you two and the medical crew will be housed on the complex to help settle everyone. As soon as the marriage contractor has had a chance to visit with everyone and solidify their roster, I want to announce it. I'd like the couples to have as much time together as possible before we depart. Oh, and when we announce the roster, I want you to be the one to do it."

"Me? Why me?" Justin asked. "That's something the marriage contractor should do."

"Absolutely not. They'd make it sound like an entertainment show. 'Come on down and meet your new husband or wife.' You and Frank have worked with them, and they trust you. It only makes sense that you should be the one to announce who they will be mated with. After the list has been presented, the contractor will spend a week going through bonding exercises with the couples.

"In the following weeks, the Houston astronaut training crew will spend time teaching the prisoners about space suits and do underwater training. The engineers will come over and give classes on the train, much like they did for you all. The medical team will spend a few days with them discussing the cryogenic process and answering any questions they might have. They'll also discuss the role of the nursing, physical training, nutrition, dental, vision and other support sections. Although everyone has had a thorough medical screening, they'll have to undergo one more comprehensive evaluation.

"Along with the evaluation, each prisoner will receive an injected tracking device. Anyone who attempts to escape will find their freedom to be short-lived. Then he or she will be removed from the mission and returned to their former residence. Since many of the classes and trainings will be held in non-secure areas, both prisoners and guards will be allowed to wear civilian clothes.

"Each prisoner, both male and female, will also receive monthly birth control injections. I know that might seem contradictory since they had to be fertile to be accepted for the mission. Couples may marry and begin cohabitation in Houston if they wish to, but the last thing we want is to have a pregnancy before the mission even begins. Prisoners will have their choice of when they marry. Some will do so right away while others will opt to wait awhile. Some may even wait until they arrive at the New World. That won't stop them from being intimate though. I hope either Colonel Straight or Frank will take care of the marriages for those who wait until they arrive at the New World."

"I'm sure Frank would be happy to perform marriages either here or on the New World," Justin responded.

"I was surprised how many of the first group decided to wait until they arrived at the New World to marry. As I recall, about thirty percent of the group opted to wait. I also want to share something that needs to remain with us," Mr. Harris continued.

"It's been confirmed there will be a construction delay of at least a month, maybe longer. I'll have to look to you and the other crew members to take over as teachers in mental health, recreation or whatever else we can think of to occupy time. I think it may even be possible to take some of the prisoners on local recreation outings like restaurants, a theme park or other places of interest. Of course, such civilian-outings will have to be carefully planned and chaperoned."

Looking at his watch, he said, "We had better get back so we can have the final group meeting."

When they arrived, the group had already assembled.

Mr. Harris stood, and addressing everyone, said, "I think we've accomplished everything that needs to be done. Make sure you have vacated your offices and turn in your prison badges. Tomorrow don't forget to check out of the guest house and clear security before you leave. When you get to Houston, check in with the space center at this number." He said, as he wrote the number on the whiteboard.

"They will direct you to your lodging or to the conference facility. Just for your information, the conference facility has rooms for more than three hundred people. It also has a large auditorium, numerous break-out rooms for small group training, plus a swimming pool for the space-suit training.

"There are a few two-bedroom suites for those of us who will be housed there. The engineering group and those involved in overseeing the construction of the train will be housed at a separate facility."

Looking over the group one last time, he continued, "Drive safely, enjoy your trip but get to Houston as quickly as you can. When you arrive, let me know. There is still a lot of work to accomplish."

12

"Look, Milton Slusser, we've got to have consistent communication. I don't trust Harris, the crew or even the other inmates at this point. We also need to have one more face-to-face meeting before we leave for Houston," Vidula barked.

"Vidula, I have some important engagements to deal with. I for sure can't run out there tonight. I'll make sure I get down to Houston within the month to see you. In the meantime, we can continue chatting over the secure communication devices. We've all had to make concessions, but that's the way these games work. We still have a deal, don't we?"

"Yes, Milton, we still have a deal. But it seems like we're the only ones doing the conceding."

"Vidula, you have no idea how hard Congressman Richards and I work to take care of you and keep things running smooth."

"Yeah, yeah," Vidula said as she punched the device off. Then she said to herself, *It may not continue to run smooth for neither you nor the congressman.*

Justin enjoyed the drive to Houston. He'd never been from Virginia to Texas, so he was seeing new country. He arrived in Houston, checked in with the Houston Space Center and was directed to the training center complex.

When he checked in the lady at the desk found his name, and said, "Oh, both you and the minister have been assigned suites. You'll be right next to the swimming pool and hot tub. We hope you have a lovely time while you're here."

"Actually he's a priest. Has he checked in yet?" Justin inquired.

"Yes, he checked in earlier this morning. He drives a flashy red sports car. Are you aware of that?"

"Yes, I am. That's how he got here so fast. I wonder how many speeding tickets he got along the way."

"Oh, he's a priest. I wouldn't think a priest would drive fast enough to get a ticket," the receptionist said.

Justin just smiled. The facility was completely walled in and must have been beautiful at one time. From its outside, it appeared not to have done well in the last few years. The buildings were shabby and needed paint. The grounds definitely needed some tender loving care. Planters and flowerbeds were overgrown with weeds and half dead shrubs. It looked like the government had taken the lowest bidder.

The first prisoners would arrive in two days with the rest following a few days later. Justin went over to Frank's suite and knocked on the door.

"Wow," Frank said. "Can you believe this place? It's a bit run-down on the outside, but the suites are beautiful."

"They do look nice. How'd you get here ahead of me?" Justin asked.

"Just put the hammer down and let the little bug have her head."

"How many speeding tickets did you get?"

"Justin my son, we've already had that conversation. What happens with me and my car is between myself and the man upstairs. Actually if you want to know, I didn't get any tickets. I just cruised along about five miles above the speed limit. They don't usually bother you if you're only a few miles over. Want to go out for dinner tonight?"

"Sure," Justin replied.

They spent the following day settling in and having discussions with Mr. Harris. The first flight of prisoners was scheduled to arrive early the next morning.

At 0430, both Frank and Justin's communication devices jarred them awake. "Be at the airport at 0600. We'll be receiving twenty-three prisoners," a voice on the other end said.

The prisoners arrived in civilian clothes and were transported to the compound in unmarked buses. The first transfer went smoothly and over the next two days the rest would follow.

For many it was the first time in many years they'd been allowed to dress in street clothes and be treated like regular civilians. For most it was exciting. There were a few, though, who felt overwhelmed. Especially those who had been incarcerated for many years. Some were experiencing institutional withdrawal. They actually felt uncomfortable without the security of the prison walls.

Frank agreed to work with Cynthia Wong, and one evening he noted, "Ms. Wong seems to be doing well. She's excited to be living in an almost-a-normal situation. But, like everyone else, she's anxious and preoccupied with whom she will be paired up with."

"Oh," Justin responded, although just the mention of her name made him dewy-eyed. "I'm glad to hear that. But why did you single her out?"

"Just thought you'd like to know," Frank responded.

The inmates were allowed to use the complex swimming pool, a small snack shop and there was a small credit union office. Many had accumulated funds while at their previous institutions. The funds were made available to them to use at the snack shop, or even on the outside for meals, etc.

One evening, a male prisoner decided to make a break for it before his tracking device was implanted. Even without it, he was apprehended within two blocks of the complex.

Meeting with Justin, Frank, Dr. Davis, and Dr. Lister, Mr. Harris said, "The contractor has solidified the final list so the marital roster can be announced in another week or so. Once it's announced, the group will be broken into four smaller work groups. I want each of you to participate in one of them. You will be there just to monitor, a contract person will be the small-group leader. They'll spend a week helping the couples learn about each other and doing bonding exercises."

On the second Saturday after their arrival, the entire group met at 0800 in the large meeting room for the marital assignments. Everyone was in a twitter as they were seated. They all seemed to be evaluating those of the opposite sex, and it was easy to see the questions on their faces. "I wonder if it could be him or her or . . ."

When everyone was assembled and accounted for, Mr. Harris welcomed the group. Looking over everyone, he said. "Ladies and gentlemen, I cannot tell you what a thrill it is to see you all assembled in one place. I see you as pioneers and trailblazers of the future. We've worked for over two years to find the best people in the system and I believe we have found you. As you know, Earth is overpopulated. Before long there may not be enough resources, especially water, to sustain everyone. You're mankind's best hope for the future.

"If we can transport you to the New World and establish a colony, then there is a hope for others. We have just a little over one month to prepare for the beginning of the cryogenic process, which should take place about the last week of March. Between now and then we are going to be busy which will make the time go by quickly. You will also undergo another medical, dental and psychological evaluation."

"For the twentieth time," someone shouted from the audience.

"Yes, for the twentieth time," Mr. Harris laughed. "And those won't be the last either. For the crew, they'll receive periodic medical checkups throughout the mission. In addition, they'll also receive ongoing mental health questionnaires, which will be administered by Mr. LeMoore and Chaplain Molony.

"For those of you in the cryogenic group, you'll be receiving regular comprehensive health and dental checkups. Luckily, you'll be spared the mental health evaluations until you are awake again.

"Remember, people, your mission is not only to get to the New World but also to provide valuable medical and psychological information which will be used in the future.

"Now, we need to have a discussion about security. Last night one of the men made an escape attempt. He figured he'd make a run for it before his tracking device was implanted." Then turning to one of the guards, he asked, "How far from the complex did he get?"

About two blocks," the guard responded. "We have cameras covering the entire complex and a mobile unit cruising around the training facility twenty-four hours a day. We had him under surveillance from the moment he tried to flee. He's now in the custody of the federal marshals awaiting return to his former facility."

"You are special people and we want to treat you like special people. We don't want to have guards on you every minute, but leaving the compound will not work. I can guarantee it," Mr. Harris said, trying to make eye contact with everyone.

"Once your tracking device is implanted, we will have you under surveillance twenty-four-seven. So don't do anything stupid. If we continue to have unauthorized departures, we'll have to have curfews, bed checks and again treat you like prisoners. As long as you behave, you'll have total freedom in the compound. If you abuse the privileges, we'll return you to the institution you left and your fellow inmates here will be locked down. Are there any questions, or do I make myself crystal clear?" Mr. Harris rhetorically asked as he scanned the audience.

There were several questions about how far they could go. Could they stay out past 2100? Could they buy beer? Could couples move in with each other?

"The quick answer to all the questions is yes, as long as you exercise self-control and follow the rules. I know you've had someone essentially telling you what to do every minute in the past. We don't want to treat you that way. Don't do anything foolish and we'll give you all the freedom possible. Are there any more questions?"

Scanning the group, Mr. Harris said, "It doesn't appear there are any further questions. Before I turn the time over to Mr. LeMoore, who will be announcing the mate selections, I hope you'll indulge me for a few more minutes."

He picked up a recorder, sat it on the podium and then again looked out over the group. "How many of you are familiar with the music of Antonin Dvorak?"

One man raised his hand.

"Sir, please stand up. How do you know of Mr. Dvorak's music?"

"Before my living accommodations were changed, I was a high

school music teacher. If I recall correctly, Antonin Dvorak was a Czech composer who briefly lived in America," the man replied.

"You are absolutely correct. Mr. Dvorak was born in 1841 and lived until 1904. He moved to the United States from Poland in 1892 and remained until 1895. While here he wrote to a friend, and said, in part, 'The American's expect great things from me. I am to show them a way into the realm of a new independent art.' Using many of the early folk songs of America as inspiration, he wrote his Symphony No. 9. I want to play you part of that symphony."

He turned the recorder on, and powerful, stirring music filled the room. Mr. Harris raised his arms, closed his eyes and led the music as if conducting an orchestra. When it finished, he opened his eyes and again looked over the group.

"Ladies and gentlemen, like Dvorak, the world expects great things of you. We expect you to show the rest of us the way into the realm of a new world, a new society. I, Colonel Straight and the rest of the crew are the conductors. You are the musicians who will make the music real."

He removed a handkerchief from his pocket, wiped his eyes and stood for almost a minute before continuing. "I hope you will forgive me. This is an emotional moment for me."

Putting his handkerchief back in his pocket, he continued, "Let me take care of a question I know will arise. Can we swap mates?"

"Yes," someone yelled from the rear. "Can we try four or five out before we make a selection?"

"The answer to that is no. We are not selling cars where you can try several models before making a choice. After an extensive trial period, if you feel you cannot adjust to the mate you have been assigned to, talk to either Justin or Frank. If they cannot reconcile the differences, then we will talk. Okay, Mr. LeMoore, I'm sure the group would like to find out what prince or princess has been selected for them."

Justin stood, walked to the podium, and said, "Thank you, Mr. Harris. Before I go through the list, I need everyone to move to the sides and back of the auditorium. We need to leave the center area open. When I call your names, please come to the front. The first couple will take the first center seats to my right, the next couple will take the next two seats and so on.

"As you are called, Chaplain Molony will give each of you a packet with your mate's name and their biographical information. Okay, is everyone ready?"

"Yes," several impatiently yelled. "Get on with it already."

"Okay," Justin said with a laugh. "Here we go." He began reading the names. For the most part, smiles were shared when the couples met. A few knew each other but most were meeting for the first time.

When Cynthia Wong and Herman Hockstrasser were called, Justin watched with interest but made sure not to make eye contact with Ms. Wong.

Dr. Momora was coupled with the teacher Victor Benchley. Victor was tall, but almost a foot shorter than Dr. Momora.

It took two hours to complete the couples list and break into the four smaller groups. Participants spent the next week playing games, taking walks together, discussing child rearing, religion, and several other subjects. Justin tried not to appear any more interested in Ms. Wong or Dr. Momora than anyone else. But of course, he was. It was with a mixture of satisfaction tinged with jealousy that Ms. Wong and Dr. Hockstrasser appeared to be bonding nicely.

The four groups began rotating through the medical,

engineering, space suit and the other training classes. Justin made sure Ms. Wong wasn't in any of his groups so he didn't see her very often.

During the second week, another male decided to make a break for freedom. With his tracking device implanted, his freedom was even shorter than the first attempt. The sad thing was the individual's wife-to-be, Ms. Elvira Strong, could also have been returned to her institution.

She pleaded for the opportunity to remain, saying, "Please let me stay. I'll marry anyone who is available." Since she was a physical therapy assistant and needed, she was paired with another male.

About three weeks after their arrival, several teams of workers showed up. Some began painting the buildings while an older Hispanic man and a boy about eighteen years old began working on the gardens and flower beds.

Justin liked to garden, so he easily made friends with Caesar Garza and his nephew Rolando. If he had a little extra time, he'd often go out and help the Garzas dig up old planters, repair the sprinkling system and plant new flowers and shrubs. Dr. Hockstrasser, Ms. Wong and several others also volunteered. Before long, Caesar became the foreman of his own work crew. Justin always made sure he was always in a different group than Ms. Wong.

There were four couples who opted to marry and begin living together. Most however, wanted more time to get to know each other. Except for two couples, everyone seemed to be doing well.

The first couple they were concerned about was Safire Strong. She was paired with a quiet man whom she constantly bullied. Although he was good-natured, both Justin and Frank kept a close eye on them. Justin could not put his finger on what bothered him about Ms. Strong, but she made the hair on the back of his neck stand up.

The other concern was Ms. Elvira Strong. After her intended mate had tried to escape, she'd been paired with another man. He was quiet and seemed to be easy to get along with. She was domineering with him and Justin had a bad feeling about her too.

The prisoner training progressed smoothly as far as Justin and Ms. Wong went until the fourth week. Justin's group was scheduled for underwater space-suit training in the afternoon. Ms. Wong had a dental appointment during the morning when her group went through the training, so she missed it.

When she checked back with the instructors to see when she could reschedule, he said, "I can take you right now. Hurry and put your bathing suit on. You can join this group."

She was given a space suit that was still damp and almost impossible to pull on. The instructor could see she was having trouble, so he handed Justin a dry one, and said, "Sir, please go over and help that person," pointing toward the back of the group.

Justin was shocked to see the person was Ms. Wong. She was struggling with the damp suit, unable to either get it on or off. There wasn't anything he could do but try to help her. When he approached, she looked up and was startled to see him. He was holding another suit and looking at her.

"Here, let me help you," Justin said as he knelt in front of her and began tugging the suit off.

"I think I can do it myself," Ms. Wong said as she continued to struggle.

"Probably so, but the instructor wants you to get this dry one on so everyone can get into the pool at the same time."

She'd managed to get the suit down below her hips but couldn't get it below her thighs.

Justin pulled at one of the feet with one hand and reached up with the other to pull the bulk down. As he pulled, his fingers touched her bare thigh. It was just a slight brush, but his heart was already beating fast. Now his legs felt like they were going to collapse.

This is crazy, he thought as the offending suit finally slipped off and he got up to leave.

"Thank you," she said as her heart pounded and her mouth went dry. "I . . . I . . . I can take it from here."

Justin said nothing, and as he left, he thought: *I'm acting like a seventh-grade schoolboy who got to touch a girl's leg for the first time. I'm a grown man and this is ridiculous.* But with her being so close, his attraction to her was overwhelming and he had to reel his feelings back in.

Holding the dry suit, Ms. Wong watched Justin retreat. On one hand she was amused to see his obvious discomfort, but was also in turmoil. *Why does he make me feel like this?* She quickly put the suit on, but could still feel where Justin's fingers had brushed her leg.

You see how you react to this man? You've got to stay away from him, Molly shouted, making her head hurt.

The medical, dental, and psychological exams were completed and for the most part the couples appeared to be doing well. By this time more than half of the couples decided to get married and begin living together. Cindy and Herman opted not to wed, or be intimate, until they arrived at the New World.

By late February, everyone was in high spirits. No one else had dropped out and many of the restrictions had been lifted. Groups of four to six prisoners were actually allowed to go to the movies or to the local malls to shop. Of course, at least two guards accompanied them.

Mr. Harris called a meeting with the medical and mental health teams and announced, "The train is at least two months behind schedule. The hull of the command and cryogenic cars are complete, but due to some changes to the guidance and computer systems, much of their interiors had to be removed and reconfigured.

"I'm afraid it'll be at least the end of May before we can begin the mission. The prisoners are through with their training, which means we'll need to come up with something to keep them occupied."

"Perhaps we could provide them with some cultural experiences in the area, like museums, the zoo or other places," Frank suggested.

Mr. Harris was a bit cautious. "We've gotten to know these people and it appears we can trust them. However, can you imagine what would happen if word got out that we have convicted prisoners, some of them murderers, out in the community sightseeing, going to the movies or the zoo?"

"We're doing it now," Justin responded. "Groups are going shopping almost every day after training and we haven't heard a peep."

"Yes, but we've been lucky. They've also been attending classes and working. If they have nothing to do, they'll get bored and want to go out and wander the community. That's a recipe for trouble. We need to come up with something constructive to keep them occupied."

"Several of the inmates have been volunteering to help the Garzas in the gardens," Justin commented.

"That's great," Mr. Harris replied, "but that only takes care of about a dozen or so of them."

"How about having a meeting with the prisoners and get their ideas?" Justin suggested.

All were in agreement, and Mr. Harris directed, "Justin, I want you to lead the group discussion."

"Mr. Harris." Milton Slusser's voice shimmered on the desk communicator. "I hope you're enjoying yourself in sunny Texas while the rest of us are still struggling with winter up here in the north."

"Other than the confounded delays, we're doing well," Mr. Harris dryly acknowledged. "How can I help you, Milton?"

Always to the point. Yes, always right to the damn point, Milton thought. "Congressman Richards is interested in your progress and wants me to come down and meet with the group. When are you going to have another inmate meeting?"

"Tomorrow morning," Mr. Harris replied.

"That's great. Simply out-of-this-world great," Mr. Slusser responded. "I'm going to have a few days of slack time between our busy congressional schedule, so I'd like to run down and see you. Is that okay?"

"The meeting is scheduled for 0900 tomorrow. If you want to come down, that will be fine with me," Mr. Harris dryly replied.

"Super. I'll catch a flight tonight and be there in the morning."

"Okay, see you in the morning," Mr. Harris replied and pushed the stop button on his device.

Someday, you old fart, you're going to be in for one hell of a rude awakening, Milton said to himself.

Mr. Slusser arrived just as everyone was sitting down. For once he was wearing an almost-ironed shirt but sweating like a marathon runner at the end of a race. He had a large white handkerchief and continually mopped his brow and jowls with it. Mr. Harris briefly introduced Milton to the prisoners, explaining he was Congressman Richard's assistant.

Mr. Slusser led off with the usual flattering political mumbo jumbo. "Congressman Richards is proud and sees you as pioneers. You are part of the greatest human adventure ever," he gushed as he again mopped his brow and jowls. Vidula and Ervin were sitting up front, but nary a smile did they show. Milton even singled them out for lavish praise about how important they'd been. By the time he finished his political discussion, everyone was either asleep or ready to lynch him.

Mr. Harris finally broke in and stopped the harangue. He thanked Mr. Slusser for his remarks, and said, "I have some bad news. I've been officially notified there will be a two-month delay in the completion of the train. We've completed your training, so we need to think about what we can do during the delay. Justin will facilitate the discussion."

"Before we start on the fun stuff," Justin said, "Chaplain Molony and I will begin meeting with each couple weekly to administer questionnaires and discuss how you're getting along. A schedule has been developed starting after lunch."

There was another collective moan. "I'm so sick of answering questionnaires I could barf. I don't think there's anything more you could find out about me. From now on I'm going to make up answers. That'll give you something to chew on," one person said, generating a laugh from everyone.

"I'm sorry, but we don't have a choice. So guys and gals, just hitch up your garters and go with the flow. We'll just have to do it. As Mr. Harris said, there's been a delay in the completion of the train. That means we'll have some slack time. We need to come up with some ideas for what you'd like to do for the next month or so. Chaplain Molony will write your suggestions on the screen."

"How about an unchaperoned thirty-day furlough?" someone shouted.

"I like the idea, but I doubt Mr. Harris would go along with it," Justin laughed, turning and looking at Mr. Harris, who frowned and shook his head. Looking back over the audience, he asked, "Any realistic ideas?"

The group came up with small groups going to movies, out to eat, to a dance hall, camping, fishing and a bunch of other ideas.

Then Ms. Wong raised her hand. "If we're going to be here for an extended time, why don't we contact some of the local colleges and universities? They may be willing to come and teach some university level classes. That would keep us busy and also give us an opportunity to learn something."

Mr. Harris was sitting behind Justin, and when he heard Ms. Wong's idea, he immediately jumped up. "That's brilliant. I don't know why we didn't think of that."

Then looking at Justin and Frank, he said, "I want you two and Ms. Wong to come to my office immediately after this meeting. We need to discuss Ms. Wong's idea further."

Justin thought it was a great idea but he was dubious about how things would work out with him and Ms. Wong. Until now they'd had little to do with each other.

Cindy, you've got to be alert. This could be dangerous. You're going to lose control of your emotions. You know you're attracted to Mr. LeMoore, Molly warned.

After the meeting concluded, Justin, Frank and Ms. Wong followed Mr. Harris to his office. Mr. Harris was all smiles, and as they walked, he put a hand on Ms. Wong's shoulder. "Ms. Wong, I think your suggestion is brilliant."

"Thank you sir," she replied.

They all entered his office, took their seats, and Mr. Harris said, "I want you three to contact several colleges and universities and see what kind of response you get. Start at the department level. There might be some graduate students who would be willing to come and teach courses. We could have medical classes, business, history, psychology and who knows what else. It would keep everyone busy, and as you said Ms. Wong, people could actually learn something."

Mr. Slusser hung around after the meeting smiling, trying to shake hands with everyone and acting like he was up for election. He wormed his way over to the Kozenskies, and asked, "Would you be free to have dinner with me this evening?"

"Yes, that would be nice," Ervin said.

"Good. I'll work it out with the guards."

Later that evening, Mr. Slusser met Irvin and Vidula at the guard house and signed them out. It was a cool evening, and Vidula clutched her jacket to her as they got into his rented Mercedes and drove toward one of the finest restaurants in Houston.

On the way, Vidula said, "This car smells wonderful. I could sit here all night and just sniff the new car smell."

"I think there'll also be some smells at the restaurant you haven't experienced for a while. You won't want to miss them either," Mr. Slusser noted.

"Why Milton, I'm shocked. Don't you think prisons hire chefs like those in the restaurants you frequent?" Vidula asked with a smirk.

"I think you'll find the aromas and tastes of our meal will be more to your liking than what the prison provides," Mr. Slusser noted.

They rode in silence the rest of the way to the restaurant. Vidula sat up front with Mr. Slusser. She was enjoying the luxury of being in a Mercedes again. Ervin sat in the back.

When they arrived, Mr. Slusser turned the car over to the valet and they went in. He had obviously informed the restaurant that he was an aide to a congressman. They were met at the front door by a waiter dressed in a black tuxedo, who said, "Good evening lady and gentlemen. My name is André."

Then in a French accent, he directed, "Please follow me." In military precision he ushered them to a table with white linen napkins, all standing at attention next to the plates. After seating Vidula, he stood erect and took their drink orders. Then clicking his heels, he said, "Very good."

Mr. Slusser looked around the room, and feeling smug, he picked up his napkin, shook it out and laid it on his lap. Then, smiling, he leaned back in his chair. "You seem to be doing quite well. I want you to know I think you made a wise choice to join the cryogenic group. Very smart. A good political move."

"We didn't do it by choice." Vidula's words hissed at Mr. Slusser as the waiter arrived with their drinks. She allowed him to retreat out of listening range, and then continued. "We had to. In part because we can't count on you or the Congressman to keep your promises. In fact, we haven't seen the good congressman for over a year now."

"The congressman is tremendously busy, but he's extremely interested in you both. I hope you know that. In fact, that's why he asked me to come and meet with you.

Vidula leaned forward across the table, gripped Milton's wrists and locked eyes with him. "Listen to me, Milton Slusser. The wrong words to the right people could cause you and your dear congressman a lot of trouble. I suggest you don't make the mistake of thinking we're out of sight and out of mind. We still have considerable influence in certain circles and could be a significant inconvenience to you. That is, if we choose to do so."

André again appeared with their appetizers. With flare, he strategically placed each plate just so in front of them. Again, allowing André to depart, Vidula continued. "To avoid such problems, we need several things done. First, we've found a supplier for the devices we talked about. They're inexpensive, only fifty-five dollars for each of the microphones. We ordered one hundred of them. The transmitters are slightly more at eighty dollars apiece. We ordered three-thousand of them."

"You've got to be joking," Mr. Slusser stammered.

"Mr. Slusser, this is hardly a time for joking," Vidula said, as she glared at him with eyes hard and cold as a serpent from the forgotten depths of hell.

Mr. Slusser got his communication device out and quickly calculated. "One hundred microphones come to $8,000. Three thousand transmitters come to $240,000. How am I supposed to come up with that kind of money? And these items can't be written off as equipment for the train."

"The problem of where you find the money is yours," Vidula coldly stated.

Then holding her glass up, she carefully swirled the contents. She then focused on Milton and in her most loveable voice, continued. "That's a pittance compared to the agreement you reneged on, so let's not quibble about a few dollars. Take it out of the congressman's slush fund or his next campaign fund. We don't care. Here are the specs," Vidula said, handing Milton a folder that she took from her purse.

"There's also another thing we need to discuss. We don't care how you do it, but Kyle Williams and Justin LeMoore must be eliminated from the mission."

Milton Slusser's face turned white and his blood turned as cold as ice. "You're not suggesting what I think you're suggesting, are you?"

"Milton, I'm not suggesting anything," Vidula said with a smile. "Kyle and Justin are dangerous for us and the congressman. You certainly wouldn't want to see anything politically untoward happen to the congressman's reputation, would you?"

"Vidula, I've had it with your demands and threats. Congressman Richards and I are doing the best we can. But neither of us will be involved in someone being hurt."

Vidula again leaned across the table. Her dark eyes were cold as ice. "There was no threat intended, just a promise. No one said anything about Justin or Kyle getting hurt, but they must be eliminated from the mission. How you accomplish that is your business. What I can tell you is this: if you can't resolve the problem, we're prepared to do so. You have one month."

Mr. Slusser was furious; his face became almost purple as he carefully wiped his mouth with his white linen napkin. He raised his hand summoning the waiter over. "André, I'm sorry. Something has come up and we must leave. Please bring me the check and let the valet know we're ready for the car."

"I hope everything was all right," André, worriedly said, looking at the barely touched drinks and appetizers.

"The drinks and food were excellent. As I said, something has come up," Mr. Slusser lamely mumbled.

André quickly returned with the bill, which Mr. Slusser paid. He then briskly led Vidula and Ervin to the parking area where the car was waiting for them. Milton tipped the attendant, and both Vidula and Ervin got into the backseat. They drove to the training area without a word. When they arrived, Mr. Slusser didn't get out of the car; he couldn't. He was having a hard time even breathing.

Seeing the car pull up, a guard walked out of the guard shack with an electronic device in his hand. Before getting out, Vidula leaned over the seat, put her hand on his shoulder and, wearing a censorious frown, said, "Mr. Slusser, your month starts tonight."

The guard arrived at the driver-side door, so Milton rolled the window down.

"Good evening sir," the guard said, handing him the device. Mr. Slusser quickly placed his thumb on the device and handed it back.

The guard took the device, and said, "Thank you sir. I hope you had a lovely evening."

"Yes, lovely," Mr. Slusser lied. He rolled the window up and drove to the nearest convenience store. He felt stiff and wooden as he got out of the car. Although the night was hot, he was cold. He had to lean on the car for several minutes to gain his composure. He kept seeing Vidula's evil eyes boring into his skull. He finally had to admit: *I think Congressman Richards and I may have bitten off more than we can chew.*

When he finally could walk, he shuffled to the men's room and relieved himself. He washed his hands and splashed some water on his face. When he looked into the mirror above the sink, he was shocked. His frightened face was staring back at him. He'd extolled the Kozenskies' virtues, pulled strings to meet their demands and fended off countless accusations from others. After tonight he was finally forced to admit the Kozenskies were everything they'd been accused of being. They were self-serving and dangerous. The congressman and he were simply pawns in their quest for power and control.

Walking to their quarters, Vidula said, "He isn't going to do anything so I'll take care of things."

"Vidula, no! We're going to start our own society and be a king and queen. Our posterity will rule the land for a thousand years. You can't do anything to jeopardize that."

"You're right," Vidula blandly said. Then to herself, she continued: *but I have a plan and in the morning I'll put it into action.*

Cindy asked Dr. Momora to help, and over the next few days, contacts were made with most of the local institutions of higher learning in the area. They were astounded at the favorable responses they received. They were inundated with offers from graduate students and even full professors to teach classes for free. Geology, health care, nutrition, stellar navigation, gardening, geometry, home canning, agronomy, literature and several other university-level classes were offered.

Mr. Harris was delighted. The prisoners not only seemed content but also excited about learning. He proudly called the classes, "My Space University."

Between March and July, there was one delay after another. The university classes continued to be a big hit, especially with Mr. Harris. All prisoners were required to attend at least two classes a day, five days a week. Attendance was carefully monitored.

On weekends, Justin, Frank, Millie and several others volunteered to take small groups out on various outings. Of course, there were at least four guards that accompanied each group, and like the classes, the prisoner's whereabouts was carefully monitored.

One Saturday, Justin and Millie took a group to the beach for a picnic, a day of swimming and some ocean fishing. It was a beautiful day. The sun was bright and the water was warm. They picked a spot where there were no other people. Everyone, but especially the men, were anxious to see Millie's bathing suit. Her bright-pink bikini didn't disappoint them. It only covered the necessities. It wasn't hard to keep track of the males, both prisoners and guards alike. Of course, she wasn't near as much of a hit with the other females.

One of the guards was an avid ocean fisherman and had brought several rods and other supplies for the group to use. Justin and a female prisoner were the only ones interested in fishing, so accompanied by a guard, Justin and the female fisherperson went about a block down the beach so they wouldn't be around the swimmers with their hooks.

Ms. Wong didn't go on the trip, but Dr. Momora was there and made a point to single Justin out. She saw him sitting on a bright-yellow fishing bucket with a padded seat and walked toward him. It was a hot day, so he wore a swimming suit and had a white towel across one leg to wipe his brow. He was contentedly staring into the surf when she approached from behind.

There was a soft breeze blowing off the water. It was full of delightfully tangy sea smells. Waves marched in rhythmic, hypnotizing chants onto the sandy shore. Gulls cried overhead and sandpipers dipped their bills into the sand along the tide line. Justin was quietly absorbing the smells, sights and sounds, which were like an embrocation to his soul. He heard something behind and turned to see a person watching him.

Dr. Momora had quietly watched Justin for several minutes before he realized she was there. When he turned, she asked, "Will it disturb your fishing if we chat for a while?"

Her voice interrupted his reverie, and he held one arm up to shield the suns glare from his eyes. Recognizing her voice, he lowered his arm and gazed back out at the water. He tried to hide his discomposure, and replied, "That depends. Fishing takes complete silence and total concentration."

"Looks to me like you're just sitting there staring at the water," she quipped.

"That my dear doctor, is the difference between a real fisherperson and a mere novice. I'm concentrating; thinking; analyzing the water, the tide, my bait and watching for the most subtle changes that would indicate a fish is ready to strike."

"Sounds boring to me. I can't see where a little pleasant conversation would hurt anything." Dr. Momora laughed, as she gazed out across the water.

"Doctor, as I've already said, fishing takes total concentration and absolute quiet."

"Okay," Dr. Momora said, looking at Justin. "Answer me a few questions and I'll leave you to gaze into the surf. I'd like to satisfy my curiosity. When you reviewed Cindy Wong's file during the prisoner selection process, did you physically experience anything unusual?"

"Like what?" Justin asked, wiping his forehead with the towel.

"I don't know. That's what I'm asking."

Without taking his eyes off the tip of his rod, Justin picked up a water bottle next to his bucket and took a drink. "Dr. Momora, I'm sure you're familiar with HIPPA, the Health Insurance Portability and Accountability Act. That says one may not discuss another person's medical file with anyone without said person's permission. HIPPA has been the law for well over two-hundred years now."

"I don't believe prisoner administrative records are covered by HIPPA," Dr. Momora commented.

"My dear lady, prisoner records contain medical, mental health and other information that is covered by HIPPA," Justin countered.

"That may be true, but we're talking about your medical and mental health experience, not Ms. Wong's."

"If it is mine, then I'm not interested," Justin tersely replied, again wiping his face with the towel.

She smiled. "Thank you for answering my question. It's obvious something significant happened in the record review. And by the way, I wouldn't take up poker if I were you. Your body language is like reading a book."

Not taking his eyes off the tip of his pole, he angrily said, "I suppose you made some kind of magical diagnosis in that length of time."

"No magic. Just good medical observation. I watched you for several minutes before I approached. When I spoke, the muscles in your back and neck immediately tightened. The sweat on your forehead increased and your mouth went dry."

"It's a hot day,"

"Yes, but your blood pressure and heart rate also increased. A sure sign of stress."

"And I suppose you had some magical stethoscope to determine all of that?"

"Nope. I didn't need one. I just watched the carotid artery in your neck. It was beating like a brass band. Justin, I'm a physician and I didn't observe anything you don't watch for in your patients or clients." With a little giggle, she then said, "Again, thanks for answering my question."

Later that afternoon, as they were ready to depart, Justin was putting the guard's fishing tackle into the bus. He was still brooding over the interchange with Dr. Momora when she walked over.

"Mr. LeMoore, I want to be your friend. I'm Cindy's friend and wouldn't do anything to hurt either of you. I also understand your concern about discretion. In that regard, I can guarantee you no one other than Cindy will ever hear a word of what we've talked about. Neither Cindy nor I were ever known for spreading rumors."

It was the first of August when Mr. Harris called the paid crew to another meeting.

"I've just been informed the mission start date has been postponed again. It could be as much as two or three additional months before we can start the cryogenic process. Thank goodness, the university classes are going well. I hope we can continue them."

I don't see why not," Justin responded. "The universities we've worked with are prepared to continue classes for as long as needed." Looking at Mr. Harris, he asked, "How much has the Kozenskies constant modifications had to do with the delays?"

"That's hard to tell. They've added some backup systems that in part have delayed things. In some cases, walls had to be dismantled so larger wiring harnesses and other equipment could be installed. Kyle continues to say the additional backup systems are unnecessary, but his bosses aren't complaining. They wouldn't though. They reap lots of dollars with each modification."

Justin was continually bothered by the interchange he'd had with Dr. Momora on the beach. One day he saw Ms. Wong sitting by herself outside the auditorium waiting for her class to start. It was a beautiful day, and she was sitting on a bench reading in the warm sunshine. She was waiting for the home garden and food storage class from the University of Texas Extension Service to begin.

She had her back to him, so he could have inconspicuously

passed her by, but he wanted to clear the air with her. As he walked to her, he again felt the familiar collision of excitement and fear he'd experienced the first time he reviewed her prison record. He walked back and forth several times before gathering his courage and taking the plunge.

"Hi, how are you doing?" he asked.

Turning around and looking up, she nervously responded, "Good. I was just enjoying the sun."

"Yes, it is a beautiful day. I thought perhaps we should chat. I assume your friend Dr. Momora told you about our conversation on the beach?"

"Yes, she told me about it. I wasn't happy that she'd taken it upon herself to talk to you. I told her so too."

"I know we've both had some unusual experiences and I'd like to clear the air," he said, feeling his heart pound like a summer thunderstorm.

Molly was coaching Cindy not to talk to Justin, but she felt compelled to continue. Nervously tucking a loose strand of hair behind her ear, and adjusting the books in her lap, she said, "All right, I'll start if you'll be honest with me. Deal?"

"Okay. Go ahead," Justin hesitantly responded, as he put one foot on the bench and looked down at her.

Looking into nowhere, she said, "It started at the prison medical clinic. I was carrying a tray of medication to a patient when I saw a vision, a face. It was someone I had only briefly met. It was your face." She turned to look at him. "I didn't know you had anything to do with the mission. That's why I was so shocked when I walked into your office that day."

Looking at Justin, she asked, "Why would I have seen your face?"

"I have no idea," Justin responded.

"Me neither. But it was your face. I'm sure of that. Actually, I saw it several times. I don't understand it. Do you?"

"No, I have no explanation," Justin replied. "But it does answer a question for me. The day I was fishing and Dr. Momora came to visit with me, she asked if I had experienced anything unusual when I reviewed your record."

"And?"

Shifting nervously from one foot to the other, he hesitantly said, "Let me start with the conference we both attended. When you were led into the room and introduced to the panel, something profound happened. I had never had such a reaction to anyone before. When I looked at you, my heart began beating like a drum. I even had a hard time breathing. I don't know if you remember, but I was only able to ask one question.

"I do remember. You made a comment about me wanting to be in prison, or something like that."

"Yes, I believe that was what I asked. Now let me skip to my initial review of your record. When I pulled up your record for the first time, I had the same reaction. Just looking at your picture made my heart beat faster. I couldn't understand what was happening. Each time I pulled your file up I had the same reaction. Even Frank was able to see that something significant had happened. I can't explain it."

"Interesting. Let me be clear, I'm satisfied with Herman Hockstrasser as a future mate. Neither I nor Dr. Hockstrasser are interested in a romantic or intimate relationship. We're both invested in our careers and satisfied to just live together without any entanglements." Looking away for several seconds, she then turned back. "And I'm not interested in a romantic relationship with anyone else either."

Very good, Molly said, *don't let him play on your emotions.*

"Sounds like you and Dr. Hockstrasser plan to just be housemates. What about children? Isn't each couple supposed to have children?" he inquired.

Justin noted a shadow cross her face before she responded. "We'll just have to wait and see how that works out. When we arrive, I'm sure we'll both be extremely busy with our responsibilities."

"Yes, and I expect I'll also be busy. I'm told the crew will only remain on the planet for a month or so before starting our return journey."

After listening, Cindy asked, "So what do you think we should do about our mutual experiences? Oh, and by the way, you could sit down. I promise I won't jump on you."

"Nothing," he said, hesitantly sitting down. "It appears we are both in agreement. Whatever happened is in the past and should be left there. You're going to marry Dr. Hochstrasser, and I'm going to be returning to Earth."

"I agree, we should just let the past be the past. Now that we have resolved that, can I ask you to do me a favor?"

"Sure, if I can," Justin said.

"Would you treat Amy Momora and myself like everyone else?"

"I thought I already did," he said, looking down and scuffing his feet in the dirt.

"Mr. LeMoore, you avoid me. You refuse to see Amy or me in counseling. You won't sit next to either of us in meetings. And if we ride in the van, you make every effort not to even sit on the same seat with us. It's gotten to the point that everyone recognizes it."

With her eyes blazing, she continued, "You don't need to worry. I won't throw myself at you, or do anything to embarrass you."

"I'm sorry if you feel I've avoided you. I'll try to be more considerate."

"Thank you. I'd appreciate that," she said as a guard came out of the auditorium holding a clipboard up to block the sun. He looked around until he spotted Justin talking to Ms. Wong. He waved, and called, "Oh there you are. Just taking attendance. Take your time, it's a beautiful day to enjoy the sun."

"Thanks," Cindy called back. "I'll be right there. We're just finishing our conversation."

Justin quickly got up, and said, "Thanks for the discussion. I need to run. Have a great day."

Also getting up, she replied, "Thanks."

But she was in turmoil: *I don't know why I feel this way? My heart's pounding, my mouth is full of cotton and I'm afraid my knees could buckle again.*

Cindy, keep your emotions in check. Your relationship with Mr. LeMoore is getting more dangerous all the time. Listen to me, Molly scolded.

I agree, she responded. *I won't let him get too close.*

As Justin walked away, he turned and watched her go into the building. He didn't know why, but it was as if a weight had been lifted from his shoulders since they had at least talked.

This is crazy, he told himself: *My mouth is as dry as a bone, and my heart is beating out of my chest*. He was even more convinced he had to maintain a professional relationship and distance himself from her.

Justin didn't tell anyone about his conversation with Ms. Wong.

Although that evening at dinner, Frank asked, "What happened today? You seem more relaxed than I've seen you in weeks."

"Nothing. I guess we're just settling into a routine," Justin responded.

Frank looked at Justin like he didn't believe him, but didn't say anything more.

The next day Justin was walking to monitor one of the classes when he passed Dr. Momora on a sidewalk. She also seemed to be in a hurry, but as they passed, she smiled, and said, "Thanks."

"Have you noticed Muriel French and Safire Strong campaigning for the Kozenskies?" Millie asked one evening when she, Justin and Frank were having dinner together. "Hell, you'd think they were running for president or something. They also seem to spend their time with the same group of men and women. From what I can tell, they've convinced most of the prisoners the Kozenskies are better than a one-night stand."

"Millie, where do you come up with that stuff?" Justin asked.

"What stuff? Hell, I'm just honest enough to call it as I see it," she tersely responded.

"I've noticed the same thing," Frank noted. "It seems like we're the only ones with reservations about Vidula and Ervin. They're not here often, but when they are, they're backslapping and trying to be one of the good ole boys."

"I spoke to Mr. Harris the other day about the same issue. He's also concerned. But again, we don't have any evidence that anything nefarious is taking place," Justin said.

"No, but we all know there is," Millie concluded.

Mr. Harris called another meeting with the paid crew and announced, "I've worked out a plan for you all to ride up to the train assembly sight. You can ride up on a transport ship so you can actually see the train being assembled. Hopefully, you can spend a few days, experience what living in space is like, and see your quarters. I am told the car with the living quarters is complete. You can each spend three or four days with one of the engineers or a crew member who is familiar with the train."

Everyone was excited and jumped at the opportunity. Mr. Harris also announced each of the crew, except Justin and Frank, could take a month off after they finished their trip.

"You two will need to coordinate with Dr. Davis and Dr. Lister. They insist they need the stress questionnaires right up to when the prisoners go into hibernation. I hate to do it, but one of you will need to be here to administer and retrieve the tests," he said, looking at Justin and Frank.

"You can separately take a couple of weeks off, and hopefully when you return, the train will be finished. If all goes as planned, we'll then be ready to start the cryogenic process."

Despite the numerous delays, morale was high among the prisoners. Of course, how could one think otherwise? They were essentially on an extended parole. They were allowed to go shopping, or to movies in chaperoned groups, they ate well, they were not living in cells and all they had to do was go to classes five days a week.

For most of the prisoners, they'd have been content for the

delays to go on forever. Justin and Frank continued to see both couples and individual prisoners weekly. They wanted to ensure no one was experiencing undue anxiety about the delays, mate problems, or even second thoughts about the mission.

Justin still hadn't interviewed Ms. Wong or Dr. Hockstrasser, even though the other prisoners had been traded off between both he and Frank. Frank was understandably dumbfounded when one day, Justin said, "I'll take Ms. Wong and Dr. Hockstrasser this time."

"Have you worked things out with her?" Frank asked.

"We've talked. I informed her we'll have nothing but a professional relationship. She's going to ultimately marry Dr. Hockstrasser, and that's that."

"So, I assume she also told you why she doesn't want to marry until she gets to the New World?" Frank inquired.

"Not really, other than she just wants to wait and see how things turn out."

"Are you still attracted to her?" Frank asked.

"I think she's a nice person. Beyond that I'll maintain the same professional relationship with her as any other prisoner," he tried to nonchalantly respond.

Justin met with Ms. Wong and Dr. Hockstrasser individually, then together. Both remained committed to the mission. Both were looking forward to getting started and said they remained comfortable with each other. Dr. Hockstrasser would be departing for the ship in a few days to start growing vegetables for the mission and Ms. Wong said she was okay with his departure.

After the interview, and as she and Dr. Hochstrasser were

getting ready to leave, she turned and said, "I understand you're going to be gone for a while after your familiarization trip to the train?"

"Are there no confidentialities in this organization?" Justin asked with a laugh.

"Although we're not currently behind bars, that doesn't change the prison rumor network. We hear about everything," she replied.

"It appears that's the reality of things. To answer your question, yes, I'm going to be gone for a while. I'm going to Kansas and spend a few days with my fishing buddy and his family. I'll be back in time for the start of the cryogenic process."

"I hope you have a wonderful time and that you are safe," she said, as they shook hands.

At least my heart isn't pounding out of my chest, and I didn't get shocked, Justin thought. *I knew I could deal with this on a professional level,* he unsuccessfully attempted to convince himself.

13

The crew had to be at the launch site at 0330 for safety briefings and suit fittings. They met at the Houston Space Facility and were taken by bus to a nondescript cinderblock building. It was about two hundred yards from where a transport shuttle was positioned on a runway. They were escorted to a large room, which was painted light green. There were several rows of folding chairs and two adjoining doors. One said, MEN; the other, WOMEN. The hall smelled like insecticide or cleaning material of some kind.

An Oriental man, dressed in a blue jump suit with a large Space Corp decal on it, introduced himself. "My name is Mr. Woo. I'm the shuttle loadmaster. Please sit down."

There were about a dozen other men and women standing off to one side of the room. Like Mr. Woo, they were also dressed in blue jumpsuits.

Mr. Woo continued, "First of all, let me welcome you to the Space Corp. shuttle area. I'll be giving you a short briefing on safety procedures and other information you'll need to know before the shuttle launch."

A large 3-D screen clicked on, and a picture of the shuttle appeared. Using a laser pointer, he said, "This is the shuttle craft you'll be riding to the assembly site. Basically, it's a flying truck. We can send fifty tons of cargo up to the assembly area each trip. The major mission of the shuttle is to transport cargo. Unfortunately, it isn't built for passenger comfort."

A picture of the interior of the shuttle was illuminated showing rows and rows of shipping containers in what looked like a long metal tube. Using his pointer, Mr. Woo continued, "As you can see, there is only a three-foot space between the shuttle wall and the containers, so there isn't much room left for passengers. The seats fold down from the wall, and once you're sitting, you'll be strapped in and completely immobilized. Of course, you'll be wearing space suits."

He walked over to a table which had several articles laid out. Holding up an adult diaper, he said, "Everyone will wear one of these. It's obvious what it's for and you'll need it. Once you're in your suit, restroom breaks are over. There are different sizes to fit each of you. Just tell the crew person assisting you what your waist size is.

"Notice, there's an elastic strip in the legs and the waist." He was stretching the elastic out. "A word of caution from personal experience: make sure the elastic strip lays flat against your skin with no wrinkles. If there's a wrinkle, it will leak and that's not good.

"I'm sure you're asking yourselves, 'How many people have worn my suit before me? And how many had leaky diapers?' The answer is probably several. But be assured the common suits, as we call them, are cleaned and sanitized each time they return from space. The suit you will be issued will be the one you'll use the entire time you're at the train. I suggest you keep the inside as clean as you can. We have no way of cleaning them on the train.

"Once you arrive, you'll be allowed to shower and clean up. Another word of caution: just before you suit up, visit the restroom and try to go. Remember what your mother used to say before you got into the car, 'I don't care if you don't have to go, try anyway.'"

He laid the diaper down and picked up what looked like a nylon bodysuit. "This will be your next item. It's a heat-protection body garment. In the event of a fire, it will keep your suit from melting onto your skin. Notice, it has feet, gloves and a hood that comes up over your head. Although we have never had a fire on a shuttle, we always want to be prepared. The shuttles also have foam dispensers which will activate should smoke or a fire be detected."

Next, he picked up one arm of a space suit. It looked like the suits they'd practiced with in the underwater training. The suit was a huge rubberized canvas-looking thing with tubes or wires of some kind protruding from the back. It also had attached gloves and boots. "This little gem weighs ninety pounds." Looking around the room at some of the women, he continued, "Not much less than some of you smaller ladies." He picked up the helmet and pointed out two tubes, "These will be attached to the ships oxygen supply and the communication cable once you are on board."

"You've all had a chance to familiarize yourself with the suits in your underwater training. These suits have one feature your training suits didn't have," he said, pointing to pack on the front of the suit. Opening the pack, Mr. Woo pulled out a device that looked like the joystick on a computer game. "This is the device you'll use to move with when you are outside the train."

He showed them two small gadgets. There was one on each shoulder. Turning the suit over, there were two more on the back shoulders. "These are small thrusters that will move you in space. For now, don't pay any attention to them. You'll be issued an oxygen pack when you arrive at the train and a crew member will show you how to use them. These other tubes protruding from the back of the suit are for cooling or heating the suit.

"Once seated on the shuttle craft, you'll be fastened to the seat. Your arms will be strapped to the armrests, your legs to the under part of the seat and your helmet will be secured to the back of the seat. You'll experience between three and four Gs of gravitational pull, which is why we want you to be completely immobilized. As pressure builds, your suits will compensate for most of it. Some of you may experience brief blackouts, especially if this is your first space flight. It isn't anything to be concerned about. Normally, as soon as we leave Earth's gravitational field, you'll revive and be fine.

"Once strapped in, you will not be released until we dock with the train. If there are other shuttles to be unloaded ahead of us, it might be three hours or more before you are released. Now you see the necessity of this," he said, again picking up the diaper.

"Use it. Just pretend you're two again. When the urge arises, do what you need to do. After we dock, you'll be able to shower and clean up.

"Okay, we'll now help you suit up. Men, follow me, and, women please follow this young lady," he said, pointing to a woman who stepped forward. "Once you are suited up, we'll transport you to the shuttle and get under way."

Once everyone was suited, and an instructor checked their suits to make sure everything was functional, they were told to carry their helmets and return to the training room.

Mr. Woo was there, also in a space suit. "Follow me," he directed. He led everyone out of the building, up a gradual ramp and onto a flat trailer-looking car. The car was barely ten inches off the ground but seemed like ten feet as they struggled in their heavy suits.

When they arrived at the launch site, they disembarked from the car and entered an elevator which took them up to the shuttle. It was huge, more than fifty yards long. It looked like a long, flattened silver cigar with two sets of stubby wings. Two large twelve-foot-diameter motors were attached to the sides with a gaping black hole in the rear. They were told the rear motor was the primary thruster. The shuttle sat on the runway like an airplane, but one of the crew members explained it was really a rocket.

"We will take off like a plane, then turn and blast straight up rolling as we go," the crew member explained.

Everyone shuffled off the elevator, inched their way into the space between the outer wall of the craft and the rows of olive-drab shipping containers. The shuttle crew was very patient and helped each person trip and bumble their way to a seat. The seats were made of tubular steel with webbing on the bottom and back. They didn't look sturdy enough to hold a person with their space suit on, but apparently were.

When Justin plopped into his seat, he wondered if he'd be strong enough to get up again. A crewman helped put their helmets on and then strapped them in. Lastly, an oxygen tube and communication cable was attached to each of their helmets. The communication cable allowed them to hear what was being said by the crew, but they weren't able to speak to one another.

Justin tried to look at the person on either side of him, but couldn't see who they were, so he just stared straight ahead.

Mr. Woo's voice came into the helmet speaker. "First of all, let me welcome you aboard the shuttle. When we begin to take off, it will be a little bumpy, but it shouldn't last long. Once we're in the air the captain will engage the primary thruster and you'll experience some pressure as we gain speed. Things might get a little noisy. The cargo containers will rattle and shake, but that's normal. Don't worry, the shuttle won't come apart. You might think it's going to, but it won't.

"I'm now going to switch your communication sets to the command channel. You may find it interesting to listen to the captain and the shuttle tower as they coordinate their final preparations."

They heard the motors start up and the shuttle felt like it was rolling. Then it stopped and they could hear some kind of mechanical noises. At first there was a slight vibration; then the engines were throttled to full speed, making everything quiver and vibrate. When the brakes were released, it felt like they were hurled down the runway. The noise was like being in the middle of a volcano.

Without windows, it was hard to tell exactly what was happening. The force was significant, and it seemed like the entire ship, and everything in it was throbbing.

As they lifted off, they felt the landing gear thump into the ship's belly. As they gained altitude, the vibration decreased until the primary launch rocket engaged. They were then propelled forward like a bullet. Although the pressure was somewhat dispelled by their suits, the force still made Justin feel like he was going to pass out.

It took about twenty minutes to fly beyond Earth's atmosphere. Then the vibration stopped, and it was as if all sound ceased to exist. Going from feeling like they were inside a tornado to complete silence was disconcerting.

The captain welcomed everyone into space, and said, "There is one other shuttle at the train, so as soon as they are unloaded, we can dock. Until we are cleared to approach, just relax. I'll turn on some soothing music."

Just then, Justin saw some strange things coming along the aisle, but they weren't walking. They were floating! It turned out to be Mr. Woo and several other crew members. One of them stopped by each person to make sure he or she was all right.

When they were cleared to dock, there were whooshing sounds as the shuttle was positioned. Then after a loud bang, the crew began moving around doing various chores Justin couldn't see. A large door in the shuttle must have opened; as there was loud rush of air.

"Welcome to the space train, ladies and gentlemen," the captain said.

They were unsecured from their seats and given a small portable air tank. "You'll be given a larger tank when you're inside," Mr. Woo said. "The gravitational mechanism isn't operational in the logistic car, but your boots have electromagnets in them which will adhere to the floor. You'll feel a little awkward at first as you walk, but you can do it. Notice how light you feel. Those heavy suits back on Earth don't feel like anything up here."

Mr. Woo, and his fellow shuttle crewmembers, ushered them from the shuttle into what looked like a large brightly lit cavern. Others in space suits were waiting for them. Truly experiencing weightlessness was unsettling. If they took a big step, it felt like they could float. They held onto bars along the walls of the cavern and were assisted by the others in space suits.

Mr. Woo said, pointing to those waiting for them, "These people are Space Corp. employees, or some of your fellow crew members. Each of you will be assigned to an escort and guide while you're here. I think they are going to take you on a short spacewalk while you have your suits on."

Justin and the person next to him, who turned out to be Millie, were assigned to Kyle Williams, which was not only comforting but exciting. Justin had hoped to meet the infamous Kyle whom Vidula hated so much. Kyle approached and they shook hands as best as they could.

"Justin LeMoore?" Kyle asked.

"Yes, I'm Justin."

"I've wanted to meet you. I was supposed to be escorting two other individuals, but at the last minute they changed the list and I was assigned to you two. I look forward to spending some time with you. I've heard a great deal about you."

"Likewise," Justin returned. "You and I seem to have a lot in common, at least when it comes to our opinion about a certain couple."

"You mean the Kozenskies? I've heard you've been an irritant to Vidula," Kyle remarked.

"More like a bur under her saddle." Then turning to Millie, he said, "This is Ms. Millie Syster. She'll be the chief nurse for the cryogenic female ward."

"I've also heard about you. Where is the chaplain? I was told the three of you are a team." Kyle said.

"I don't know who he was assigned to, but I'm sure you'll meet him while we're here."

"I look forward to it," Kyle said. "If you're up to it, we'll start off with on a short tour around the outside of the train. Then you can go to your quarters, remove your suits, and clean up."

"Sounds exciting," Justin responded.

"Great," Kyle said. "I know you would like to get cleaned up, but I think a quick tour will give you a sense of the magnitude of the operation. There are over two hundred construction employees working to assemble the various sections of the train as they're transported up. Once the sections of a car have been ferried from Earth, they're assembled. When a car is complete and checked over, it's then linked to the train."

Pointing to another person, Kyle said, "That's Leif Udall, the loadmaster for the train. He's responsible for loading and cataloging all supplies and equipment that will be taken on the mission."

"Yes, we know each other. We went through the crew orientation and training together," Justin commented.

Leif had a cart with a stack of larger oxygen tanks on it, and a set was issued to each person.

Kyle helped Justin and Millie put their tanks on, and said, "Okay, we're ready to go."

They were standing next to an open door and could see other workers unloading the cargo containers from the shuttle they'd just arrived on. It was mind-boggling how those large containers that weighed many tons were pushed out of the shuttle door and moved by space tugs that looked like yellow forklifts without wheels. Each container was moved to a specific area with dozens of other containers tethered together like large metal balloons.

Kyle said, "Remove the joystick from the front of your suits and turn them on." He helped them both accomplish that task. "Now, step out of the door like this." He floated. Turning around so he could see them, he directed, "Hold the joystick in your right hand and move it in the direction you want to go. Push the stick forward to go forward, back to go back, left for left and right to move right."

Both Justin and Millie stepped out of the doorway and they were floating!

"Oh this is wonderful!" Millie squealed as she floated out of the door.

It took a few minutes of practice before they were comfortable moving and changing directions, but they were soon moving effortlessly like birds in the sky. Both were laughing like a couple of kids.

Kyle and his two charges moved about two hundred yards directly away from the train. Then Kyle said, "Turn around."

They sucked in their breaths as they saw the train with the sun reflecting off the hull. It was hard to believe what they were seeing. About twenty-five of the total sixty cars were attached to one another. Each car was more than forty feet high and one hundred yards long. The sight was overwhelming. The immensity of the train was almost incomprehensible.

Kyle allowed them time to absorb what they were seeing, then asked, "What do you think?"

"Unbelievable," Justin said.

"It's the most magnificent thing I've ever seen. It's almost a religious experience," Millie breathlessly whispered.

As they looked around, they could see Earth far beyond another group of shipping containers. "We don't have enough completed cars to accommodate all the supplies that are being delivered, but you know how the government is. Each container is to be delivered by a specific date. So although we're not ready, the stuff just keeps coming."

"Unfortunately, some of the construction contractors are behind schedule, and many of the cars haven't been completed. The project is so massive that cars, or pieces of cars, are being made in factories all over the world. And every time there's a change or modification it slows the project down. Sometimes we have to send whole sections back to Earth to be modified which takes even more time. It's the Kozenskies," Kyle spat out as though his mouth were filled with acid. "It seems like they're making constant changes, and each time they do, it throws everything behind another month."

"Why does everyone put up with them?" Justin asked. "It seems like everyone kowtows to the Kozenskies. It's almost like somebody's been bought off and they're running the show."

"Congressman Richards and his sidekick, that's who's been bought off. They especially cater to Vidula. Whenever she whines, Slusser is immediately putting pressure on someone. I don't know where they get money for the delays and cost overruns, but whatever the Kozenskies want they get."

Looking at the hundreds of cargo containers floating in groups, Justin asked, "How do you keep track of all the stuff floating around out here?"

"It may look like disorganization, but Leif knows where everything's at and exactly where it will go. Come over here and I'll show you," he said, moving toward one of the container areas.

Using their suit propulsion systems, they maneuvered over to a group of containers as big as tour buses. As they were moving along, Justin and Millie noticed more of the space tug's relocating containers from one area to another. Some were pushing containers toward cars attached to the train, others seemed to be sorting and moving containers into or out of the various groups.

They approached the first group and Kyle pointed out a label on each container.

The tug operator watched Kyle and the two others leave the train and head for one of the container corals. The two with Kyle acted like children, floating, turning, laughing and having a fun time. He tuned his communication device so he could hear Kyle. He was delighted to also hear Justin LeMoore. He smiled. *The list has obviously been changed and they're together.* He took one last sip from his drinking tube, tucked the bottle into his suit and carefully lined the shipping container up on the forks of his tug.

As he waited for the threesome to get into the right position, a stampede of memories flooded his mind. The memory of marrying Margaret. She was so young, so beautiful and they were so in love. They were poor, but happy. Then Danny was born. The doctors said he had a congenital brain disorder and would never be able to live on his own. They were encouraged to put Danny into a facility, but Margaret refused. "How can we simply put him away? He's a part of us. I love him."

Work was hard to come by and Danny required so much of Margaret's time that over the years their relationship somehow just drifted apart. His drinking didn't help either. He went from job to job barely making ends meet. When he got the job with Space Corp. they were excited. Finally they'd have a steady income and Space Corp. paid well. He tried to control his drinking but just two months ago a bottle of liquor was found on his carry-on luggage as he was clearing security on his way to work.

Liquor was prohibited on the worksite, so he was dismissed. Since he was laid off they'd been squeaking by on unemployment and the few dollars Margaret made cleaning houses at night.

Then he'd received the anonymous call. "Are you interested

in returning to work at Space Corp.?" It was a voice he'd never heard before. "If so, be at the post office parking lot at 1300 tomorrow."

That's strange, he told himself. *Why would Space Corp meet a prospective employee at a post office parking lot?* However, he didn't ask questions.

"How will I know who to meet?" he'd asked.

"We'll find you," the voice said. "Just be there."

He didn't tell Margaret about the call but was at the post office parking lot the next day as instructed. He sat for almost a half hour before a white van pulled alongside of his old, battered Toyota truck. The side door of the van opened and two men waved for him to enter. Over the next few minutes he was told about the job and offered an unbelievable salary. It would be a one-way ride, but he didn't care. His life was worthless and Margaret and Danny would be taken care of. It was the least he could do for them.

"Be at this location tomorrow at 0500," he was told.

He was then given a briefcase, which he opened. It was filled with packets of money.

As he reverently fingered the money, one of the men said, "As agreed there is two million dollars there. Don't get any ideas about skipping out with the money. You'll be under constant surveillance until you're on board tomorrow. Go home, and don't leave the house tonight. Be here at 0500 in the morning. We'll be waiting."

He rushed home and told Margaret that he'd been offered his job back at Space Corp.

"I'm supposed to meet a carpool at the post office at 0500 tomorrow morning."

"That's strange," Margaret replied. "You've never carpooled before. I've always driven you to the gate."

"It's something new they've started," he said.

Although Margaret volunteered to drive him in the morning, he refused. "You stay in bed. I'll leave the truck in the parking lot. You and Danny can walk down and get it later. It will give you something to do."

The next morning, he got up, showered, dressed and before leaving put the briefcase next to the table with a note for Margaret. He expressed his love for her and Danny. He also told Margaret not to tell anyone about the money. He instructed her to leave the area, go to another city and only put part of the money in the bank.

He then drove to the post office parking lot, arriving at 0445. The white van was waiting. He parked his truck next to it, got out and the side door of the van opened. He got in, the door closed and bright lights were turned on. He was told to sit in a chair.

"We need to make a few changes to your face," a lady said.

They then trimmed and colored his beard and put makeup on his face. Lastly, they put a pair of contact lenses into his eyes. After the woman was finished with his makeup, he was told to get into another van that was waiting for him outside.

"They will take you to the Space Corp. gate," one of the men said as he leaned over and fastened a security badge to his shirt. He was then handed a small duffel bag. "Once you clear security go to the restroom. Someone will meet you there."

He cleared security at Space Corp. without incident; even the retina check was no problem. Once through security, he went to the restroom as he'd been directed to do. A man immediately approached with a duffel bag exactly like his.

"Give me your bag," the man said, handing him the other one.

"Your directions are in the bag along with what you will need.

You'll again be under constant surveillance so don't even consider backing out. Do you understand?"

"The label tells which car the container is to be sent to, and where the contents are to be stored," Kyle said.

Since they were all looking at the label, no one saw the tug operator maneuvering the container behind them and gaining speed. The tug was pushing a container directly toward them; then suddenly the operator reversed his thrusters, causing the container to slide off its forks and move with surprising speed on its own. It was hurtling directly toward Justin, Kyle and Millie. Kyle happened to see a shadow out of the corner of his eye and turned just as the container was about to crush them. He instinctively grabbed Justin's suit and pushed him away. He then pulled Millie in the opposite direction as the moving container slammed into the stationary one. There was almost no sound as the two containers collided in the vacuum of space.

Because the moving container didn't squarely hit the stationary one, it spun around knocking Justin hard on the back and tearing his oxygen tube loose. The valve in his helmet automatically closed as he began gasping for air. He tried to reach for his air hose but couldn't find it. Gasping like a fish out of water, he began tumbling and rolling into the black of space. The pain in his back was lancing, enveloping.

I'm going to die, he thought, and then something very strange happened. He saw Ms. Wong's face as clearly as if she were there. *My life is being sucked out of me*, he thought, as everything went black. His arms limply spread out and he slowly tumbled away.

Kyle saw Justin's distress and hurriedly moved to him. He immediately saw the dangling air tubes spewing oxygen and at first inspection thought the tube had just become unattached from his helmet. A closer look revealed the tube had been severed. He took three big breaths of his air, then detached his air hose and connected it to

Justin's helmet. It took less than a minute for Justin to begin breathing again. He continued to switch his air hose back and forth between his helmet and Justin's helmet until Justin opened his eyes.

"Your oxygen tubes have been damaged, so we're sharing mine," Kyle said. "Take several deep breaths. Then I'll switch it to my helmet."

Several others had also seen what happened and with a flurry of activity, tugs and people came from all directions. Someone brought a small emergency oxygen bottle from one of the tugs which they attached to Justin's helmet. Once Justin was breathing normally, several others began pushing him toward the train.

Seeing that Justin was being taken care of, Kyle looked for Millie. He spotted her not far away holding onto one of the containers. Hurrying to her, he asked, "Are you all right?"

"I think so," she responded but continued to hold fast to the container.

He had to pry her gloved fingers from the bar she was holding onto and then guided her toward the train.

Those who were helping Justin moved him toward a specific car and an airlock opened, then closed behind them. Another door opened with loud swooshes and several people dressed in white with a gurney were waiting for them. Still in his spacesuit, Justin was loaded on the gurney along with the auxiliary oxygen tank. He was whisked down a hall, into an elevator, up to another floor, down several more corridors and finally into a door that read, MEDICAL CLINIC.

He was pushed into a room with an examining table where someone removed his helmet while two other individuals undid his suit and removed it. They cut his body suit up the middle and attached numerous leads to his head, chest and sides. Justin tried to protest, telling them he was fine and didn't need anything, but to no avail.

There was a commotion just outside the clinic and Justin could hear Kyle shouting, "Kozenskies! No accident! On purpose!"

Finally, the doctor closed the door, and said, "My name is Dr. Owen Francis. I'm contracted by Space Corp. to provide medical services to the workers during the assembly of the train. I'll also be accompanying you on the mission."

After a quick physical examination, he continued, "It appears you haven't suffered any broken bones, although you have a nasty bruise on your back. I'm going to do a quick neurological exam. If that checks out, I don't see any reason to detain you further. If it's all right with you, I'd like to ask you a few questions."

"Sure," Justin said, "but I think it's a waste of time. I feel fine."

"Well then, humor me," Dr. Francis said as he held up three fingers. "How many fingers do you see?"

"Three," Justin replied.

"Who is the president of the United States?"

Justin again replied correctly.

"Do you know where you are and what day it is?" Dr. Francis asked.

Justin replied correctly and again said, "Doctor, I feel fine."

"I'm glad," Dr. Francis replied. "As far as I can tell you haven't experienced any problems from your brief blackout. I'm happy your accident didn't turn out any worse than it did. Since we had to cut your body suit off, we'll get you a dressing robe to wear."

By the time Justin was released, Millie and Kyle were waiting for him in the corridor. He was delighted to see them both. Millie had obviously been allowed to clean up as her hair was still wet.

"Millie, you look quite fashionable in your blue jumpsuit.

Somehow, though, it doesn't look like your color," Justin laughed, giving her a quick squeeze.

"Nope, it isn't my color. And if this is what we have to wear, I'll sew some pink lace around the collar," she noted.

Without his suit, Justin noted Kyle was only about five foot four inches tall, slender with intense blue eyes and a blond crewcut. He had long, thin fingers and a face that didn't look like it knew how to smile.

As they walked down the hall, all Justin could think to say was, "Millie, were you dry?"

"Hell no, I was wet from my boobs down. That diaper didn't even start to hold what I did."

Justin laughed. "I think mine is a bit damp too. I'll be glad to get it off and take a shower."

"I'm taking you to your quarters so you can clean up," Kyle said, as he led them toward an elevator.

It seemed like they walked forever before arriving at a corridor with door after door. Each door had the name of a crew member on it. They came to one on the left that read JUSTIN LEMOORE, MENTAL HEALTH. Next to his door was one that read FRANK MOLONY, CHAPLAIN.

Millie said, "My room is a few doors farther down the corridor on the right."

There was no doorknob, just a keypad with a button next to it.

"Currently the quarters are open, but you can put your own code in which will lock your room. I'll show you how to do it later when you start bringing your personal stuff up," Kyle noted.

"Great," Justin responded, pushing the button.

The door slid into the wall with a whoosh of air and they

walked in. The walls were painted a light-yellow color. There was a small bathroom with a toilet, shower and a sink on the right. The bathroom created a narrow hall for about six feet. The room looked to be about eighteen feet long with a single-size bed at the end. A narrow cupboard sat between the foot of the bed and the wall.

A desk and a swivel chair were on the right side of the wall along with a recliner and a row of bookshelves. An entertainment screen was attached to the left wall. A large closet was farther along the same wall.

Looking around, Justin said, "So this is home."

"Yep, this is home," Kyle said. "It isn't big, but for a spacecraft, it's pretty roomy. I know you want to clean up, so we'll go down to Millie's room until you're ready. When you're finished come down. I know Colonel Straight wants to talk to you about our mishap. There are boat shoes, underclothes and jumpsuits in your closet. When you finish dressing, come down to Millie's room. It's four or five doors farther down the hall."

"It smells like paint," Justin remarked as Kyle was leaving.

"It is paint. The walls are made of a carbon fiber which is a dull-gray color. To make it a little more pleasing, they paint the walls. The smell will go away once you begin living here. I'm going to go check on Millie."

"I'll clean up and be right down," Justin noted.

Kyle had just departed when there was a knock on the door. Justin pushed the button thinking it was Kyle who had forgot something, but it was Frank.

"Frank, I'm glad to see you. Isn't this magnificent?" Justin said.

"Yes, it's overwhelming. I can't say the ride up here was that great though." Looking serious, he added, "I heard what happened. Are you all right?"

"A bit shook up and my back is sore, but other than that I'm all right. I haven't had a chance to clean up yet, which I need to do. You're welcome to come in while I shower if you want."

"You know my room is right next door," Frank said as he sat in the swivel chair.

"I know. I saw the sign on your door," Justin replied from the bathroom.

"Justin, do you think someone was trying to kill you and Millie?"

"I don't know about Millie, but I have a bad feeling someone wants Kyle and me out of the way," Justin responded from the shower.

Frank said no more until Justin had finished. He came out with a towel around his middle. He got underclothes and a jumpsuit out of the closet and then went back into the bathroom to dress. He soon came out combing his hair.

He found socks and boat shoes in the closet, which were just his size. "They've done their homework," Justin said, as he put the shoes and socks on.

"Justin, this is serious. Everyone around says the chance of what happened being an accident is impossible. It had to be the work of the Kozenskies."

"That's what Kyle thinks too. Millie and Kyle are waiting for me in her room. I'm supposed to go there as soon as I'm dressed."

"Do you mind if I come along?" Frank asked.

"I don't mind," Justin replied.

They walked down the hall until they found a sign on the door that read MILLIE SYSTER, CHIEF NURSE. He tapped, pushed the button by the door and it opened. Millie was sitting alone in the swivel chair shaking like a leaf.

"Do you really think someone was trying to kill us?" Millie asked as Justin and Frank entered.

"I hope not," Justin responded as he went to stand by her. "But it certainly seems suspicious."

"Hi," Frank said, "you've certainly had an interesting time."

"I'm not sure I'd use the word *interesting* to describe it. *Terrifying* is more like it. I can't believe someone would actually try to kill us. I've never been so scared in my life. What if someone tries to do it again?"

Justin was about to answer when there was a knock on the door. Kyle and another man walked in. Kyle was obviously agitated, and the other man was trying to calm him down. The man with Kyle was tall with a thin dark mustache, black slicked-back hair and dull-gray eyes.

He walked over to Justin, put his hand out, and said with a French accent, "My name's Alex DePaul. I'm the security supervisor with Space Corp." Turning to Frank, he asked, "And you are?"

"This is my friend Chaplin Frank Molony," Justin replied.

"Okay," Mr. DePaul replied. Turning to Justin and Millie, he went on, "First of all, let me apologize for the accident today."

"Accident my ass," Millie replied.

Looking surprised at Millie's remark, Kyle followed up. "She's right! What happened was no accident. DePaul, you know as well as I do someone tried to kill the three of us! Oh by the way, we call Alex by his last name most of the time."

"Kyle, I'm in charge here. So, if you can't remain quiet, you're invited to step out," Mr. DePaul directed.

"Well, as you said, we've never had an accident like this in the four years the train has been under construction."

"That's true, and we're investigating everything. We'll get to the bottom of it. Right now, I need to talk to Mr. LeMoore and Nurse Syster alone." Looking at Kyle and Frank, he said, "Would you mind stepping out?"

"Not at all," Frank replied, as he and Kyle departed. Once they were out of the room, Mr. DePaul turned to Justin and Millie. "Kyle is pretty passionate about what happened."

"Yes, he seems to be fervent about his position when he feels he is right," Justin responded. "Millie and I just met him today. We're sure glad he was there."

"I'm glad he was there too. It was a fluke, because he was supposed to escort two others, but the list was changed at the last minute."

"Yes, Kyle told us. He said someone came down from logistics with the roster change just as we were coming off the shuttle."

Stepping to the door, DePaul said, "Kyle, will you come in?"

"Sure," Kyle replied, walking back in.

"You said someone changed the list of who you were to chaperone. Is that right?"

"Yes, some guy walked up with a clipboard and said something like, 'I was told to give you this. I think it changes who you're supposed to escort.'"

"Do you remember who it was that handed you the new list?" DePaul asked.

"Nope. He was in a space suit and I didn't pay any attention. I just assumed it was somebody from administration."

"A man or a woman," DePaul inquired

"A man. It was definitely a man."

"That might help a little. We're working to determine who made the change," Mr. DePaul said, taking his communicator out and making a call.

After concluding his call, DePaul turned to Kyle, and said, "You can step out again if you don't mind."

As Kyle departed, Mr. DePaul sat back in his chair. He looked at both Justin and Millie and continued. "First of all, I want you to know we are aggressively following every lead. We know tug 1369 was involved in the accident. There are cameras posted around all the cargo corals. As soon as we find the operator, we'll hopefully know what happened."

Producing a small 3-D video recorder, he asked, "I need you to give me a statement with as much detail as you can remember. Would you please go first, Mr. LeMoore?"

Justin said, "I can't tell you much. It all happened so fast. Kyle pushed me, then something hit me in the back and I couldn't breathe.

"You're lucky Kyle was there and was so quick to help you," Mr. DePaul noted.

Millie told her story as she continued to tremble. "We were reading the shipping label. Kyle was explaining how Leif knows where each container is to be stowed. All of a sudden Kyle pushed me and I saw the cargo container coming at us. If Kyle hadn't seen it coming, it would have crushed all three of us. Now I see that container bearing down on me every time I close my eyes."

"I can only imagine how frightening it must have been," Mr. DePaul empathetically replied. "I'm sorry such a thing happened. Do either of you know of anyone who would want to harm you?"

"There's a couple back in Houston who are reported to have orchestrated these kinds of things prior to their incarceration. We haven't exactly seen eye to eye on several issues," Justin replied.

"I assume you're talking about the Kozenskies?" Mr. DePaul asked. "Have they ever actually told you they want to harm you?"

"Not in so many words, but Vidula and I have had some pretty heated exchanges. I'm sure she'd love to get me off the mission. I think I've been an irritation to her. And if she doesn't get her way, she throws a fit. It seems like she's groomed about six or eight fellow prisoners whom she was adamant about being part of the crew. Several of us have been vocal about blocking them because they were unqualified, or not as qualified as others who had applied. Vidula argued unsuccessfully for them to be added to the list."

"I'm familiar with the Kozenskies, especially Vidula," Mr. DePaul noted with a frosty look in his gray eyes.

"How about you, Ms. Syster? Do you know of anyone who'd want to harm you?"

"Like Justin, I've had several arguments with Vidula about some of the people she wants to have on the mission. She wanted me to accept a male nurse assistant that wasn't at all qualified. We had some pretty heated words over him."

Justin, Millie and Mr. DePaul chatted for another half hour. Then DePaul said, "I hope you'll excuse me. I need to go check on several things."

As he was leaving, Colonel Straight came in. "I heard about your mishap. I'm sorry about it. I know Mr. DePaul will aggressively pursue the issue." Then without further conversation, he asked, "I suppose you think the Kozenskies were behind it?"

"Hell yes, we think the Kozenskies were behind it. Who else would be that brazen?" Millie demanded.

Looking at Colonel Straight, Justin replied, "If it wasn't an accident, the Kozenskies certainly seem to be the most logical ones to have coordinated it."

"Neither Vidula nor Ervin are up here, and I don't think they had anything to do with it," Colonel Straight concluded.

"I hope you're right," Justin replied. "If it was an accident, then that's all we can say. If it wasn't, then I don't know of anyone else who would want us gone."

"It wasn't any damn accident, and everyone knows it. And you don't think Vidula and Ervin would be up here when it happened, do you? But you can bet your sweet ass, they set it up," Millie angrily grumbled.

They talked another few minutes, and as Colonel Straight was leaving, he said, "I'll wait for Mr. DePaul to finish his investigation before I make any judgments."

14

The operator of tug 1369 parked his tug in a group of several other tugs and sat quietly for several minutes. He knew he'd failed. He remembered the briefcase of money he'd left Margaret and thought, *At least she and Danny will be well taken care of.*

He took another long pull on his drinking tube and then sat for several minutes letting the alcohol take effect. The man he'd met in the Space Corp restroom before being shuttled up to the train had given him a duffel bag with a bottle of vodka and a pistol in it. Knowing what he'd agreed to do, he extracted the pistol from his suit. He looked at it for a moment, then with one swift movement placed the barrel to his helmet and pulled the trigger. The bullet shattered the plastic and went through his brain. With the helmet's integrity breached, the vacuum of space made his head burst.

Not long afterward, a security patrol found the tug with the operator's lifeless body still strapped inside.

The secure communication device rang in the Kozenskies' quarters. Vidula hurried to grab it. Just one word was spoken. "Down."

That was the prearranged code for failure. Although upset, Vidula never said a word and did not respond. She simply pushed the red button canceling the call and placed the phone back on the table.

"What was that?" Ervin asked.

"Nothing," Vidula responded. "It must have been a wrong number." Ervin saw an almost-imperceptible shadow cross his wife's face and knew she'd been up to something. Since Milton Slusser was supposed to be the only other person who had the code to their encrypted communicator, how could there be a wrong number?

Several hours later, he insisted on watching the news. A special report came on about an accident at the space train assembly site.

The narrator stated: A cargo container got away from a tug and almost crushed three of the space train crew who will be on the upcoming New World mission. Mr. Kyle Williams, a communication worker with Space Corp; Ms. Millie Syster, a nurse with the mission medical team; and Mr. Justin LeMoore, the mission mental health coordinator were all involved in the accident. The mishap is the first major accident reported at the space train assembly site in its four years of construction. There seems to be a mystery associated with the accident which is being investigated. The tug operator who was involved in the incident was found dead in his space tug, having shot himself.

Ervin looked at his wife, and said, "You arranged this, didn't you?"

"Now darling," Vidula countered, "something had to be done. Milton and the congressman weren't going to take any action."

"Vidula!" Ervin exploded, "we agreed not to attempt anything that could compromise our chance to be a part of the mission. I've found what we need. The opportunity we've dreamed of will be ours."

"Nothing can be traced back to us. It was washed between at least a dozen operators and none of them knew where the original order came from."

"To hell they can't! The last time you pulled a stunt like this, you also guaranteed it couldn't be traced. But it was! That's what landed us where we are today. You have got to back off! Neither Justin nor Kyle are worth risking our dream over. When the time comes, we can cull out anyone who isn't an asset to our future. Just have patience and it'll all come together. But if you keep bullying people, or trying to eliminate everyone you don't like, our house of cards will come tumbling down."

"Oh, darling, we're smarter than anyone on this entire project. But if it will make you feel better, I'll mind my own business. I'm just trying to eliminate roadblocks to our success."

Turning away, she told herself, *And the next time I'll make it happen.*

"What do you mean?" Mr. DePaul shouted. "The operator got up here somehow?" He picked up the operator's identification badge, which had been removed from the body and turned it over and over in his hand.

It seemed to be genuine. It had a retina chip in it. But they were finding even that could be breached. To avoid counterfeit badges being made, every identification card was given a specific code. Even the operator didn't know what the code was.

"I want to see the body," he bellowed.

"That isn't going to do any good," his colleague said. "When his helmet was punctured by the bullet, his head exploded. What you can see isn't a very pretty sight. It's almost impossible to recognize anything. The only way of verifying the body is the same person as on the identification badge will be from dental records and DNA."

"Then I want to see his dental records and have his DNA checked," Mr. DePaul shouted. "Have x-rays taken and match them with the records from the person on the badge. The cardholder's DNA should also be on record. In addition, check to see if he had contact lenses. That may be how he got through the retina scan."

Giving his colleagues a hard look, he continued, "I want that information within the hour. Do you understand?"

Within thirty minutes, the results were back. Mr. DePaul was in his office looking at the security films of the shuttle crew leaving for work earlier in the day. At a quick glance the operator looked like the person on the badge. He had the same hairstyle, same beard, same color of eyes and about the same height. We looked to see if he had contact lenses and found none. If he used contacts to get past the retina check, he'd already taken them out before he died.

One of DePaul's security men rushed in and reported, "The tug operator was not the same person as on the identification badge. Neither his dental records nor DNA match. I also just received word the worker who owned the badge was found dead."

"That doesn't surprise me. I've been reviewing the security tapes myself. If you look carefully, the tug operator was not the person on the badge," DePaul said, holding the badge up. "This was a carefully planned professional hit. From now on I want a retina scan and a DNA check on every person who comes up to the assembly site. And have every person checked for contacts. I also want to know everything about the dead tug operator. Who he was? Has he worked here before? Where is he from? Is he married? Does he have an alcohol or drug history? I want to know everything."

"Yes, sir," his colleague replied. "But I have a bad feeling we're going to run into a brick wall. As you said, this was a professional job and professionals don't leave trails."

"I don't care what it takes, I want every stone turned over, and I don't want it to take very long either. Give me a report on your progress at least every hour."

"Are you up to another tour?" Kyle asked Justin and Millie at breakfast the following morning.

"Sure," Justin replied. "I doubt lightning will strike the same place twice. I heard they found the tug operator and he'd committed suicide. Is that true?"

"Yes. DePaul told me earlier this morning. It seems to have been a professional operation. The original operator was also found dead. His ID had been stolen. Then they, whoever they were, found someone who closely resembled the person on the badge. The fake operator was able to come up with the other workers. They are trying to determine if the dead tug operator had worked here before. He seemed to know what he was doing. If you're still up to a tour, we can start up at the command area," Kyle said.

All three got up from the breakfast table and Kyle led them toward the command area.

Two men fell in behind them, and Justin asked, "Who are they?"

"A couple of DePaul's boys. Don't pay any attention to them. They'll just tag along," Kyle noted.

The command car was two cars in front of the dining car. They had to go through the living quarter's car, up to the top floor, then through several corridors to reach it. Colonel Straight, Colonel Forrester and Captain Quest's quarters were all just outside the command suite. They walked through a sliding door into a large room. There was a maze of computer screens, dials, handles, knobs and an entire bank of multicolored communicators.

No one was on the bridge, so Kyle led them to the front. He walked over to a dark windshield, which was like looking into a black well. He pushed a button and a screen parted in the middle, retracting into the walls on each side.

"We didn't get to see the command car from the front. It's shaped like a wedge. The front, to include the windshield, is designed and reinforced to deflect meteors and other space debris up to the size of a small car. The front window is eight inches thick of tempered glass and ground so there is no distortion. Like the other cars, the walls are made of a composition material eighteen inches thick. The train also has long-range sensors which can detect objects several million miles away. That allows the command crew to take evasive action if necessary," Kyle said.

"It doesn't seem like a train this big would be very maneuverable," Justin noted.

"It isn't," Kyle responded. "That's why we need to know what's out there, especially when we're traveling faster than the speed of light. Even at that speed, a small tweak can change the course enough to miss pretty large objects.

"Our last defenses are two cannons. They can shoot a nitro mass over a million miles away in the vacuum of space. They can blast a rock the size of a large building into sand. They'd rather not use the cannons, but it's comforting to know they are there."

"Now that's what I call coyote hunting," Justin said with a laugh.

Kyle didn't know how to react to Justin's comment about coyote hunting so he just ignored it. "I know this place looks overwhelming, but most of what it takes to keep the train operating correctly is computerized. The various stuff you see here would only be used in case of a computer failure."

As they departed the command car, Justin asked, "Out of curiosity, where do all the construction employees live while they're up here working?"

"The first logistic car has been fitted with removable walls making two-person rooms. There are male and female restrooms and showers for every hallway. Normally workers spend about two weeks at a time up here. They work twelve hours on and twelve hours off. There are workout, recreation, movie rooms and other places like a library where workers can relax. We'll walk through all of them," Kyle noted.

As they were walking down one of the gray metal corridors, a man approached, and said, "I assume these are the two who were with you when that container got away yesterday."

"That container didn't just get away," Kyle indignantly stated. "It was deliberately pushed at us."

"Yes, I talked to DePaul this morning. Sounds like it was well planned. What have you done to warrant something like that?" Matt asked.

"What do you think? We all have challenged the Kozenskies. Oh, by the way, this is Justin LeMoore, the mental health coordinator, and Ms. Millie Syster, the chief nurse for the female cryogenic ward."

Then indicating to the other person, Kyle said, "This is Mr. Matt Alton. He's the life-support engineer. Matt keeps all the life-support equipment going from the oxygen generation units, water, heating and cooling systems."

"Yes, I remember both of you from the train briefing we gave to the crew. I'm glad to see you again," Matt said, extending his hand.

"Likewise," both Justin and Millie replied.

After shaking hands, they again began walking down the brightly lit corridor.

As they walked, Justin said, "Kyle mentioned water. I'm curious. Will the train be able to carry enough water for the entire mission?"

"Yes and no," Matt replied. "The living quarters and dining facility car have several tanks with a combined capacity of over a million gallons. The other cars, which only have small restrooms or showers, have smaller tanks. I'm sure you're aware that water's main components are hydrogen and oxygen. Those two components are among the most abundant elements in the universe. We think of space as being void of water, but did you know in 2011 a gigantic cloud of water vapor was discovered with one-hundred-and-forty trillion times more water than all of Earth's oceans combined?" Matt asked.

"No, I didn't. That's interesting," Justin returned.

"It is interesting," Matt replied. "Each car with a restroom or other water requirements has a generation unit that can harvest hydrogen and oxygen as we go. We lose some water all the time through evaporation, so we must continually add water to make sure we have enough for our needs. Our waste water is recirculated back into potable water."

"You mean we're drinking reconditioned sewer water? Hell, that's appetizing," Millie said.

"I guess you could say that. But then we do the same thing on Earth. We call it the hydrologic cycle. I'm sure you're familiar with the process. It's the continuous exchange of water within the atmosphere and the Earth's surface. Water evaporates from the Earth's surface, which could even come from sewer ponds. Purification takes place as the water evaporates, leaving the impurities behind. We're able to do the same thing on the train. It's a bit more complicated, but the simple explanation is that each car that requires water has a regeneration unit. Used water goes into an evaporation tank where it's heated and the steam is turned back into potable water. The solids that remain are discharged into space." Matt said.

"So we're not only drinking sewer water, but we're also polluting space. Right?" Millie asked.

"What we discharge into space is so minuscule it won't matter much. Hey, I've got to run. I told Leif I'd help him this morning. It was nice seeing you both again and I hope you don't have any more mishaps," Matt said.

They walked back to the crew quarters car and took an elevator down one floor to the prisoner crew quarters. The rooms there were about the same size as Justin's, but each would house two prisoners.

Each had a bathroom and two single beds with a clothes locker on each wall. There was also a small desk, two chairs and an entertainment screen on one wall.

Taking another elevator back up to the top floor, Kyle took them back to the dining facility. Although they'd eaten there, he wanted them to see the kitchen. It was huge and as well-equipped as a middle-sized restaurant.

"We've used this large eating area to feed the construction crew for well over a year now. The space has also been handy for meetings, parties and other activities. The kitchen will be downsized and completely refurbished before the mission starts. As of now, we plan to leave the eating space as is. Although larger than we will need, it will also be handy for parties and meetings," Kyle said.

They then toured the medical clinic. This time it looked different to Justin. It was bright, clean and neat. It looked efficient. It had two doctors' offices, a nursing station, two examining rooms, a room with diagnostic and other equipment and four treatment rooms. As they were looking, Dr. Francis came in.

"How are you feeling, Justin?"

"I'm feeling fine. My back is a little sore, but other than that I feel great."

"I'm glad. It could have turned out much worse if they hadn't got to you so quickly," Dr. Francis said.

"Yes, I'm sure you're right. As I said before, I'm glad Kyle was there."

"I'm taking Justin and Millie on a tour of the train," Kyle noted.

"That's great. I need to run. I'm due for a meeting with Colonel Straight in about two minutes," Dr. Francis said.

Justin thanked Dr. Francis again.

Then as they left the medical clinic, Kyle said, "My favorite place is the library."

Both Justin and Millie were impressed how bright the corridors were. There were lights every fifteen or twenty feet. They were so bright they cast shadows. The library was also large and bright with about twenty reading devices. Many were occupied, and Kyle noted, "With these reading devices we can access almost every book ever printed."

Walking toward the back, they found a movie room. "Our movie system has several-thousand movies on demand."

Then off to one side there were six cubicles where one to four people could watch a movie in private.

They made their way to the exercise facility, which was down one level. It was also well equipped and several men and women were using the various machines. Apparently, the news of the accident had spread, as everyone stared at the threesome and the two men following them. Just off the exercise room were male and female saunas and two whirlpools. All were in use.

There was a full-size gym with a basketball court, two handball courts and two bowling lanes. Kyle laughingly said, "If you're bored here, it's your own fault."

Not far from the gym was a small chapel. It looked like it would hold about twenty people. It also had different-illuminated fake stained glass windows. One had the Ten Commandments, one had a menorah and there was one with a Koran. There was even one with a picture of John the Baptist baptizing Christ.

"We have Catholics, several Baptists, a few Jews and at least one Muslim," Kyle said. "I can't remember what faith you are."

"I belong to the Church of Jesus Christ of Latter Day Saints. Some people call us Mormons," Justin replied.

"Oh, no. What special requirement do you have in architecture or symbols?"

"None. This room will do very well."

"Don't you have a gold book or something?" Kyle asked.

"We have the Book of Mormon. It was translated from gold plates, but we don't have any special requirements. And we don't need a fake stained glass window."

"That's a relief. We don't want to put any more windows in if we don't have to. How about you, Millie?" Kyle asked.

"God and I don't talk very much, so I'm kind of everything. My family was Baptist, but I couldn't get into all the preaching and Bible thumping. I haven't found any denomination that I'm all that comfortable with," Millie responded.

"Great, that makes it easy. You'll like the next place I'm going to show you. The entire car is devoted to food. The bottom floor is a giant freezer. The middle floor is a world-class greenhouse. Dr. Hochstrasser is already growing all kinds of vegetables. The top floor is a nonperishable storage area," Kyle said.

"I imagine this car was a comfort to Frank," Justin remarked.

Kyle gave Justin a curious look.

"Frank is the chaplain. Food is important to him. One of his biggest concerns about the mission was what kind of food we'd be eating," Justin said.

"He should be happy then. Not only do we have all kinds of frozen food, but as I said, Dr. Hockstrasser is already growing fresh vegetables and even fruit in the greenhouse. I'll show you. It's just one floor down."

They went down a set of stairs to the middle floor. When they exited the stairwell, they were in a large open area. There were dozens of tables. Each table was about twenty feet long with eight-inch sides and hanging lights above them. There were also areas on the floor with eighteen-inch walls with fruit trees growing in them.

"Dr. Hockstrasser can grow just about anything in here," Kyle said.

He then led them to an area with rows of shelves with glass containers sitting on pyramid-shaped racks. "This is the hydroponic area where tomatoes and other vegetables can be grown. Dr. Hockstrasser will be coming back in the next few days to stay. He's currently on Earth purchasing more seeds and transplants he wants to take."

After finishing the tour, Justin and Millie went to their rooms to freshen up. They had lunch with the other members of the crew, and of course everyone wanted to know from the horse's mouth what had happened with Justin, Kyle and Millie. As they were talking, Mr. DePaul walked in.

After listening for a few minutes, he said, "So far nothing has turned up. Colonel Straight and Mr. Harris feel until the investigation is complete, you all could still be at risk. As a result, we've been informed you will be leaving tomorrow morning."

There was a collective groan from the group. Everyone was disappointed. Some even suggested if Justin left, they didn't think there would be any further problem.

"We don't want to take any chances. You have had a good look at the train and seen your quarters, which was the goal of the visit. Until the investigation is complete, we feel it would be safer to have you back on Earth. You have the afternoon to yourselves. You're welcome to use any of the recreation facilities or just wander the train," DePaul responded.

Since the afternoon was open, Millie, Frank and Justin roamed through the train looking at everything, with the two security men following. After dinner, Kyle asked if he could chat with Millie and Justin in private.

"Of course," they both said and walked to Justin's room. When the door was closed, Kyle sat in the swivel chair, Millie in the recliner and Justin on the edge of the bed.

"I don't want to frighten you, but I think we could be in trouble. I don't know how they managed to pull it off, but over the last two months, Vidula has almost rebuilt the main computer. My concern is that many of the programs have been encrypted. In both the men's and women's cryogenic wards, Vidula has had computer units installed as big as refrigerators. I can't help but be suspicious. I've almost been cut out of seeing the blueprints or having anything to do with the installation. I don't understand why there are so many secrets. I can't tell you what to do, but if I didn't have so much invested in the project, I'd bail out.

"On top of that is the so-called accident we experienced. Don't get me wrong, I trust DePaul explicitly. But he isn't going to find anything, even though we all know who orchestrated the attempt on our lives," Kyle said.

They talked well past midnight and all three explored resigning. In the end though, none of them wanted to give up. They decided the best thing was for everyone to watch, listen and keep one another informed. Justin knew Frank would agree, and there were several others who'd also do the same.

Kyle finally said he was tired. Kyle left first, and then Millie followed.

When she got to the door, she turned, saying, "Justin, we've both been through a rough couple of days. I know you're pretty straight arrow, but if you need, well, you know, something to help you relax, I'd be glad to stay."

"Millie, you're a dear friend and I love you like a sister. Let's not complicate our relationship with something else."

"I figured you'd say that, but just thought I'd offer. If you change your mind, please let me know." With that she left, closing the door behind her.

The next morning, Justin was at the dining facility when Millie arrived. He was sitting alone, and after getting some toast and coffee, she sat down.

Looking at him, she said, "Justin, I'm sorry for last night. I was out of line."

"It's all right, little sister," Justin said, giving her a smile and a pat on her hand.

"Are you ready to go back?" she asked.

"I am. This has been an interesting couple of days, but we've seen the train and I'm ready to return. I've got a lot of things to do and there isn't much more to be seen here."

The crew had been informed they were to be at car nineteen at 0900 to suit up. Kyle didn't show up for breakfast. After eating, Justin and Millie returned to their quarters and packed the few things they'd brought. When they arrived at the suit-up area, Kyle was there waiting for them.

"I just came from DePaul's office to see what he'd learned, which is nothing. Like we already knew the tug operator acquired someone else's ID and came up to do just what he did. Now that he's dead, the chance of finding who hired him is going to be slim to none. As we know, someone changed the chaperone list so you'd be with me and that's still a mystery. I'm going to stay on DePaul and if I find anything out, I'll let you know."

"Thanks," both Justin and Millie said in unison. They both liked Kyle.

Justin was given a new body garment before the team suited up. Once everyone was in their suits, they boarded an empty shuttle and were buckled into their seats. The shuttle was freed from the train and it moved away as if in slow motion.

After receiving clearance from Houston control, they glided into a lower orbit and then into the atmosphere. The shuttle began making long turns and at first it was almost soundless. It didn't take long before a small vibration started to be noticeable. Then as they descended farther there was a slight noise which increased until it was a loud screaming howl. There was a smell like something hot, but as Justin looked around, as best as he could, the crew didn't seem alarmed. He took a deep breath, sat back and thought about all that had happened over the past two days.

Although there were no windows to see how close to Earth they were, after about thirty minutes the shuttle seemed to level out and slow down. They heard the landing gear descending and knew they must be near. After a few minutes more, the craft nosed up, the tires screamed and they were back on Earth.

"Welcome back to Earth folks," the captain said. "I understand the trip was pretty exciting for a couple of you. On behalf of Space Corp, let me apologize for the accident. We're always concerned with safety. Hopefully, another such incident will never happen again."

Mr. Harris was waiting for them when they arrived. He

welcomed everyone back, and asked, "What did you all think about your visit?"

Someone yelled, "Ask Justin and Millie. They had the most fun."

"I want to hear about their fun, as you call it, but I'd like to hear what the rest of you think about the train."

Comments like "overwhelming," "mind-boggling," "like a religious experience," "spectacular," "wonderful," and several other positive adjectives were tossed out. After some discussion, Mr. Harris dismissed the rest of the team but asked Justin and Millie to remain for a few minutes.

"I've talked to Kyle and Alex DePaul several times. They're both convinced the Kozenskies were behind the incident. Both Vidula and Ervin have been questioned, but of course neither said they knew anything about it."

"It wasn't an incident. It was an attempt on our lives," Millie indignantly stated.

"Whatever it was, you'll never get anything out of the Kozenskies. If they arranged it, they'd have covered their tracks so no one could implicate them. From what I've heard, they're experts at this kind of thing," Justin caustically said.

"I fear you're right. All I can tell you, is if I can find so much as a thread of evidence, they'll be off the mission."

"Forget it," Justin repled. "It's a waste of your time to even look."

"I am not giving up, but from everything I'm hearing, it was a well-planned job." Looking at Justin, he asked, "Not to change the subject, but can you meet with me and Frank tomorrow morning? We need to coordinate some time off for the two of you before we start the final preparations. I'd like to give you both a month off, but I'm afraid it may only be a couple of weeks each. I assume you'd like to go back to Wyoming and see if you can catch that big fish again."

"I'd like one more crack at the lunker, but I doubt I'll get there. I'll go up to Colorado and say good-bye to my sister and her family, then on to Kansas to see Ted and his family. Barring any weather problems, I think I can accomplish what I need to do in two weeks," Justin remarked.

"I appreciate your willingness to work with me."

"I'll see you in the morning," Justin agreed.

Next morning, Frank and Justin walked to Mr. Harris's quarters where he cooked breakfast to Franz Schubert's Symphony no. 5 in B-flat Major. They decided Justin would take the first two weeks and Frank would go when he returned. Mr. Harris said not to say anything about when they were leaving or where they were going.

"You're too late," Justin laughed. "Before I left, one of the prisoners said she'd heard we were going to get some time off after visiting the train."

"You really don't think anyone would try something again, do you?" Frank asked.

"I doubt it," Mr. Harris said almost under his breath. "I don't want to take any chances though. I fear we're dealing with people who will go to any length to accomplish what they're after."

Thinking this would be a good time to solidify the issue of taking guns on the mission, Justin said, "When I signed on, I asked if I could take a few guns along. I hope that still stands," Justin asked.

"A few? As I remember, you asked if you could take a gun," Mr. Harris said.

"Naw, I'm sure I specifically said 'a few.' I need a shotgun for birds, a large-caliber gun for big animals and a small-caliber rifle for small game," Justin replied.

"So exactly how many are a few?" Mr. Harris asked.

"Well sir, I can't rightly say until I've thought it through and looked at the guns I have."

"We are in agreement that if you take 'a few guns', you'll put them in the arms room and, you won't have access to them until your arrival at the New World?" Mr. Harris inquired.

"Absolutely. I won't touch them until we land."

"I'll contact Leif and let him know you'll be bringing 'a few' guns. When you return, call him. He'll be expecting you and will help you get them onto the train. Don't tell anyone about this. The only ones who need to know is you, me, Leif and I guess Frank since he's sitting here. Are we agreed?"

"Absolutely. I won't tell anyone," Justin said.

Justin worked hard for the next three days seeing as many prisoner couples as possible and ensuring everything was still on track"

He spent the evenings with the Garzas and several prisoners working in the gardens. Justin was always impressed with Rolando, and as they worked, he asked, "Are you still going to medical school this fall?"

With obvious pride, Rolando said, "Yes, sir. I'll be going to the University of Texas Medical School starting in September. I've spent the summer saving money to buy a truck and for my tuition. Uncle Caesar is helping me build an equipment trailer. When I go to Austin I'm going to set up my own landscaping business to help make money. He's going to give me a mower, power rake and some hand tools to get me started. We've been doing lawns before coming to work here every morning, so I'll know what I'm doing."

Justin was shocked. "You do lawns before coming to work here? What time do you do those?"

"I get up at 3:00 AM so I can get everything ready and be on the job by 4:30 or 5:00 AM, depending on how far I have to drive. I'm using Uncle Caesar's truck, so after I do a lawn or two, I go back home. By then he's up, we have breakfast and then drive here to work. After work we can usually take care of two more yards. It doesn't get dark until almost 10:00 PM."

Justin was amazed. "When do you relax, chase girls or just have fun?"

"I can't afford girls or fun right now. Maybe after medical school I'll have time for those things," Rolando replied.

"How much will it cost for school?"

"About $150,000 a year. And that's cheap. That's why I'm going to the University of Texas. I can get in-state tuition. If I went to an out-of-state university, it could cost as much as $300,000 a year."

"I don't want to be intrusive, but may I ask how much you've saved up?" Justin asked.

"Not enough," Rolando gloomily responded. "As I said, Uncle Caesar will help me, and I can get a student loan. Although I don't want to take out a loan if I can help it. I don't mind working hard for what I get."

"What kind of a doctor do you want to be?"

"A family practice doctor. I plan to work in the poor areas of Houston. I'd like to work with families who can't afford medical care. I watched both of my parents die from the lack of medical care. My father was a farm laborer and couldn't afford medical insurance. He was helping load large boxes of cabbage on a farm when one of them slipped off a forklift and crushed him. The farmer refused to pay anything. He laid at home suffering for more than two weeks before he died.

"After that, Mother tried to take care of herself and me by working eighteen hours a day at two different jobs. Even then we still just got by. She worked in a laundry during the day and then cleaned houses in the evenings. She'd only get two or three hours of sleep at night. I think it was the fumes from the laundry that killed her. She died from some kind of lung problem. I was only seven. That's when I came to live with Uncle Caesar and Aunt Ester. They didn't have any kids so I've really been raised by them. I owe them a lot."

"Wow, you've had a hard life. I admire you for what you're doing," Justin replied.

15

Justin left before dawn and was well out of Houston heading west toward San Antonio on Interstate 10 when the sun came up. He hoped to arrive in Amarillo by the end of the first day. It would be a long day, but he was sure he could do it.

As he traveled west, it was as if a weight had been lifted from him. He was alive again, there was open space and he was relaxed—more relaxed than he'd been in several months. Although later in the day it would be hot, the morning air was relatively cool and smelled like sage.

He found a classical radio station and lowered the window in the cab of the truck. The wind was refreshing on his face. To look for miles in any direction was more than a treat. For the past months, he'd been cooped up and engrossed in a new environment, making new friends and with what seemed like constant emotional confrontations. And then there was Ms. Cynthia Wong.

He drove around the outskirts of San Antonio to Highway 83 north, then took Highway 87 toward Lubbock. The hours gave him time to think and his mind returned to Ms. Wong.

Why do I automatically keep returning to her in my mind? He couldn't deny his attraction to her, but he'd vowed to remain professional. Although that was even a farce. Every time he saw her, his heart raced and he felt like a schoolboy with his first secret crush on a girl.

The Kozenskies were also difficult to push out of his mind. As was the attempt on his life. In addition, Rolando's willingness to work eighteen hours a day to get to school intrigued him.

Just past Lubbock he was shocked to see a thin dark line on the horizon. He found a news station and the newsman was warning everyone between Lubbock and Amarillo to be on the alert for a large dangerous dust storm. He intently watched the line as he got closer. It seemed to be alive—rolling, tumbling and twisting. It looked like a dark demonic monster.

He watched it as it got closer and his stomach tightened. As he drove into the orange-gray maelstrom, the truck shuddered and lurched. It was like wrestling a bull to keep it on the road and his visibility was reduced to less than a hundred feet. He put the windshield wipers on and tried the washers. That just turned the dust to mud. The howling wind was blasting tumbleweeds, sticks and gravel into the truck.

Due to the lack of visibility, he had to reduce his speed to less than twenty miles an hour. His biggest fear was running into someone else, or being rear-ended himself.

His fear was realized when he almost ran into a car that was stopped partially in his lane and partially in the oncoming lane. He screeched to a stop and at first was irritated.

What idiot would park like that? He asked himself.

There was someone in the car, but he or she wasn't moving. He forced his door open and was instantly assaulted by the wind and dust. He made his way to the car and found a young woman with her head bowed and her hands clenched to the steering wheel. He had to tap on the window several times before she acknowledged him. Finally she turned; her face was white. She was crying. The window lowered about an inch and he could also hear children crying from the rear seat.

Looking in, he asked, "Ma'am, are you all right?"

"I can't do it," she wailed. "My father was killed in a dust storm like this. He was hit by a semi-truck. I just can't do it."

Looking more closely, he could see two small girls. Both were crying at the top of their lungs.

"I know we're all going to die," the woman sobbed.

Almost unable to speak for the dust in his nose and mouth, Justin croaked out, "No, we're not going to die. Put your headlights and emergency flashers on. I'll pull ahead of you with my flashers on. Follow me. But watch closely in case I have to suddenly stop. Can you do that?"

"I don't know. I'll try," she responded with tears still running down her cheeks.

Justin returned to his truck. His mouth, nose, ears and eyes were packed with dust. His hair was stiff and his clothes were covered with sand. He drank a mouthful of water, then spit it out trying to rinse the grit out. It didn't do much good. He sat for several additional moments trying to clear the sand out of his nose and eyes before he could see enough to drive.

When he could see, he slowly pulled ahead of the woman and watched to make sure she was following. For thirty minutes, they slowly drove through the dark swirling dust. Several times they passed cars off to the side of the road. One time a car traveling in the opposite direction almost ran into him. Another thirty minutes passed before they came to another car off on the side of the road.

Justin was going to pass it by, but as they neared a woman quickly stepped out and frantically waved. Justin stopped as the wind whipped her dress and hair. He lowered his window and the woman screamed, "My husband has emphysema. He can't breathe."

Justin quickly got out and followed the woman to their car. Her husband was sitting in the passenger seat with an oxygen mask on. He was blue and gasping for breath.

"The oxygen in his tank has run out," she yelled above the wind.

"Do you have another one," Justin yelled back.

"Yes, in the trunk, but I can't lift it," she cried.

"Pop the trunk and I'll get it out."

She did so and Justin quickly got it out. He carried the tank around to the front of the car, opened the passenger door and helped her hook it up.

"Thank you," she yelled.

"Turn your headlights and emergency flashers on. Then follow the car behind me," Justin instructed.

The woman nodded her head as she ducked and got back into her car.

Justin got back into his truck and as before, it took all he could do to keep it on the road. Suddenly there was a warning beep alerting him that his engine temperature was climbing. He and the two cars behind pulled over. Quickly running back, he informed the two cars his truck was overheating.

"I'm sure my cooling system is plugged. I'll try to clean it out."

He had to lean into the wind to stand up as he moved to the front of the truck. He carefully opened the hood so it wouldn't blow away. He found the front grill and cooling system crammed with tumbleweeds, sticks and dirt. He pulled as much out as he could, but his cooling radiator was chock full. He knew he wouldn't be able to go very far before having to find someone to clean the system. Checking his GPS, the closest town was Corner, Texas, about fifty miles away.

He had to turn the air-conditioner off, and even with that the temperature gauge was in the red. To make matters worse, he couldn't roll the windows down. The cab of the truck was stifling hot. He pulled out with the two cars following and nursed the truck along for another hour. As they drove north the wind finally began to slow. It was still blowing but had diminished enough so they could see a block or more ahead. Justin was concerned about the temperature gauge and was relieved when fifty minutes later they came to a sign that read CORNER, TWO MILES.

Within a minute or so, they came to another sign that read,

CORNER

POPULATION 3,500

ELEVATION 728

There was a small cluster of houses and buildings in the distance. Although what he could see didn't look like much.

He pulled over and both cars followed. He got out of the truck and went back to the woman with the two little girls. They were both now asleep. "I can't thank you enough. When you found me, I was praying for someone to help. I think you were sent to do just that," she said.

"I'm glad I could help. Are you going on?"

"Yes, I need to get home. My husband will be worried."

"Drive carefully," he said as she pulled out.

He next checked on the elderly couple and the woman said, "My husband is doing much better. We live in Amarillo so we're going to push on. You'd be welcome to stay at our home for the night."

"Thanks, but I need to see if there's someone who can clean my cooling system here in Corner. If I can't find anyone, I'll have to go on to Amarillo. If I do, I'll call you."

"Please do. We'd love to have you stay with us. I don't know what I'd have done if you hadn't stopped."

They exchanged contact information and the couple departed.

As he entered the town, he saw an elderly man walking along a sidewalk, holding on to his hat. He stopped alongside of him, lowered his window and the man looked up.

"Excuse me sir, I'm looking for someone who can clean my cooling system. Is there anyone here in Corner who can do that?"

The old man had a face like wrinkled shoe leather. He flashed a friendly smile, and said, "Burt can do it." His hands were large, gnarled and looked like they'd worked hard for many years.

"You can't miss his place. It's 'bout two miles or so down this here road," he said, pointing in the direction he should go. "The road ain't paved, so it's a might dusty. You can't miss it though. It's a big metal shed with a few cars parked around it. The place don't look like much, but Burt's honest and knows what he's doing. Tell him Wilbur sent you. That's my name, Wilbur Jenkins. He knows me. You tell him Wilbur sent you."

"Thank you sir," Justin said. Then making conversation, he continued, "That was quite a dust storm."

"Oh shucks, that weren't nothing. You should've been here in '53. Blew like that for three weeks straight. We had to wear wet rags around our nose and mouth just to breathe. It made dust drifts more'n six feet high. Buried whole herds of cattle."

Then looking at the sky, he continued, "Looks like it's about blowed out. Go see Burt, he'll take care of ya."

Justin thanked the man for the advice and drove west in the direction he had indicated. He'd only gone a couple of miles when he came to what could only be Burt's garage. There were about a hundred cars parked in a large field. They looked like wherever they'd stopped is where they'd been left. Some were facing one way, some the other. Some were up on blocks and most had their hoods and trunks open.

As Justin neared, he saw a line of cars along the road with

several people standing in a cluster. Justin parked at the back of the line, walked over to the group, and asked, "Is this Burt's garage?"

"If you can call it that," a man with New York license plates sarcastically said. "Actually, I think it's just a damn junk yard. I hope he knows what he's doing."

"Are you all waiting to have your cooling systems cleaned?" Justin asked.

"Yes," several responded at the same time.

"Wish I could get to Amarillo where there is a real shop. I don't think I could make it though. My car was hotter than a firecracker," another man replied.

"Yes, and I was told he's the only mechanic in town," a lady chimed in.

"I was told the same thing," Justin confirmed. "Is that old tin building his shop?"

"Yep, that's it. And the inside looks the same as the outside. It's almost impossible to get into it for the junk. I don't see how he has room to work," a man angrily commented.

"I guess I'd better go get my name on the list. Thanks for the information," Justin said, as he walked toward the building.

On the way, he noticed a shabby lean-to tucked up alongside the shop with a sign that read, OFFICE.

He walked around the tin building into what looked like a dark, door-less cave. As he entered, he was immediately accosted by the smell of diesel, rancid grease, coolant and dust. The light coming through the only window showed dust swirling around and settling on everything. He had to walk sideways to get past the piles of cooling parts, rusty axles, greasy motors and other assorted parts.

He saw someone in old greasy coveralls draped over the fender of a car, so he walked in that direction. The person was grunting and groaning. He also had a vocabulary much like Millie's, only worse. The voice sounded like a man, so he said, "Excuse me sir. Are you Burt?"

"Yeah, that's me," the man replied without looking up.

Justin took a step closer. All he could see was a greasy hat with strands of gray hair escaping from under it.

"I just met a man up town by the name of Wilbur Jenkins. He said you might be able to help me. The cooling system in my truck got plugged up in the dust storm. Now it's overheating."

"Wilbur Jenkins! Is that old coot still around? He's a rancher. Been around here for more than eighty years. I heard he retired," the voice said, discharging another volley of cuss words. "What kind of outfit you say ya got?"

"It's a Dodge pickup."

"Got one of them damn new-fangled carbon motors in it?" the voice asked.

"Yes, sir. It's never given me any trouble until this happened. I think the dust storm plugged it up. I hope it hasn't damaged the motor from the heat."

"Hate them damn motors. Ya gotta be a contortionist to work on one. I'm gettin' too old for that stuff. You know there are lots of other folks ahead of you. Won't be able to get at it 'til tomorrow morning."

"I can see you're busy. Tomorrow morning will be fine. Do you want me to move the truck?"

"Where is it?"

"Out on the road."

"Naw, it'll be okay there. Go to the office. It's around the side.

You can pay my wife. She keeps the books. It'll cost four hundred dollars and I need payment up front. You can leave the keys with her. I'll move it when I can get to it."

"My luggage is in the front. Will it be all right?"

"It'll be fine. Nobody'll bother it."

"Okay, thanks," Justin replied. He went around the side of the building to the lean-to. He gingerly opened a squeaky, gray, paint-chipped door and took a step inside. A large woman was sitting behind a plywood counter with a fan blowing on her. She had a stack of papers which was held down by a red brick. The papers were all flapping like birds trying to escape.

"I spoke to your husband about cleaning the cooling system on my truck."

"We always do a brisk business after a blow," she said. "You know there's about a dozen people ahead of you. Did he say when he'd be able to get at it?"

"Not until tomorrow morning. He told me to pay you and leave the keys."

"He say how much it'll cost?" she asked.

"He said four hundred dollars" Justin replied, getting his wallet out.

"That's about right. Damn, it's hot. It's always hotter than hell after a blow. Supposed to rain tonight though. That always helps a little."

"Are you aware of a motel within walking distance?"

"Yeah, the Corner Motel, if it ain't filled up. There's only one motel in town. Burt's sister runs it. Go back up the road and when you get to town, take your first left. You'll be able to see it from the corner. There are a couple of bigger ones outside of town toward Willie Nelson's place. Be a long walk to go clear out there though."

"Thanks. I'll try the Corner Motel first."

Justin went to his truck and retrieved his overnight bag. He'd just started walking when an old rusty, beat-up Ford truck pulled up. The truck was so covered with dust Justin couldn't see what color it was. The fenders had big rust spots which showed clear through to the bed. Looking into the truck, Justin saw a boy with the happiest face he'd seen in a long time. The boy rolled the window down as he continued to smile.

"You wanna a ride to town?" he asked.

"That would be great," Justin responded, noting the boy looked to be about fifteen and had Down's syndrome.

The driver said, "Come on Little Toad, slide on over here so the man can get in."

The boy opened the door and slid to the middle. Justin got in and the man said, "They call me Toad." And he extended his hand. "They call this guy Little Toad."

"That's an interesting name," Justin remarked.

"It's a nickname. Everybody around here has a nickname."

"How did you come to be called Toad?" Justin asked.

"When I was a boy, I had several warts on my hands, so the kids started calling me toad. It just stuck, so that's what everybody calls me."

"My real name is Dickson Franklin Schmidt the third," the boy proudly said. "My dad is Dickson Franklin Schmidt the second, and my grandpa was Dickson Franklin Schmidt the first. He was the first to have that name."

"Well, Dickson Franklin Schmidt the third, I'm glad to meet

you," Justin said, extending his hand, which Little Toad pumped furiously.

"Having car trouble, are ya?" Toad asked.

"Yes. My cooling system got plugged up in the dust storm. Burt can't get to it until tomorrow though. His wife said there's a motel in town," Justin said.

"Yep, the Corner Motel. Burt's sister owns it. Her name is Nancy Perkins. It's the only one left. Used to be two in town, but one closed down. Nancy's husband died about three years ago. Her kids want her to give it up and move to California where they live, but she refuses. Several of us go over when we can and help with little odds and ends around the place. Needs a lot of work. Wish she'd break down and give it up," Toad noted.

"That was quite a dust storm," Justin said as they drove along.

"Hell, that weren't nothing. Ya should've have been here in '53. It blew for three weeks straight."

"I met Wilbur Jenkins on my way into town. He said the same thing," Justin replied.

"Wilbur! Hell is he still alive?" the man asked. "I heard he died."

"I guess he's still alive. I met a man who said he was Wilbur. He told me about Burt's shop."

"That old farts got to be ninety. He's a rancher. I think his kids are running the outfit now."

They pulled up to a white stucco house with a sign on a pole that read CORNER MOTEL. It had nine rooms attached to it. A sign on the front door read, OFFICE.

"I'll go in with you to make sure she's got a room. If not, Little Toad and I'll take you out to Willie Nelson's place.

They all got out and walked into the office. The room had a couch, fireplace, lots of plants and a plywood counter with a sign that read, RING FOR SERVICE. Little Toad walked up and began pounding on the bell.

A voice from the next room called, "I'm coming. You don't have to keep ringing that damn bell." An elderly woman came out of a back room wiping her hands on a towel.

"Little Toad, you're going to wear that damn bell out. Stop it or I'll have to break your fingers."

Little Toad just smiled.

Then looking at Justin, she asked, "Can I help you?"

"Yes, ma'am. I'm looking for a room for tonight."

"Burt sent him up here. His truck got plugged up in the blow," Toad said.

"I'm so sorry. I just rented my last room out a little while ago."

"Don't you have that room with the busted air-conditioner," Toad asked.

"Yes, but I can't rent that out until the AC is fixed."

"Don't you have a fan he could use? It's supposed to rain tonight, so it'll cool down. Otherwise, he'll have to go out to Willie Nelson's and that's too far," Toad stated.

"I guess if you're willing," she said, looking at Justin. "I haven't cleaned it since the air-conditioner broke, and that's been a month. I guess we can walk over and look at it. If you want it, I can quickly clean it. Since it don't have an air-conditioner, you can have it for free."

"I wouldn't feel good about taking it for free. How about I pay half price?" Justin said.

"That would be sweet of you. And I'd appreciate it. I sure could use the money. The part for the air-conditioner is five hundred dollars. I've had some doctor bills and haven't been able to save any money. Half price would be forty-five dollars."

"That'll be great," Justin agreed.

"Let's go over and check it out," she said.

They walked over to the room and Nancy opened the door. The room looked like it had been the epicenter of the dust storm. Everything was covered with a thick layer of dust. Justin threw his bag on the bed causing a puff of dust to fly up around it. He walked into the bathroom and the floor was covered in dust. The toilet had a brown ring around it and the shower had mold along the tile floor.

"If you want it, I'll clean it up and bring a fan over," Nancy said.

"I think it'll be all right," Justin replied, handing her the money.

Taking the money, she continued, "I'll be right back to clean it. Here's the key."

"Well, at least you've got a bed and a roof over your head," Toad said. "Little Toad and I need to run. I'm sure Nancy will take good care of you. Oh, by the way, my wife has gone to Amarillo to see her sister for a few days. Little Toad and I are going to supper at Maggie's Café about seven. Would you like to go with us?"

Little Toad piped up, "You need to have the chicken-fried steak. It's really good."

"That does sound good," Justin replied.

"Come on, Little Toad. We've got to go check on those cows on the north field. That blow may have broken the windmill again and they won't have nothing to drink. We'll pick you up about seven."

"Great. I'll be ready," Justin replied.

There was a knock on the door and Nancy walked in. Her cart was just outside the door, and she was pulling a vacuum. "I'm ashamed to rent this. Since the air-conditioner stopped, I've ignored it. With the wind here, it doesn't take long to get dusty. Don't be concerned though, I'll get it cleaned up."

"I wouldn't worry about doing too much. I'll only be here one night."

"That's all right. I need to get it cleaned anyway. If I have a good month, I should be able to save enough to get the air-conditioner fixed."

She immediately busied herself dusting and vacuuming. As she worked, she said, "Did Toad say Burt is fixing your truck?"

"Yes, ma'am. He can't get to it until tomorrow morning though. It was his wife who recommended that I come up and see you about a room."

Taking the bedspread off, she said, "Burt's my little brother. He's a damn junk collector, but he's a good mechanic."

"Toad told me Burt was your brother. I've also heard from several people that he's a good mechanic."

Nancy was still fussing around cleaning when Toad and Little Toad came to pick Justin up.

Justin got in the truck, and noted, "The wind is still blowing pretty hard."

"For Corner, this is just a breeze," Toad said.

The café was only a block from the motel. It was a whitewashed building with a big red-and-white sign on the roof that read, MAGGIE'S CAFÉ.

As they got out, Little Toad took Justin's hand, and said, "You should have the chicken-fried steak. It's so good."

"I think I will," Justin said, giving him a pat on the back.

They walked in and it smelled wonderful. There was a large table in the middle of the room with booths around the outside. Several men were sitting at the table. They were all wearing muddy rubber boots.

One of them said, "Toad and Little Toad. What are you two doing here? Your wife finally kick you out or something?"

"Naw, she's visiting her sister in Amarillo." Turning to Justin, Toad said, "This is Justin LeMoore. Burt's working on his truck. He's staying at Nancy's motel. Let me introduce you to these reprobates. This is Curley." He was indicating to a bald man. "The goofy guy next to him is MoJo, next is Gert, then Snake and finally Windy."

Little Toad poked Justin, and whispered, "You know why they call him windy?"

"No," Justin whispered back.

Whispering in Justin's ear, Little Toad said with a giggle, "Cause he farts a lot."

"Oh, my," Justin replied. Then looking at the group he said, "I'm glad to meet you all," "You all sure have interesting nicknames."

"Heck, if anyone called us by our real names, we wouldn't know who they were talking about," Snake said. "Seems like nicknames get started when we're young, and they just stick."

"So what are you doing up here in this neck of the woods?" Curley asked.

"I'm on my way to see my sister in Colorado Springs and then to see a friend in Kansas."

"You live in Kansas?" MoJo asked.

"I did for a while. I used to work at the federal prison there."

"What do you do now?" Snake inquired.

Justin was telling the boys about the space train when a lady wearing a black dress with pink lace around the neck and sleeves and a white apron walked up. She had bright-pink lipstick, blue eye shadow and pink fingernails.

Wow, she could be Millie's sister, Justin thought.

Putting her hand on Justin's shoulder, she said, "What's a nice guy like you doing hanging around these old coots?"

"Maggie, go get lost. We're educating him on life in Texas," Curley replied.

"Don't listen to a word they say. They're all full of sh——. Well, you get the picture." Then taking a notepad out of her apron pocket and looking at Justin, she asked, "What can I get for you?"

Little Toad leaned over and whispered loud enough for everyone to hear, "Get the chicken-fried steak. It's really good."

"I believe I'll have the chicken-fried steak," Justin said, winking at Little Toad.

Little Toad smiled. "I'm gonna have the chicken-fried steak too."

While they waited for their food, Justin continued answering questions about the upcoming mission. After eating, the group sat around talking until finally Toad said, "Boys, we've gotta go home. Little Toad and I have to get up early to move the irrigation water on the pasture. Justin, you want a ride?"

"Yes, that would be great."

They dropped Justin off, and Toad said, "We'll pick you up at 6:00 AM for breakfast."

Justin opened the door to his room and was dumbfounded. The

room was as clean as a whistle. Everything had been dusted, there was a fan on and even the mold in the shower was gone. He also noticed a note on his pillow, which read, "I forgot to tell you. In the morning just drop your key off in the slot by the office door. Thank you for coming. And thank you for taking the room."

Justin woke early, so he got up, showered and prepared to check out. He found an envelope in the nightstand next to the bed and wrote a note: "Thank you for cleaning the room so well. I appreciate you going to all the work it took." He took five one-hundred-dollar bills out of his wallet and tucked them into the envelope with the note. He was just slipping the envelope into the key slot at the office when Toad and Little Toad pulled up.

"Good morning," they both said. "How was your night?"

"It was great. When I got back from supper the room was clean, and there was a fan on. It was a little warm at first, but then it started to rain, which cooled things down. I went to sleep and didn't wake until morning."

"That's great," Toad said. "Nancy has always been a worker. I just don't know how much longer she's going to be able to do it."

When they arrived at the café, the same round table was again surrounded by men. Some had muddy rubber boots on; others were in cowboy boots with cow manure on them.

"There you are," Snake said as Toad, Little Toad and Justin walked in. "This is the astronaut I was telling you about," he nodded to a person Justin hadn't met.

"I'm not really an astronaut," Justin replied.

"You're going to fly in a spaceship, aren't you?" Snake asked

"Yes, it's called a Space Train."

"Well, that makes you an astronaut in my book." Then looking toward the counter, he yelled, "Hey Maggie, get your butt over here and clear these dishes away so these paying customers can sit down."

Maggie was doing something behind the counter. She turned and gave Snake and the others a dirty look. "Can't you see I'm working? Clear the damn things off yourself. Your arms ain't painted on, are they?"

"Dang, she's testy this morning," Snake said as he got up. "Bull, help me."

"I'll help," Little Toad said, as he gathered up several plates and carried them to the counter.

Little Toad returned and sat down by Justin. He leaned over, and said, "Get the Corner omelet. They are really good."

Maggie finished her chore behind the counter and walked over to the group. Looking at Justin, she said, "I thought I warned you about these old shit-kickers. Look at them, mud and cow shit on their boots. And not one of them has the courtesy to take their boots off before they come in."

"Maggie, get off it. That's why we tip so well. We each leave at least a dollar."

"A dollar," Maggie scoffed. "I have to mop the floor every morning when you stinking old cowboys finally get out of here." Then turning to Justin and the two Toads, she asked, "What would you like?"

"I believe I'll have the Corner omelet. I hear it's really good," Justin said.

Little Toad's face turned into one big smile. "You're gonna like it. It's really good." Then looking at Maggie, he said, "I want a Corner omelet too."

After breakfast and answering a million more questions, Justin,

Toad and Little Toad got up to leave. Everyone had to shake Justin's hand, and Maggie wouldn't even let him pay.

Toad drove him to Burt's place, and said, "After the mission we'd love to have you come back. We'd like to hear all about your trip."

"You've got a deal. I'll make a point of coming back."

When they arrived at Burt's garage, and after shaking hands with both Big Toad and Little Toad, Justin got out.

"You come back and see us," Little Toad said as they drove away.

As he watched them go, it felt like he was leaving good friends. *Over the past day, I've met some of the nicest people I've ever encountered,* he told himself as he watched their dust recede out of sight.

He looked around, and not seeing his truck, he walked into the shop. Burt was just finishing and wiping his hands on a greasy rag. Justin recognized the greasy coveralls and hat from the day before. Burt's bearded face, hands, hat and coveralls were all equally greasy.

He had a big toothless smile, and said, "'Bout done with it. She was plugged tighter than a toilet after Thanksgiving dinner. I got it all cleaned out though. I just gotta put a little more coolant in her. She'll be good as new."

As he worked, he continued, "I seen you got a space sticker on yur truck. You some kind of space man or something?"

"I work for NASA. The sticker is my parking permit," Justin replied.

"What ya do for them folks?" Burt inquired as he poured coolant into the radiator.

Justin quickly told Burt about the train and the mission.

"Yep, I seen something about that on the entertainment gizmo.

Thought once I'd like to be a space man, but I'd be afraid of flying around up there in the stars. Don't it scare you?"

"No, not really," Justin replied.

"Well, it's better that Hazel and me stay here. Flying around up there is for young people like you. Our kids are always trying to get us to fly out to New York and see them, but neither Hazel nor me like to fly."

Having finished, he wiped his hands on the rag again, and said, "I'm glad to meet you. An' when they show you leaving, I'll be proud to have worked on your truck."

He patted Justin on the back. "You go ahead and go on now. Your truck should be just fine."

"Do you think the motor was hurt from the heat?"

"Naw. I changed the oil and checked her over. She's fine."

Justin thanked Burt for his work, backed his truck out and was finally on his way again.

As he drove away, he couldn't help but think about Corner and the good people he'd met. They were just ordinary simple folks with no ostentation that he could see. They lived in an unpredictable world with the uncompromising forces of nature. They didn't have much, but everyone had been friendly and helpful.

Maybe I should just bag the mission and move here. I don't need the Kozenskies and their conniving. I could take over Burt's shop or Nancy's motel, wear muddy boots and eat breakfast and dinner at Maggie's Café every day. I could even have my own nickname. I don't know what more I could ask than living in a small place like Corner with good friends.

Even with the delay, he hoped to arrive in Colorado Springs by late evening. As he drove, his mind returned to Rolando and his intense desire to get into medical school.

I need to sell my truck as soon as I get back to Houston. I can rent a car for a few weeks until the mission gets under way, he told himself.

As he thought about it, a plan began to take shape. *Perhaps I could do something to benefit Rolando with my truck. It's almost four years old, but I've taken care of it and it still runs well. It's paid for and titled in Kansas. While I'm there I'll go see what I'd have to do to transfer it into Rolando's name. I also still have most of the advance money they gave me, and I could also give that to Rolando. I certainly won't need it and he could use the money to get into his first year of medical school.*

He arrived at his sister's home late in the evening. After spending two days with her and her family, he left to go see Ted and his family.

It took just over twelve hours to drive to Kansas City, and again he arrived late in the evening. Ted and Eve were excited to see him again.

Eve's first question was, "Tell us about your accident."

"It wasn't much," Justin said. "A shipping container got away from a tug. That's all."

"But the news said you were hurt," Eve followed up.

"When the containers collided, one of them spun around and hit me in the back. It severed my oxygen hoses which cut off my air supply for a few minutes. I blacked out but Mr. Williams saw what happened and gave me some of his oxygen. They took me to the medical clinic where they carefully checked me over. They said I was fine."

"The news intimated it might not have truly been an accident. Is that possible?"

"They still don't know yet. It's still under investigation," Justin replied.

"You make it sound like a walk in the park. Weren't you frightened? I'd have been scared out of my wits for something like that to have happened," Eve said with a grimace.

"It happened so fast I didn't have a chance to think. After it was over, I was a bit concerned. What can you do though? It's over now, and nothing terrible happened, so I just keep going."

"We're just glad it wasn't worse than it was," Eve said.

They talked well into the night catching up on all the news of one another.

The next day was Sunday and they all went to church. Afterward Justin and Ted sat around swapping old hunting and fishing stories. Justin also got his guns out, cleaned them and decided which to take with him.

Although he enjoyed being with Ted and Eve, he often had an intrusive, recurring vision come to his mind. He would see Ms. Wong.

On Monday, Justin went to the motor vehicle section at the courthouse. After explaining what he wanted to do, a very nice lady helped him arrange for the transfer of his truck to Rolando. He then went to his storage shed. He boxed up his reloading equipment, got his fishing stuff out and selected the rods he wanted to take. He also checked his fly-tying kit and determined what he would need to replenish it.

Justin was playing with the boys in the backyard when Ted got home from work. "You should stay here and have a passel of kids. You'd make a good father," Ted said as he watched.

Justin laughed. "Yes, I think I'd enjoy being a father."

That night was family night for Ted's family. They had a little lesson on being kind to one another; then Eve served cake and ice cream.

"Okay," Eve directed, as the boys finished their ice cream. "It's time for bed. Go get your pajamas on and then you can give Uncle Justin a hug. The boys quickly ran screaming upstairs and did as they were told. Running back down, each boy gave Justin a bear hug.

The older boy said, "Thanks for coming Uncle Justin. Mommy and Daddy said you're going to a new world in the stars. They said you'll be away for a long time. Will you come back and see us?"

"You bet I will Tiger," Justin said, giving both of them a hug and a kiss on the forehead.

"All right, come on boys. Let's go brush your teeth. Then it's to bed for you both," Ted said, as he herded them back upstairs.

As they ran laughing and screaming up the stairs, Justin thought to himself, *If I could have a family like this, I'd be a contented man.*

The next day Justin went to a sporting-goods store he used to frequent. He knew the owner very well having done business with him before. They shared greetings and he had to again relate the story about the accident.

Finally the owner asked, "What can I do for you?"

"I need a big-game rifle, ammunition, reloading supplies and some fly-tying material."

"I've got just the big-game rifle you want," the owner said. "I just received a couple of .62-caliber sniper rifles with 12×36 power scopes. They'll shoot more than a mile. I've seen groups of four inches at that distance." Taking the gun off the rack, he handed it to Justin. It was a rifle like he'd never seen before. "It uses that new nitro powder. It's hotter than a firecracker."

"I'll bet this thing kicks like a mule," Justin said as he hefted the rifle.

"It's not as severe as you'd think. As you can see, the stock is thick. The forearm accommodates a recoil device inside. The device absorbs about 60 percent of the shock, so it isn't bad to shoot. I'll take you out to the range if you want to try it. I'm convinced this baby could bring down a dinosaur."

Justin looked the gun over, and said, "I'll take you up on going to the range if you've got the time."

"Let's go," the owner said as he picked the rifle up. Then he yelled, "Sam, Justin and I are going to the range. Keep an eye on things."

The day was sunny and hot as they drove to the range. Luckily there wasn't anyone else there, so as usual Justin went about setting up a target at a hundred yards. The owner just laughed. "A hundred yards for this baby is the equivalent of ten yards for any other gun."

Using a golf cart he had in the back of his truck, they drove to the farthest target stand on the range. It was a thousand yards away. They stapled a standard target on the backboard and returned to the shooting tables.

"Go ahead Justin," the owner said, handing him the rifle and three bullets. The bullets were four inches long.

Justin timidly inserted the rounds into the gun's magazine and looked through the scope. He had to dial it to the range, but once he did, the target looked like it was no more than the standard hundred yards away.

He sat down at the shooting table and loaded a round into the chamber. Then using a sandbag to rest the rifle on, he got ready to shoot.

"Don't give it any elevation. Put the crosshairs on the target, snug it to your shoulder and touch it off. The scope has a range finder in it, which will adjust to the distance. The trigger is set for two pounds. If you prefer it a little heavier or lighter, it can be adjusted."

Justin adjusted his ear protectors and snugged the rifle to his shoulder. He put the crosshairs on the target, inwardly braced for the kick and slowly squeezed the trigger. The gun bucked, but unlike the instantaneous kick of a standard rifle, it was more of a steady push.

"Go ahead and shoot two more, then we'll ride down and see what you did," the owner directed.

Justin shot two more rounds, and said, "I like the smell of the nitro powder." He opened the bolt and laid the rifle on the table.

They rode the golf cart back to the target to see how Justin had done. Justin couldn't believe his eyes. At eight hundred yards the three shots were less than two inches apart and the holes in the paper were each the size of a nickel.

"I've got to have one of these. How much is it?" Justin asked.

"For you I'll make a deal you can't refuse. I'll sell you the gun at my cost if you'll let me take a picture with you holding it. I'll put it up at the store."

"I don't think the agency would go along with that," Justin replied. "I'd better pay full price."

"I understand." Then quickly thinking and rubbing his chin, the owner continued. "I'll tell you what. I'll still let you have it at cost. I'll make my profit on the ammunition and other supplies."

"I think I can make it worth your while," Justin said.

They loaded the golf cart into the truck and drove back to the store. Justin ordered twenty-four boxes of loaded ammunition, fifty pounds of powder, plus primers, bullets, cleaning supplies and a set of reloading dies for his new rifle. In addition, he purchased a passel of fly-tying supplies.

"I'm leaving early Thursday morning. I'll come by Wednesday evening, pay you and load all this stuff into my truck," Justin said.

"I'll put all the bullets and reloading stuff on a pallet and have it shrink-wrapped for you."

On Wednesday evening, Justin and Ted drove to the store, backed the truck up to the loading dock and they went into the back of the store. The ammunition and reloading supplies were neatly stacked on a pallet covered in shrink wrap plastic. The owner came into the backroom with a list of everything he'd bought and handed Justin the bill.

When Justin saw it, he said, "Whew, I could almost buy a new truck for that amount."

"Don't whine. I gave you a baker's dozen on all the ammunition. You did okay," the owner said.

Justin transferred the amount, they placed the pallet into the back of the truck and strapped it down. It was amazing. The supplies on the pallet was almost three feet high. His fly-tying material was in a separate box, but that didn't amount to much. To keep it dry, they tied a tarp over everything. Justin thanked the owner and they drove to Ted's.

Justin took Ted, Eve and the two boys to dinner where they talked about all the great times they'd enjoyed together. It was an emotional time for them all as they wondered if it would be their last evening together.

The next morning, Justin was up and on his way before anyone else was stirring. He headed south toward Houston, hoping to make it in one long day.

As he was leaving Kansas, Justin called Leif Udall to see if he was on the ground or at the train.

"I'm on the ground supervising the packing of some shipping containers. Mr. Harris said you'd be calling. I understand he's authorized you to take a few guns and some ammunition on the mission. I want you to know I'm not thrilled about it. But since Mr. Harris said to do it, I guess I don't have a choice. Give me a call once you're in Houston and I'll meet you."

Justin got on Interstate 71, which would take him all the way to Houston. At first he made good time, the roads were dry and there was very little traffic. By the time he got to Texarkana, it started to rain and the farther south he went, the harder it rained. He called Leif's cell phone when he got to the outskirts of Houston.

Leif said, "Meet me at the crew parking lot at 0400."

Justin stayed in a motel that night and was at the logistics crew parking area at 0330. It was still pouring rain so he had the guns in the front seat of the truck to keep them dry. When Leif arrived, he jumped out of his car, ran to the truck and opened the door to get in. He took one look and was dumbfounded at how many guns there were.

Wait a minute," Leif said as he scooted into the seat. "How many guns have you got here?"

"Seven," Justin replied.

"Seven? I thought you were bringing 'a few guns,' not an arsenal. I don't have room for all of these," Leif anxiously said.

"Seven is a few. Besides, I saw how big the train is. You can surely find a place to put seven little guns in," Justin pleaded.

As Leif closed the door, he asked, "If seven is a few, how many is a lot?"

"Eight or more," Justin replied. "Besides, two of them are pistols. They shouldn't count." Then thinking quickly, he noted, "Besides, some of them are for you and others who'd like to go hunting with me when we arrive at the New World."

"Justin, I can't accommodate this many. Can't you pick just one or two to take?" Leif asked.

"Come on, Leif, I can't do that. You need more than one type of tool to get a job done and I need more than one kind of gun."

They bantered back and forth as they made their way to the security gate. Leif put his coat over the guns so the guard wouldn't see them. When they pulled up, Leif leaned over, and said, "This is Justin LeMoore. He's on the train crew. We're bringing some of his personal items to be transported up."

"Yep, the departure must be getting close. Several others have brought their personal stuff to be sent up. I'll need to scan your ID card," the guard said to Justin.

He quickly dug it out of his wallet and handed it to the guard. He scanned his card, then handed it back, and said, "I'm sure tired of this cursed rain."

As they drove away, Leif said, "Actually it was good that it was dark and raining. The guard didn't even look in the truck. I hope you realize you've just made a dang gun runner out of me."

"You're a good man," Justin replied.

They drove to a warehouse and Leif opened a large double door for Justin to back the truck into. Leif hadn't looked in the back, and when he did, he was again astonished. "Tell me all of this doesn't go?"

"Yes. I hope it will," Justin quietly replied as he pulled the tarp off.

Leif's jaw dropped. "What is all this stuff?"

"Just a few bullets and some reloading stuff."

"Justin, there was no mention about reloading stuff. What's in that pile anyway?" Leif demanded.

"As I said, bullets, primers and a little powder."

"Gun powder?" Leif asked.

"Yes, but it's harmless until loaded into bullets," Justin said with his tongue in his cheek.

"Justin, I may be a city boy, but I'm not stupid. Gunpowder isn't ever harmless. You're not planning on starting a war up there, are you?"

Then again looking at the pallet of stuff, he said, "Justin, I can't take this much stuff. The train is big, but every square inch is accounted for. Besides, do you know what they'd do if anyone found out we were transporting guns and ammunition, not to mention gunpowder?"

Justin looked pleadingly. "Please, with all that's going on, we may need this stuff."

"You do know you won't be able to shoot any of this in the train, don't you?"

"Yes, I know. But if we arrive at the New World, what's to say we won't need it? Do you think the Kozenskies are just going to roll over? You and I both know they've been conniving to get the personnel they want on the mission. You can bet they want them for a reason. I fear it might be to take over once we arrive. They also don't want certain individuals on the mission like Kyle and me. In addition, you know that so-called accident up there at the train was no accident."

"We have phasers on board. They could be used for defense," Leif noted.

"Sure, if we're in control of them. What if we aren't? Then what?"

Leif paced back and forth, then got into his briefcase and took out about four inches of papers bound together with wire stays. He also took out his computer and turned it on.

"Okay, Justin, here's the deal. I've got to have your absolute agreement and promise. If I risk and take your guns and all this crap"—he was gesturing to the mound of stuff in the bed of the truck—"everything has to be locked up. You won't have access to any of it until we arrive at the New World. Agreed?"

"You bet," Justin replied.

They shook hands.

"I hope I don't regret this. You need to know the arms room is programmed so that any access into it triggers an alarm in the command suite. Once the guns are locked up, there won't be any way to get to them without alerting command," Leif said, as he leafed through his paper documents and mumbled to himself.

He kept searching his papers, which were covered with marks and calculations in the margins. Finally he said, "Stay here. I'll be back in a few minutes."

Justin sat on the tailgate of his truck and impatiently waited as the rain continued to pelt down outside. As he looked around, he saw dozens of large shipping containers stacked up.

I wonder if they are waiting to be loaded on a shuttle.

About fifteen minutes later, Leif returned. He was riding on a baggage tractor with a small aluminum shipping container on a trailer. They spent the next hour carefully packing the guns, ammunition, and reloading supplies into the container. Leif said he'd have the fly-tying gear and fishing equipment put in Justin's quarters.

He made notes on his paperwork and then typed something into his computer. He plugged a small printer into the computer and printed a label, which he affixed to the container. It listed the contents as "medical equipment." It noted the container would be stored in a larger shipping container and gave the exact storage location. Leif printed one more label, which he handed to Justin.

"This is so you know where it is, just in case. By the way, what kind of guns are you taking?"

"A .62-caliber game rifle for big critters, a .300 Magnum rifle for kind of big animals, a 25-06 rifle for cow-size animals, a 12-gauge shotgun for birds and a .17-caliber rifle for small animals. The pistols are a .41 Magnum, and a .357 Magnum for protection. That's all," Justin said.

"That's all?" Leif said, shaking his head.

16

Justin drove back to the training facility and reported to Mr. Harris. "I'm glad you're back safe and sound. There's not been any new developments in the investigation. The Kozenskies have been interviewed over and over. But of course, they deny any involvement."

"They won't admit to anything. They're as slippery as a can of worms."

"I assume nothing out of the ordinary happened on your trip?" Mr. Harris inquired.

"No, nothing. I got into a dust storm between Lubbock and Amarillo and had to have the cooling system on my truck cleaned out. I spent the night in a little town called Corner, Texas. I met some of the nicest people I've ever encountered. It makes me wonder if all of this is worth it. Other than that, nothing happened."

"Hopefully the problems are at an end," Mr. Harris said. "I've been informed by Congressman Richards' press secretary, and of course Milton Slusser, that they want a big send-off prior to the departure of the train. I had hoped to keep the beginning of the mission a low-key affair, but it looks like it will be a media event. Everyone knows Congressman Richards is maneuvering for the White House. So, he can't pass up an opportunity for publicity. And I guess it's even deserved. He's been the financial driving force for the mission."

"When you say a big send-off, what do you mean?" Justin asked.

"I haven't been given the exact details yet. I expect it will be held at the Houston Space Center. The congressman will make a brief appearance and be off again. However, it's just part of the game. We don't have a choice."

"Didn't they do the same thing for the first New World mission?" Justin asked.

"Yes, but the difference is that Congressman Richards wasn't the daddy supreme. The first mission was supposed to be the only colonization mission with just periodic supply runs and checkup missions after that. It wasn't until the good congressman happened to meet the Kozenskies that the current colonization mission was conceived."

"So this mission really is built around, or perhaps for the Kozenskies?"

Mr. Harris just smiled. "When an additional mission was conceived, I was all for it. The first one was a mammoth success and I wanted to be a part of a second one. It was touted to be a huge economic boon to the nation, so it was all positive, a no-brainer. It was not until months after the public announcement that I even heard about the Kozenskies.

"Even then, all I knew was what I had heard about them on the news. They were eccentric, brilliant geniuses according to everyone who met them. I really didn't care about them. It was the bigger picture I was interested in. As time went on though, it was obvious if they were geniuses, they were from the dark side. They wormed their way into every aspect of the mission. And Congressman Richards, and of course Milton Slusser, were there every step of the way to tout their brilliance."

"It almost seems like the Kozenskies have something over the congressman and Slusser," Justin mused.

"Politics is a dirty business," Mr. Harris said almost to himself as he stood. He stared out the window for several seconds as if looking into eternity. "At times, I feel like I'm living at the bottom of a cesspool."

Then turning back and looking at Justin, he continued, "As I said, we don't have a choice about the send-off, and in addition we've got to get ready for the start of the mission. What Congressman Richards does is just part of the game. I am glad to have you back, and I know Frank is excited to start his leave."

Justin hadn't paid attention to Mr. Harris, but looking at him, he'd visibly aged over the past several months. His hair was grayer and he slumped as if carrying the world on his shoulders.

I wonder how much more he knows about the filth of politics, Justin pondered.

"What did I tell you, Ervin? No one is as intelligent as we are. They've tried to trick an admission out of us in their silly interrogations, but yet again we've outsmarted them all. Actually, I'm rather enjoying our little mental gymnastics with these morons."

"Vidula, we can't take any more chances. There are too many others out there who can be tripped up and expose us. We've got to go with the flow until the time is right. Then we can execute the real mission. Promise me you won't do anything else."

Vidula smiled, walked over and kissed Ervin on the forehead. Still smiling, she said, "I promise not to set anything else up."

Ervin looked hard at Vidula. "What do you mean by 'anything else?'" You've already set something up. Haven't you?"

"Oh, darling, stop worrying. We've got to get rid of a couple of nits, that's all. You know what they say, one rotten apple can spoil a whole barrel."

"Vidula, you've got to stop. Hasn't this last fiasco demonstrated how dangerous it is?!"

"Ervin," Vidula said with fire in her eyes, "Justin and Kyle have both been troublemakers. They've messed up our plans. They're dangerous. I don't want them on the mission."

"Vidula, please don't do it. You're risking everything. We have the chance to start an entire new civilization. It's an opportunity no other mortal man has had and you're risking it all to eliminate a couple of fleas—fleas that can be eradicated after we arrive."

"Oh, Ervin, get off it. Why take vermin along when we don't need to? They contribute nothing to our vision and could complicate things if left unattended. You used to be a risk taker, making things happen. Now you snivel around like a little girl. Everything is set and it's out of my hands. Just sit back and enjoy the show." With that, Vidula stomped out of the room.

Just because you've lost your nerve, Ervin, doesn't mean I have, Vidula said to herself.

Justin went over to Frank's room and met with him for the rest of the day. "Sounds like we're going to have a circus in a few weeks. I just saw Mr. Harris and he told me about the political send-off event."

"That's all anyone's talking about. Finally, we'll be able to meet Congressman Richards. I even heard the president might attend," Frank said.

"Mr. Harris didn't say anything about the president coming, but I guess he may not want to be left out of the publicity. Maybe I could go fishing about that time." Justin laughed.

They spent the next couple of hours reviewing each couple and discussing what Frank had been doing during Justin's absence. Of course, Frank had to place special emphasis on Ms. Wong and Dr. Momora.

"As you know, Dr. Hockstrasser has now relocated to the train to work on his gardens. Ms. Wong states she's doing fine though. It's obvious both Dr. Hockstrasser and Ms. Wong are independent people who don't mind not being together. I suspect the primary reason they're comfortable with each other is they can both do their own thing without worrying about the other feeling neglected. I'm told Dr. Hockstrasser works eighteen hours a day. He just takes little catnaps from time to time. Not many women could put up with that for long."

"No, I suppose not," Justin replied.

"Dr. Momora and Mr. Sharma seemed to also be doing well. Dr. Momora's been working long hours at the medical clinic, but they seem well suited. Both say they're comfortable with each other."

"That's great," Justin commented.

By the afternoon, they'd completed the reviews and Frank wanted to get ready to depart on his leave.

Justin left so Frank could pack and found Mr. Garza. He took him aside and quietly told him of his plan to assist Rolando. He was in tears, and both agreed not to tell Rolando until just before Justin departed for the mission.

The next two weeks while Frank was gone were a blur. Justin administered the last stress questionnaires the prisoners had to take before they departed. He met with all sixty couples, except for Dr. Hockstrasser. None expressed any reservation about leaving.

By the time Frank returned, the train was ready for the cryogenics to begin. It was expected the mission could start within the next sixty days. The medical crew wanted the cryogenic patients to be in hibernation for at least a month before the train departed to ensure there were no problems. The Kozenskies insisted on being the last to go into hibernation so they could allegedly make sure everything was working correctly. Of course, they got their way.

17

The big send-off postponed the mission for two additional weeks. The president decided to definitely attend, which complicated everything with the required extra security. The president's attendance was inevitable though. He still had three years left on his first term in office and Congressman Richards was already posturing to make a run against him. Congressman Richards and the president were in different parties, so the President couldn't afford to let him take all the credit for the mission or garner any political advantage.

The day of the big send-off event was hot and muggy with heavy gray, overcast skies. There was a steady rain falling as the prisoners were bussed to the space center. A large hangar had been converted into an auditorium for the occasion.

For the first time since their arrival, the prisoners were forced to wear new orange prison jumpsuits. Besides being colorful, it gave the public the appearance the prisoners were under control. Little did they know they'd been shopping, going to the beach, eating out and living among them in civilian clothes for the past almost nine months.

For this event, it was important that they looked like prisoners. The only thing better would have been to show them in leg irons and handcuffs.

The media had their field day showing the prisoners filing off the buses as couples and taking their seats. After they were all seated, the dignitaries were ushered in along with swarms of US Secret Service men. The president and Congressman Richards filed in first and took their seats. They were followed by other congressmen and representatives from Texas. A raft of other dignitaries and straphangers then filled in and took their seats behind the more important individuals. By the time everyone was seated, there were almost as many on the stage as were in the audience. Mr. Milton Slusser wasn't to be seen, although Justin and Frank were sure he was lurking somewhere close by.

Mr. Harris stood in a gray pin-striped suit and red tie looking as distinguished as ever. In his booming command voice, he welcomed everyone. Turning, he made note of each dignitary and introduced them by name. He also gave a brief description of the role they'd played in the mission. After the introductions, he turned the floor over to the president.

The president was a tall, thin man with steel-gray hair and an honest-looking face. He was dressed in a dark suit and also had a commanding voice. "I want to speak to the intrepid desire of man to explore and take control of his environment. We humans are builders, and many of you have helped design and construct the most advanced space machine ever built. Since the beginning of time man has looked to the sky and dreamed of exploring it. We have known there was something special out there and longed for the power to go see for ourselves.

"I want to recognize and compliment you for being willing to be pioneers. Space pioneers. You are some of the first from our planet to colonize a new world."

Looking around at various individuals, he continued. "I also want to thank all of those who have made this mission possible. It has taken thousands of people to bring the mission to fruition. I want each of you to know how grateful the world is for your accomplishments. This mission is not just an achievement for America, it is also an accomplishment for the entire world. We have pioneers and explorers who will be on the mission from many countries around the globe.

"Many countries have also assisted in developing a space vehicle unlike any the world has ever seen. It is the first vehicle of its size to travel significantly faster than light, making it possible to colonize another planet so far away. We could not have achieved such a success without a global effort."

The president concluded by thanking Congressman Richards for his untiring interest and dedication to the mission. "He deserves credit for watching out for the funding and making sure the mission had all it needed to be a success beyond measure. Please join me in giving him and his staff a big round of applause."

The president's speech was clear, to the point and dignified.

After the president spoke, an aide unobtrusively moved a stool into place behind the podium. Congressman Richards deftly stepped onto it, making him appear several inches taller than he really was. The Congressman was a small man, barely five foot two inches tall. He wore a dark double-breasted suit and a garish red-and-yellow tie.

He began by thanking the president for his remarks, which was the only kind thing he had to say about him. The good congressman then launched into a campaign speech telling about the uphill battle he'd waged to get and keep funding for the mission.

He not so subtly gloated about the thousands of jobs he claimed to have created. He spoke of the larger economy and his vision for a more prosperous future for America. "With dreams like I have, a visionary man can change the course of the entire world," he shouted, making his voice reverberate off the metal walls of the hangar.

Justin leaned over to Frank, and said, "Sounds like he's been hanging around the Kozenskies."

After more than forty-five minutes, he finally began to wind down but not before giving credit to the Kozenskies for almost single-handedly designing and building the train. He even had them stand in their bright-orange jumpsuits.

"Just a few years ago, they were seen as world villains. Now they've been vindicated. They have dedicated themselves to the mission and the betterment of all mankind," he shouted again, raising his arms high into the air.

Several other dignitaries were scheduled to speak, but Justin had heard enough and left after Congressman Richards's nauseating self-proclamation.

The prisoners would be moved to the train in groups of five couples at a time starting the morning after the departure ceremony. Physicians from John Hopkins Hospital, Tulane University, the Naval Academy, and other facilities around the world with cryogenic research units had flown in. Most were already on board the train and each was ready to assist the medical crew.

It was anticipated it would take two to three days to process each group of ten individuals. Either Justin or Frank would be on the train throughout the process to provide support and comfort. They decided to divide the duty. One would remain at the training site and one would go to the train. The process would be a seven-day-a-week affair to complete everyone as quickly as possible. Frank took the first shift on the train. Justin stayed back to work with the prisoners waiting for their turn. Justin spent evenings and Saturdays helping the Garzas.

Frank called back to Justin, and said, "You can't believe what's happening up here. Vidula is glad-handing everyone. At first, she was seeing each person going into hibernation and giving hugs and kisses. I got with the physicians and we put a stop to her entering the cryogenic preparation area. That didn't stop her though. She spends time at dinner with each person the night before they are processed. She even goes to their rooms to talk. It's like she's campaigning for something."

"Sure," Justin said, "she's campaigning for when the trip ends. There are supposed to be elections when they arrive to determine who'll be the community leaders. She wants to be at the top of the list."

Justin took the second shift. Like Frank, he held hands,

supported, reassured and encouraged each prisoner as they were prepped for the cryogenic procedure. He saw the same thing Frank had noted. Vidula was everywhere shaking hands, slapping backs and expressing her love and concern. Everyone except Justin, that is. She went out of her way to avoid him.

While on the train, he spent his evenings setting up his quarters and helping Dr. Hockstrasser in the greenhouse. He helped assemble tables, plant seedbeds, thin or water plants and many other little chores. Dr. Hockstrasser worked his usual sixteen to eighteen hours a day. He was already harvesting lettuce, chard, radishes and had summer squash coming. He had beds of potatoes, corn, turnips, beans, peas and other vegetables planted in addition to his dwarf orchard. He hoped within six months to have apples and peaches ready to pick.

Justin and Frank continued to rotate every seven days. The medical team along with the other physicians and nurses were getting more proficient in accomplishing the cryogenic process. They were now easily able to do four people a day. With those numbers, they anticipated being able to complete the entire process within a month. The medical crew would then spend a month monitoring everyone to make sure everything was working properly.

Everything went well until the fifth group when for no apparent reason one of the men had a heart attack and died during his preparation. The death was sobering for those who had not gone into hibernation. It highlighted the risks everyone was taking on the mission, both prisoner and crew alike.

His mate, Safire Strong, had not been processed and was returned to the training center. An alternate couple was selected to take their place. Since she was a physical therapy assistant and not in the cryogenic group, both she and Vidula lobbied for her to be allowed to return as a single person on the crew. Their request got all the way to Congressman Richards's office. After some heavy-handed congressional pressure, Safire was allowed to return to the ship and join the crew as a single person.

Vidula continued her public relations campaign with everyone on board. She cried about the death, praised everyone for their bravery and told each person how much she loved them. She also made sure they all knew about the many safety features she and Ervin had added to the train.

"I look forward to our arrival at the New World where we will all work together to build a perfect society," she told anyone who would listen.

It was Justin's turn to be at the training center. He was sitting by the pool reading when Ms. Wong came out. She was hoping to wring out her last chance to enjoy Earth's sunshine before going into hibernation. Justin's heart immediately began to race as they acknowledged each other. Neither spoke as she walked by and settled into a lawn chair. The magnetism he felt toward her was overwhelming.

She opened a book and began reading but was acutely aware of Justin being there. After several minutes, he got up, walked over to her, and asked, "Are you ready to enter the cryogenic group?"

"I guess so," she replied, closing the book and putting it in her lap.

She looked at Justin and suddenly felt dizzy. Her heart was pounding and her mouth went dry. They talked for several minutes about the university classes and how the Garzas had transformed the training center landscape.

Then without thinking, she blurted out, "Do you think you could be there when I go into hibernation?"

Cindy, you idiot, you don't want him there. You need to get away from him, Molly screamed in her head.

Ignoring Ms. Wong's request, and stalling for time, he asked, "When do you go up?"

"I'm in the ninth group. I know you're supposed to be with the even-numbered groups."

Justin was caught totally off guard, and astonishment somehow vetoed prudence. "Ah, well, I guess I could see if Chaplain Molony would mind trading a shift with me."

Something in his head said, *Have you lost your mind? Why in the world did you say that? The best way to remain professional is not to be around her, especially in emotional situations.*

Molly was likewise screaming, *Cindy, you idiot. You don't want him there. You've got to stop. You're setting yourself up for trouble and heartache. Mark my word.*

Adjusting the book in her lap, Cindy said, "I'm sorry. I don't know where that came from. If you're uncomfortable being there, it's okay."

Instead of coming up with some reason not to accept, and still bewildered that she had asked, he said, "I'll see what I can do."

Cindy, are you crazy? You have no idea what you're getting into. You're acting like a little girl. You're leading him along knowing nothing good can ever come from a relationship, Molly angrily shouted.

Cindy knew Molly was right, but she didn't stop. *Why am I so attracted to something I can never have? He might as well be from an entirely different species, or as the Bible states, an untouchable. I can't help it though. For some reason, I'm drawn to him. I know I'm playing with fire and nothing can ever come from a relationship, but oh how I wish it could. I don't care. Who knows what will happen on the mission. I want him there.*

Okay, Molly responded, *but don't forget what I've said when you get in over your head. I'll tell you that I told you so.*

Realizing what he'd committed too, Justin was in a panic. "I have to go. I've got some paperwork to do," he said.

The reality of what he'd agreed to rushed in and wrapped a frosty grip around him. *What have I done? And what am I going to tell Frank?*

Unfortunately, Frank was more than willing to trade, but asked, "Why do you want to?"

"Well, there are some people I'd like to be there for when they go into hibernation," Justin limply stated.

"Like Ms. Wong?"

"Oh, I didn't know she would be in that group," he lied.

Frank was good enough not to press the issue.

Although Justin asked himself a thousand times why he'd accepted Ms. Wong's request, and despite wishing he hadn't, the time for group nine arrived. With trepidation, he flew up to the train on Sunday afternoon.

Ms. Wong transferred to the train on Monday morning. She was to be the first patient processed on Tuesday. She spent Monday afternoon in the greenhouse helping Dr. Hockstrasser. He even ate dinner with her at the dining facility. It was the first time he'd eaten there. They sat by a port and marveled at the beauty of space.

"I can't believe how many stars there are," Cindy said.

Justin arrived and got a tray. Dr. Hockstrasser invited him to sit, but he said, "I need to talk to Leif. I'll go down to the greenhouse after I eat."

When Justin arrived at the greenhouse, Dr. Hockstrasser asked both he and Ms. Wong if they'd help plant, water and harvest lettuce and chard. When they finished, he then asked them if they'd mind taking two large baskets of produce to the kitchen.

They were both uncomfortable about going together, but did so. They chitchatted on the way about little things like who was already in hibernation, who was to be processed the next day and other insignificant things.

As they walked along, Molly warned, *You're headed for disaster. You're going to have your heart broken and do the same to Mr. LeMoore.*

She ignored Molly's warnings, and as they were returning, Ms. Wong said, "I appreciate you being here for my processing tomorrow."

Justin suddenly had a rush of emotion and felt like he was falling through air with no way to stop. Hesitantly, he said, "I'm happy to do so."

They walked the rest of the way in silence. In fact, for the rest of the evening neither spoke much. About 2100, Justin said, "I'm tired. If you don't mind I think I'm ready to turn in for the night."

Neither Cindy nor Dr. Momora slept well that night. Cindy got up a little after 0300, had a shower and put the scrubs on she'd been given to be processed in. She then curled her hair.

Dr. Momora was awake but didn't get up until 0500. She looked at Cindy, and said, "You're beautiful, but I don't think you needed to curl your hair for the processing."

"I couldn't sleep," Cindy responded.

Yes, and I suspect it's also for the benefit of Justin LeMoore, she said to herself.

Since Ms. Wong was to be the first person to be processed,

she'd been told to be at the female cryogenic processing site at 0700. Unable to contain her anxiety, she and Dr. Momora were there at 0600.

When they walked in, two of the cryogenic nurses were just finishing setting the equipment up for the day. "You're early," they said to both Cindy and Dr. Momora.

"You must be excited to go to sleep." The other nurse smiled. "It's all right. If I were in your shoes, I'd be nervous too."

"You're right. I am nervous. I couldn't sleep so I thought I'd come down. I'd like to get it over with."

"We're set up, so if you want, we're ready to get started. This is your hospital bed," the nurse said pointing to it. "If you're ready, go ahead and lie down."

One of the nurses handed her a small plastic cup with a pill in it and a cup of water. "Take this," she directed. "It's a mild sedative. It'll help you relax." They put a blanket over her and continued, "We'll take you into the visiting room so your friends can see you before you're processed."

Justin also had a hard time sleeping and arrived at the preparation area at 0630. When he walked in, Ms. Wong was lying on the hospital bed with Dr. Momora at her side. Cindy's hair was curled and arrayed around her face, making her look like an angle. He stared at her with a dreadful fascination. He was instantly engulfed in a flood of hot emotions.

When Dr. Momora saw Justin, she said, "I need to talk with Millie," and stepped out. Almost immediately, Dr. Hockstrasser arrived and moved to the left side of her bed. She smiled and took his hand. Justin moved to the right side of her bed, putting his hands on the side rail. She immediately reached up and put her hand over his.

Justin didn't know what to do and quickly looked at Dr. Hockstrasser to see what his reaction was. He didn't seem to be bothered in the least.

In fact, he smiled, and said, "We both appreciate you being here."

Thank goodness, Dr. Momora and Millie walked in and joined them at Cindy's bed. Justin stepped back and both gave her hugs.

Dr. Momora looked at Justin, Millie and Dr. Hockstrasser, and asked, "Would you mind if Cindy and I were alone for a few minutes?"

The three of them walked out together and Millie looked at Justin "Are you all right? You look pale."

"Yes, of course. Why wouldn't I be alright?" Justin testily answered, giving Millie a look like thunder. His voice was gruff with emotion.

Millie just smiled and put her arm around him. "No reason. I was just wondering."

They stood and quietly talked for several minutes before Dr. Momora called them back. When they returned, Dr. Momora was holding Ms. Wong's hand. It was obvious there had been lots of tears shed. To Justin, Ms. Wong looked small and helpless. As Justin and Cindy's eyes met, a cataclysmic explosion took place in both of them.

Dr. Momora and Millie were both openly crying, and to his mortification, Justin felt tears of frustration welling up in his eyes too. Dr. Hockstrasser was the only one with dry eyes. Ms. Wong was clinging to Dr. Momora's hand but also reached for Justin's hand. Then she looked directly at him and choked out, "Will you do me a favor?"

"Sure, if I can," he responded through a gulf of confusion.

"Call me Cindy."

Now for sure you've gone way too far, Molly screamed. *You need to get behind the wall with me. Can't you see what has happened? You've lost total control of your emotions. You've got to remember that you are nothing but damaged goods. Neither Justin nor any other man will ever want you.*

Justin didn't know what to say. Dr. Hockstrasser, Dr. Momora and Millie were all there, but Ms. Wong only looked at him. He was trying to remain calm, but his composure was fragile and it felt like the air had been crushed from his lungs.

Thinking quickly, he stammered, "I guess when we get to the New World. Ah, ah, maybe that could be arranged."

Several other attendants had come in and stood quietly for several minutes. Then one of them said, "I'm sorry. If we're going to remain on schedule, we need to begin Ms. Wong's processing."

Dr. Momora gave Cindy one last hug. Then she, Millie and Dr. Hockstrasser all backed away. Cindy looked at Justin with yearning eyes one last time. It was as if her eyes bored into his soul.

A mask was placed over Cindy's face and her eyes immediately closed. With everyone watching, the nurses pushed the bed into the processing room.

As Justin watched, he sensed a longing well up inside him that he never imagined possible. His life suddenly felt empty and unfulfilled. Over the past months, and despite his best efforts, his feelings for Cindy had evolved into something he never thought possible. His life as a bachelor had provided a life of freedom to do what he wanted, but now he felt empty. It was as if his life had crashed down around him and it shook him to his very core. The feeling was the most powerful emotion he had ever felt.

Dr. Hockstrasser immediately left, but Justin just stood. He couldn't move. He closed his eyes and took a deep breath trying to steady himself. He took another breath, then another, yet his heart continued to pound in his chest. He was finally able to take a step back where he slumped against the wall.

Millie quickly went to him, and asked, "Justin, you are pale. You're not all right, are you?"

Dr. Momora heard Millie, and also went to him. "Justin, you look sick. Come sit down," she said, pointing to a chair. She reached for his wrist to take his pulse, but he pulled away.

"I'm fine," he mumbled. "I must have a touch of motion sickness. I just need some air." He quickly excused himself, leaving the two women watching as he departed for his quarters.

When he arrived, he laid down on the bed, stared at the ceiling, and rummaged through the wreckage of his emotions. He was miserable, humiliated and angry. He loathed himself. His sense of guilt and shame was like a burn on his skin which continued to be painful long after the flame had gone away. He had helped dozens of prisoners begin their cryogenic process, and here he was, worse off than the patient.

Why did I ever come up here? Neither of us want a romantic relationship nor have feelings for each other, he tried to convince himself. Yet he was both stimulated and tormented by her. *Why did I have such an emotional reaction to her? I don't love her and we aren't emotionally connected. Yet just the thought of her lying there looking at me caused my heart to race. I've never experienced such exhilaration or such a feeling of despair. I'm a professional failure. How will I ever face Dr. Momora, Millie or even Dr. Hockstrasser? And what will happen when we arrive at the New World? If I can't control my emotions now, what will happen then?*

Just thinking of what a fool he'd made of himself, filled him with rage. *How could I have been so stupid? I've made a fool of myself in front of everyone. It's over and I know what I have to do.*

There were still three more patients to be processed, so he had to return. He washed his face and went back to the processing area. Luckily, neither Dr. Momora nor Millie were there. He got through the rest of the day without incident. Yet in his mind he kept seeing Ms. Wong, or Cindy as she asked to be called, lying there looking at him.

After the last prisoner had been processed, Justin again returned to his room feeling even more like a failure. He didn't go to dinner. He just couldn't face anyone. He had to apologize to Dr. Hockstrasser though, so he went to the greenhouse.

Dr. Hockstrasser was working in a carrot bed. Looking up, he greeted Justin like usual.

Justin didn't know how to begin, so he blurted out, "I'm sorry."

Dr. Hockstrasser turned and quizzically seemed to ponder him. Justin was sure he could see into his mind and heart. "What are you sorry for, Justin?"

"For being unprofessional. I let my emotions get away from me. I'm so sorry. I don't know what came over me. I've never done anything like that before."

"Justin, sometimes you have to adjust your mind to hear what your heart already knows. You and Cindy care for each other. That's been evident for a long time."

"That's silly," Justin denied. "I feel close to everyone I've worked with. And besides, you're going to be her husband. She loves you."

"We care for each other, we respect each other, but we don't love each other as a husband or wife. You see Justin, I'm married to this," he said, spreading his arms wide and walking between the growing tables. "Even as a child I liked to grow things and I've always been in love with my work. After I immigrated to America, I invented a way to genetically alter plants to create strains that could produce three and four times as much as ordinary plants. My work was stolen from me and I killed a man over it."

He stared into space for several seconds as if wondering how

330 | LaMont G. Olsen

that had happened. Turning to Justin, and looking him in the eye, he continued, "Cindy cares for me as a friend but not as a husband. Like me, I think she's in love with her work. We've discussed it and agree, if it's meant to be we'll marry. If it's not meant to be, we're not going to be hurt or bitter. I don't know what the future will bring, none of us has control over that. What I do know is Cindy is a strong woman, and when called upon, is capable of controlling some very complex situations. I also think she has the strength to accept whatever is in store for her. Do you?"

Listening to Dr. Hockstrasser, he thought; *For the first time in my life I don't truthfully know if I do have that kind of strength. I always thought I could control most every situation in my life. Now I feel overwhelmed and at a loss of what to do.* "All I know is that I wasn't professional," he responded.

"Justin, I've watched you go out of your way to be nothing but professional in your dealings with both Cindy and myself. But you're also human. We don't know what's in store for any of us. So all I can say is continue to be professional, but also keep your heart open. If a higher power has a plan for you, it will be revealed. Until then I have a bed of peas that is ready to plant and I could use some help." He started to walk away, then turned to face Justin. "I wonder if you'd do me a favor."

"Sure. What is it?" Justin asked.

"Call me Herman."

Justin was about to respond when the door opened, and Dr. Momora and Millie walked in.

"We've been looking for you," Millie said. "You didn't go to dinner, and we've gone to your quarters several times, but you weren't there."

"We're both worried about you," Dr. Momora said.

"I'm all right," Justin responded, feeling momentarily irritated.

"Bullshit, you're all right," Millie stoutly stated. "I know you better than that. You're hurting, whether you'll admit it or not. You finally had to acquiesce to your emotions and be human. Didn't you?"

Justin looked at Millie and again felt a torrent of emotions threatening to overpower him. Then like a dam that burst, everything began to tumble out. "I know I'm attracted to Ms. Wong. I wasn't able to control it, but as a professional I should be able too. I've never allowed myself to get personally involved with clients. I've worked hard to keep my feelings about Ms. Wong under control, but I failed. I don't know what come over me. All I know is that I made a complete fool of myself."

Dr. Momora locked eyes with Justin, and asked, "Do you know how hard Cindy has also tried to do the same? I was astonished that she even asked you to be at her processing. In fact, she wasn't sure what possessed her to ask you. She changed her mind a dozen times and wanted to tell you not to come, but there was something overpowering her. As you know, she's had a hard life and is committed to not having an emotional relationship with a man. Yet she has been uncontrollably drawn to you. And obviously, you feel the same way about her."

"I can't deny that I'm attracted to her, but I shouldn't be. She's a prisoner and I'm an employee. Nothing could ever come from such a relationship."

Then looking at Dr. Hockstrasser who had been standing impassively by, Justin said, "She's going to marry you and that's the end of it."

"You know you're not infallible, Justin LeMoore. When I was in nursing school, I fell head over heels for one of the doctors. I've heard Frank say he was attracted to some of his parishioners. Professors sometimes feel emotionally attracted to students. Although you don't seem to believe it, you're as human as the rest of us. For some unknown reason, you and Cindy are attracted to each other and there isn't anything you can do about it," Millie firmly stated.

Justin's thoughts were a cyclone of twisted agonies as he responded. "As I've already said, I admit to feeling attracted to Cindy, but nothing can come from such an attraction. And there is something I can do. I can resign from the mission and remove the temptation," Justin said, again feeling tears welling up in his eyes. "Please excuse me. I'd like to be alone for a while."

Several days later when Justin finished the group he'd switched with Frank, he returned to Houston. It was late evening when he arrived at Frank's quarter and the incident with Ms. Wong was still raw on his mind. Frank knew he'd had an upsetting week. When Justin walked in and sat wearily down, Frank stated, "It looks like you had a rough week. I'll be glad to take the last two groups." He then asked, "Justin, something is bothering you, isn't it?"

"Well," Justin hesitantly stammered, "perhaps. I guess."

"It has something to do with Ms. Wong, doesn't it?"

Justin glared at Frank, and asked, "What do you know about it?"

"Millie called me and said I should check on you. She said something happened when Ms. Wong went into hibernation."

"You know the two of you are pains in the neck. You both think you can intrude on my life anytime you wish." Then without thinking, he blurted out, "I've decided to resign from the mission."

"What brought that on?"

"Frank, I don't know what happened. You know I've been attracted to Ms. Wong, but I've worked hard not to let anything unprofessional happen between us. Then I made a complete fool of myself up there. If you hadn't agreed to trade, this would never have happened," Justin weakly stated. "I can't go on. In the morning, I'm going to give Mr. Harris my resignation."

"Justin, you can't resign. You're a leader and many of us look up to you."

"The only ones I'm a leader for is you and Millie. And you two just want me to do your dirty work."

"That's not true. Many on the staff see you as a leader. You're the one who stands up to Vidula. You have a special relationship with Mr. Harris and can talk to him in a different way than the rest of us can. If you resign, you'll be making the biggest mistake of your life."

"I've already made that. I did that the other day," Justin said with his head in his hands.

"Look blockhead, people have emotional attractions to other people all the time. Priests are sometimes attracted to someone in their parish, or a doctor may be attracted to a patient."

"I've already had that lecture from Millie," Justin retorted.

"Okay then, listen to this. It's not the attraction. It's how you handle the attraction that makes you a professional. You've maintained a professional relationship with Ms. Wong for over nine months now. Almost everyone on this compound recognized you two had feelings for each other. But what could they say? You were always professional and appropriate. You've nothing to be ashamed of."

"Real professionals don't break down and get emotional when their clients go into hibernation."

"That's nonsense. Tell me you've never got emotional when a client died, or when you've worked forever trying to make changes in someone only to have them revert to their old lifestyle? You care for her. Showing emotion isn't wrong or unprofessional."

"Frank, I've seen bunches of clients go into hibernation. I didn't get all weepy and emotional over them."

"Sure, but you didn't feel the same way about them as you do for Ms. Wong. That's the difference."

"That's exactly what I'm talking about. Frank, I'm so mixed up. I wish I'd never signed up for this mess. I just want to go back to Kansas, do my job, and look forward to simple things like a hunting or fishing trip."

They talked for over two hours, and in the end Frank's recommendation was the same as Herman's. Remain professional and keep an open mind. Justin wasn't convinced and went to his suite with a heavy heart.

He was unable to sleep a wink that night. The troubling feelings that had been brewing over the past days finally crystallized.

If I can't control my emotions toward Ms. Wong, I have no choice. I must resign.

He got out of bed, and after several attempts wrote a letter of resignation. At 0600, he called Mr. Harris asking if he could come over and talk.

"I just got up, but come on over," Mr. Harris said.

Mr. Harris answered the door in his bathrobe. "I slept in this morning," he said running his fingers over his rumpled hair. Walking into his office, he motioned to a chair. "Sit down."

Mr. Harris then walked behind his desk, plunked into his chair and yawned. Justin could feel his weariness. George Frederick Handel's Water Music Suite no. 3 was playing softly in the background. This was the first time he'd ever seen Mr. Harris when he wasn't impeccably dressed. Without any hesitation, he reached across the desk and laid the letter of resignation down. "I want to resign," he quietly said.

Mr. Harris didn't even look at the letter before saying, "Don't you just love Handel's music? He is one of my favorite composers. Do you know what piece this is?"

"I think one of his Water Music Suites."

"Very good. You always impress me." Looking at Justin, he said, "I've already heard about what happened with Ms. Wong."

"News travels fast," Justin angrily noted. "I assume you received a complaint from the medical crew on the train."

"Nope. Chaplain Sylvester Frank Molony called me late last night. In fact, he woke me up." Then he leaned back in his chair and intently looked at Justin's face.

"Why would he call you?" Justin demanded.

"Because he's your friend. And he's the mission chaplain."

"I'm not his client and it wasn't any of his business," Justin angrily retorted.

Mr. Harris leaned forward in his chair, and never removing his eyes from Justin, said, "You know I've been waiting for this. I knew your feelings about Ms. Wong would come out sooner or later."

Justin couldn't believe what he was hearing. *How did Mr. Harris know anything about my feelings?*

"Sir," Justin stammered, "I was unprofessional."

"Why do you say that?"

"Because I disgraced myself, the federal prison system and the mission."

"Wow, that's quite a lot of disgrace. Justin I've watched you for nine months and it's been obvious you've been battling your attraction to Ms. Wong."

"Was it that obvious?" Justin weakly asked.

"Let me start from the beginning. You gave Ms. Wong's file a ten plus—the only ten plus given to a convict by any panel member. Then you viewed the file forty-two more times after voting. And there was the interview tape of Ms. Wong. That was more than interesting. When you got to Houston, the agreement was for you and Frank to assess and counsel everyone. You refused to see Ms. Wong and Dr. Hockstrasser. You wouldn't even sit by Ms. Wong or Dr. Momora in meetings as the educational classes were coordinated. Then you suddenly decided to switch with Frank and be there when Ms. Wong was processed for hibernation."

"I didn't know you kept track of such things," Justin lamely stated.

"Justin, it was obvious to everyone who had eyes to see. I was concerned and spoke to Frank and Millie about you several times over the last months. I've been closely watching you and have been impressed that despite your feelings, you continued to be professional. If you'd been anything but professional, I'd have called you on it and asked you to resign. As I said, I've heard what happened from Millie and Frank. Now I'd like to hear it from you—in your own words."

Justin exhaled and related the embarrassing details as best as he could. Looking at Mr. Harris, he concluded, "That's why I have to resign."

Mr. Harris looked at him for several seconds before saying, "I can't accept your resignation, even if I wanted to. It's too late. I don't have time to hire another mental health professional. And in addition, if you departed now, it would destroy the cohesion of the crew."

Justin was looking at the floor.

"Justin, look at me."

Justin reluctantly did, as Mr. Harris asked, "You didn't propose marriage to her, did you?"

"No, of course I didn't propose to her," Justin pointedly stated.

"Did you tell her that you loved her?"

"No I didn't."

"Did you kiss her good-bye?"

"No, I didn't kiss her."

"Well, then I'm not concerned. Ms. Wong will be in hibernation until you arrive at the New World. Then hopefully you'll be so busy hunting and fishing you won't have time to do anything stupid." Without ever reading the letter, he tore it up and threw it into the trash.

"I expect you to continue being professional and I trust you will. I need you. The mission needs you. Just do your job and everything will be fine."

Standing up, Mr. Harris said, "Now get to work. I need to get dressed and I'm sure there's something you need to be doing."

"Sir, I don't feel right about what happened and I'd really like to resign," Justin continued.

Placing his big hands partway across his desk, and leaning forward, Mr. Harris angrily said, "Justin, what words didn't you understand? It is too late to resign. If I was worried about inappropriate behavior from you, I'd gladly accept your resignation. As I've told you, I'm not. I'm sure you still have work to do, so go do it and stop sniveling."

He then reached over and turned the volume up on his entertainment device. "What you need to do is go to your room, sit quietly and let Handel's music cleanse your soul."

Justin didn't know what to say, so he just got up, mumbled a thank you, and left.

Frank had no right calling Mr. Harris. Especially after I confided in him, Justin thought as he stomped toward Frank's quarters. *And I can't believe he and Millie have been talking to Mr. Harris behind my back. I thought we were friends.*

By the time he was at Frank's door, he had worked himself into a first-class fit of pique. He didn't even knock, just stormed in. Frank wasn't in the room, so he shouted, "Frank, what gave you the right to talk to Mr. Harris last night? I talked to you in confidence. It was none of your business to go blabbing to him. And in addition, what gave you and Millie the right to talk to him about me behind my back? I've had it with the two of you."

Frank came out of the bathroom in a bathrobe. He looked at the anger on his friend's face, and said, "Justin, sit down. I'll try to explain."

"There's nothing to explain," Justin said, glowering at Frank. "I thought you and Millie were my friends and confidants. Then I find out you two have been meddling in my business for the past several months. This time you've both gone too far."

"Justin, sit down. You're acting like a child," Frank forcefully directed.

Justin sat but continued to look at Frank like he'd like to knock his teeth out.

"Now, are you still a crew member?"

"I suppose so. Although I wish I wasn't! Mr. Harris wouldn't accept my resignation."

"Okay then, let's get to the bottom of this. First of all, I'm the mission chaplain. My job description states I'm responsible for the religious and emotional well-being of everyone on the mission, both prisoner and crew member. That gives me the right to discuss the mental health of anyone on the mission with Mr. Harris. You were making a rash emotional decision. Mr. Harris needed to be aware of what you were contemplating. In addition to that, you're my friend. My best friend. Millie's also a friend and she's concerned about you too. We've tried to look out for you. And as far as talking to Mr. Harris behind your back goes, we didn't. He came to us. We simply answered his questions and reassured him, from our perspective, you were doing nothing professionally wrong. You can call that meddling if you wish. I call it looking out for each other. Justin, we all need you. You can't resign. Think what it would do to the entire crew."

Frank then went over to where Justin was sitting, put his hand on his shoulder, and asked, "Now can we talk?"

18

The rest of the processing went well, and the entire crew prepared to move to the train for the one-month shakedown. Justin chose the Friday before he was to depart to turn his truck over to Rolando and give him the money for his first year's tuition. He'd deposited the money into an account in both his and his uncle's names.

He worked with the Garzas during their last afternoon at the center. Rolando was unusually quiet. When Justin queried him, he said, "I can't start school until the winter semester. Since we will no longer be working here, the finances just aren't there. I'm going to need to buy a truck so I can continue doing yard work both here and when I go to school. Hopefully by winter semester I'll have enough saved up."

Justin was tempted to tell Rolando about the truck and the money, but decided to wait until he was ready to go home. The workday finally came to an end, and with both Caesar and Rolando there, Justin asked, "What kind of truck do you want to buy?"

"Just one that will run. I don't care what kind. It just needs to be reliable so I don't spend all my money fixing it."

"Would one like mine do?" Justin asked.

"Of course, but I don't have money for one that new. I'll have to get one a few years older and hope it will last."

"I'll tell you what. If you'll promise me you will devote yourself to your studies, I'll sell you my truck. I won't need it for several years and I don't have a place to store it."

"I'd love to have your truck, but I can't afford one that new."

"Could you spare a dollar?"

"A dollar?" Rolando winced, looking cautiously, expecting some kind of trick.

"Here's the title," Justin said, handing it to Rolando."

He gingerly took it, read it and then held it as if it was a hot potato.

"It has your name on it as the buyer," Justin said, taking the title back and pointing at it. "If you look right here, the sales price says one dollar. Can you afford that much?"

"You're kidding," Rolando said, staring at the title. It did have his name on the buyer's line, and the sale price of one-dollar was clearly there. But he still couldn't believe it.

"Mr. LeMoore, I can't accept this. Your truck's worth a lot more than a dollar," Rolando said with tears in his eyes.

"It's a good truck. It has a carbon engine, it runs well and she's been well maintained. The oil was just changed, it has new tires and I even had it washed. If you take good care of her, she'll last you a long time."

Still in incredulous shock, he stammered, "I don't know what to say, Mr. LeMoore. Are you sure?"

"I'm sure if you're willing to pay." Then giving him a wink and a nudge, he continued, "I still haven't received payment."

Rolando quickly pulled out his wallet and handed Justin a dollar. "Thanks. This is the best dollar I've ever made," he said, handing Rolando the title and keys. "I almost forgot." He removed the bankbook from his pocket, and holding it out to Rolondo, said, "This is for your first year's tuition. I expect reports every month on how my investment is going. Here, take it."

Rolando's hands were shaking as he timidly took the book. He opened it, looked at the amount and almost collapsed. "Oh no. You can't. I could never repay this much."

"You don't have to repay it. Call it an educational investment. You'll still have to work and save for your second year, but this will get you started. Perhaps you can get a scholarship if you do well."

Rolando was trembling. It was inconceivable. Caesar gave him a hug and also had tears in his eyes. "I don't know what to say either. You're truly an unusual friend. I'll never forget you. Would you honor us by coming to our home for dinner this evening? My wife makes the best tortillas in the entire world. We'd be proud if you'd have dinner with us."

"I'm the one who'd be honored," Justin said. "I'll need a ride though. I just sold my truck."

"I'll take you wherever you need to go." Then turning to Rolando, he said, "Take your truck and get on home. Tell your aunt we'll be along shortly."

With a big smile, Rolando got into the truck. He drove through the no-longer guarded gate and onto the city street.

"He's on his way, driving east. Are you ready?" the voice on the handheld radio asked.

"We're ready," another voice replied.

The sedan slowly pulled out and followed a block behind the pickup truck. Just two blocks from the training center, as Rolando was crossing an intersection, a tan SUV barreled through the stop sign and T-boned the truck so hard it knocked it across the street.

The driver of the SUV unbuckled his seatbelt and pulled an already-dead body over behind the steering wheel. He then quickly opened the door just enough to slide out. He immediately stood and began shouting for help. Running to the truck, he tried to open Rolando's door, but it was damaged so bad it wouldn't open. By then people were running toward both vehicles, so the individual melted into the group. He then slowly walked to the waiting sedan, got in and the two occupants slowly drove away.

The supposed driver of the SUV was slumped over the steering-wheel with blood running down his face.

Justin and Caesar heard the crash and Justin's blood ran cold. They both jumped into Caesar's truck and drove the two blocks to the crash site. Caesar drove right into the intersection, jumped out and ran to Rolando.

Justin couldn't believe what he was seeing. *No, it can't be! Please, no, it just can't be!* He said over and over to himself.

Caesar got to the truck, looked in and collapsed in a heap. The police arrived almost immediately and when the first officer looked into the truck he began pushing people away. Another officer helped Caesar to his feet and screaming, he struggled to again get to Rolando. "I have to help him. He's my nephew. Please," he said again with tears running down his face.

"I'm sorry, sir," the officer replied. "There's nothing that can be done for him. Come with me and sit down." The officer gently led Caesar to his patrol car. "Please sit here. An ambulance is on the way. Please don't go to the truck."

Police cars continued to come from every direction. They immediately blocked the streets while several officers began taking statements from witnesses who saw the accident.

Justin couldn't move. He leaned against Caesar's truck knowing if he tried to walk, he'd collapse.

After Rolando's body had been removed from the truck, it was taken by an ambulance. A policeman drove Caesar and Justin to Caesar's home while another officer drove Caesar's truck. Caesar had called his wife. Both were in shock. When they arrived at Caesar's home, Justin embraced them both and said how sorry he was.

"It should have been me," he said. "I wish it had been."

Before long the house was filled with twenty-five or more relatives, friends and people from their church. All were trying to comfort the Garzas.

Justin excused himself for a few moments, called Mr. Harris and briefly told him what had happened. "Sir, you and I know exactly who did this. It was that bloodsucking Vidula who set this up. It was me they were after. They didn't know I'd just sold the truck to Rolando."

"I'll come and get you," Mr. Harris said. "I also want to see the Garzas."

Mr. Harris soon arrived and hugged Caesar and his wife. "I want to tell you how profoundly sorry I am for your loss."

Justin and Mr. Harris stayed about an hour and then left for the training center.

On the way back to the center, Mr. Harris called a friend at the FBI center in Virginia. After a long discussion, his friend said he'd contact his colleague in the Houston office. They would immediately begin an investigation.

At the same time as Rolando's accident, Kyle was on the train and received a call on his communicator. A voice he didn't recognize, said, "A transformer in car fifty-three has shorted out. Tegan is busy and asked me to call you to see if you could take care of it."

Kyle was a computer specialist, not an electrical engineer. He was competent with electricity, and felt comfortable fixing the problem—especially if Tegan asked him to do so. It made no sense though. Transformers almost never failed. Especially when there wasn't a heavy load on them.

"Are you sure Tegan asked me to change the transformer?"

"Yes," the voice said. "I'm one of the cargo handlers. Tegan is working on an outside door down here. He asked me to call you."

"Okay," Kyle said. "Tell him, I'll take care of it."

"Thanks, I will," the voice said, and then disconnected.

Kyle went to the equipment room, got a battery-powered floodlight out, and pushed it to the transformer cabinet in car fifty-three. He went to the main power switch for that car and made sure the master switch was turned off. Although all the lights went off, he double-checked the switch again to make sure the power had been disconnected. The emergency life-support system was on, but it was independent of the main power source in the car.

He went to the electrical storage area, pulled a transformer from the storage shelf, loaded it onto a dolly and wheeled it to the panel that housed the failed transformer.

He opened the electrical panel, put on heavy rubber gloves and confidently disconnected the wires leading to the transformer. He pulled the lead wires out and although the electricity was off, he made sure the two leads did not touch. He disconnected the transformer from its mounts in the panel and began sliding it out. There was no way of removing it without the case touching the metal cabinet. He wasn't concerned though because he'd disconnected the main switch and also disconnected the leads. While he was wrestling with the heavy transformer, the lights suddenly came on, and a bolt of lightning jumped from the transformer, knocking Kyle to the floor.

A warning buzzer went off on the bridge and Colonel Straight saw there was an electrical surge in car fifty-three. Surges were not uncommon, but normally Tegan or someone called ahead to tell the bridge they were working on something. Since no one had called, it concerned him enough that he called Tegan.

"I'm not aware of any electrical work being done," Tegan replied.

"There was a significant surge in car 53. You'd better go see what's going on," Colonel Straight directed.

"Okay, I'll go check it out."

Tegan quickly looked for someone to go with him and found Leif. They ran to the car and when they entered, the lights were on. Kyle was lying unconscious on the floor next to the transformer. They immediately called the medical clinic and informed Dr. Francis, "It appears Kyle has been electrocuted."

"Is he breathing?" Dr. Francis asked.

Tegan listened, felt Kyle's chest and said, "Yes, I think so."

"Good. Can you carry him?"

"Yes, Leif is here with me," Tegan replied.

"Get him here as fast as you can."

They carried Kyle to the medical clinic, and Dr. Francis was waiting for them. As he was checking Kyle over, he began regaining consciousness. "I want to check his brain and nervous system before he is fully awake," Dr. Francis said, giving him a shot. "His arm's been burned, and I'll take care of that too."

Once Kyle was being taken care of, Tegan and Leif went back to the car fifty-three. They found Alex DePaul already there. The lights were on and DePaul was looking at the transformer cabinet.

"Who turned the lights on?" Tegan asked.

"They were on when I arrived," DePaul said.

"Holy mackerel," Tegan replied, "come to think of it, they were on when we arrived too. The juice should have been turned off. That doesn't make sense though. The flood lamp is still on, so he must have turned everything off. By the way, how did you already hear about this?"

"Colonel Straight called me," DePaul replied. "Can you tell me what happened?"

"Not exactly. First of all it's a mystery why Kyle was even here. I'm the one who should have been called about a transformer problem. I assume someone called him, but I don't know who or why," Tegan said.

"If the transformer had blown, why was there power in the car when Kyle was working on it?" DePaul asked.

"There shouldn't have been. If the transformer had shorted out, it would have automatically tripped the master switch. In addition, protocol requires that all power must be shut off to the entire car when we're working on something like a transformer. But even if there was power, Kyle would have turned the master switch off himself. That would have killed everything," Tegan angrily noted.

"Then he must have forgot to turn the switch off," DePaul said.

"The power was on when we arrived, so either Kyle forgot to turn it off, or someone else turned it back on. Either way my guess is Kyle would have been sitting on his haunches when he tried to pull the transformer out of the cabinet. Once the transformer leads were disconnected and the mounting bolts removed, there's no way it could be pulled out without touching the metal cabinet."

The transformer was lying half out of the cabinet, and looking at it, Tegan said, "The power leads were properly disconnected, so there shouldn't have been any power in it. Even if it touched the metal cabinet, nothing should have happened. Somehow the power was still on and attached to the transformer. If that were the case, it would arch across to the cabinet and short out. You can see where it arched." He noted pointing to a large black hole in the cabinet and a corresponding black mark on the transformer.

"His rubber boots and gloves stopped him from being grounded, so although the charge burned his arm, it didn't go through his body. That would have killed him instantly. I'm going to turn the power off so I can look at the transformer," Tegan said, walking to the breaker box and pulling the switch down.

Everything went dark. He put his rubber safety gloves on, walked back, turned the battery-powered flood lamp on and pushed the transformer over. Looking closely, he said with amazement, "There they are." He pointed to two small black marks on the transformer. "Somebody hooked a set of unauthorized leads to the transformer."

Then looking at the lead cables, he said, "Look, there are also two small holes in them. These marks are where the two additional wires were attached, and that is why the transformer was still hot." Then looking at everyone, Tegan said, "This transformer was deliberately hot-wired to kill Kyle."

"You're telling me someone deliberately set this up?" DePaul asked.

"There's no doubt about it, DePaul. This was an attempted murder."

DePaul immediately stood, took his communicator out and made a call. "Shut the train down. No one comes in or goes out without my authorization. And stop all earthbound shuttles. No one is to leave the area without checking with me. I also want to see the surveillance disks of this area so get them set up. Detain Dr. Ervin Kozenskie. I'm on my way to find his wife. Also, make sure they're kept apart."

Vidula was working in the female cryogenic unit, programming the new backup computer when her communicator device vibrated in her pocket. "Excuse me, I need to step out for a moment," she said to the medical staff as she hurriedly walked out of the room.

She clicked her device on and heard three words, "Done and done."

Vidula and Ervin were not scheduled to go into hibernation until the month-long shakedown was complete, so she had time to savor her accomplishment.

Finally rid of Justin and Kyle, she told herself.

Vidula returned to the computer she'd been programming and was again working when DePaul located her. Walking directly to her, he said, "Dr. Vidula Kozenskie, my name is Mr. Alex DePaul. I'm the chief of security."

She looked up with all the grace of cold steel, and relied, "I know who you are. What do you want?"

"You're to be detained and immediately returned to Houston."

"You have no jurisdiction or authority to do anything with me. Besides, why would I need to be detained?"

"You're to be detained as part of an investigation into a murder and two attempted murders."

"And again sir, may I remind you that you have no jurisdiction over me?" Vidula said, still continuing to work.

"Madam, you have two choices. You can either leave with me peaceably, or I'll stun you and remove you to the launch center on a gurney." Mr. DePaul pulled his phaser out and pointed it at her.

"Okay, after I finish this," Vidula said, returning to her work.

Mr. DePaul fired, the computer clattered to the floor and Vidula collapsed writhing in pain.

DePaul turned to the stunned group of physicians and nurses, and asked, "Do you have a gurney I can use?"

Millie quickly retrieved a gurney and helped Mr. DePaul pick Vidula up and strap her to it. DePaul pushed her out, and by the time they arrived at the transport area, she was recovering. She was madder than a hornet. "I'm going to have you arrested for kidnapping. When I get through with you, no one will hire you."

"Madam, don't threaten me or I'll stun you, gag you and after that you'll be sedated. All I want from you is to keep your mouth shut and cooperate. Put this space suit on, and if you so much as twitch, I'll stun you again. And that's not a threat. It's a promise. Do you want an adult diaper?"

With a growl, she yanked the suit out of Mr. DePaul's hands and pulling it on, said, "You can go to hell!"

When she finished putting the suit on, DePaul restrained her hands behind her back. When another security officer arrived, he said, "Watch her. If she moves an eyelash, stun her. I'm going to check on the other Kozenskie."

Vidula stoically sat staring at the security person but thinking; *It's worth a little harassment to have Justin and Kyle out of the way. They can never link their deaths to me or Ervin.*

While sitting there brooding, a fearful thought intruded into her mind. *Mr. DePaul said a murder and two attempted murders. If one died, why did he say two attempted murders? It sounded like at least one died, and if that's the case, which one?*

The other Dr. Kozenskie followed without a word. Inwardly he was seething mad and afraid something might be found that could incriminate them.

Later that evening, Tegan, Leif, and DePaul went to visit Kyle. Kyle was alert, but Dr. Francis said he wanted to keep him overnight to make sure he hadn't suffered any neurological damage.

"Kyle, we're glad to see you awake. You could have been killed. Why were you even working on the transformer? That's my job," Tegan pointedly inquired.

"I received a call from someone who said you were working on an outside door. He said you had asked him to call and have me to do it," Kyle responded.

"Who called you?" Tegan asked.

"He didn't identify himself. I think he said he was a logistic worker."

"That's strange," Tegan mused. "Did you cut the power to the transformer before you worked on it?"

"Of course!" he indignantly replied. "I disconnected the knife switch and also tripped the circuit breaker!"

"Kyle, someone tried to kill you. Someone installed a second set of leads to the transformer housing so when you removed it, and touched the metal case, it would short across. Someone must have been watching you and turned the power on as you began pulling the transformer out. They must have thought you were dead and quickly removed the second set of leads. Of course they were gone before we arrived. By the way, did you see the lights come on as you were pulling the transformer out?"

"I don't remember. But with the floodlight on I might not have noticed."

"This was no Mickey Mouse operation. Someone knew exactly what they were doing. There was nothing wrong with the transformer you were taking out. Someone wanted you dead. Mr. DePaul has shut down the train and his people are interviewing everyone. He's also detained Vidula and Ervin, but they'll never admit to anything. Even though we're all sure they set this up.

"I called Mr. Harris, and he said someone also tried to kill Justin. He'd just sold his truck to that gardener kid at the training facility. Thinking it was Justin driving, a big SUV deliberately ran a stop sign and plowed into the side of the truck. It killed the poor kid instantly," Tegan said.

"That's terrible," Kyle remorsefully stated. "He seemed like such a great kid. As I recall, he was saving his money and planned to begin medical school in the fall."

"Yep, he's the one. Like the attempt on your life, it was well orchestrated and professionally executed," Tegan replied.

Kyle looked stunned, and looking at his friends, said. "You all know darn well who are behind these attempts. It has to be Vidula and Ervin Kozenskie."

"I'm sure you're right," DePaul replied. "But proving it is another matter. I've taken both Vidula and Ervin into custody for questioning. They've been separated and returned to Earth, but I doubt there'll be any way to link either attempt to them. It'll be just like when someone tried to kill you and Justin. Everyone knew the Kozenskies were responsible, but people like them don't leave a trail."

The FBI, the Houston police, and even investigators from the Federal Bureau of Prisons spent three weeks interrogating and investigating both Kozenskies. Nothing was found. The coroner said the person who allegedly was driving the SUV was a homeless drunk and was dead before the crash. Other than that, nothing was found at the train or on Earth. Yet everyone knew the Kozenskies were behind both attacks.

Justin and Mr. Slusser were in Mr. Harris's office. "We all know the Kozenskies were involved in both the truck crash and Kyle's so-called electrical accident," Justin angrily noted.

Looking at Milton Slusser, Mr. Harris responded, "There's no doubt about it. But after three weeks of investigation we still have no proof."

"You're right. There's no proof and we can't keep the train in orbit indefinitely. The Kozenskies need to be returned to the train. They've still got to wrap up a few communication tasks before they go into hibernation. Then you won't need to see them again until you arrive at the New World. Unless you want to resign," Mr. Slusser challenged.

"You'd like me to resign, wouldn't you?" Justin angrily stated. "If I did, you and the Kozenskies would win. I don't know what you and they have up your sleeves, but whatever it is, I want to be there to squash it. You can assure yourself I'll probe under every slimy rock while I'm gone. When I get back, whatever I find will be turned over to the authorities. So, don't get too comfortable, Mr. Slusser.

"And I'll be doing the same here," Mr. Harris said, looking directly at Milton.

With that Mr. Slusser stood up, smiled at them both, and left the office.

Mr. Harris and Justin talked another hour and both agreed to keep each other informed about what they found. Both were sure the Kozenskies were involved in the crash that took Rolando's life and neither would rest until Vidula and Ervin paid for what they did.

"Keep the Kozenskies here on Earth," Justin said. "If they're not on the train, we won't have a problem. I'm sure they're up to something."

"I'd like to," Mr. Harris replied, "but there's overwhelming congressional pressure to get the train on its mission. The Kozenskies will be returned to the ship and allowed to proceed. I know it isn't right, but my hands are tied."

Rolando's funeral was held on Sunday at the St. Mary Catholic Church. The funeral exploded into a media frenzy with hordes of journalists and cameramen camped outside. Justin, Mr. Harris, Frank, Millie and several other crew members attended.

"This should never have happened to him," Justin sadly stated. "Every time I close my eyes, I see Rolando, so excited about going to school and making a difference. Then I see his mangled body knowing the evil person who caused his death is going free."

After the funeral, Caesar found Justin, and said, "I need to give your money back to you."

"No," Justin replied. "Please keep it. Find some other young person with a dream. Give it to him or her." They both hugged and said they'd never forget each other.

Vidula and Ervin were returned to the train. The FBI and the other agencies would continue their investigation. If anything was uncovered prior to the train's departure, they'd be arrested. Of course, no one was optimistic anything connecting them to the murder would ever be found.

Almost immediately after returning to the train, Vidula made a call. "Thanks for your support. Slusser, you're truly a worthless slime ball. Now you listen because we're going to have a little farewell chat."

"Vidula, I'm tired of your complaints, accusations and demands. You orchestrated those botched attempts to kill Justin and Kyle. In the end, all you did was kill an innocent kid. Right now, the only thing I want to hear from you is that you're in hibernation. There's nothing Congressman Richards nor I can or want to do for you. Please don't contact me anymore."

"Milton, Milton, Milton," Vidula viciously cooed. "Let me read you something." She began reading from a document about when they first met, about deals they'd made, money in numbered overseas accounts and political opponents that had been eliminated. Additionally, she also shared details on campaign spying, which had been accomplished by individuals who couldn't be traced. She even had the names of the various levels of hit men that had been used along the way. "Do you want me to go on?"

Mr. Slusser was numb and silent as Vidula spoke. Each word was like an acid burn to his brain. Finally, he asked, "Vidula, what do you want?"

"First of all, the document I'm reading from is only one of six copies. The other five are with trusted friends. Each copy is preaddressed, one to the FBI, one to the *Wall Street Journal*, one to the House Committee on Ethics, one to Fox News and the last to the president of the United States. My friends will post all five copies upon my direction. The sixth copy I'm keeping as a backup, just in case. Here's what we want you to do in order to avoid the immediate release of the documents. Ferrell Logan, the nurse assistant who was disqualified, is to be on the train before we go into hibernation. That gives you four days. So—"

"Vidula," Milton broke in. "You know that's impossible. Mr. Logan is in the Beaumont, Texas, federal penitentiary. Do you think I can just walk in there and take him for a ride? Vidula, be reasonable!"

Silence hung in the air like a knife blade for several seconds before she continued. "I can call and have the documents released today, so don't give me a bunch of political mumbo-jumbo. You can make anything you want to happen, happen. Ferrell Logan will be on the train within the next four days or the documents will be on their way.

"If Mr. Logan isn't on the train, watch your e-mail. Better yet, watch the evening news. Now, just to be sure we clearly understand each other, I'm going to send you the first page of the document to your secure communication device. That way you can verify the authenticity of it. Four days, Milton. You have four days. Actually, you don't have time to be chatting. You've got work to do." And she disconnected her communicator.

The shakedown went like expected, constant little things going wrong but nothing that was a showstopper. Most important was the cryogenic wards seemed to function flawlessly. The cryogenic consultants would remain on board to ensure everything continued to go well until the mission was launched.

Kyle, Leif, Brent, and Tegan were solidly against the Kozenskies. Yet above their objections, Colonel Straight allowed Vidula to finish programming several of the computer modules. The engineers, both on the train and on earth, continued to fight with her about programs being encrypted and making everything more complex than necessary.

In one heated exchange, Kyle said, "Vidula when you're asleep, I'm going to go through every program and straighten it out. I'll expose you as nothing but a dangerous, conniving wench."

The laundry van pulled up to the final Beaumont prison check gate. The guard walked to the rear, opened the doors, turned his scanner on, checked the laundry bundles and returned to the driver's window. He pressed his thumb on the driver's data device and was given an envelope, which he discretely tucked into his jacket.

The van drove to a local high school where a noisy basketball game was just letting out. A large man got out of the van wearing a laundry uniform. He walked to a waiting car and got in. The car departed, drove to where they could enter Interstate 10, and proceeded the two-hundred-and-forty-four miles west to Houston in just over four hours.

The two occupants in the front seat, and the person in the back never spoke. The car exited the interstate about 0200 and pulled into a truck stop next to a delivery van.

The big man in the rear seat was given an envelope and told to give it to the people inside the van. He got out, and the rear doors of the van opened. Once inside and the door was closed and bright lights were turned on. He was standing in a small beauty parlor. There was a chair and he was directed to sit. Once seated, two women went to work.

A flexible latex mask was placed over his face, and for the next three hours the women worked on his hair, face and neck. Lastly, contact lenses were placed in his eyes. When they finished, he was provided a white shirt, suit and tie. He was told to put them on. Once dressed, he was handed a briefcase, another envelope, and was told, "Give them both to the people in the car that is waiting for you outside."

A nondescript gray car with government license plates was waiting. At 0500, the man got into the car as directed. He handed the envelope to a person in the front passenger seat. The front passenger opened the envelope and extracted two additional envelopes, plus one sheet of paper. He read the paper and then handed it to the driver. There was another man in the rear seat who didn't speak. He just reached over and pinned a NASA security badge on the individual's lapel.

They drove directly to the Houston Space Center cargo area and pulled up to the gate.

The driver handed an envelope to the guard at 0530, and said, "We're bringing Dr. Manson to the shuttle."

The guard opened the envelope, checked the papers that were inside and found Dr. Manson's name on his log. The guard walked around the car and the rear window was lowered. He flashed the retina scanner in the individual's right eye, and a picture came up on the device. He checked the retina scan one more time, again matching the face to the picture on his screen, then told the driver to proceed.

The car drove to a hangar where they were met by a logistic worker. The second envelope was given to the worker and the man was escorted into the hangar.

He was told, "Take your makeup off and put it into this bag." A bag was held out to him.

Once that was completed, he was helped into a space suit with an oxygen tank. He was escorted into a cargo container that was then picked up by a forklift at 0615 and driven to a waiting space shuttle.

When loaded, the cargo worker shouted, "That's the last of it. You can button her up."

"Thanks," a voice shouted back. "This has held us up for over an hour. I hope whatever's in that container is worth it."

The cargo worker just shrugged his shoulders.

It was the day before the Kozenskies were to be processed. Vidula was completing her work on the new computer module in the women's ward when she received a message on her secure communicator.

She opened the device, and the message read as follows: 29-103986-44826. She smiled to herself and left.

With adrenaline surging through her system, Vidula walked briskly to logistics car twenty-nine. She quickly located container 103986; then using the code of 44826, she opened the lock on the container.

"Welcome. You know what to do."

"Yes, ma'am," the large man responded.

It's amazing what a few dollars and a crooked congressman's assistant can do, she said to herself as she returned to the women's cryogenic ward.

Although still in protest, the following day Vidula and Ervin went into hibernation. Many felt relieved to finally have peace and quiet.

Both Mr. Harris and Mr. Slusser went to the train to bid the crew farewell the day prior to its departure. To everyone's surprise, Mr. Harris informed everyone that Mr. DePaul had decided to go on the mission in light of the attempted murder of Justin and Kyle.

As usual, Mr. Milton Slusser spent a half hour rambling about all the good things Congressman Richards had done for the mission. He made no mention of the Kozenskies at all. Even more curious was that he wanted to see Vidula and Ervin in their hibernation cocoons, as if he was not sure it had happened. The command team, along with Justin, Frank and several others walked with Mr. Harris and Mr. Slusser to the cryogenic wards.

On the way, Mr. Harris took Justin's arm, and they slowed down until they were several steps behind the rest of the group.

"Justin, I'm not convinced the threats against you or Kyle are finished. I want to give you one last chance to resign. I don't want to put you in harm's way."

"I tried to resign. Remember?" Justin said with a sly smile.

"Yes, and I almost wish I'd accepted your resignation," Mr. Harris lamented.

"Who would replace me at this late date? And do you think Frank could manage alone? I can't see how he could do all the crew interviews, administer the mental health questionnaires and also deal with crew issues that might come up."

"No, I don't think he could. But I don't want to put your life at risk either."

"Sir, I'm fine. Now that the Vidula and Ervin are in hibernation, I don't think there'll be any more issues. Besides, I don't like to be run off like a scared rabbit. I also want to make sure nothing happens when we arrive at the New World. Many of us think the Kozenskies have something nefarious planned for when we arrive. We just don't know what, or of course when."

"I figured you'd say that." Then turning to Justin, Mr. Harris said, "Justin, you've become very important to me. I want you to keep your eyes open and let me know if you see anything suspicious—and I mean anything! Milton is acting mighty strange, and I am not sure what to make of it. I don't trust him or the Kozenskies, even though they are in hibernation. Call me on my secure device day or night if you see or suspect anything out of the ordinary. Deal?"

"Deal," Justin replied, and they shook hands.

"Oh, and one more thing," Mr. Harris said with a wink and a mischievous grin. "I'm glad you didn't let the issue with Ms. Wong cause you to resign."

"Sir, I . . . I'm not . . ."

"Justin, we've had this discussion before. Neither I nor anyone else was blind. I don't know what is ahead, but I trust whatever it is, you will do what is right."

They embraced one last time, and Mr. Harris said, "I'll pray for you every day. I have faith that God will watch over and guide you."

"Thank you sir, that means a great deal to me," Justin replied.

It was the first of October, seven months after they had expected to leave. The crew was anxious to get started. Mr. Harris, Mr. Slusser, the cryogenic consultants and the remainder of the construction crew departed the train to an awaiting shuttle. From there they watched as Colonel Straight engaged the massive motors and the train slowly glided away.

"I hope we're here to see them return," Mr. Harris said.

Mr. Slusser did not respond.

ACKNOWLEDGMENTS

I have worked on the *Space Train* series for over twelve years. I first must recognize and express my appreciation to my wife, Linda. She has graciously allowed me the time to write, rewrite and rewrite again each of the six books.

Several friends and family members also made valuable comments and suggestions. My sister, Shirlene Davis; my sister-in-law, Sandra Olsen; my cousin Clark Howard; my former boss Janice Crow and Ms. Pat Oetting all read the manuscript and gave insightful criticism. Ms. Susan Gallego also reviewed the manuscript with an eye for detail. She found errors even after the manuscript had been reviewed by professionals. Her attention to the smallest detail was greatly appreciated.

My army friend Retired Colonel Matthew Carp read and edited the book with his always-critical eye for detail. I worked for Matt for many years, both in and out of the army. I never produced a document without his making it better. Such friends are rare and I love him like family.

Two individuals require special recognition. I almost abandoned the project when I was encouraged to have Ms. Debbie Pollock, a retired Panguitch High School English teacher read the manuscript. Debbie corrected my grammar, suggested ways of making the story flow better, and made numerous other invaluable suggestions. Without her encouragement, I would never have kept going.

The second is Ms. Shawn Cane, the Panguitch High School computer teacher. From the time she heard about the book, she has encouraged me, and although extremely busy, has helped format the manuscript numerous times. Without her patience, friendship and assistance the project would not have happened.

Lastly, I have to acknowledge Green Ivy Publishing, and especially Ms. Darleen. Her expertise and patience are more than appreciated. She has formatted and reformatted my work and scolded when needed. I have nothing but appreciation for her work. I also appreciate Brittani S., the managing editor for Green Ivy Publishing, who did a magnificent job with a rough manuscript. Thanks to Ms. Darleen and Brittani S. If we should publish volume 2 in the *Space Train* series, I will be better at making the manuscript ready the first time. If a first time author is contemplating publishing for the first time, I would highly recommend Green Ivy Publishing.

CPSIA information can be obtained
at www.ICGtesting.com
Printed in the USA
BVOW11s0905060717
488538BV00008B/152/P